GW00322952

£2.99 ②

The Riddle of the River

The Riddle of the River

CATHERINE SHAW

Allison & Busby Limited
13 Charlotte Mews
London W1T 4EJ
www.allisonandbusby.com

Hardcover published in Great Britain in 2007.
This paperback edition published in 2008.

A CIP catalogue record for this book is available from
the British Library.

10 9 8 7 6 5 4 3 2 1

ISBN 978-0-7490-7903-1

Typeset in Sabon by
Claire Bezzano

Printed and bound in the UK by
CPI Bookmarque, Croydon, CR0 4TD

Vanessa Weatherburn's Case Diary
Summer 1898

'Well, Vanessa,' cried an eager voice in my ear. 'Who do you think she might be, then? Any ideas?'

I straightened up abruptly from the scone upon which I had been engaged in spreading a thick layer of clotted cream, preparatory to inserting a small portion of it into little Cedric's expectantly open mouth.

'Pat!' I exclaimed. 'How you startled me, coming up the garden path so quietly.'

'I wasn't particularly quiet,' he retorted. 'It's you who were concentrating so deeply you didn't hear anything. It happens every single time I come here, you know. I don't think I've ever seen you glance up like a normal person!' He laughed comfortably, then reverted with typical single-mindedness to his original topic.

'So – do you have any ideas about our newest mystery?'

'Oh, Patrick,' I sighed. 'I'm sure you mean that you've written some exciting article lately that I ought to have read. I'm really sorry to say that I haven't seen it. I don't have time to look at the newspaper as regularly as I should, I'm afraid. I just don't know where the hours and the minutes go, day after day.'

'Didn't see it?' he said in a slightly theatrical tone of amazed disappointment. 'And here I wrote it specially with you in mind. What a pity! If I'd thought for a moment you hadn't seen it, I'd have brought a copy with me.'

'That's probably all right,' I told him. 'Arthur takes the *Cambridge Evening News*; it comes here every day. It must be lying around somewhere inside. Which day was it – yesterday? Goodness, you *are* impatient! Here, then, I'll go and look for it now.'

I recklessly abandoned the whole of the scone and cream into Cedric's chubby hands. The unexpected boon occupied his attention fully, allowing me to hasten indoors and rummage amongst Arthur's newspapers for two entire minutes.

'Here it is,' I said, finding yesterday's copy, snatching it up, and returning quickly outside in the hopes that no serious domestic disaster had yet occurred, to find Pat actively encouraging Cedric while discreetly and hastily removing cream from them both with the corner of a napkin. 'What page should I look at? What is it all about?'

'Murder!' he said gleefully. 'It's on the front page, what do you think? A scoop for me again – but it could be even greater, if you'd help me!'

I read the article aloud, startled by his words.

Drowned body found in the Cam

The body of a young woman was found floating at the edge of the Cam between the Lammas Land and Sheep's Green, yesterday morning, by a passer-by who was taking his dog for an early morning run along the footpath. The police, immediately alerted, had the body removed from the water and taken for post-mortem examination. It is as yet uncertain whether the cause of death was actually from drowning, as certain marks on the girl's neck, partially obliterated by a station of some hours in the water, may in fact indicate death by violence. Dressed in a white evening gown, the young person carried nothing which could reveal who she was, and since no missing person of her description has been declared, her identity remains a total mystery. Any member of the public who has information about a young lady of between twenty and twenty-five years of age, with curly or wavy blonde hair and wearing a flowing ivory-coloured gown with embroidered flowers, probably last seen on the evening of Tuesday, June 21st, is requested to notify the police at once.

'Well?' Pat interrogated me eagerly. 'Are you willing to take it on?'

'What, the case? Of course not, Pat. I am not the police – I'm just an amateur detective! I only take on cases when I am hired to do so. Nobody has hired me yet, as far as I know.'

'Oh, I didn't mean take on the murder case,' he said quickly. 'I realise that is too big a job.'

I knew he was only trying to make me indignant and rejected the bait with a shake of my head and a smile.

'What I meant was that you could try to identify the lady,' he continued quickly. 'If anyone could manage to find out who she was and what she was doing in Cambridge – it really doesn't seem possible that she actually lived here – I'm sure you are that person. Then I would get an even bigger scoop, and the police would be better able to get on with their work of finding the murderer.'

'Is it clear that there really *is* a murderer?' I asked doubtfully. 'Perhaps this poor young lady came from somewhere else to make away with herself, on account of some personal unhappiness.'

'Oh, no,' he said seriously. 'She was murdered, I do know that. My brother-in-law's on the case; you remember Fred Doherty. The full post-mortem report came in last night, and he showed it to me, though I'm not to publish anything of it yet. She had a problem, that is true enough – she was expecting a baby, Vanessa.' He blushed slightly and glanced around the perfectly empty garden, as though someone might hear him speaking of scandalous things to ladies. 'And she wore no wedding ring,' he went on. 'Yet she didn't kill herself. The post-mortem was clear. She was killed; strangled, if you like, by pressure applied to the throat.

It's a very quick death,' he added as I paled.

I paused, thinking. The girl was dead; how could I help her now? Pat had succeeded in intriguing me, yet one could not simply take up a case directly from the newspaper because it was intriguing. And even if I did wish to help identify her, it was difficult to see how to begin.

Pat put on his most persuasive and wheedling Irish expression, and began again.

'My editor will hire you, up at the paper, if I ask him to,' he said. 'They couldn't offer any big fee, of course, but just for the identification – they'd be interested in that, I'm certain. News makes sales, Vanessa.'

'What a vulture you are,' I remarked. 'Listen, the thing is that even if I wanted to, I simply don't see how I should go about it. Why don't you simply put an advertisement in the paper?'

'We did,' he said. 'That article of mine is an advertisement. It hasn't received a single answer so far. I don't think the girl can have been from here. But listen! Don't say no. Just give it a chance; come with me this evening, to have a talk with my brother-in-law. Let him give you the details. Perhaps there will be something that can start you off.'

'Well,' I hesitated, 'I suppose I will, if Inspector Doherty is willing. I can't see anything wrong with that. Let me not agree to do anything until we have met with him, and I hear what he is willing to tell me, and think it over.'

'Oh, he'll be willing!' he exclaimed as joyfully as if he had just been offered a gift. 'He needs any help he can get on this! It's smooth as a marble sphere for the moment; no handle anywhere. I'll come by and pick you up tonight after supper, then, shall I?'

We did not go, as I expected, to Inspector Doherty's home on George Street, not far from where I had lived as a young teacher before my marriage. Instead, Pat directed me to the too-familiar police station on St. Andrew's Street

'Fred is on duty tonight,' he explained, 'and it's just as well.'

'Does he know I am coming? He might not be pleased,' I said quickly. The visit to the police station made my involvement seem so much more official, more formal than a simple house call. I wasn't at all sure that was what I wanted.

'Fred will be delighted,' said Pat. 'He knows all about you, you know that. And even though it seems probable that Scotland Yard will soon be called into the case, especially if it turns out that the girl came up from London, he would be pleased to have something concrete to show them when they come, if that could be managed. Remember,' he added slyly, 'we are talking about identification here. Only identification.'

He was not mistaken. A smiling Inspector Doherty welcomed us into his small office, which was littered with a medley of interesting items of all descriptions, and lit by three or four small lamps placed on different articles of furniture, giving the little room an odd, contradictory glow: bright here, dim there. Like Pat, Inspector Doherty was a British Irishman; he had perhaps never set foot in the Emerald Isle in his life, but it was all reflected in his bright blue eyes, his snub nose which insisted on remaining boyish in spite of a hairy growth underneath it intended to increase its dignity, and in the sheen of his dark hair. A different model from red-headed Patrick, yet equally typical. Our Irish contingent.

'Hullo, hullo,' he greeted us warmly. 'Once again, I have the honour to meet the famous Mrs Weatherburn. A pleasure.

Pat has told me that you are most interested in the case of the drowned girl he wrote about.'

'Oh?' I said. It had seemed to me, rather, that it was *Pat* who was interested. I am not a sensation-monger. I opened my mouth to say something of the kind, but suddenly realising that I actually *was*, by now, most interested in the case, I changed my mind, and said,

'It seems nobody has the slightest idea who she is.'

'No. And no missing person of her description has been reported since the death,' he said, plunging without hesitation into the facts. 'Of course, we looked into the records of missing persons from well back, as we thought she may have gone missing some time ago, and now the result makes things difficult the other way. Far too many blonde girls have gone missing in the last few years. Run away, I should think, most of them, but you never know. It'll all have to be verified.'

'How do you do that?' I asked.

'We start with physical particularities,' he said. 'The girl had a small, heart-shaped birthmark on her left elbow. For that matter, her nose had a rather special shape, too. There was a little wave in it, seen from the profile. Those pieces of information eliminated all the girls from the families we've been able to interrogate up to now.'

'If you found a girl that seemed to correspond, what would you do?' asked Pat.

'Family members would have to come and have a look,' responded his brother-in-law. 'Somewhat uncomfortable, in a case like this. The body has undergone post-mortem. And it had already spent some hours in the water. It is...it is not very presentable, you know. Not too presentable, but we show only small morsels at a time, avoiding the cut areas.

It's not nice,' he added, making a face.

'Oh,' said Pat. 'Is she that bad? Can't one make out what she looked like?

'Oh yes,' he said. 'I meant it is not nice for the families in general. This particular case is not so dreadful, apart from evidence of the post-mortem. Long periods of immersion in water cause swelling and wrinkling, but in this case the body cannot have been there for more than three or four hours. And one or two of the photographs taken before the post-mortem would be quite usable in case of positive response to the preliminary questions.'

'Photographs? Let's see them,' said Pat with authority.

The inspector shuffled about in a drawer and extracted two or three large photos, which he handed to us. I looked at them, studying each one for some time, with Pat staring and breathing over my shoulder. They showed the dead girl lying on a stretcher on the bank, after having been removed from the water. Her hair, though still wet and matted, had lifted into heavy waves. Her features were small and delicate. She looked very dead. One of the photographs was a portrait, showing only her face. I gazed, fascinated, at the slight shadow of her eyelashes, the curve of her cheek, the drops of water clinging to the hair at her temple. The powerful, inexplicable difference between life and death arose from the photograph like a vapour. 'She is wearing an unusual dress,' I said, trying to make out the details from a full-length photograph in which the body lay stretched on the bank, and pointing to the lace collar around her neck.

'Yes,' he assented, touching a box on the floor at his feet. 'Her effects are all here.'

'You've got more photographs in there, haven't you?' asked Pat, indicating the drawer with his chin.

'Er, yes,' replied the inspector. He opened it again, with some reluctance, then finally resigned himself to withdrawing the whole sheaf of pictures. He sighed. I waited.

'Some of these are not so easy to look at,' he told me. 'Here she's still in the water; we haven't touched her yet,' and he handed me the first one.

'Ophelia,' I said, astonished. I had unconsciously braced myself for a scene evoking murder; instead, the image in front of me was one of sublime and peaceful beauty quite incompatible with that notion. The grass and flowers, all the little life that flourishes on the edge of a stream, formed a frame for the figure of the floating girl. She lay face down in the water, caught in the rushes near the edge, her hair fanning out like algae, and her white dress forming a poetic, ghostly shape as the lines of those parts of it which floated under the water were deformed into waves. The back of her head emerged from the stream, and the wet hair floated, echoing the ripples of the Cam itself. My river – my river contained this mermaid. She was murdered.

'I don't like to show these others to a lady,' said Inspector Doherty uncomfortably. 'Photographs of the corpse as we took it out. I don't think you would learn much from them, actually. It's not that it's as horrible as many other murders I've encountered in my career. But there's something weird, ghostly about these images.'

'Oh, be a good fellow,' said Pat, exactly as I was about to say that I didn't want to see them. Shrugging, the inspector handed them over, obviously not wanting to seem superior or to put obstacles in the way of help. Pat spread them out. I took one look, and shuddered. There was no horror, nothing spectacular, nothing overtly revolting, yet they emanated death. My eyes were held by an image of a hand, a dead, limp hand, hanging down as they lifted her onto the bank, white against the dark background. I turned away, and picked up the portrait photo again. It was the only one whose image spoke more of the living girl than of her miserable demise.

'May I see her things?' I said after staring at it for a while.

He took the photographs back and stuffed them into his desk drawer with some relief, I thought, then lifted the box onto his desk.

'If anything could tell you something, it might be these things,' he said. 'Here is where a lady's knowledge can be useful. The quality, the make, all that.' He opened the clasp, and lifting back the lid, began handing me the items one by one. I examined them carefully, starting with the underwear: a pair of Dr Jaeger's woollen knit combinations, plain white cotton corset, white cambric corset-cover and petticoat with a simple ruffle and no lace.

'These are very standard items,' I said. 'Such things can be purchased in any number of large shops, or by catalogue. They are mass produced.'

'Well,' he said, disappointed, 'suppose I asked you to tell me what they reveal about the young woman herself. Would such items tend to indicate a person of good family?'

'Good, perhaps, but middle class,' I replied. 'They would not belong to somebody dressing at the height of fashion. That is confirmed by the corset strings; you see how they are marked by the lacing holes? They were loosened to remove the garment, but look: this is how she laced herself. A pretty form, as you see, but not as tightly pulled as today's fashion seems to encourage.'

'She wouldn't be,' he said, 'given her, uh, condition.' He looked at me carefully to see if I was aware of the situation.

'True,' I concurred, nodding briefly. 'But the corset shows no signs of ever having been laced more tightly.'

'But it looks very new. Don't you think it must have been purchased recently?'

'It is practically new,' I agreed. 'What is odd is that all these garments seem to be new – the, well, undergarments, I mean. Obviously, people buy themselves new items as the old ones wear out, but one's garments do not usually all wear out at the same time; that's why it seems a little odd. Girls often do keep a collection of new things aside, of course, in their wedding trousseau. However, they are not supposed to be worn before the wedding. I wonder if this girl had a particular reason either to use her trousseau, or to completely renew her wardrobe.'

'It's a little unfortunate,' he remarked. 'The newness of the things makes it impossible to deduce anything about her ordinary habits. The dress is different, though. Have a look at it.'

I took it from him, and gave an exclamation of surprise. Made of silk, it was loosely cut, and embroidered with a scattering of pansies and green sprigs. I turned it over, then inside out, and examined it closely, studying the seams.

'It's an unusual gown, isn't it?' he remarked.

'Quite unusual,' I agreed. 'In fact, I have never seen a pattern just like it before. It's not a true evening gown; it's more like a tea gown. Although peculiar even for that. It must have been very pretty. Oh, I know what it might be – Aesthetic Dress!'

'An aesthetic dress? I should hope that all dresses are aesthetic,' he said.

'No, I mean Aesthetic Dress, with capital letters. It's a movement, the Reform Movement in Dress, you know. It's rather old already, decades, I should think; it gained a little popularity when Oscar Wilde adopted it and began wearing the clothing and writing about it—'

'Oscar Wilde? The playwright-turned-convict?'

'If you want to put it that way,' I answered with a sigh. There would be a great deal to say about the fate of the once celebrated and adulated writer. But this was definitely neither the time nor the place. I turned the conversation quickly back to dress. 'The clothing was inspired by the work of the pre-Raphaelite painters,' I went on, 'Rossetti, Morris, and the others. They painted women wearing loose, romantic draperies. They just meant it artistically, but the reform movements, Aesthetic Dress, Rational Dress and so on, were inspired by those images to create very beautiful, very comfortable clothing for both men and women. Never cinch the waist; hang from the shoulders, that was one of their main creeds for both beauty and health.'

'And such dresses would have been fashionable...when?' he asked, eyeing the white dress with its old lace and sparse scattering of embroidery doubtfully. 'I don't believe I've ever seen any like the ones you describe.'

'I don't think such dresses ever actually became the fashion, in the sense that they were not adopted by the majority,' I replied. 'But there are still women who are known to wear them frequently. I am thinking of some rather well-known figures such as Ellen Terry.'

'The actress?'

'Yes, such dresses are typically worn by ladies who wish to appear – or really are – artistic and bohemian.'

'Interesting. So do you think we can conclude that about this particular young lady?' he asked, fingering the silk.

'I wish we could conclude something more precise than just a reflection on her character. She was no conformist, that much is certain. But it is impossible to say whether she dressed in this manner from personal taste, or as an echo of some artistic profession, or, let me be very frank, quite simply because she found this style of dress more comfortable in her condition.' I peered at the dress slowly, then turned it inside out.

'You know,' I added, 'this is rather curious. The seams of this dress are stitched well enough, but they have not been finished! That is very odd.'

'Oh, girls nowadays,' replied Inspector Doherty with a wave of the hand. 'Don't know how to do things properly any more. Only think about what will show on the outside.'

'That seems unlikely,' I said. 'It is foolish to leave the seams unfinished; even the most inexperienced seamstress is taught that one cannot leave them like this – they would begin to come undone after just a few wearings, as the edge of the material frays. No one wants to find themselves with an unravelling seam in the middle of the day. Also, this dress has been altered, and probably more than once. It was originally sewn to fit a different person, someone rather larger. You can see the traces where the seams were undone and redone. Here are the marks of the former seams; at the waist, and on the shoulders and under the arms. And the extra material on the inside has not been trimmed away.'

'Perhaps the dress was borrowed, and would need to be

altered back to the way it was before? That would explain not finishing the seams, wouldn't it?'

'It could,' I said, 'though it seems like going to a lot of trouble. Still, it is possible. The thread is obviously fairly new, whereas the dress itself looks to me as though it has been worn quite a number of times, and washed many times as well. We'll keep that in mind; a borrowed, altered dress.'

'She didn't have any handbag or reticule?' asked Pat hopefully, as I put the dress aside and turned to the other items.

'No. It may have been taken from her, or else it floated off down river. It may still be found. But look at her jewellery. This is quite interesting, don't you think?'

He handed me a remarkable bracelet of intricately carved ivory beads threaded on a silken twist. I looked at them intently.

'It comes from the East,' he said. 'Now, where might she have got hold of an Oriental bracelet? I've never seen one like it.'

Hmm, I thought to myself, looking at it.

'The ring holds a single pearl set in silver. Banal, though pretty enough. Do you think you could discover anything about any of it?' the inspector asked me. 'It's annoying: the purchased items seem too typical to trace, and the personal ones too original to have been purchased.'

I fingered the bracelet of ivory beads, wondering if I had not seen something quite like it...not long ago. Surely – yes, surely...Pat's eyes met mine, and he stood watching as I tried the bracelet on my wrist, slipped it off, and stood holding it, thinking, and wondering. He stood up and began helping the inspector to pack the unknown girl's affairs back into the box. They rolled up the dress with pansies and put it away, and I watched them, and thought of the young body itself lying under the scalpel on a brightly lit post-mortem table...and from thence to a hard, dark coffin. Pat piled up all the undergarments and placed the sad little pair of water-soiled slippers together on top. He looked at them a little wistfully.

'Where is the ring?' said Inspector Doherty suddenly, glancing suspiciously at his brother-in-law.

'Here it is, everything is back in the box,' said Pat cheerfully, placing the ring carefully inside a shoe. Inspector Doherty closed the lid and snapped the clasp firmly, then handed me the portrait photograph.

'Pat says you're willing to see what you can do in the way of identification,' he said. 'Sometimes locals can find out things more easily than the police. Take this, if you think it might be useful. I can spare it, I have all the others.'

'I will see what I can do,' I said, rising and taking it. Not that I could really imagine myself using it. Going around showing photographs of dead faces to people – what better way to look like a policeman? Goodness gracious! Yet I did want the photograph, if only for myself. I wrapped it in a piece of paper and slipped it into my bag.

Pat accompanied me home in a silence quite unusual for him. I had expected him to inundate me with questions as to my intentions. But he seemed wrapped up in his thoughts, and when he did speak, it was not about the murdered girl, but about quite other things. He shook my hand warmly when we separated, and told me to let him know about anything particular which came my way. His handshake was unusually long and firm, and when he dropped my hand, I felt something unfamiliar slide onto my wrist.

'Pat!' I called, but he was already striding off into the distance. I looked down unwillingly. The Chinese beads hung there looking innocent. They gleamed and winked at me in the darkness.

'All right,' I said to myself. 'I knew he was going to do it, that is, I didn't really know, but really, I did. I saw that he saw I was thinking about them. So there we are. I think these beads are going to be useful, and I shall use them – and then it will be up to Pat to make his misdemeanour good.'

I returned home and placed the ivory beads carefully in the little alabaster dish on my night-table, where I habitually put my jewellery when going to bed if I intend to wear it again in the morning.

A Chinese ivory bracelet – I saw such things not long ago, and right here in Cambridge. Not just like this one, to be sure – carved ivory bangles, rather, and bangles and beads of jade. Yet they all differed from each other, and this one may have been among them. I plan a little investigative shopping trip for tomorrow.

1874

The servants, tenants and farm workers pressed into the large bedroom to admire the new baby, snuggled in its mother's arms. Still weak, she made the effort to smile at them from her bed.

'Goodness me, what enormous ears he has,' observed old Vornelli, who had lived and worked at the villa for forty-four years and had the right to make remarks.

The mother looked up at him.

'He will hear the still, small voice of the air,' she replied softly, running her fingers over the baby's fuzzy head.

It is one of the moments of the day I love best; the children are in bed, and a peaceful silence has descended into every corner of the small house, which is nestling quietly in shadows relieved only by the glow of the lamp. This is the only moment at which I can take up my pen to write down the events of the day without fear of instant disturbance of one kind or another, whether it be visitors, tradesmen, urgent household duties or scampering twins. So here I am with my notebook, freshly begun yesterday, in front of me, and the inkpot conveniently to hand. Oh. Arthur has looked up from his newspaper.

'Hum,' he said. 'Not writing letters? Fresh notebook? What does this mean, Vanessa? Have you a new investigation on hand?'

'I have, since yesterday,' I said. 'A case of identification.'

I do prefer to recount things when I feel ready to do so and not before. In any case, Arthur seems to know most things without being told, but as he says little, it comes to much the same. He contented himself now with glancing at me penetratingly before returning to his newspaper. So I shall proceed to my task and recount my search for the origin of the Chinese bracelet.

As it happens, I had seen a number of similar bracelets for sale recently, amongst a large selection of varied decorative objects newly imported by Robert Sayle's from China. I had visited the sale with little Cecily, but we had not paid much attention to the ivory beads and bangles, her gaze having been captured more vividly by the exotic objects such as fans and conical hats, whereas I spent my time examining the brightly coloured silks, of which I ended up buying a length for my own personal use. And how many ladies in Cambridge, I wonder, did not purchase some object, however trifling, from the far-off land of oriental dreams, during the three days that the sale lasted?

Upon rising this morning, I slipped the bracelet onto my wrist and scrutinised my memories. I could not recall having seen this precise bracelet, yet it seemed to correspond well enough to the kinds of objects spread over the shop counters. I carried it to the nursery and showed it to Cecily, who, with a large napkin around her neck, was deeply engaged in manoeuvring a spoonful of bread-and-milk to her mouth without letting fall a single drop. I waited until the operation had come to a successful conclusion before showing her the bracelet; not, however, with much hope that her three-year-old mind could contain any really useful memories.

'Ooh, pretty,' she remarked, admiring it.

'Do you remember the big shop with bracelets like this, Cecily?' I asked her, but she merely stared at me, shook her head, and thrust her hand through the circle of beads. I had some difficulty in recovering it from her firm grasp. Dropping a kiss on top of her silky brown head, I returned it to my wrist and set off to Robert Sayle's shop on St Andrew's Street by myself.

It is always a pleasant walk, if somewhat long, up the Newnham Road towards the centre of town. The sun was bright and strong, and I failed to open my parasol, letting the warmth radiate down instead upon my hat, comforting and inspiring. The shadows fell, dark and sharply outlined, on the pavement, and all looked so open, so reassuring, so free from secrets that my heart was lifted by a little wave of pure well-being, until the vision of the hand came, unbidden and undesired, floating into my mind. That limp, drowned hand lying like a withered lily on the edge of the photograph, my eyes fixed on it so as not to see the rest, the face, the staring eyes. I quickened my steps, and was glad to finally enter the shop and cool my forehead in its quiet shade.

There were few clients at this hour, and those were essentially concentrated about the areas selling useful items. The counter where jewellery and imported items of all kinds were presented was deserted. A girl sat on a stool behind it, her dark eyes filled with melancholy boredom. I stared at her, wondering, although I did not exactly recognise her, if she might not be the very same girl who had sold the Chinese items on the days of the sale. I could not quite remember – yet if it were she, if this girl had sole charge of the counter, and if my guess about the bracelet were correct – why then, she herself may have seen the dead girl alive...

I shook myself quickly, severely. If I could barely remember her face, then how could she, who sold dozens, no hundreds of objects, possibly remember a single client? There was nothing for it but to ask her. I made my way over to her; lost in her thoughts, she perceived me only as I arrived in front of her. Then she jumped to her feet, arranging a polite, albeit artificial smile upon her features. Her simple white dress bordered with black lines outlined an astonishingly firmly laced waist, whose strained tininess provoked me to an enormously deep inhalation, for the sheer pleasure of feeling my lungs expand. In spite of the prevailing fashion of tight-lacing, which has been if anything reinforced by the controversy swirling around it, I really cannot endure lacing beyond a certain, very reasonable point. I like to breathe, not to mention the frequent necessity of bending down. And I consider that as a mature matron, I have the right to do as I please on this score. Anyway, Arthur says that a womanly figure has just as much charm as a young girl's, if not more. The girls one sees on the streets, however, seem to vie with each other to achieve waists of such small dimensions that they sometimes resemble ants more than young women. I recalled that the dead girl had not entered into this rather frightening game.

Before addressing the girl, I let my eyes rove over the items spread out in front of her. Today they seemed to be Indian rather than Chinese; a collection of boxes, some of fragrant carved wood and others of gaily inlaid stone, decorated the surface of the counter, and the glass case underneath contained a selection of heavy silver jewellery, necklaces and earrings set with large turquoises. Perching my elbows amongst the things, I leant towards her in a confidential manner and slipped the bracelet off my wrist.

'May I ask you a question?' I said engagingly, trying to meet her eyes, for she seemed vaguely absent even as she prepared courteously to come to my assistance.

'Certainly, ma'am,' she replied without any show of interest. I imagined her forced, no doubt, into a tedious and wearisome job by the economic straits of a struggling family, and nourishing secret dreams of rising in life to some higher position, thanks, perhaps, to nothing more than her waist measurement. I felt tempted to talk to her about herself rather than about the bracelet, but I did not want to annoy her needlessly or to waste time, and I was afraid another customer might arrive at any moment. So I simply reached out with the bracelet and showed it to her.

'Do you recognise this? Could it have come from here?' I asked. 'Is it possible that you sold it yourself?'

She took it, examined it closely, letting it run through her fingers a moment, while I thought of the many negative answers she might give: never saw it before, was not working here during the Chinese sale, couldn't say. Then, unexpectedly, she nodded.

'Yes, I think so. This was among the collection of Chinese bracelets we had here a week or two ago. I am almost certain that I remember it. It is so pretty – look how it is carved. Each bead is hollow and the surface is carved with tiny flowers, or perhaps it is just ivory lace. It is incredible to be able to make such things. Most of the other bracelets were made of a single piece; this was the most exquisite and complicated one. Some of the others still remain,' she added, searching a key out of a drawer and unlocking the cupboard which was low behind the counter, at the level of her knees. 'We keep the things for the next time we bring out Chinese goods,' she explained, taking out some items and setting them in front of me. 'It is not good to allow the public to become tired of the same things, or used to them, or to see that they are not sold. They must think that everything disappeared very quickly.' She smiled again, her kind, disillusioned smile. I looked at the bangle she held out to me, and at a decorative object in a circular glass window. I had not noticed these things particularly when I had visited the sale, but now I was unable to take my eyes off the almost unbelievably intricate carving protected between the two glass discs. A pagoda stood on a rock, trees made of inexpressibly delicate needles surrounded it, and a stork pointed its threadlike beak into the air. The whole scene seemed to have been created by the hands of fairies, not the thick, clumsy fingers of men (even Chinese ones, whose fingers must be lighter and quicker than our own). I stared into the magic disc, entranced.

'May I buy this?' I said suddenly.

'It is not for sale now,' she said. 'I am not allowed to take out these things and sell them.' She glanced around nervously, for her superior, no doubt, but the shop was functioning peacefully, each lady busy with her own stock, and nobody was watching us.

'It doesn't matter,' I said. 'I will come back and buy it the next time you have Chinese things.'

'I should like to sell it to you, since you want it,' she said softly. 'It is beautiful, isn't it? I also look at it sometimes. I look at it quite often, when I am here alone. It is even more delicate and miraculous than the bracelet.'

'Keep it for me,' I said. 'I will buy it some day, and in the meantime you can go on looking at it.' I looked at her sober dress, and felt for a moment how it must be to see, touch and hold pretty things, frivolous things, luxurious things all day long, and probably never have the chance to own even one. I turned back firmly to the subject of the bracelet and proceeded to recount a string of falsehoods that I had prepared while on my way to the shop.

'I found this bracelet on the street,' I began, 'and was almost certain that it must come from here. I thought I would try to return it to its rightful owner if I could possibly identify her. But it would probably be too much to ask, that you should remember to whom you sold it. If it was you who sold it at all – it might of course have been someone else?'

'Oh no,' she said. 'This is my counter. I'm here all day, every day, except Sunday, of course.'

'It must be tiring,' I said.

'Oh, well. It's not such a bad place,' she answered quickly. 'I help gentlemen choose gifts, I sell beautiful things, and I see different kinds of people. By the way, I do remember who bought the bracelet,' she added, and then looked up at me, surprised at my sudden access of tension, although I said nothing. 'I don't know who they are, of course,' she amended, 'but I remember quite well what they looked like.'

'They?' I asked.

'Yes, it was a couple. A rather elderly gentleman bought the bracelet for a – for a woman. A young person. They hesitated over any number of things first – she tried them all on, I think. That's why I remember it.'

A woman? A *young person*?

'Was there only one such bracelet? Were there not several similar ones?' I asked, just to be certain.

'Oh no. There were no two the same. Each one was different. This was the only ivory one with beads, as a matter of fact.'

'Ah! Well then, tell me what the people who bought it were like. Can you describe the girl?' I said, and my heart beat till the blood rushed in my ears. Those limp fingers...

'She was...well...she was very pretty and friendly,' she said guardedly. 'And curious. She kept on trying things and laughing. The gentleman seemed fond of her. But, well...'

The photograph was in my bag – I reached for it, then

hesitated. I was afraid that it would turn our cheerful chat into an investigation, and that she would become suspicious and silent.

'But what?' I said.

'She wasn't a lady,' she replied shortly. There was a world of meaning, of contempt, of resentment, of jealousy, in her words. A *young person*, being offered jewellery by an *elderly gentleman*, whilst she herself remained forever a prisoner behind her glass counter, a *good girl*. Thumbnail sketches of the dramatis personae of British society passed in front of me.

'And the gentleman? What was he like?'

'Oh, he was distinguished, with a cane and silver grey hair. He had a rather loud voice, and a lot of authority. I don't know who he is, but I think he lives in Cambridge. I see him sometimes, passing in the street.'

'Ah!' I cried, as the import of her words sank into me. This fact presented an astonishing opportunity to succeed in my task.

'Well,' she added, 'at any rate, I believe I've seen him passing in front of the shop more than once. I spend a lot of my time staring out at the street.'

I turned involuntarily, and followed her gaze out of the broad display window. The sunlit street appeared like an aquarium, with brightly coloured fish floating past, deprived of their legs by the lower wall.

'I wonder how I could manage to find that gentleman?' I said.

'If all you want is to give him back the bracelet, then why don't you simply leave it here with me? I can dash out and catch him next time I see him passing by, and give it back to him.'

'No!' I said, struck suddenly by the awful image of a man suddenly being handed, in bright daylight, a bracelet he knew to belong to a dead girl – *a bracelet he may even be aware that she was wearing when she died.*

It could be dangerous; he could see it as a preliminary to blackmail...

'No, no. No thank you. What I really want is to meet this man myself,' I said firmly. 'Will you help me?'

'Why do you want to meet him?' she asked, looking up at me directly, her curiosity awakened.

The position was most awkward. I disliked telling the truth – goodness, how dishonest that makes me sound – but I have found it immensely useful to have my professional identity utterly hidden while detecting. Yet it was clear that there might be much to be gained by telling her everything, now, at once. And indeed, I could not see any other way to obtain the information I needed.

'I can tell you, and I must,' I decided quickly, looking around to make sure no one was within earshot. 'I need your help, and I see that I cannot ask you for it without making you aware of the facts.' And with a quick gesture, I withdrew the portrait of the dead girl from my handbag and placed it on the counter in front of her.

'That's the woman who bought the bracelet!' she said at once. 'But – how strange she looks! What is this picture? Is she sleeping? She looks as if she were dead!'

I felt the taut, narrow possibility of imminent success stretching before me, so fragile, so easily snapped.

'She is dead,' I said. 'Her body was found floating in the Cam, and the bracelet was on her wrist.'

'Oooh,' she breathed, staring at me. 'Was she killed?'

'It seems she might have been,' I admitted.

'Are you from the police?'

'No,' I said quickly. Nothing causes witnesses to close up like clams so much as the mention of that hard-working, earnest and deserving body. 'I'm just a friend,' I continued, both vaguely and untruthfully. 'I thought that I recognised her bracelet as coming from here, and offered my help in trying to identify her. You see, the body is completely unidentified. Nobody has any idea who she is.'

'Oh,' she breathed thoughtfully. 'And the gentleman that I saw – is he the *murderer*?'

'Very likely not,' I said. 'It would be a bit too dangerous for him to have done it, wouldn't it, after all kinds of people like you had seen them together?'

'Well, but he might be,' she insisted. 'That kind of gentleman wouldn't think anything of being seen by people like me. People like me don't even exist for him.' She gave an impatient little gesture of frustration.

'Well, that's as may be,' I said. 'People do tend to take more care if they are about to commit a murder. I don't know, but I do think that if we can find the gentleman you saw, he will at least be able to tell us her name, and that is all I want right now.'

'Oh,' she said. 'Well, if that's all, I could just run out and ask him about it, next time he passes.'

'No!' I said quickly. 'Don't speak to him – I definitely advise you not to speak to him at all if you see him, least of all about the young woman or the bracelet.'

She gave me a quick, penetrating glance. 'So you do think…' she murmured.

'I don't really, but of course we must remain on the safe

side,' I said firmly. 'We don't know, that's all there is to it. It would be best if he were not even to lay eyes on you. What I would like to ask you to do, next time you see him passing, is to follow him a little way and see where he goes. Then send me a message at once.'

'But I'm not supposed to leave my post,' she hesitated.

I looked around. To the left of the exotic items was a stand selling silk scarves, and to the right several handbags were on display. There was a young woman behind each of them, and neither of them was doing anything.

'Well,' she admitted, following my glance, 'I could run out for just a few minutes if I see him again.'

'How often do you think you see him?'

'It's hard to tell. But fairly often, I think. Every few days, maybe? Though I don't believe I've seen him since the Chinese sale.'

'If you see him, have a note sent to me immediately,' I told her, writing down my name and address on a piece of paper which I handed her together with a modest financial encouragement. She flushed.

'I can't take this,' she said.

'This is a job I am asking you to do for me,' I said. 'It is work, honest work. It is quite all right. In fact, it is very important – you do realise that? A girl hardly older than yourself has died. We must find out who she was and how she died.'

'Yes,' she said. 'I do see that. Even if she was just a…even if, well, what I mean is, whoever she was, she was enjoying her life and didn't deserve to die. I see what you mean. Even if she is dead, this is still like giving her a helping hand. I'll do it.'

Our eyes met across the counter, scattered with its litter of objects, delicate, frivolous, artistic objects, all made uniquely for pleasure – the pleasure of young girls. Her eyes like deep pools showed me anxiety, concern, a consciousness of suffering, a search for meaning.

'She shouldn't have died,' she said again, thoughtfully. 'She was happy.'

'That's an interesting remark,' I said. 'Do you think she was in love with the gentleman?'

'Him? Oh, no. That was just – well, professional. She was very nice to him. He was a gentleman friend. And she liked the bracelet. No, she was just happy in general, I think, happy and excited. Maybe a little too excited. Maybe almost nervous. I can't remember exactly.'

An unwed girl, 'professionally' befriending an elderly gentleman, a baby on the way…and yet the impression she gave – to another girl of her own age, no less – was of being happy. Why happy? Would not a girl in such a situation be rather fearful and troubled, if not in despair? Yet she seemed happy. And days later, she was dead.

'Vanessa – you're waiting again,' said Arthur, after dinner had been cleared away and the twins sent upstairs to be put to bed.

'Who, me?' I said, dropping a ball of wool which I had taken out of my workbasket and put back twice already.

'Yes, you. Listen, nothing is easier to observe than a waiting Vanessa. You fidget and don't do anything.' Rising, he came to lean over me and smiled.

'I won't ask you what you're waiting for, but I will ask you if you'll have to wait long.'

'I don't know, that's the trouble. It could be days and days. Oh, Arthur, you're right, I do hate waiting and not being able to do anything. It's my worst defect, I know. I really ought to cultivate the Eastern art of patience.'

'Well then,' he said, 'since you haven't done that yet, let me suggest instead that you relieve the anxiety by spending the weekend in London with me. You know Ernest Dixon and his wife have been inviting us for ages – they have an extra room in their flat. He's just written to me about it again, and he even asked what we'd like to see. Do let's go, it would do you good.'

'Oh, I would love to,' I said eagerly, thinking secretly that Robert Sayle's is closed on Sundays anyway. 'But how can I leave the children for a whole weekend?'

'Stuff,' he said. 'Sarah will spoil them rotten and they'll simply love it. And we'll come home on Sunday. We'll spend just one night away.'

'But what if the message I'm waiting for comes while I'm gone?' I worried. 'I don't expect it so soon, and yet that is just what *would* happen, isn't it?'

'Well, there I can't give you any advice, as I don't know what kind of message you're waiting for. Once it comes, what need you do?'

'Well, that will depend on what it says,' I admitted, wondering what the shopgirl – whose name I suddenly realised I had stupidly omitted to ask – could possibly write, even if she did spot the familiar gentleman. *Come at once – he's in the tea-shop?* Or better, *Have managed to talk to him and found out his name?* No, no, she mustn't do that!

'Yes, do let's go,' I said.

'Good! I knew you would want to!' he said happily. 'And I

simply can't face a whole weekend at home with you waiting. I'll send Ernest a telegram. Let's have a look at the paper to see what plays are on.' He rustled the pages of his newspaper to the theatre section and read over it with undisguised pleasure.

'There's *Hamlet, Lear* and *Midsummer Night's Dream*,' he said in a faintly hopeful tone, 'but we've seen all of them already, of course.'

'Many times,' I agreed.

'So perhaps you'd like something different,' he continued. 'How about this? *The Second Mrs Tanqueray* has come back after a break, with the same cast, at the St. James. Do you remember? It was a great hit about two years ago.'

'I remember hearing something about it,' I said. 'It's one of Pinero's comedies, isn't it? We couldn't go at the time.'

'It isn't a comedy. It's supposed to be rather a powerful critique of social mores. It was the big revelation of the actress Stella Campbell, who's become very famous since then.'

'Oh, I remember now! It's the play about a woman with a past!' Indeed, I had been intrigued at the time, both by the 'dangerous' content and by the flamboyant reputation of the young actress impersonating the main character. But the twins were tiny, and travelling had been out of the question. I had not even had time to think about it again since.

'Yes, that's the one. It made quite a splash. What do you say? Shall we go?'

'Yes indeed, if the Dixons haven't already seen it.'

Like a magician, Arthur had eased the anxious pressure which seemed to constrict me, and filled my mind with eager anticipation. While not necessarily the most exotic thing in the world, a day in London, a visit to friends and a trip to the theatre is a sufficiently rare event in my quiet life for it to cause quite a stir and a ripple there. Taking my candle, I went upstairs to pack a few small items in readiness for a departure early in the morning, glancing out of the window as I did so.

The sky was clear and starry, and beyond being pleased that the weather seemed fine, I felt moved by its endless depth. But my joy was suddenly marred by the thought that that infinity of twinkling eyes had looked down so recently on this same garden, on the road which ran past the bottom of it, on the Lammas Land beyond, on the river which flowed and whooshed softly through it, and on the corpse of the dead girl floating there, carried by the current, held by the weeds.

The four of us sat together at a table beautifully laid with white cloth and crystal glasses, awaiting the arrival of the fish. Ernest and Kathleen had quite insisted on bringing us to this little restaurant near the theatre, a newly discovered favourite of theirs, perfect for a late dinner after the play. I settled down contentedly and indulged in feeling experienced and cosmopolitan.

'So what have you been working on lately?' Arthur asked Ernest, unfolding his napkin and spreading it on his knee. Ernest is of course primarily a physicist rather than a mathematician, and an experimentalist, at that. But Arthur is fascinated by any and all sciences.

'Still the old magnetism experiments,' replied Ernest. 'It's just extraordinary, the power they have. I showed Kathleen some field lines the other day. You know – if you put iron filings on a sheet of paper and hold it over a magnet, the filings literally shift into a picture of force lines, going from one pole to the other. It looks like this,' and he began scratching out a picture with a point of his fork onto the tablecloth. 'It's extraordinary. It means, you must realise, that those lines are more than just abstract pictures of the directions of force. They represent physical action on the atoms! That's the direction of my present work.' He completed his thumbnail sketch and displayed it to us proudly. 'If you do this with a magnet, you literally see in which direction the forces of the magnet's poles will pull the iron filings. But if you know the theory, you don't need the experiment!'

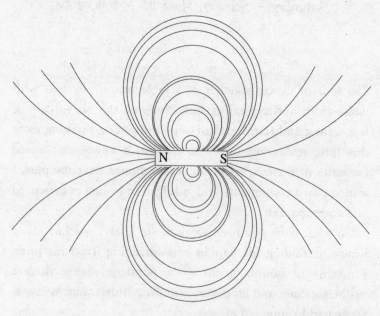

'No physics during meals,' said Kathleen in a hurried whisper, cutting short his enthusiasm as the waiter arrived balancing several dishes on his arm, and hastily rubbing over the scratches with her fingers, 'and stop spoiling the tablecloth!' 'Got to stop them, dear,' she added, turning to me with a smile, 'otherwise they'd be at it all night. I simply can't stand science at the table.' She shook a finger playfully at her husband to smooth the prickle behind her words, but she meant business clearly enough. Personally, I find these discussions quite interesting, although I am but a poor contributor. However, Kathleen preferred to talk about the play.

'Mrs Campbell is sublime,' she said. 'Goodness, how I love to watch all that spunk and fire up there on the stage for all to see! What a difference with Ellen Terry. Terry can portray the divine in woman as no one else can, I'll grant you that. But Campbell gives you a flavour of the devil.'

'Redhead that you are,' said her husband.

'Well, Mrs Campbell may not be a redhead, but she might well be Irish, if you ask me,' said Kathleen.

'Campbell is hardly an Irish name.'

'No, but it's her married name. I've no idea what her own name might be. She likes to be known as Mrs Patrick Campbell – it keeps up some semblance of respectability, I suppose.'

'That is an interesting point,' I said. 'It makes her sound just like the woman in the play.'

'Yes, you're right, poor Mrs Tanqueray, trying so hard to tear some respectability from the fabric of her life, and discovering the thing to be impossible. The whole play is about nothing else, really.'

'Yes, and yet it's dramatic, tragic even. It's odd that a notion like respectability should take on such importance that tragedy can be based on it. What is wrong with our time? Shakespeare would never have employed such stuff for his plots. Since when has social approval been given the power of life or death over us?'

'Oh, well – the power of life or death? Let us not exaggerate.'

'But yes, in the play it does, doesn't it? After all, Mrs Tanqueray takes her own life at the end. Is she not destroyed by the realisation that her sinful past will prevent her ever obtaining a respectable social position?'

We all four fell silent, trying to understand why Mrs Tanqueray had committed suicide, or, rather, why the author had caused her to do so, after she had managed to pull herself out of the mud of loose living by contracting a marriage with a gentleman.

'I think it was because of guilt. She felt guilty about having revealed to the pure young girl that her fiancé had been her own ex-lover,' said Ernest after a moment.

'No,' argued Arthur. 'She didn't feel guilty, for it was her own choice to reveal it; she clearly says that she would feel guilty to hide it.'

'It wasn't that at all,' said Kathleen. 'It was because she realised that her past would not leave her alone, that she would always meet people in society who knew about it. Marriage or none, in fact, respectability was simply out of her reach.'

'I think perhaps it was because she found respectability itself disappointing rather than unattainable,' I said. 'Her husband is so stuffy, the girl Ellean is cold and the life is portrayed as being horrendously stifling. I think that once she found it, she was disillusioned and found she could not stand it.'

'Man is a fool,' hummed Ernest, 'when it's hot he wants cool, when it's cool he wants hot, he always wants what he has not. And woman is worse, of course.'

'How unfair,' said Kathleen. 'Women's lot is a difficult one, and if they dream of something better, they are accused of not knowing their own mind.' And she pinched his ear, nearly knocking over his glass of wine as she did so. I noticed that droll or tender gestures always accompanied and attenuated the echo of bitterness in her words.

'Well, your lot may be hard,' remarked her husband, 'but

think how you'd hate it if you had to be respectable like Mrs Tanqueray.'

'Ho! I am respectable, thank you very much.'

'Are you sure?' he teased. 'I don't see you dying of boredom in a country house.'

'That was only because Mrs Tanqueray had a past! All the truly respectable people in the play live in London and visit the Continent and go to restaurants and have dinners, and no one has a word to say about it!'

'The whole thing is like a supercomplicated game of chess with a thousand subtle rules,' observed Arthur. 'If one has not done such-and-such before, then it is all right to do such-and-so now, but not this other thing, whereas if one has done it before, then such-and-so is unthinkable now.'

'It is not so complicated as you make out,' said Ernest. 'There's really just a single rule. Stay straight on one matter – let me make myself clear, just a single one – then everything else is open to you.' He blushed as everybody stared at him, open-mouthed at such plain-speaking. Although now that I write the words down, it occurs to me that plain-speaking is not such a good description. Indeed, he did not pronounce the words *stay straight on all that concerns love*. Still, we all understood him perfectly, a sign, perhaps, that our minds are not as pure as they might be.

'No,' said Kathleen sharply. 'That's far too simple. For one thing, what you just said applies only to women. No, don't deny it, don't even bother. You know it perfectly well. And for another, a woman can be as virtuous as you like, and yet put herself outside the bounds of respectability by her profession. Just take Mrs Campbell as an example. Do you think she could ever be invited to a bourgeois home?'

'Well, an actress,' said her husband, with a little, secret smile.

'There, you see? You are simply assuming that an actress cannot be virtuous! But why?'

He considered the question for a moment.

'Well, she might *be* virtuous, but she can never *appear* virtuous, because she's public,' he said finally. 'That's the whole point, really, isn't it? Virtue is essentially private.'

'I don't see that,' said his wife. 'Mrs Tanqueray in the play had lived with a man without being married to him, before she married the stuffy fellow. That was perfectly private.'

'No, it was public, because everyone knew about it. She had a "set", remember? All her friends knew, and they didn't care, because they were just the same themselves.'

'The real question is, why should we care?' said Arthur surprisingly. 'And why women particularly, indeed?'

'What an awkward conversation,' said Kathleen; 'we keep having to stop and think.'

'In order not to find ourselves giving out easy formulae or pat words,' I added. 'I wonder, if each one of us admitted to the first answer that came into our heads at Arthur's question, if we would not find out something rather disagreeable about ourselves?'

'You mean when he asked why we care? Because society's dictates have power over our thoughts,' said Kathleen. 'That's what you call a disagreeable thing, isn't it? But we should be praised for at least trying to resist, should we not? I'll admit to my first thought in answer to his question: I thought that we care about respectability in – in much the same way we care about cleanliness. Because we don't like to be soiled. But I know that Arthur could then just as well ask me why living with a man without being married to him should necessarily be perceived as *soiling*.'

'I thought of those women you see on the street, late at night, in the West End, when you come out of the theatre alone,' said Ernest. 'The ones who come up and say "Cheerio, ducks", and things like that.'

'What things?' enquired Kathleen with great interest.

'Oh, nothing important – just things like that. What did you think in answer to your own question, Arthur?' Kathleen looked both fascinated and alarmed, while Arthur, to his credit, looked merely thoughtful.

'I thought that I should not like to share my wife with anyone else,' he said simply. I laughed.

'What did you think of, Vanessa? Tell the truth – the whole truth, and nothing but the truth,' ordered Kathleen energetically.

'I remembered a woman I met once who had a little restaurant,' I said. 'She was that kind of woman, and what of it? She was very kind.' I glanced at Arthur, recalling how I had burst into tears on that surprised person's ample bosom at a point when the outcome of his trial was looking particularly frightening. Having never told him about my hasty visit to London, I perceived that he was staring at me in surprise.

'Oh, it was long ago, long before we were married,' I said quickly, in order to ward off any questions. 'But seriously, Ernest – you don't really believe that all actresses are immoral?'

'Oh, I don't know, and in fact I don't really care to know,' said Ernest. 'I like to see them where they are, on the stage, I mean, and shouldn't like to see them in my own drawing room. That's all I mean.'

'The bourgeoisie may feel like you, but swells do marry

actresses sometimes,' said Kathleen. 'Why, Pinero's most recent play is about that very subject! It hasn't been put on yet – they're rehearsing it now. We're attending a reading tomorrow. It's to be about a rich young man who falls in love with a juvenile-lady from Sadler's Wells.'

'Falling in love is different,' said her husband. 'No one can explain why that happens. You see a hundred women on the stage – why fall in love with one of them in particular? And yet it happens. One among hundreds. I – I saw a lovely Ophelia last month.'

'Oh,' said Arthur eagerly. 'Where was that?'

'The Outdoor Shakespeare Company. It's quite new. Have you heard of them? It was all put together by a bright young fellow called Alan Manning; he puts on Shakespeare's plays, and other plays too, in fields and things on the outskirts of London. They have a kind of tent for when it rains, but they don't play in the winter, of course. It's very fetching, I can tell you. They like to set up their stage where there are trees, when they can. Ophelia actually floated away – literally floated away down a little stream, out of sight. It was most poetic, although in reality, she must have been cold and wet, poor thing. *The Tempest* was impressive as well, with Ariel darting about all over the place, disappearing behind things and turning up somewhere else. He was played by the same girl. Ivy Elliott is her name. A lovely creature.'

'That sounds both charming and intriguing,' said Arthur. 'I wish we could see one of those.'

'You can,' said Ernest. '*A Midsummer Night's Dream* is running now, out in Hampstead. We haven't been yet.'

'And shan't, if you keep on praising that actress to

the skies,' said Kathleen sharply. Ernest crimsoned.

'Is she playing Hermia or Helena?' enquired Arthur smoothly.

'Neither; she's booked for Titania on the programme. She couldn't be Hermia, as she's blonde, nor Helena, as she's rather small. You should go, really. There'll be a matinée tomorrow, even though it *is* Sunday – these bohemians don't respect anything any more! What time did you mean to leave for home?'

'Oh, our plans for tomorrow are not firm yet,' said Arthur. 'Shall we, Vanessa? What do you think? We can go to a matinée and still arrive home before the children are in bed.'

'I'd love to,' I said, putting my hand on his. 'It will be quite a psychological leap, won't it, from Pinero to Shakespeare.'

'Interestingly enough, it won't be as much of one as it might if it were any other play,' observed Arthur, irresistibly entering his stride. 'We were saying before that Shakespeare did not deal with such seemingly artificial questions as respectability and social strictures in his tragedies, being concerned with much more powerful human driving forces—'

'Like ambition—'

'Like jealousy—'

'Like passion—'

'Yes, all that. Shakespeare expresses the fundamental drives that define the *human* condition, not only the *social* condition. Yet those social questions make their appearance as well. Often, in fact – especially in the comedies.'

'Do you think so?' asked Kathleen. 'I never thought of the comedies that way. They always seem to be delving into stories of awful complications due to mix-ups, misidentifications, and confusions.'

'Yes, but think how often he creates those mixed-up situations by raising questions about one's "place in society",' persisted Arthur. 'Think of all the girls dressing as boys, the women who fall in love with young men who are actually other women, the various comical punishments endured by those who would infringe the sacred rules of marriage – Falstaff, Katharina, Titania also for that matter.'

'I guess,' I said slowly, 'that the point is that the questions which concern Pinero also concerned Shakespeare, but what Pinero sees as tragic, Shakespeare saw as the stuff of comedy. He actually perceived all the rules people make to keep every person in his own little box as funny, and even funnier the mishaps that occur when the prisoners attempt to escape.'

'Oh, he knew what he was doing,' said Arthur. 'It's no accident that our sympathies always lie with the shrew rather than the tamer, with Falstaff rather than the merry wives.'

'It's much less dramatic put that way,' remarked Kathleen, 'one loses that exciting feeling of being surrounded by *bad* people whom one mustn't know, but who live secret, sinful lives.'

'Yes, Shakespeare's characters are allowed to flow in and out of naughtiness,' said Ernest. 'But that was another century. It's not so easy any more. Or perhaps it was difficult even in his time, in reality.'

'So you think that Pinero is representing reality?'

'Well, as it is now; today's reality. Yes, I think so. Perhaps it was a little exaggerated to make Mrs Tanqueray commit suicide, but the description of her social isolation was accurate enough, I would say, and it's understandable that such a situation can lead to despair.'

'I believe you have a point,' said Arthur with a shade of surprise in his voice. 'We tend to be thankful for the times we live in; we tend to assume they are better than those that came before. But our society must be horrendously more difficult than it used to be, for some.'

This conversation was still floating vaporously in my mind as we took a bumpy omnibus to Hampstead, carrying our bag and a picnic basket generously filled by Kathleen and covered with a chequered cloth. The streets were full of people in their Sunday best, and the sunshine gilded dusty London with a golden glint.

'Enjoy yourselves,' she had said good-heartedly on seeing us off. 'You're lucky with the weather. I hope it lasts.'

'Wouldn't you like to come?' I asked.

'Oh – I think not,' she replied quickly. 'We're going to the Pinero reading, I told you; a friend of Ernest's will be reading one of the main parts. And anyway – well, no. It's better not.'

We walked for some distance after descending from the omnibus, asking our way several times, until we reached the expanse of meadow where the play was to be held. Large signs with directions had been installed in its vicinity, making the last part of the walk easy enough, and we arrived more than an hour early, and settled ourselves a short distance away from the bustle going on around the tent and caravan that were being set up near a little grove. The tap-tap of a hammer rang through the still, warm air. Bees buzzed, other small creatures came to investigate our meal, and Arthur removed his jacket and reclined upon it, accepting the large wedge of bread and cheese I handed him. Kathleen had put in a piece of meat pie as well as a bottle of water and several fruits. I leant against Arthur and allowed myself an hour of dreamy respite from life's responsibilities.

When the play was soon to begin, we gathered up our things, swept off crumbs, shook out the cloth and made our way to the makeshift ticket stall which had been established in front of the clearing which was to serve as a stage, upon which the long-stemmed Queen Anne's lace and the reedy grasses had been carefully shorn. For an extra penny one could rent a cushion; we took two, and settled ourselves in an inviting spot. There were few people as yet, but as the minutes passed they began to arrive in a trickle which turned into a steady stream, and by the time the three knocks signifying the raising of the non-existent curtain were to be heard, we were surrounded by a human swarm clad in shirtsleeves, muslin and straw hats.

The Greeks entered upon the scene, in white swathes and sandals, and the severe scolding of Hermia for loving a man not of her father's choosing began. I found myself concentrating on the familiar words – and realised with a shock that I never had listened to them properly before.

Theseus: *What say you, Hermia? be advised, fair maid:*
To you your father should be as a god;
One that composed your beauties, yea, and one
To whom you are but as a form in wax
By him imprinted and within his power
To leave the figure or disfigure it.

Hermia's fundamental sin is to *possess a will*. For this, she is

given the choice between obedience – murder of the will,
death – murder of the body, or perpetual reclusion – murder
of the soul. And she chooses the last.

Hermia: *So will I grow, so live, so die, my lord,*
Ere I will yield my virgin patent up
Unto his lordship, whose unwished yoke
My soul consents not to give sovereignty.

And I perceived in these words the eternal and fatal circle of
transgression and punishment, where previously I had seen
nothing but a poor maiden crossed in love, but certain to
triumph in the end. I poked Arthur in the ribs with my elbow,
and he glanced at me, shrugging very slightly.

There it was, in Shakespeare's own words: what are you,
what are we all, but *forms in wax*, controlled by authority,
destined to yield or die?

Was this comedy? Were we meant to laugh or cry?

To laugh, of course. We all know that Hermia will wed her
beloved in the end.

Yes – thanks to supernatural help. The price of her
rebellion is paid by Titania, whose own submission is a work
of sorcery. I was reminded of my mother, who invariably
added a benign hunter to Perrault's Little Red Riding Hood,
who kills the wolf and rescues the previously devoured child
and her aged grandmother. I was stunned when I first read the
story for myself and discovered that in fact it ends abruptly
after the wolf's repast. Was the hunter truly nothing but a
little show of magic destined to console and reassure the
tender listeners, who would be shocked and frightened by the
plain reality?

'Look,' whispered Arthur suddenly, interrupting my train of thought. 'It's Puck's scene. Ernest's flame will soon appear!'

I shifted on my cushion, rearranged my posture and observed the mischievous youth cheerfully recounting his exploits, until the fairy shushes him out of the way for the advent of the Queen.

'What a silly Ernest is – that's obviously a wig!' I whispered into Arthur's ear, as a lady stepped forth wielding a sceptre, followed by a ragtag band of fairies carrying her lengthy train. She was not young, but her gait was strong and elegant, and the blonde mane which streamed nearly to her knees was crowned with a wreath of leaves and berries. The effect, while very unlike my personal vision of Titania, was not unqueenly, and the reproaches she immediately proceeded to heap upon her wayward husband reminded me faintly of Kathleen. I noticed Arthur smiling privately.

I continued to stare at Titania curiously during every scene in which she appeared. Stately rather than fairy-like, I actually thought she would have been better as Helena – except –

'Ernest is odd,' I said, smiling, as we rose a little stiffly, and gathering up our wraps and basket, made our way across the broad meadow over which the slight dimming of the late afternoon sun was beginning to be perceptible. 'Too small to play Helena and too blonde to play Hermia, indeed! Why, if anything, it's the opposite. She's quite tall, but if her eyebrows are anything to judge by, I think she's really dark-haired.'

'Yes, I noticed that,' agreed Arthur. 'Careless of them. Surely they could have lightened them up a little, to match the wig.'

And he teased Ernest about it, as he and Kathleen met us to deliver our small bags and join us in a final cup of tea before we boarded our train.

'So you took the lovely Titania for a true blonde?' he said laughingly. 'Vanessa and I have a theory that she isn't really. Her eyebrows were too dark. It's particularly strange as they took such pains with the costumes. They were really most successful. I wonder how theatres manage it – so many costumes, for so many different plays!'

'And even worse – the same ones in a different size, any time they change the actor for a given role,' I added. 'All those alterations...' I stopped suddenly, struck by my own remark.

'According to the play we have just heard – *Trelawney of the Wells*, it's called – some actors are obliged to purchase their own costumes,' said Kathleen. 'They must share, though. It's too expensive for the beginning ones, on their tiny salaries. After all, theatre costumes are no ordinary clothes. They are both special and expensive. The actresses in the play shared everything, although Ernest's friend told us he keeps his own things for himself. But there isn't anything about the theatre that Pinero doesn't know.'

'You mean that the play you heard was a play about acting?' I said curiously.

'Exactly. It was about the life of actors and actresses in a small London theatre. But the true subject is not so different from what we were discussing yesterday. Rose Trelawney is an immensely popular, successful young actress, but she falls in love with a rich young man of good family, and gives up the stage for him. Yet she cannot get used to the life of his family and social class. She suffers from the restraint, and from agonising boredom, exactly like poor Mrs Tanqueray. Only this play ends on a much happier note, with Rose returning to the theatre, and her young man running away from home and becoming an actor himself in the hopes of winning her back.'

'And does he succeed?'

'Well, yes, although it doesn't seem too realistic. He gets his heart's desire, his career, and the forgiving acceptance of his parents as well. All very positive, and done with humour. Yet it's easy to see that it's all just a happy ending to make sure the play is perceived as a comedy and not a tragedy. The pain, the sensation of bitter failure during the scenes showing the clash of the classes, that's what carries the force of the play.'

'Yes, it is a tragedy disguised as a comedy, and it won't be so easy to perform,' agreed Kathleen. 'It's difficult for an actor to succeed well in both tragedy and comedy. And the more so as one tends to get used to the actor in one persona, and have difficulty admitting of his appearance in the other, so that even if he is doing a fine job, one feels somehow put out.'

'Or else one cannot help feeling the tragedy behind his comedy, or vice versa!' added Arthur.

'No, but there are actors and actresses who can do both, extraordinarily,' said Ernest enthusiastically. 'Their tragedy is not heavy, and their comedy contains tears. That is exactly what I admire in Ivy Elliott. I've seen her in both types of role and she is totally convincing in both.'

'But you saw her in both types of role in Shakespeare, isn't that right?' said Arthur. 'It's a bit different, because there is no question that all of Shakespeare's characters spring from the same family, whether tragic or comic. Like the strange kinship, or twinship, between Lear and his Fool.'

'Yes, that is true. Playing Shakespeare is a whole art in itself. I'd like to see Ivy in a play by someone else – then we'd see what she's really capable of!'

'Pah!' interrupted Kathleen. 'A girl who wears a wig, they

say, and you don't even notice it! I'll take Mrs Campbell, myself. You've only seen her in Pinero – but we saw her as Mélisande not four months ago. Maeterlinck, you know – *Pelléas and Mélisande*. Now, that's an actress. It's not that I'm really taken by that symbolic stuff – it's all rather too heavy for me. But Mrs Campbell played Mélisande as a waif-like lost girl that made me cry.'

'Well, if anyone was wearing a wig, it was she in that role!' said Ernest, harping a little unnecessarily, as I thought.

'That's different,' argued Kathleen, 'it's symbolism. Mélisande's long blonde braids are part of the play. You can't do without them, and no one has such braids in reality.'

'Rubbish,' said her husband.

I started to smile, until I caught sight of Kathleen's face, and all of a sudden felt a little stab of worry.

1887

Two little boys knelt at the edge of the road, giggling uncontrollably, concealing something under the bushes with busy hands.

'It will never work,' said one of them, covering his mouth to stifle the sound, as he scrambled to hide from some elegantly dressed passers-by.

'It will!' exclaimed the other. 'It will! You'll see. All we need is a thunderstorm.'

They both looked up at the endless, perfectly blue Italian sky, and doubled up with laughter again.

The weekend at the theatre helped greatly to soothe the impatient turmoil of my feelings, and to maintain me in a state of relative calm, although I had to restrain myself daily from dropping by Robert Sayle's. After four days of waiting, my patience was rewarded by a little letter which arrived, somewhat unexpectedly, through the post.

Dear Mrs Weatherburn,
I have a little information for you; not much, but it may help.
Please visit me when you can.
Estelle (from Robert Sayle's).

I dropped it on the table and pulled on my gloves at once, calling for Sarah to let her know that I was going out for a while. She nodded cheerfully.

'I'll give the twins their dinner, then,' she said.

The walk into Cambridge seemed longer than usual, though I love walking, and know every detail of the way from dusty Newnham to the lovely university buildings of the centre. I arrived a little dishevelled, feeling as though I had been running, although of course I had been doing nothing of the kind. Yet my heart was pounding exactly as though I had, and I felt dampness on my forehead, under the edges of my hair. Estelle was sitting composedly behind her counter, just as she had been the first time I saw her. A young man was examining some wares that she had spread out in front of him, but even though she was serving him, her expression remained distant, as though it did not make the slightest difference to her whether or not he bought anything, though she was perfectly courteous. I observed her from a distance for some time, while ostensibly examining silk squares and handkerchieves, and waited for him to leave before approaching. She lifted her eyes and saw me.

'Ah,' she breathed in a little voice, glancing hastily around.

'What have you discovered?' I asked her quietly, half-pretending to examine the articles on the counter. She began to remove and put away the different trinkets and knick-knacks she had taken out to tempt the customer.

'I saw *him* passing in the street outside yesterday,' she told me. 'I asked Emma to watch my counter for a moment—' she nodded towards the stout lady at the corset counter ' – and ran out after him. I followed him for a few minutes as you told me, then I had to leave him and return. I stayed away ten minutes; I really could not stay any longer.'

'I understand,' I said. 'And what did he do during the ten minutes that you followed him?'

'He went into Heffers bookshop,' she said. 'I think you may be able to find out more about him there. Through the window, I saw him talking quite familiarly to the man behind the counter. I looked at the time; it was almost exactly a quarter to four. I am sorry I couldn't do anything more, but I did think that the shop assistant at Heffers spoke to him as though he knew him. You may be able to find out simply by asking him who the gentleman who came in yesterday at a quarter to four was; he's tall, silver-haired, and was carrying a cane. I don't know the assistant, that is, I don't know him personally, but I've heard something about him. The girls say he's the heir to a gigantic fortune, but obliged to work for his living while he waits for it.' She smiled, and added, 'Who wouldn't like to make *his* acquaintance?'

I laughed, and thanked her warmly and concretely for this information, which struck me indeed as being potentially very useful. She promised to keep me informed if she saw him again, and to help me further if need be. I left the shop thoughtfully, and my feet led me naturally straight to Petty Cury.

Heffers bookshop was, as always, comfortably populated with clients, not a few of whom were occupied in turning the pages of books with a studious concentration more suggestive of reading than purchasing. There were two or three comfortable leather armchairs between the shelves, and the general impression was welcoming and cosy. I entered, my arrival signalled by a little tinkle, and hesitated briefly on the threshold, wondering how to identify the clerk that Estelle had seen. I thought it likely to be the very man who was there now, briskly serving a small group of customers, with a nod and a friendly smile for each. I decided to proceed on the supposition that he was the right man, given that Estelle could always accompany me to the bookshop later on if further identification should be necessary. Ah, how reassuring *facts* are, and how useful an observant spirit and a good memory for faces.

The clerk appeared to be something over thirty years of age; he was well-mannered and distinguished, humorous and pleasant, with nothing of the obsequiousness or the vulgarity that sometimes distinguishes salespeople. His confident air and the advice and counsel that he freely offered to those who asked him for suggestions made me suspect that he was, in fact, more than a mere salesman; a manager, perhaps, or something more responsible. This feeling was strengthened when I saw him call a younger man who was supervising the shelving of new books from a large box, and ask him to replace him at the counter for a few moments while he consulted a catalogue to see whether a particular edition requested by an elderly gentleman was still in print. Entering a small, glass-windowed office behind the counter, he could be seen turning over the leaves, after which he took up a telephone, requested a number, and spoke silently (as it seemed through the window) into the machine at some length. He then returned and proceeded to give a comparative analysis of the different editions in existence to the elderly man, explaining to him that the one he wanted, while no longer available, was also no longer particularly desirable since more scholarly ones had been compiled since.

I stood by, listening with half an ear, until the peevish old man departed, having stubbornly refused all advice and counsel. Suddenly the personable clerk stood in front of me, asking engagingly if he could be of help.

'I have to ask you a rather awkward question,' I said, fabricating hastily. 'I do hope you will forgive me. I – I met a most interesting gentleman recently at the house of a friend, but I simply cannot remember his name, although he was introduced to me. However, it so happens that – that I saw the very same gentleman in here yesterday, so I thought you might know him. I should so like to meet him again!'

'Good Heavens,' he said, 'but many dozens of people come in here every day! How can I tell whom you mean?'

'He came in yesterday, at about a quarter to four,' I said, neatly parroting Estelle's words. 'He is quite tall, and silver-haired, and carries a cane.'

'Oh-oh!' he said, with a sudden, amused smile. 'Why, you must be talking about my father! So you've met him and would like to meet him again? I *see*,' and his eyes suddenly roved up and down me in a slightly provoking manner. Instinctively, I buried my left hand in my dress to hide my wedding ring, although there was no real need to do so, given that I was wearing gloves. But it was a reflex, for it suddenly appeared obvious to me that the best way to become acquainted with the elderly gentleman was to be a young woman of the type of the dead girl – frivolous, light, possibly even somewhat loose. I smiled much more widely than was natural, and flickered my eyelashes, deciding instantly that my sprigged muslin and beribboned hat, although both proper and elegant, were not so excessively ladylike as to contradict my attitude. I altered my stance, leaning on one foot and crossing my ankles, as advanced young ladies often did.

'He'll be charmed,' said the young man with a smile that was a little too meaningful for my taste, although it had appeared through my own fault. 'Listen, my father lives outside Cambridge, towards Grantchester. Here, I'll write down his name and address for you.' He took up a pen from the counter, dipped it in the ink, and wrote:

Geoffrey Archer, Esq
Chippendale House
Grantchester Meadows

'Oh, thank you very much,' I said, taking the paper and glancing at it attentively. 'I do hope I will meet him soon. May I take it that your name is Mr Archer, too?'

'Julian Archer at your service,' he replied with a slight bow.

I returned to Robert Sayle's before making my way home after this most satisfying interview. I could not prevent my mind running, as I walked jauntily along, on the manner in which I would present Pat with the information that his little puzzle was already solved. But I checked myself firmly. There was still work to be done.

'I've found out his name, but I need you to identify him positively before I do anything else,' I said to Estelle.

'I don't want to meet him!' she said hesitatingly. 'That girl – that girl *died*.'

'No, of course not,' I said quickly. 'You must not get involved at all; you must not meet him.'

'But then what can I do?'

'Well,' I said, 'if you are willing, the best way is to wait in front of his house for him to come in or go out or pass in front of a window. It can be boring and last some time, I am afraid, but it really is the best and safest way. We will do it together, if you wish. Are you willing to try it with me this evening?'

'All right,' she agreed. 'If we're together I won't be frightened.'

Returning home, I found Arthur in the sitting room with the twins on his knees, putting together a small train with pegs whenever he had both hands simultaneously free, while Cecily tried to figure out how to untie his cravat and Cedric tried to push her aside and get more space for himself. Their ringing cries filled the room chaotically. I gave up my half-formed plan of asking his advice.

'Ernest and Kathleen answered your thank-you note,' he said, looking up at me and smiling as I removed my hat. 'Their letter's on the table.'

I picked it up and read it through. They spoke warmly of the pleasure they had had in our company and our shared interest in theatre, and invited us to return soon. I looked over at Arthur and the little scene in front of me, and sighed.

'Their note sounds almost lonely,' I remarked. 'Do you think a happy couple living in London can be lonely?'

'Of course,' he said, peeling off some little arms that were clinging too tightly to his neck. 'I think they wish they had a family.' He smiled, kissing Cecily's dimpled fingers.

'Oh,' I said, turning over the note and reading the postscript on the back. 'Look, Ernest says he's coming up to Cambridge on Monday to give a lecture.'

'Yes, I saw,' he said. 'Can we have him here?'

'Oh, yes, if you like,' I replied. 'Why not? We mustn't tease him too much about his blonde – actress, though...'

I put down the letter, suddenly struck by the word *blonde* which had already been so much in my head because of the dead girl. I turned to Arthur to make the remark, but he was taken up with the noisy, vigorous little pair, so I sat down on the sofa instead, and proceeded to think.

Ernest had said Ivy Elliott was small and blonde. The actress we had seen was undoubtedly dark and rather tall. Could it possibly be that we had seen a different actress? And if so, why was Ivy Elliott not playing her role? Where was she?

No, I was being silly.

Yet he had admired Ivy as Ophelia – and I had thought of Ophelia at once...

Yes, but who would not associate a young girl floating in the river with the eternal image of Ophelia?

Yet it would explain the strangeness of the dress, the ill-sewn, altered white gown with its scattered pansies.

...and there is pansies, that's for thoughts.

Ophelia, in her theatre costume, floating in the green water?

I shook myself and rose. I had set up a logical procedure to identify the dead girl, and I should follow it through. There was no need to speculate or jump to conclusions.

'Arthur, I must go out again,' I said as soon as supper was over. As the time of my meeting with Estelle approached, my desire to confirm Mr Archer's identity as the purchaser of the bracelet was becoming irresistible. He looked up at me queryingly. I crossed over to him and put my hand on his shoulder.

'You are taking care of yourself, of course,' he said in a matter-of-fact tone.

'Oh, yes,' I said. 'Nothing much is happening, Arthur. It's just a matter of identification. I'm not even working under false pretences at this point. I'm not letting myself be seen at all.' He smiled, relieved, and I put on my hat and left, trying not to let my sense of urgency drive me into an unseemly show of haste.

Mr Archer's imposing manor house was easy enough to find, a mere twenty minutes' walk from my own. I realised as I located it that I had passed in front of it uncountably many times on my rambles, but I had never actually seen it, since it

was set deep within stately grounds filled with trees and was not
actually visible from the street. We crept through the wrought
iron double gates and walked quietly up the curving main drive
until we came in sight of the house. Dusk was falling, and the
lamps were lit in all the rooms of the lower floors.

'Oh, be careful,' whispered Estelle, even though there was
not a soul within hearing distance. She seemed nervous; she
breathed rapidly, and I could not help glancing at her trim
figure and wondering if she ought not to have prepared for
her adventure by relaxing her tight-lacing a little.

'There's somebody there!' she gasped, snatching my hand.
'There is somebody in that room!' and she pointed to one of
the large, lit front windows.

'Let's go nearer,' I said.

'Up to the house?' she squeaked.

'No, no,' I reassured her. 'Just near enough to see through
the window.'

'Ooh,' she said. 'What if someone comes out and chases us
away?'

'It's all right,' I said, 'then we will go away. We'll ask if
Mr...Mr Lighthorn lives there, and say we made a mistake
with the address. Nothing bad can happen to us, Estelle.'

The whole identification procedure took us, in the end, no
more than ten minutes. We did not continue up the drive, but
skirted it, moving quietly under the shadow of the trees and
approaching the house from the side. Several windows looked
out onto the side where we now stood, one of them a large
french window giving onto a terrace with stairs leading down
to the garden. As we approached cautiously, moving from tree
to tree, this door suddenly opened a crack, and an arm
appeared, holding the knob from inside.

'I thought I heard something out here, Spokes,' a voice tossed back into the room, and a man emerged onto the terrace and stood looking out into the night. He moved down a few steps, and Estelle and I froze behind a rather large oak.

'I'll put out a trap, sir,' said the butler from the doorway. 'It might be a fox or a rat.'

'All right. Bring me a whisky and soda, and then you can lock up,' said his master, returning into the house and shutting the door behind him.

'It's him all right,' cried Estelle ungrammatically, in a loud whisper. She was squeezing her hands together enthusiastically. 'That's the very gentleman who bought the bracelet! I know him for sure. It's him! Oh, ma'am, *do* you think he murdered her? Do you?'

'I don't really,' I said. 'It would be too obvious, somehow. Still, one never knows, so I now advise you to forget about everything we have said and done together. Whatever you do, do *not* try anything further.'

'Oh, I don't want to,' she said. 'Just doing this has frightened me to death! But perhaps you will come and see me when it's all over and you have found out who did it. Will you do that?'

I smiled as I drew her away, and tried to explain that I was not investigating the murder. Yet my task was not complete, and certainly not without its own importance. I spent the rest of the walk home puzzling deeply over the best way in which to accomplish the next step in my investigation. I now knew the name and residence of a man who had bought a bracelet for the dead girl. From there to discovering her identity seemed but a short leap – yet not an easy one! In fact, I simply could not think how to go about it. I could not figure out a single reasonable way of initiating a conversation with a gentleman with whom I was absolutely not acquainted, on the subject of a girl with whom he obviously had illicit relations, and whom he may or may not know to be dead – and, for all I had said to Estelle, who may or may not be her murderer. I was still wondering what I should say to him in the event that I could somehow wangle a meeting when I reached home. Upon entering, I discovered that Pat was there, enjoying a late drink with Arthur.

'Already back?' said Arthur, extremely surprised to see me arrive so soon after I had left. 'I thought you'd be out for the evening.'

'It was quick,' I said.

'Well, here's someone who will be delighted to hear that,' he said. 'Pat considers me but a poor substitute for your company, Vanessa.'

'I'm an impatient man,' said Pat apologetically. 'It's been a while, Vanessa, and you haven't written or let me know anything. What have you been doing? Where have you been this evening? Have you found out anything? You can talk – I told Arthur everything anyway.'

'Oh, Pat,' I sighed. 'I do hate sharing the details of an investigation at this stage. It isn't ripe yet!'

'Well,' he said pitilessly, 'too bad. Do it anyway.'

'Oh, all right,' I said. 'I will, because I'm in a bit of difficulty about how to proceed, so I'll ask your advice. What I have discovered is that the girl's bracelet was bought in Robert Sayle's last week when they had their Chinese sale. I went to the sale myself, that's how I thought of it. The bracelet was bought by an elderly gentleman who was accompanied by the dead girl. The shopgirl recognised her from the photograph.'

'Fantastic!' cried Pat. 'Now we just have to find the old gentleman!'

'His name is Archer, and he lives in a manor not very far from here. It's called Chippendale House.'

'Chippendale House!' he exclaimed. 'Why – don't tell me you're talking about old Geoffrey Archer?'

'Yes, I am,' I said in amazement. 'Why, do you know him?'

'Well, I do,' he replied proudly. 'I'm a journalist, you know; I know all the major citizens of our fine metropolis.'

I laughed.

'I do indeed, you can believe me or not. I've interviewed Mr Archer myself, on a question of financial matters. I remember him very well. It was a little matter of funds for the restoration of Little St Mary. The paper did a great splashy project to help raise the money, and a couple of us journalists were sent around to solicit interviews with a list of wealthy people we felt might be induced to contribute. We were instructed to be ready to write up a flattering article on each major contributor. I was assigned several, and got plenty of pounds and shillings from them altogether, I must say. But Mr Geoffrey Archer said he couldn't do it, so he never did get his article.'

'That's odd,' I said. 'He must be very rich. I wonder why he wouldn't contribute?'

'Actually, he told me. He explained it all quite frankly,' said Pat. 'Only I can't recall exactly what he said. He asked me not to write anything about it. What was it now? Something about his estate being all tied up so he didn't have the right to touch anything, not anything significant, anyway. He gave me ten pounds and said let it remain anonymous, he'd rather be seen publicly as giving nothing at all, rather than a trivial sum. Ten pounds was a very nice little sum for the church, of course, but I can imagine that a gentleman would like to make a bigger mark than that. I remember feeling a bit sorry for him; he keeps up such a train of living, in that big splendid house, that one can't help thinking he's very wealthy, and so he is, but all the money is administered by trustees or some such thing.'

'Interesting,' I said. 'It might be true, I suppose, although he did buy the girl a bracelet. But what's a bracelet? Still, the impression of the shopgirl from Robert Sayle's was definitely that she was a kept woman. How much does it cost to keep a woman, I wonder?'

'Vanessa – what a question!' said Arthur.

'A lot, if you have to pay rent,' said Pat pragmatically. 'But let's get back to the point. This man obviously knew the girl well enough, kept or not. Now we know who he is, but we don't know who she is, or was. So what are you going to do about it?'

'I don't know,' I admitted. 'I was rather stuck on that point. I wish we could just ask him. What I was thinking of doing was asking Mrs Burke-Jones if she knows him. I might be able to become acquainted with him through her. She moves in quite good circles, and given that her brother is a don, she has managed to surround herself with a rare social mixture of town and gown. She might easily have met our Mr Archer somewhere.'

'But that could take days,' he said, echoing my own thoughts, 'and even when you do meet him, how on earth can you ask the question? You can't just go up and say "What was the name of that girl you bought the bracelet for?" No, I have a better idea. How about if I do it? I can get at him easily. I'll interview him!'

I kept silent about the vague thought that was tickling the back of my mind. If the dead girl was one and the same as the actress Ivy Elliott – and if I simply brought the conversation round to theatre and mentioned how much I admired her, might he not be led to react? No, but I couldn't mention the idea to Pat yet, it was too silly; I should make a fool of myself. Ivy Elliott was very likely the bewigged Titania.

'But you'll have the same problem as me,' I said instead. 'If you pretend to be interviewing him for some newspaper business or other, then you can hardly bring up facts from his personal life.'

'I'll take care of it, leave it to me. I'll think of something,' he said confidently, already on his way out of the door. I felt a little envious. Being a real journalist is a fantastic cover for a little detective work. Simply going up and ringing Mr Archer's bell and asking to speak to him was admittedly a legitimate possibility under such circumstances. It was not obvious that he would succeed, but the chance was there. And he ought to have the best chance possible.

'Pat!' I called impulsively, as he was already disappearing down the path to the gate. 'Pat, listen. This may be all wrong – this may be wrong and simply silly, but – I just have a hunch that the dead girl might have been an actress. Perhaps it might give you an idea about how to talk to him. And another thing, Pat – please take this back! I don't need it any longer.' And I thrust the Chinese Bracelet into his hand, and latched the gate behind him.

1887

They gathered them together, sisters, brothers and cousins, and swearing them all to secrecy, made them pray for rain every day. Weeks went by before the longed-for black cloud was perceived on the horizon. And then the grown-ups could not understand why the youngsters were so tumultuous and so excited – not only were they not annoyed at being penned inside the house by the downpour, but they were all crowded together in Guglielmo's room, and they didn't even seem to be talking, except for bursts of whispers and hushes.

The grown-ups didn't even hear the tinkle of the tiny bell. But they heard the burst of applause and the children's screams of joy.

Saturday, July 2nd, 1898

Even though I knew that Pat had an advantage over me, and that he might be speaking to Mr Archer at that very moment, I could not resist taking myself off, yesterday, to pay a call on Mrs Burke-Jones. In order not to seem too goal-directed, I brought Cecily with me, proudly dressed in her best with new patent leather shoes on her minuscule feet. I found Mrs Burke-Jones enjoying a peaceful afternoon by herself, school having let out for the holidays some days ago. She was cutting the heads off the dead roses and piling the withered flowers in a basket on the grass at her side. I paused, admiring her upright carriage and well-tailored dress. I do find that the modern fashion of skirts closely fitted near the waist and sweeping into a gentle flare as they descend to the ground becomes her better than the stiff bustles we used to wear when I first met her ten years ago, which seemed to underscore rather than soften her somewhat stern and authoritarian style.

'Why, Mrs Weatherburn,' she said – our friendship, although warm, having begun on too unequal a footing to ever admit of the use of Christian names between us – 'how unexpected and what a pleasure. Do join me in the garden. Would the child like a biscuit?'

Cecily registered due enthusiasm at the suggestion of a biscuit, and holding it tightly, went to stand in front of a large flower-bed which was buzzing with an astonishing number of busy bees.

'Bzzz, bzzz, bzzzz,' she said to herself, quietly, observing them.

'Oh dear,' said Mrs Burke-Jones, 'aren't you afraid she'll get stung?'

'No,' I said. 'She won't disturb them. She likes to watch. She looks at things very carefully, and can tell you quite a lot about them afterwards.'

'She'll be a good pupil, then,' she said, 'if you mean to send her to school.'

'Well, naturally I'll send her to your school, *and* her brother,' I laughed, recalling a time when her school used to be my little school and the audacious idea of including small boys in its composition came to us together. That idea of ten years ago seems almost banal now, as schools of its kind have sprung up all over the country. What had seemed so daring, so original to us, had apparently struck the mind of an entire country all at once.

'But it won't be for a long time yet,' I went on. 'They're only just three – they're practically babies still. They need far too much sleep and love and play to even think about learning anything yet!'

'Why the bees say bzzz?' said Cecily suddenly, turning around.

'It's the sound of their little wings,' Mrs Burke-Jones told her, agitating her hand quickly in illustration of her words, 'going back and forth very very fast, like this: bzzzzzzzz.'

'Oh,' said Cecily seriously, and turned back to her observations. Mrs Burke-Jones laughed.

'They may be readier than you think!' she said.

The maid brought out a tray containing tall glasses and a pitcher of fresh lemonade, which she placed on a little iron table. Mrs Burke-Jones poured out a drink and handed it to me. I settled myself to perform a certain number of indispensable social tasks before proceeding to my true purpose.

'How is Emily coming along with her studies?' I asked.

'Very well indeed,' she said, with a satisfaction that contrasted sharply with the consternation I well remembered when Emily had first declared her intention of attending university to study mathematics. 'She says that her dissertation is advancing, and she expects to finish it within the next two years. Unfortunately, it seems out of the question for her marriage to take place then, for Roland is only just beginning his own dissertation now.'

'Of course,' I said, 'Arthur told me that he was Senior Wrangler this year. Emily must be extremely proud.'

'Oh, it was not much of a surprise,' she said. 'Hudson of King's has been the best mathematics student in his year since he arrived. His sister Phoebe – Hudson of Girton, they call her – is in her second year now, and favoured to achieve Wrangler status as well, and there is a third sister who will begin at Newnham in September.'

'I met the Hudson family in London once,' I recalled. 'They seem quite astonishing.'

'Emily says that Roland will hopefully complete his dissertation within three years, and is planning to be married then. It seems a long time. Why, I should have been furiously impatient to be married, in her situation. They have already been engaged for nearly a year! But she seems quite content.'

'I was engaged for four years myself,' I said, 'and found the time very pleasant. I wanted to marry, to be sure, but I clearly remember also feeling a tinge of fear at the idea of abandoning all of my professional activities and remaining unoccupied at home. Even if I *was* only a teacher of small children, I led a busy life.'

'Emily talks of continuing to do mathematics after her marriage,' said Mrs Burke-Jones, looking as though she did not believe that any such wild plan could be put into execution. 'Well, we will see,' she added. 'Now that Edmund is at university and Robert is already a lad of fourteen, I am beginning to look forward to having small children about the house again. Your little girl is a delight. That age is so extraordinarily charming. I suppose she and her brother keep you extremely busy?'

'I am busy,' I assented, 'but I have nevertheless found the time to take on a case recently; a case of identification. In fact, I must admit that there is something I thought you might possibly be able to help me with.'

'What is it?' she asked. Mrs Burke-Jones is always very serious about such things as work. Her attitude towards mine has never been disapproving, although she is both discreet and incurious. Still, I felt that I could count on her help if necessary.

'Are you,' I asked, 'by any chance acquainted with a certain Mr Geoffrey Archer, who lives in a large manor called Chippendale House, in the direction of Grantchester?'

'Geoffrey Archer,' she repeated thoughtfully. 'It rings a bell. I don't really know him, yet the name is definitely familiar. Where might I have met a Mr Archer? Is he old or young?'

'He's not young,' I said. 'He can hardly be less than sixty, I should think.'

'Sixty,' she said, 'that narrows it down. I know – yes, I believe I have it. Is he a tall man with good bearing and white hair, and a rather loud voice? I think I may have met him at the Darwins.'

'The Darwins?' I said. 'Do you mean Darwin as in Evolution, or Darwin as in my neighbours in Newnham?'

'It is the same Darwin,' she said with a smile. 'The same family, that is. Your neighbour George Darwin is Charles Darwin's son. Didn't you know?'

'Really, no, I didn't!' I said, startled into a new respect for the querulous, bearded gentleman I saw frequently passing down the Newnham Road, well wrapped up and leaning heavily on a cane even on the loveliest day.

'Why yes,' she went on, 'Charles Darwin had a number of sons, and several of them live in Cambridge. Your neighbour has a lovely American wife. Now that I think of it, their house is only a few minutes from yours, isn't it?'

'Just a short walk,' I said, 'and I pass in front of it almost every day. Most of Cambridge does, I think, living just off the Silver Street bridge as they do! The children like to run wildly along the top of the garden wall, and even when I don't see them, it is easy to hear them playing in the garden. They are an adventurous bunch, I think. However, I am not acquainted with them. I should quite like to be. But my real goal is to meet Mr Archer. Do you think there is any chance that something might be arranged?'

'It really should be possible,' she said, 'assuming that I haven't made a mistake about Mr Archer. But no, I am quite sure I remember him from a dinner party at the Darwins. I will call on dear Maud and see what I can do. The Darwins receive very frequently.'

'That would be wonderful,' I said eagerly, wishing that social conventions did not leave me so powerless to hurry events along, but exhorting myself inwardly to be grateful for small blessings. 'Just – I must ask you another small favour. I hope you don't mind.'

She looked questioning, so I continued quickly.

'It's only this: if you mention me to Mrs Darwin, it would be best to call me by my maiden name. I – hum – for purposes of detection, I really *must* be taken for a single woman. And please, please do not be surprised if I behave a little strangely. My goal is to begin a friendship with Mr Archer.'

She raised her eyebrows and said nothing, merely nodded in discreet acquiescence.

So excited was I by the prospect of progress in this quarter, that the ringing of the doorbell, early this afternoon, sent me jumping out of my seat, wondering if Mrs Burke-Jones could have worked the miracle so quickly. But I was not surprised when upon throwing open the front door, I perceived Pat upon the step. A comically dejected, deprecating look painted itself upon his features as he saw me.

'Failure,' he said, sitting down at the dining room table and throwing his hat on it crossly. 'It was easy to get at him, as I told you it would be. I interviewed him – standing on the doorstep, since he wouldn't let me in – and took notes of everything he said. But I couldn't get anything useful out of of him at all. Not one dashed thing, even though I tried using what you said about the girl possibly being an actress.'

He pulled a couple of folded pages of notes from his pocket and slid them to me across the table with a rueful smile. I took them and read.

Notes of interview

P O'S: I'm here from the *Cambridge Evening News*, sir, to ask you if you would be willing to be interviewed for our new series of articles called Arts and Society. Our goal is to raise public interest in artistic productions by presenting the opinions of important members of society on them.

G A: Well, I'm afraid I don't have much to say on the subject. I don't get out much.

P O'S: Surely a gentleman of your standing has a busy social life, sir, if I may make so bold as to say so.

G A: Well, I go out of an evening on occasion, but I prefer to dine with friends than to go to a show.

P O'S: What are your feelings about paintings? Do you visit museums, or collect?

G A: No, I'm afraid I don't. I'm more interested in machines.

P O'S: *(Afraid the interview is about to be summarily ended)* Well, how about the theatre? Surely you go to see a play from time to time, sir?

G A: Well, from time to time, I suppose I do.

P O'S: Can you tell me the title of the last play you saw?

G A: Now, you're not going to be pleased, young man, but I can't. I really don't remember.

P O'S: *(Never discouraged)* How about artists, sir? Are you personally acquainted with any artists? That would do just as well for an article in the paper.

G A: I don't believe I know any artists, no.

P O'S: No painters? How about actors? Actresses? Ah *(afraid of being too explicit)* – singers? Musicians?

G A: The problem is that although I've met such people on occasion, I really don't have anything particular to say about them. Individually, they're – why, they're just individuals, some pleasant and others unpleasant, no different from anyone else. And as for their work, I really don't have an opinion on such things.

P O'S: Could you at least give me the names of some artists you are personally acquainted with?

G A: I'd rather not, because I have a suspicion that you'd manage to make more newspaper copy out of what I've told you than it deserves. I'd prefer not to appear at all in your series of articles about Arts and Society. Come back when you start one on Technology and Society.

'That's when he stepped back inside and closed the door rather firmly,' grumbled Pat. 'I can't even say he was disagreeable – but he certainly wasn't friendly. Well, you see how it was.'

I couldn't help laughing at his discomfiture, and even more at the style of his notes. But I was brought suddenly back to earth by his next words.

'Vanessa, we're going to have to take this to Fred. It's too important to go on playing with. This Archer *must* know who the girl was, and the police will get it out of him if we can't. I feel we don't have the right to waste any more time.'

'You are right,' I said slowly. 'I have begun arranging a possibility for myself to meet Mr Archer, but I am almost certainly going to run into the same difficulty as you, apart from the fact that it may take days if not weeks to organise. We can't wait so long. You are right; we must go and see Inspector Doherty.'

'And this very minute,' said Pat. 'I feel bad already about not going yesterday. As far as I know – and he promised to keep me abreast – he's got nowhere as yet with the stuff from the Missing Persons Bureau. Come along, Vanessa, get your things on!'

'Hm,' I said, thinking how uncomfortable it was going to be to explain about the identification of the bracelet. 'Do I have to come? Can't you explain it all to him yourself?'

'Nonsense. He's sure to have questions to ask you,' he said obliviously. 'Come along, do – it won't take much time. He's not working tonight. We'll find him at home.'

I yielded, ran upstairs to explain my errand to Arthur, and left with Pat, buoyed up by a comfortable feeling of relief at the idea of delivering the whole puzzle over to the capable hands of the police. Yet when we reached Inspector Doherty's little terraced house on George Street, I felt a little nervous again. What if I was about to disturb an important policeman with nothing but a heap of nonsense? I wished I had been able to conclude the investigation with all its details by myself. But it was too late, and too urgent for that.

'Vanessa's found out who she is, Fred,' announced Pat with his characteristic careless haste, as soon as the door opened, whilst poor Inspector Doherty was still peering half-blind into the darkness to make out who his visitors were.

'No, I haven't,' I objected quickly.

'Oh, Pat dear, how nice of you to come by,' said a friendly voice from within, and a female version of Pat appeared in the hall behind him, complete with red hair, freckles and irrepressible gaiety.

'My sister Molly,' he told me, drawing me inside as though the house belonged to him, pushing freely past his brother-in-law, and kissing his sister warmly on the cheek. During this time, the inspector slipped quickly back into the dining room, where we found him seated at an imposing mahogany table which dwarfed the humble room, in front of the remains of what looked like a most appetising plate of ginger pudding.

'Don't mind him,' said Molly Doherty. 'He's just finishing. Here, Fred, run along to the sitting room and talk. I'll take the things out to the kitchen.'

'I'm not done yet,' he protested, hastily scooping up the last morsel as she swept his dish out nearly from under his fork. 'Oh all right, Pat. I see you're just bursting with the discovery, and I'll admit that, pudding or no pudding, I'm longing to know what you've found out.' He rose, and leading us to the little adjoining parlour, he looked at us expectantly.

'Vanessa had better tell it,' said Pat.

'I really wish I had more to tell,' I began. 'Unfortunately, it isn't true that I know who the girl is. But I believe I have found someone who must know.'

'All right,' he said, 'that sounds like a good start. Who is it, and how did you find the person?'

I hemmed for a moment, wishing but not seeing how to avoid mentioning the bracelet.

'What happened is that, as soon as I saw the dead girl's Chinese bracelet in your office, I believed it might have been sold at Robert Sayle's,' I finally chose to say. 'They had a whole collection of such items for sale a week or two ago. I enquired with the girl who sells them, and she remembered the bracelet quite well. She said it was one of a kind, for most of the other bracelets in that lot of imports were carved ivory bangles, whereas this one was a string of intricate beads.'

'She recognised the bracelet from a description?' he asked, eyeing me sharply.

'No, Vanessa showed her the bracelet,' intervened Pat, rescuing me. 'I – ah, borrowed it temporarily. Did you notice it was missing?'

'I did,' said Fred. 'It didn't occur to me it might be you who took it, you rascal. I couldn't think where it had got to. But then I found it again – oh, I see, you actually put it back when you came by the other day! Now I know why you asked to see the girl's things again.' He glared at Pat. 'You made off with Crown's evidence, Pat. That's very bad; I'm astounded at you. Believe me, this is the last time I'll show you anything in my office.'

'But it was useful, Fred! It was in a good cause,' said Pat. 'You see, as soon as Vanessa took a look at the bracelet, I saw the cogs in her brain begin whizzing like mad. So I knew that she needed it.'

'You should have told me that right away,' he said.

'But I wasn't certain,' I answered quickly. I was about to add that I had never suggested Pat steal it for me, but decided this was too childish and that my share of the blame must be accepted with no moral detours.

'That doesn't matter. The right thing to do was to tell me then and there,' he said severely, then relaxed somewhat. 'Well, all's well that end's well. Go on. Let's hear your story.'

'All right', I said meekly. 'So, as I was saying, the girl remembered selling the bracelet to a man who was accompanied by the dead girl. She identified her from the photograph you gave me. But the main thing is that she actually recognised the man as a person who passes fairly regularly in the street in front of the shop. She promised to write to me the next time she should see him, and she did so. She had managed to slip away from her counter for a few minutes, and followed him as far as Petty Cury, where she saw him go into Heffers bookshop and enter into conversation with the clerk there. I then spoke with the same clerk, and discovered that the person in question is apparently none other than the clerk's own father, a gentleman by the name of Geoffrey Archer. He lives towards Grantchester, in a manor called Chippendale House. The girl from Robert Sayle's confirmed the identification of Mr Archer as the gentleman who bought the bracelet, accompanied by the dead girl, whom she identified from the photograph. That's all I've been able to find out up to now. But you will probably be able to get the girl's identity from Mr Archer directly.'

The inspector had drawn a pad towards him and was writing busily.

'We thought we'd come to you with this,' said Pat, wisely

suppressing all mention of his unsuccessful interview attempt. I supposed that he felt that the inspector would view that as a piece of clumsy interference.

'I'll see him tomorrow,' he said. 'If this turns out to be correct, it's going to be very useful. I'm grateful for your help. Now, listen to me,' he added, fixing me with a look of authority. 'Don't you go meddling in this business any further. You must realise that it may be dangerous. The girl was murdered, and any person you encounter while meddling around might be the murderer. You realise, don't you, that you can't be allowed to take that risk. This absolutely and completely goes for you, too, Pat. Out of it. Right?'

'It's our meddling that brought you this key information,' grumbled Pat resentfully.

'Yes, but it mustn't go any further! I'm saying what I'm saying for your own safety,' retorted his brother-in-law. 'And for mine, too. Your sister will kill me if I let you go stumbling into danger.'

'All right, all right,' said Pat, 'I'll stop detecting if you promise to tell me what you find out from Mr Archer and I can put it in the newspaper. Will you do that?'

'It's a bargain, for the girl's name at least. I'll let you know, and you *keep out*.'

I remained silent, but Inspector Doherty turned to me relentlessly. 'Thank you again, Mrs Weatherburn. Good work,' he said. 'That's quite enough for now, please. You can leave the rest of it to the police.'

The boy stood alone on the edge of the stream, concentrating so deeply he lost touch with his surroundings. He had borrowed the family's dishes for an experiment, and was attaching them all together with a complicated arrangement of knotted string. His first thought, as the entire pile went crashing and splashing onto the wet rocks below, was that his experiment had failed. Only afterwards did he wonder if his father might not be angry.

'Remember that Ernest is coming here tonight,' said Arthur, as he settled himself at the breakfast table and poured out a cup of pleasantly steaming coffee. 'His lecture is this afternoon. Shall I bring him home for dinner?'

'Certainly,' I said. 'Let me see, what shall we have? Roast beef, I think, don't you? What is he lecturing on?'

'Recent experiments in electromagnetism,' he replied. 'Interesting stuff, though rather far from my speciality. Perhaps, if I don't understand his lecture, you'll manage to get a translation for laymen out of him at dinner.'

'If I feed him well enough, maybe,' I said. 'All right, I will try. Gravy, perhaps...'

'Gravy, by all means,' he laughed, gathering up papers and putting on his coat. 'He was looking peaky in London, don't you think? Thinner and paler than usual. Hope he's all right today.'

I spent the day as domestically as can be, playing in the garden with the twins while Sarah went to the shops for some ribbon, then discussing the details of the menu with Mrs Widge, then out with Sarah for the afternoon walk. It was only after we returned and the children were taken off to the nursery for their supper of bread-and-milk that I found myself alone, and only then did I realise with what unconscious anxiety I had been waiting for news from Pat. I started up eagerly when, towards six o'clock, I heard the little jingle of the bell of the garden gate. But it was Arthur and Ernest who appeared, divesting themselves of their jackets and settling themselves on the grass, in the rays of the late afternoon sunshine. There was a silence.

'How was the lecture?' I asked, taking it upon myself to break it. Ernest closed his eyes and did not answer.

'Most interesting,' said Arthur. 'Quite revolutionary stuff, some of it. You must tell Vanessa more about it, Ernest.'

'Oh, quite,' he said, not opening his eyes. There was another small silence.

'Ah, is Kathleen well?' I asked, gathering the twins onto my knees, as they suddenly formed a small crowd around me, eyeing the stranger suspiciously.

'Very well, very well,' replied Ernest a little moodily, and the conversation lapsed again. He seemed to be in a dreadful mood. I rose and went into the kitchen, hoping that dinner would provide a diversion.

The roast was done to a turn, surrounded by new potatoes and glazed carrots. Mrs Widge was stirring the gently bubbling soup while Sarah, momentarily free from twins, was adding a large bowl of flowers, as a finishing touch, to a table already pleasantly laid with the pretty Limoges porcelain that Arthur had had delivered in a large box after his last visit to France, and which we kept for use only in the presence of guests.

'Everything is ready, ma'am,' she said as I glanced over the table to see if anything was missing. 'I'll put the children to bed now.'

Fresh and dainty as always (when she might well have presented an exhausted and harassed appearance, given the infinite quantity of hard work she performed every single day), she stepped into the garden and announced, 'Dinner is served.'

This rather formal statement roused the gentlemen, who were now lying propped on their elbows, while Arthur recited 'The Charge of the Light Brigade' with suitable drama, both twins draped heavily over him and clamouring for more every time he stopped to draw breath.

'Time to go in now,' he said, sitting up and shaking them off. They responded unanimously with a wail, containing various primeval shrieks and long-drawn-out syllables.

'Now, now,' said Sarah, taking over and scooping them up. 'What kind of behaviour is that? Come with me at once – we'll go upstairs and have games and stories.'

Their screeches diminished in volume at once. Arthur kissed them and brushed grass off his trousers. We settled ourselves around the table and Mrs Widge brought out the soup, and I tried once again to make small talk, hoping that Ernest's mood was not going to render the evening endless and heavy. Fortunately, he seemed to realise that the necessities of politeness demanded that he respond to my encouraging questions, and taking refuge in science, he became first courteous, then loquacious, and finally positively excited.

'The world is trembling on the verge of fundamental discoveries, explaining the true nature of all things!' he told me.

'All things?' I replied, taken aback by the megalomaniac echo in this somewhat overglorious statement, but attempting to look duly impressed.

'Far more than you would believe,' he said. 'If I told you

that we were approaching a complete understanding of the nature of light and matter, and force and energy, you would perhaps not blink an eye. But I and others believe that these things will lead even further, to discoveries about the very nature of life and death, and the soul itself.'

'There speaks the physicist,' I said. 'Surely you are not one of those who believe that thoughts and emotions can be reduced to equations!'

'No,' he said. 'But I believe the universe around us is filled with mysteries that are not, in fact, impenetrable, if one approaches them with an enquiring, but not a doubting mind.'

'Well, yes,' I assented. 'I suppose that all scientific discoveries may be thought of that way.'

'They can, certainly. But most of them tend to centre on the physical world which surrounds us. My belief is that tremendous progress can also be made by applying such methods to human phenomena! I am not claiming to quantise or predict feelings; no. But such well-known and yet insufficiently understood, insufficiently proved, insufficiently mastered experiences as out-of-body motion or communication with far-away people, both dead and alive, should and must have scientific explanations.'

'Oh!' I said. 'Perhaps I am too much of a rationalist, but I have always wondered if such things were not fairy tales or hoaxes.'

'No. They are not always hoaxes,' he said. His expression grew intense, and he leant over the table towards me till he nearly dipped his shirtfront into the soup.

'Have you read H G Wells's latest story in the *Strand Magazine*?' he asked. '*The Stolen Body*? On the man with an incredible out-of-body experience?'

'No,' I said, 'but I have read *The Plattner Story*. Of course, it is fascinating and most entertaining, the description of the parallel world inhabited by Plattner after the explosion. A very interesting idea. But still, Wells only means such tales to be purely amusing fiction to entertain us for a moment, does he not?'

'No,' he replied flatly. 'It would be pointless to invent such stories. There would be no use for authors. Every one of us can invent some answer to the question: imagine that you left your body; where would you be, and what would you see? No, the power of Wells's tales is that they are based on true experiences. *The Stolen Body* is astonishing. He explains in detail how a man can achieve his aim of departing from his own body, not by some gimcrack explosion, but after weeks of effort and intense concentration.'

'And where does he go?'

'Nowhere. He remains in London, something like Plattner, but he can hover above it, see into people's rooms and minds; not exactly reading their thoughts, but making some kind of contact with a deep part of their brain, so that in certain cases they can perceive or hear him.'

Arthur was too polite to comment, but threw me a little look that clearly said 'nonsense'. I smiled. There are times when I am truly pleased to be a woman. A man must either be above taking such childish rubbish as anything more than fairy tales, or struggle against the silent contempt of his fellows. A woman may serenely allow herself to entertain such fantasies and let her imagination roam, without being required to classify herself strictly as a believer or a disbeliever.

'It is rare to find a scientist who believes in psychic phenomena, is it not?' I asked non-committally.

'Rare, perhaps, but certainly not non-existent,' he replied. 'Why, I myself learnt about all this and became interested as a student up in Liverpool, thanks to my own professor of physics.'

'Not Professor Lodge!' exclaimed Arthur.

'Yes, Sir Oliver Lodge. One of our great physicists if anybody is.'

'Indeed, he has made some extraordinary mechanical discoveries, according to what I have heard,' said Arthur. 'But didn't he also design some experiments to detect the ether?'

'He did, although they are generally considered to have been unsuccessful,' said Ernest. 'The results are difficult to interpret. But then, so are the results of Michelson and Morley's experiment, which is always hailed as a great success!'

'The Americans, Michelson and Morley, designed a most astute experiment to measure the speed of the ether wind, about ten years ago,' explained Arthur, turning to me. 'Instead of which, their experiment seems to have established the non-existence of ether as a material substance.'

'I know the ether is supposed to be whatever fills up the universe, where there is no matter,' I said. 'But I didn't know it was supposed to be a wind.'

'It isn't; that's the whole point,' said Ernest. 'It's supposed to be at rest throughout the universe. That's why something that goes rushing through it at great speed should cause a resistance which would be felt as a wind. Our Earth is constantly moving, both rotating around the sun and spinning around its own axis, so one would expect to find an ether wind, analogous to the air resistance you encounter if you run swiftly forward.'

'Exactly,' said Arthur. 'Michelson and Morley compared

the speed of light along the direction of the Earth's motion – so where you would expect to get most resistance from the ether – with the speed of light in the perpendicular direction, where there would be less resistance. They found that the speed of light was identical in the two directions.'

'How could they do that?' I wondered. 'How can one measure the speed of light?'

'One can, actually, but that's not what they did. They didn't actually measure the speed. They compared the two speeds by sending out a single light ray through a piece of glass which was half-transparent, half a slanted mirror. The slanted mirror sent its half of the light ray off at a right angle to the other half. Then, by means of other mirrors some yards off, they sent the two halves of the ray back together again. They arranged the apparatus so that the interference fringes were perfectly matched; that is, one saw dark and light alternating lines on the screen they set up to catch the rays. The apparatus functioned over several months, so that eventually by the earth's motion, it had turned to a right angle from it original position. The light ray that had been along the earth's circumference was now perpendicular and the perpendicular one was now in the direction where some resistance from the ether wind might be expected. If the two rays were travelling at slightly different speeds, it would have been reflected in the interference fringes, which would have been shifted. But in fact, they were exactly as before. So they concluded that there was no ether wind which could make any difference to the speed of light.'

'It's not hard to come up with ether theories that don't contradict Michelson-Morley,' said Ernest. 'Professor Lodge thinks that the Earth's atmosphere might drag the ether along with it, so that an experiment close to the Earth's surface wouldn't detect the wind.'

'Why does one need ether at all?' I asked. 'Why can't the universe just be empty for the most part, with stars and planets and things here and there?'

Both men began to answer me at once, but Ernest's voice was the louder.

'Because we have understood that the behaviour of light is a wave-behaviour,' he explained. 'Light behaves just like waves you see propagating in the sea, or ripples in water when you drop in a stone. Physicists have been able to determine the speed and the wavelength now; the wavelengths, I should say, because each colour has its own. But what is a wave, Vanessa? Do you know?'

'Ah,' I said, 'a movement in the water?'

'Yes,' he said. 'But what many people don't realise, is that the water only moves *up and down* when a wave passes through it. When you see a wave coming towards you on the beach, you may have the false impression that *water* from far off is coming towards you. But if you throw a rubber ball some distance away and watch its behaviour, you will see at once that it is lifted by the passage of the wave, and then lowered back to the place where you originally threw it. Actually, except at the very edge of the ocean, the particles of water are only temporarily displaced by the wave.'

'Yes, well, all right,' I said.

'So the wave is just a force acting on the water, locally moving it up and down as it passes,' he continued. 'And that is how waves work in general. Sound, also, travels by waves – through the air. But our air is not emptiness, it is made up essentially of nitrogen, with some oxygen and a dash of other elements. It is a kind of gas, with a certain thickness, which can be moved and shifted, as you can easily feel when you fan yourself. So it supports the motion of waves. Now, our air, or atmosphere, thins out to nothing as it goes up – virtually nothing is left after eighty miles or so. It's just a kind of halo around the planet Earth. The question is: what lies outside it? Something must, for light reaches us through the space which is far beyond the atmosphere, from stars which are inconceivably distant. So, since light is a wave and a wave is a force acting on some material, we conclude that there must be some substance out there.'

'Yet Michelson and Morley could not detect it, nor Sir Oliver, for that matter. I don't say it isn't a puzzle,' said Arthur.

'Oh, it's there, all right,' said Ernest. 'The greatest minds believe in it, in fact the greatest minds invented it. Newton explains it in the *Opticks*, simply by the operation of removing air from a glass tube and leaving a vacuum behind. Light shone from the outside across the tube still goes through – ergo something is still in the tube, carrying it. He calls it the Medium – the "Etherial Medium", and explains all refraction and diffraction of light by following its density, which will obviously be greater in the wide open spaces than within solid bodies. For that matter, according to Newton, the "Etherial Medium" explains every phenomenon of vision or perception or motion you can think of.'

'Is that so?' said Arthur. 'I don't remember studying ether in the *Opticks*. But then again, I haven't opened it since I was an undergraduate.'

'And even then, you probably skipped that part, you mathematician,' said Ernest. 'Give me your copy, and I'll show you.'

Arthur abandoned his dinner long enough to fetch the book from his study, and Ernest neglected his to read us out a passage or two, with the result that my plate was empty while theirs were both still well-garnished. I helped myself to more carrots and listened to Ernest:

May not Planets and Comets, and all gross Bodies, perform their motions more freely, and with less resistance in this Etherial Medium than in any Fluid, which fills all Space adequately without leaving any Pores, and by consequence is much denser than Quick-silver or Gold? And may not its resistance be so small, as to be inconsiderable?

'There, you see? That would explain Michelson-Morley, that right there. And now, listen to this.'

If anyone would ask how a Medium can be so rare, let him tell me how the Air, in the upper parts of the Atmosphere, can be above an hundred thousand times rarer than Gold. Let him also tell me, how an electrick Body can by friction emit an Exhalation so rare and subtile, and yet so potent, as by its Emission to cause no sensible Diminution of the weight of the electrick Body, and to be expanded through a Sphere, whose Diameter is above two Feet, and yet to be able to agitate and carry up Leaf Copper, or Leaf Gold, at the distance of above a Foot from the electrick Body? And how the Effluvia of a Magnet can be so rare and subtile, as to pass through a Plate of Glass without any Resistance or Diminution of their Force, and yet so potent as to turn a magnetick Needle beyond the Glass?

Is not Vision perform'd chiefly by the Vibrations of this Medium, excited in the bottom of the Eye by the Rays of Light, and propagated through the solid, pellucid and uniform Capillamenta of the optick Nerves into the place of Sensation? And is not Hearing performed by the Vibrations either of this or of some other Medium, excited in the auditory Nerves by the Tremors of the Air, and propagated through the solid, pellucid and uniform Capillamenta of those Nerves into the place of Sensation? Is not Animal Motion perform'd by the Vibrations of this Medium, excited in the Brain by the power of the Will, and propagated from thence through the solid, pellucid and uniform Capillamenta of the Nerves into the Muscles, for contracting and dilating them?

He clapped the book closed.

'There you have it,' he said, 'from a Cambridge man if there ever was one. We ether supporters are not beaten yet! Professor Lodge believes that ether is the main medium of contact, of transmission, in the universe,' he went on quickly. 'He believes it explains every contact of every kind that occurs. Including that between ourselves and the – ah, the afterlife.' He glanced at us both quickly, with a tinge of aggression in his eyes.

'The universe is still an utterly mysterious place,' observed Arthur evenly.

'This is all fascinating,' I said warmly. 'I really should like to hear more.'

The pudding had come and gone during this discussion, which had allowed Ernest to recover his usual animation and colour. I smiled at him, and rose to leave the gentlemen a moment alone with their drinks.

'We won't be long,' said Arthur, already hunting about for a decanter in the sideboard, as I moved out of the dining room by myself. 'Let's see, Ernest, what can I offer you? A little drop of liqueur? Or brandy, perhaps?'

I betook myself dutifully away from the alcoholic regions, and busied myself arranging the drawing room until they should emerge, but I was interrupted quite soon by a sharp rat-tat upon the front door, accompanied by an anxious ringing of the bell. I opened it at once. Pat, whom I had entirely forgotten for once, stood upon the doorstep, shaking his shoes and wiping off the drops of a misty drizzle from his forehead, where it appeared to have caught him unawares.

'Oh, Pat, come in,' I said quickly, ushering him forward to the detriment of the floor. 'Have you got news?'

'Yes, I have. We have her name,' said Pat. 'And I have a lot to tell you.' He took off his hat and dropped it over the umbrella stand, while I helped him to divest himself of his dampened overcoat.

'Who was she?' I urged him.

'She turns out to have been an actress in some kind of roving theatre company no one ever heard of,' he began.

I closed my eyes for a moment, then opened them and looked at him.

'Ivy Elliott,' I said.

He stared at me for a moment as though I were a magician or a mind-reader, gaping. Then he nodded slowly.

'Still waters run deep,' he said reproachfully. 'You knew it all along, even while you sent me off on that ridiculous chase. You knew it – why, you even told me you thought the girl might have been an actress! What a lot of trouble you could have saved us. Why didn't you say?'

'I couldn't,' I said. 'It was just a wild guess. I never had time to find any proof.'

At that precise moment, the door of the dining room flew open, and Arthur and Ernest emerged. Arthur was his usual sober self, but Ernest had an odd gleam in his eye.

'Oh, hello, Pat,' said Arthur. 'Vanessa, guess what? Ernest went to see *A Midsummer Night's Dream,* and he says the Titania we saw simply isn't the same actress as the one he meant. She's a replacement.'

'The very idea,' added Ernest, 'of imagining that I can't tell if a woman is large or small, or wearing a wig.'

'And Ernest says she had to be replaced suddenly, because she seems to have disappeared,' went on Arthur.

'She's absolutely gone,' added Ernest bitterly. 'They say she's ill, up at the theatre, but I've asked around all my acting acquaintances, and something fishy is going on. No one knows where she is. She was all set to play Titania last Monday, and never turned up. They gave the role to her understudy, who was herself booked to play the First Fairy.' He glanced at me, and paused suddenly, becoming aware of something. I glanced at Pat, and saw that he had grasped the situation. He looked seriously at Ernest.

'Are you talking about a missing actress?' he said with unusual gentleness.

'Yes,' replied Ernest. 'Missing since last Monday, and no one seems to know where she has gone.'

'What was her name?' was the next, inevitable question.

'Ivy Elliott,' he replied, the little glint intensifying in his eye. I felt Pat grow tense next to me, bracing himself. Ernest's passionate feelings were quite manifest, and they reared up like a massive wall, preventing us from speaking openly and naturally about the dead girl.

'Why, what is going on?' said Ernest suddenly, growing both defensive and aggressive. 'Why are you all silent?' He looked from me to Arthur accusingly. 'Do you know something that I don't?'

'Not me,' said Arthur. 'Do you, Vanessa? Obviously you do. Perhaps you had better tell it as it is.'

'A young woman was found drowned, here in Cambridge, last week,' said Pat, once again intervening to spare me a most distressing statement. 'She has only just been identified.' He looked at Ernest, sorry and a little helpless.

The portrait photograph of the dead girl lay in the bureau drawer just behind Ernest. I felt myself move towards it, inexorably, unwillingly.

Arthur, who, floating in an academic world of ideas, had heard nothing of the murder, stared at me, surprised. Ernest watched me in silence, and stepped aside as I reached behind him, opened the drawer, and drew out the photograph. It was as though we were bound by an invisible thread of intense electric tension. I handed it to him. He fixed his eyes upon it. The silence was long and dreadful.

'How did she die?' he said suddenly.

'She – she was found in the river,' I said uncomfortably, anxiously, doubtfully. There was much more to say on the subject, but I found myself unable to say it.

'She drowned herself?'

'The police believe it was murder,' said Pat. 'She didn't drown. She was strangled.'

'Who did it?' snapped Ernest, in a tone for which, had I known the answer to his question, I would have hesitated to give it to him.

'Ernest, we don't know. No one knows.'

'Well,' he said, 'you're going to find out, Vanessa. You are going to find her killer for me. I am hiring you, if you will take the case.'

It was so unexpected that I fluttered momentarily.

'I – I don't know where to start,' I began.

'But I know. Come down to London with me tomorrow, and I'll show you.'

'You're not really going to take this on, Vanessa?' said Arthur, as I sat in our bedroom half an hour later, brushing my hair. We had sent Pat away, plied Ernest with promises, camomile tea and laudanum, and sent him to bed. The nervous tension of the evening had left us both feeling drained and exhausted. I wanted to sleep. The ivory-backed brush almost slipped from my fingers. I put it down and went over to the bed, pulling back the covers, touching the fresh white sheets, welcoming their soothing, restful contact. Arthur blew out the dressing-table candle, leaving only the two little ones on our bedside tables burning. Their flames cast two soft round glows upwards to the ceiling. It is so much easier to talk in the near darkness.

'I think I am,' I said thoughtfully.

'But what is Ernest's call to hire you?' he objected. 'What has he to do with this actress? Just because he admired her!'

'How stupid men are,' I sighed. 'Can you not see that Ernest was mad about her? She occupied his mind and soul, that much is clear.'

There was a hesitation.

'But Kathleen...' he said meekly.

'I know,' I said. 'But it happens. And the girl is dead. He

will remain obsessed unless the thing is solved and the murderer brought to justice. Legal justice, of course. Ernest must be prevented from taking anything into his own hands.'

'The police will find the murderer,' he said.

'Well and good,' I assented. 'I won't object if they reach the solution before I do.' I lay back and watched the flickering light on the ceiling.

'Will you go to London tomorrow?' said Arthur, propping himself on his elbow and facing me in the glow.

'Yes,' I said, looking into his brown eyes. He reached over and put his hand on mine. Then he took his candle and blew it out. A little puff of fragrant smoke wafted across the room. I took mine and did the same. Darkness, silence and tenderness settled over us.

1892

Bread and salami for lunch	*0.25*
One apple	*0.05*
Stabling for the donkey	*0.50*
Total	*0.80 lire*

'Bother,' said Guglielmo to himself. 'My money's already practically gone, and I haven't even got the metal and batteries yet. Perhaps the cobbler will buy my shoes from me. I can go back barefoot.

When I came downstairs in the morning, I found Mrs Widge standing in the doorway to the dining room, holding a tray containing a large silver coffee pot, a toast rack, a covered dish and a fragrant, steaming sponge cake, and looking offended.

'He's gone off, ma'am,' she said, 'he's gone, Mr Dixon is. He left a note.' She gestured with her two chins towards the dining table, where an envelope was propped against the vase which decorated its centre.

'Oh, Mrs Widge,' I said, 'had you prepared an extra-lovely breakfast for our guest? I'm sure if he'd known he would have stayed for it! But as it is, we shall have to enjoy it ourselves. The sponge cake will be much appreciated in the nursery, I know.'

I extracted Ernest's note from its envelope and read it.

Dear Vanessa,

Can't face the friendly family breakfast. You'll understand. You know I'm counting on you. I've heard about the cases you've solved. Don't fail me. I feel I'm staring death in the face – not sure whether it's hers, mine or HIS, whoever he is.

Come to 10 Heron Lane in Islington, at 9 o'clock this evening. And thank you.

Ernest

Goodness, I thought to myself, as I sat alone at the table in front of the large quantity of succulent things that Mrs Widge was setting upon it. *I wonder whose address that is? Whom does Ernest want me to meet? Some of the girl's friends, I suppose. He seems to know all kinds of people in the acting world. Islington, though – that's hardly the kind of place where actors live!*

Arthur came down a few minutes later, freshly shaven, and poured himself a cup of coffee before sitting down. His eye roved appreciatively over the table.

'Mrs Widge has outdone herself,' he remarked. 'Where is the happy beneficiary of all this effort?'

'Arthur, right or wrong, he learnt last night that the girl he loved is dead,' I said. 'Do you expect him to be interested in sponge cake?'

'Well, I don't know about sponge cake, but sausages, maybe?' he said, lifting a dish cover and spearing one with a fork. I opened my mouth indignantly, but shut it again. He cannot help it. The idea that Ernest should be in love with an actress while being married to Kathleen is not an admissible one in Arthur's moral world. He would not deny, in theory, that such a thing can happen, and there are even moments when he might be brought reluctantly to speak of it, but certainly not at table in the clear light of day. One cannot change people.

'He left early,' I contented myself with saying. 'He must have caught the first train, and he's left me a note asking me to meet him in London at nine o'clock this evening.'

'To meet *him*?' he said, surprised.

'Well, to meet someone. He just left an address.'

'A bunch of murderers, probably,' he said.

'Nonsense, Arthur. I suppose he wants me to learn something about the dead girl's friends and relations.'

'One of whom killed her, unless she was killed by a passing tramp.'

'She might have been,' I said thoughtfully. 'She was found in the river in the early morning, and had not spent more than a few hours there, Inspector Doherty told me. She must have been killed in the middle of the night.' I wondered if the police knew more or less precisely at what time she actually died. Post-mortems do allow them to determine such information. I realised that I knew almost nothing about the circumstances of her death, and that my first task should really be to find out more.

To this end, I proceeded to the police headquarters after breakfast and enquired if Inspector Doherty was available. He was in, and seemed quite pleased to see me.

'An excellent tip, that one about Geoffrey Archer,' he told me. 'Good work. I am very angry with Pat for stealing the bracelet, obviously. But he insists that he did it entirely without your knowledge. You should have brought it straight back here when he gave it to you, you know that. In fact, you ought to have told me immediately that you thought it might have come from Robert Sayle's. Still, let bygones be bygones. Our talk with Archer was conclusive. The girl has been identified beyond a doubt.'

'I suppose Mr Archer is not the murderer?' I asked, thinking suddenly of Estelle's anxiety on that score.

'No,' replied the inspector. 'Do you think we didn't ask ourselves that question at once? We questioned him about his relationship with her, and found out that although he was not precisely keeping her, he did give her the occasional gift of money for services rendered. The child she was expecting might have constituted a motive of sorts, though it's not clear why it would represent a threat to a man in his position, but some people panic about such things; perhaps she was threatening to make a public scandal. However, be that as it may, he's out of the running with a cast-iron alibi.'

'Oh, that is interesting,' I said. 'Are you allowed to tell me what it is?' If I had asked him straightforwardly, he might have been reluctant to give me details out of pure official discretion or the fear of my continuing to meddle (little did he know...), but the word 'allowed' had the hoped-for effect of piquing his sense of importance.

'Certainly I can tell you. The girl Ivy Elliott was last seen at a party at Mr Archer's home on the evening of 21st June. Mr Archer was present, obviously, and there was a fairly large number of guests. Sergeant Forth and I questioned them all.'

He handed me a list of some twenty names. Although not personally acquainted with any of them, I saw more than one that I recognised as belonging to people of the highest social standing in Cambridge. The testimony of each witness had been taken down and signed. I read rapidly through the statements. Most of them had virtually nothing to say on the subject of Ivy Elliott's presence at, and departure from, Mr Archer's home on the night of the dinner party. They had simply not taken any notice. A few were more observant.

Miss Elliott left a few minutes before midnight. She said she was tired and would go home; she was staying with a friend. Mr Archer spoke with her for a few moments in the hall before she left. He opened the front door and let her out himself. I saw her walking away down the drive. She was easy to make out in her white dress. The path was lamplit, and the weather was so warm that she had only a shawl over her shoulders.

The party took place in Mr Archer's drawing room, which has large windows giving over the front garden. Miss Elliott was in the drawing room for most of the evening. She did not exactly act as hostess, but took care of the material aspects of the service, telling the servants when to bring liqueurs and biscuits, which curtains to draw and which to leave, when to light the outdoor lanterns and so on. She left quite late. I did not look at the time, but it must have been near midnight. A lot of the guests had already left at that point. Miss Elliott seemed tired, and going up to Geoffrey, she told him that she thought she would be on her way. She said she was going to a friend. He asked her if she was sure she wanted to leave, and pressed her to stay a little while longer. She did so, but after a few minutes she said that she was very tired, and would leave. He went out into the hall with her to bid her goodbye. He cannot have been out of the room for more than five minutes. She left, and Mr Archer returned and remained with us for the duration of the party, which continued until past two o'clock. He did not leave the room again. I am certain of it, as I was sitting on the sofa next to him for the entire time. He simply rose to his feet once or twice to say a few words to the butler.

After letting Miss Elliott out, Mr Archer came back to the drawing room, where he remained with us for more than two hours. He did not leave the drawing room again, I am certain of it. In fact, we were both sitting on the sofa during the whole of the conversation that followed. My husband does not support the same parliamentary candidate as Mr Archer, and this led to quite an argument. Spokes came in once or twice to see if anything was needed, since Miss Elliott had left. After Miss Elliott's departure, the servants brought new drinks as well as tea for two ladies who desired it, and several trays of small cakes. At one point – it must have been an hour or so after Miss Elliott left – Mr Archer sent the servants to bed. Several guests left before Miss Elliott, and she sent out for cabs for some of them. The remaining ones, myself, my husband and four or five others, left together. It was already after 2 o'clock in the morning.

From seven o'clock to midnight, when she left, Miss Elliott was the one who would come here to the kitchen whenever anything was needed. She didn't oversee the dinner service, she sat at the table with the others. But she made sure the drawing room and dining room were arranged properly before the guests came and after. She did the flowers herself and made sure everything was dusted. After the dinner was over, there was music, and more refreshments were served throughout the evening. That was how Mr Archer wanted things. It's not our place to question that. Miss Elliott was pleasant and polite in her ways. We had nothing against her. After she left Mr Spokes went in to the drawing room to see with Mr Archer what was wanted.

Miss Elliott played the role of housekeeper during the party, making sure that all ran smoothly. The whole pretence was perfectly shocking, if you ask me. Miss Elliott is not a housekeeper, and I was surprised that Mr Archer permitted such a person to mingle with his guests, when we all know what she is. Had I known she would be present, I should not have accepted the invitation. Indeed, I was quite surprised that she actually left. She claimed that she was staying with a friend. She and Mr Archer avoided showing any signs of vulgarity in our presence, but I saw them standing in the hall when she left, and he was holding her hands in his, and then he pulled out a roll of bank notes and pressed them into her hands! Yes, he certainly did. No, I cannot guess how much money passed between them, but it was no trifle, I assure you! I was both shocked and disgusted. I shall not set foot in Chippendale House again.

'Did you notice that he gave her money?' I said to Inspector Doherty, surprised by the vehemence of this last statement.

'Well,' he said uncomfortably, 'what do you expect?'

'Oh, I know,' I said, 'I didn't mean that. I meant that it's strange that the money was not found on her. Or was it?'

'No, it wasn't,' he said.

'Where did she put it?' I wondered. 'Was she carrying a bag of any kind?'

'We asked Archer that. Look here.'

He separated Mr Archer's statement from the others, and handed it to me, pointing to the lines at the end. I read:

As far as I remember, she was not carrying anything. Yes, I did give her money as payment for her services during the evening. I gave Miss Elliott three pounds. She folded the notes and slipped them into her dress. I then bid her goodbye and opened the front door for her. She walked out and down the drive. I shut the door and returned to my guests. I did not leave the party at any time. I never saw Miss Elliott again.

'It's all very odd,' I said, looking up. 'Where can she have been going, all by herself, on foot, at midnight? Why on earth didn't she simply stay at Mr Archer's home?'

'Read Archer's statement from the beginning,' he counselled me. 'It's quite interesting.'

I met Miss Elliott through friends two years ago. To be more precise, these friends, who are very fond of theatre, had invested some money in a newly formed theatre company and were invited to a cast party after their first successful production. I was visiting these friends at the time, and joined them there. I met Miss Elliott upon that occasion.

I developed a strong affection for this charming young woman and used to employ her services from time to time, because I enjoyed her company, and also in order to aid her financially. She was an actress, but her position was obviously quite precarious; she earned very little and was not with any established theatre, although I believe that she subsequently found work with an experimental roving company, which plays in tents, or open fields, or some such thing. At any rate, it wasn't very serious, and she was in straitened means, so I was pleased to be able to contribute to her welfare.

I saw Miss Elliott regularly, but not very frequently; perhaps two or three times a month. Sometimes I saw her in London, other times I wrote to her to propose some little service up here in Cambridge, and if the schedule did not interfere with her rehearsals, I would then send her a train ticket and she would come. I did not become involved in the rest of her life in any way. As far as I know she was a busy young lady with a great many colleagues, friends and acquaintances, but I am not acquainted with any of them. I was not in the habit of interfering in any way in her personal life.

Yes, I bought her the ivory bracelet a week or two ago, on one of her visits to Cambridge. She had come up to help me sort some old pictures. It was a pleasure to me to be able to offer her a small gift. She was really a good-hearted young person. At that time, I asked if she would be willing to return to Cambridge on the twenty-first of June, in order to help me with the organisation of the evening dinner and party for twenty guests. I much prefer organising things this way to having the servants come in to get their orders, or going out to the kitchen continually myself, or having a fixed and rigidly timed plan beforehand. Yes, I do have a housekeeper, of course, but I preferred to have Miss Elliott in and out of the drawing room than Mrs Munn.

I really do not know where she went when she left my house. She told me that she was tired and wished to leave, even though the party was not quite over. I thought it a little strange that she wished to walk into Cambridge at midnight, but she said she was going to a friend's and that there was nothing to worry about. Let me be blunt; the streets at night hold no terror for young women such as she. I did not think much about it and let her go.

As far as I remember, she was not carrying anything. Yes, I did give her money as payment for her services during the evening. I gave Miss Elliott three pounds. She folded the notes and slipped them into her dress. I then bid her goodbye and opened the front door for her. She walked out and down the drive. I shut the door and returned to my guests. I did not leave the party at any time. I never saw Miss Elliott again.

'So this is his alibi?' I said. 'The fact that he remained at the party until two o'clock in the morning? What did he do after that?'

'It doesn't matter,' he told me. 'After that she was already dead. As it turns out, she must have been killed very shortly after midnight. The post-mortem showed definitively that she was killed within an hour of leaving the house at the very most.'

'Really!' I said. 'That's strange, very strange. How can they be so sure? Isn't the time of death usually rather vague?'

'When you have to guess it from the condition of the corpse itself, yes,' he said. 'But in this case, there were the, ah, the stomach contents.' He glanced at me apologetically. 'You see, the meal was partially although not much digested, but the stomach contained fragments of practically undigested food...actual biscuit crumbs. They were identified as almond-flavoured wafers. We were able to determine that Mr Archer had a tray of such biscuits served at eleven-thirty, and not before. Given their state, the pathologist claims that they must have been in the stomach for a period of half an hour to an hour.'

'She could have eaten them any time between eleven-thirty and midnight,' I said.

'Yes. So we can narrow down the time of her death to the half-hour between twelve-thirty and one o'clock,' he replied.

'It's so peculiar, though,' I said. 'Didn't you tell me that she had been floating in the river for about three hours? What time did you say the body was discovered?'

'At seven. Yes, I agree that it is very odd. The results of the post-mortem clearly indicate that she was strangled before one o'clock and placed in the water around four or even five o'clock. Even by stretching the medically established times, the two events cannot possibly be brought to within less than three or four hours of each other.'

'So she was killed somewhere, and her body transported to the river later?' I asked.

'Who knows? She was found in a place almost directly on her way from Chippendale House to the centre of town, so at first I wondered if her body had not been left on the bank of the river, and rolled or slipped in of itself after some lapse of time. But there were no stains of grass or mud on her clothing to substantiate that idea, nor could we find a specific imprint where the body might have lain, even searching some distance upriver. We may never know exactly where she was actually dropped in, but we can estimate the farthest possible distance, since drowned bodies sink after some time if they do not become caught, as this one did. We searched up and down both banks over the whole area, but the trouble is not that there are no marks, but that there are far too many. The riverbank is constantly being trampled by people and animals. We found nothing conclusive. Still, as far as Archer's involvement is concerned, his alibi seems final. We're looking into the circumstances of the girl's life in London.'

'Well,' I said, deciding that I had better confess at once and get it over, 'so am I. My services as a detective have been retained by a friend of hers.'

He stared at me.

'I know you told me not to,' I went on quickly. 'And I certainly would not have gone on meddling in your investigation on my own. But now I have a client, and, well, I want to propose something to you, Inspector Doherty, if you will allow me.'

'Who is your client?' he barked abruptly.

'Oh, I can't reveal his identity,' I said, feeling a little guilty at having openly disobeyed his injunction to stay out, and now refusing his very first request.

'Any friend of hers might be or know the murderer,' he said.

'It does not appear possible to me that the murderer would retain my services, and the rules of my profession do not allow me to divulge my client's identity at this point,' I said anxiously. 'However, I did want to tell you that if I discover anything at all that seems to have a bearing on the case, I will tell you about it at once. I do not want to enter into any kind of competition with the police, but simply to add the results of my investigation to theirs.' This promise afforded me some relief. It seemed to me to be more than likely that Ernest would plunge into acts of inexcusable and irreversible foolishness were he to learn the identity of the murderer of his idol before the police had seized him. Inspector Doherty allowed himself to smile.

'You do that, Mrs Weatherburn,' he said. 'I cannot stop you from investigating, much as I would prefer to, but since you insist upon it, I would much prefer that we work together. I believe I can work with you – and I wouldn't say this about just any private detective, you know. Stay out of danger, see what you can do, and let me know.'

I thanked him profusely and shook his hand. I really do not want to arouse the hostility of the police. Such a worthy, able and admirable institution.

I boarded the London train in the early evening with a feeling of rising tension. Had Ivy Elliott been murdered by a passing tramp or common thief, for the money he snatched from her dress? Or was somebody waiting, waiting for her outside Mr Archer's home, knowing that she was there, biding his time, planning, pulling on the gloves of the strangler, perhaps...

Then he would have carried her body to the river – but why not throw it in directly? Why wait three or four hours?

No, she must have been killed somewhere else, and the body transported somehow to the river later on. Midnight was too early; there were people in the streets, Mr Archer's guests were being driven home. Three or four o'clock in the morning seemed a much safer hour for disposal of bodies. It began to make more sense. The question was to discover where the girl could have been strangled and kept, secretly, for three or four hours.

In Mr Archer's house, for example? Could her departure have been nothing more than a gesture of politeness, to save appearances? Could she not have slipped quietly back into the house through some other entrance? And could not Mr Archer have known it and darted quickly upstairs – a mere minute of absence – to strangle her?

This idea so excited me that I had to remind myself firmly that I was in a train to London, and that there was no possibility of immediate communication with Inspector Doherty. I sat back and breathed deeply. I might be wrong, of course. Ernest had something important to show me. I should complete my task in London. Cambridge and its police force – and for that matter, very probably London's police force as well – would still be there upon my return.

The train drew into Liverpool St, and I stepped out, collected my little valise, gave up my ticket, and proceeded to the exit, where I found a cab to take me to Islington. Heron Lane turned out to be a small, curved street with a line of little houses built along it, separated from each other by small gardens with high walls. From what I knew of her, I thought it a rather surprising place for a girl like Ivy Elliott to be frequenting, but I pushed all preconceived ideas to the back of my mind, walked up the path, and rang the bell firmly.

The door was opened at once by a plump, buxom lady who seemed too decoratively dressed to be a housekeeper. She wore a long, ample turquoise gown with flounces, and an aqua-green silk shawl embroidered with butterflies was draped over her shoulders and hung almost to her knees. Around her neck was a heavy necklace of large, irregular stones, shells and feathers.

This lady immediately seized me by the hand and drew me into the house.

'You must be Mrs Weatherburn, dear,' she said kindly. 'We are expecting you. Come in, come in and meet the others.' She divested me of my wrap and led me into a rather small, stuffy drawing room, lit with electric lights – the first time I had seen them in a private house. Several men and women were already there, seated on numerous little sofas and hassocks. Their presence filled the room to overcrowding. The air was permeated with a strong fragrance of incense; I perceived the slim little stick burning and smoking in a corner of the room.

Ernest rose to greet me as soon as he saw me in the

doorway. He came forward and pressed my hand, nodding at his hostess.

'I am glad you came. I'll admit it; I was not sure you would,' he said. 'All I ask you, Vanessa,' he added in an undertone, 'is to let go of your prejudices completely for one hour. Just one hour.' He eyed me significantly, and I assented with some surprise. Were these good people so very disreputable as all that? I glanced about me, and saw a little drab woman with red eyes and a hat decorated with flowers, two portly gentlemen, one bearded and the other moustached, a young man afflicted with a complete absence of chin, a stern young woman with spectacles and a notepad, and my genial hostess. Who *could* they be?

'We are all here, are we not, Mrs Thorne?' said one of the portly gentlemen, rising from his seat. 'Perhaps we should begin.'

'Certainly, Mr Doyle,' replied my hostess with great respect. He smiled at me, a kind of friendly walrus, looking somewhat uncomfortable in his formal collar. Then suddenly he hoisted up his large armchair in his arms, and shoved it unceremoniously against the wall.

To my surprise, the guests all now rose in unison and began to move the furniture, pushing all of the sofas and little tables to the edges of the room, and carrying a round table to its very centre. Around this they arranged eight chairs. Mrs Thorne turned off the electric lights with a flip of a switch, and the room fell into utter darkness. For a moment I was quite blind, but after a few moments, the tiny glow of the incense stick sufficed to allow me to make my way to the table and seat myself together with the others.

'Place your fingertips on the table,' said Mrs Thorne, and I realised that I was participating in a spiritualism séance – and understood why Ernest had exhorted me to forget my prejudices. I saw him glancing anxiously in my direction now, and stifled a nervous giggle of apprehension. Was he – could he seriously be expecting the dead girl to communicate with us?

We sat in silence for a long time, while I repressed a series of powerful urges to cough, to scratch, to yawn, to look at the time. Not that I was in the least bit bored; these irritating urges seemed to appear uniquely because I was not in a position to satisfy them at once. I ignored them in deed, and tried sincerely to ignore them in thought, although nobody had told me what to concentrate upon instead. So I gazed alternatively at Mrs Thorne and at the shiny table-top.

Suddenly, I felt it vibrate under my fingers. Mrs Thorne was rocking softly back and forth in her seat, her eyes closed. There was a tremendous atmosphere of tense expectation around the table. Then, after several minutes, I felt the table tilt and rock. Two or three sharp raps sounded against it. I glanced around the table, and saw all the hands of those present simply resting on it, as mine were.

Mrs Thorne took a deep, shuddering breath, and began to speak.

The effect was startlingly unexpected, amazing, horrifying. The voice which issued from her mouth was absolutely not hers. It was a man's voice, deep and slightly raucous.

'Louise? Louise? Louise? Louise?' it repeated, again and again.

The drab little woman with the flowery hat burst into excited sobs.

'Oswald?' she squeaked. 'Oswald? Is that you?'

'Louise? It's me, Oswald. I'm here, Louise. I'm near you, I'm near you. I watch over our children – always.'

'Oswald?' said the woman again. 'Oswald – what is it like there?'

'It's good, Louise. It's good here. Good. Only – they all want to speak. I must go.'

Mrs Thorne shivered and fell silent for a moment. Oswald appeared to have departed. Louise was weeping and helplessly wiping the tears which were running down her face. I tried to check the many thoughts which flashed through my mind. *Drop all prejudice.*

I jumped half out of my seat with shock, as Mrs Thorne now burst into a shriek of manic laughter – ha-ha-ha-ha-ha-ha-ha-ha-haaaaaaaah. This was accompanied by a frenetic series of raps.

'It's Macky!' cried a shrill voice. 'Macky is here! Ha-ha-ha! Let me speak! Let me speak!'

It continued in this vein for a minute or two, until Mr Doyle suddenly said, in a stentorian voice,

'Go away, Macky. Go away now, unless you have a message to transmit.'

'*He* doesn't want to be dead,' said Macky. '*He* doesn't like to be dead. He wants to come back. You know who I mean! ha-ha-ha-ha-ha-ha-ha!' The weird staccato laughter rang out mockingly.

'What rubbish,' said Mr Doyle firmly. 'Let him stay dead. I shan't resuscitate him.'

I found this quite incomprehensible.

Mrs Thorne fell silent again. Her eyes were closed, her face chalky white. After some time, a sad, throaty voice emerged from her mouth.

'Is my son here?'

'Is that you, Mother?' cried the young, chinless man. The bearded professor did not speak, but looked as though he hoped it might be his mother.

'Nobody loves like a mother loves her son,' said the voice.

'I know, Mother,' said the young man, and appeared at a loss for words. 'Are – are you well?' he said after a second's hesitation, and then blushed furiously at the stupidity of the question.

'Be well,' said the sad voice. 'Goodbye.'

There were several further interventions of this kind. The spirits, some acquainted with the members of the circle, others strangers, came and went at will, sometimes rudely pushing each other aside. The young woman with spectacles was never addressed by any spirit. The members of the circle did not seem to be allowed to call up whomsoever they wished, although several times I felt that one or another of them would have liked to do so. I saw Ernest frame the word 'Ivy' with his mouth more than once, as though trying to silently summon her. I could not help wondering how much Mrs Thorne knew about the lives of the people surrounding her, and in particular how much about Ivy. Surely Ernest would not have informed her – his desire for knowledge was intense and genuine.

Suddenly the electric lights in the room flashed on, all together, and then off again. All the faces seemed white and strained in the brief glare. Mrs Thorne began to rock more quickly, more agitatedly.

'Murder,' she wailed in a strange, sing-song voice. 'Murder, murder, grisly murder.' This was not accompanied by raps, but by a strange swishing noise. I started, wondering if I was hearing the lapping of water.

'Ivy?' gasped Ernest, in a half-whisper, obviously not sure of himself. I wished he would keep silent.

'Who wants to know about murder, here? Who is thinking about murder?' said the chanting voice.

'I do,' he said with stiff lips. 'I am.'

'The dark box,' said the lilting, softly wailing voice. 'Oh, the dark box. Oh, the dark box.'

I had a horrible vision of Ivy, still young and fresh, struggling miserably in her coffin. Ernest winced.

'Who killed you?' he asked.

'The ba-a-ad man,' wavered the voice. 'The bride will never see the church, oh, oh, oh, oh, oh, oh,' and it tailed off into weak sobbing.

Ernest glanced at me doubtfully.

'Are you Ivy?' he said.

'Yes, Ivy. I am Ivy. Poor Ivy,' said the voice.

'Go away, Ivy, go away!' shrieked another, violent voice. 'Macky is back! Macky is back, ha ha ha.'

'No! You go away!' said Mr Doyle severely. But Macky had displaced Ivy once and for all. He proved immensely difficult to get rid of, and no other relevant messages came for anyone present. Mrs Thorne fell silent for longer and longer periods, and finally she appeared to be sleeping deeply. After about five minutes of total silence, Mr Doyle said,

'It is over. We should wake her.'

He leant forwards and touched her gently on the shoulder once or twice. She opened her eyes, and sat up.

'Finished, ducks?' she said kindly, although she appeared extremely worn and tired.

'Yes, Arabella,' he replied. 'You were wonderful, as always. Shall we ring for tea?'

The guests were rising, pushing back their chairs. Mrs Thorne tottered to the wall, pressed the electric light switch, and rang the bell. A neatly dressed maid appeared, carrying a large tea-tray containing a pot of tea, several mismatched pretty porcelain cups piled in each other, and a plate of biscuits. Obviously all had been kept in readiness for this moment. The sofas were pulled out and placed about the room, and we all sat down to partake of refreshments. It was most peculiar.

'Did everyone get a message?' asked Mrs Thorne.

'Not I,' said the girl with spectacles.

'Nor I,' said the bearded gentleman.

'Nor I,' I said meekly, but nobody heard.

'Who were you expecting, Professor?' asked the medium.

'Oh, no one in particular,' he replied. 'I'm interested in the science of the thing. How do they reach you, Kate?'

'I've no notion, dear,' she said. 'It just takes me. I don't remember a thing.'

'It is my dearest wish to understand what makes some people into better mediums than others,' said the professor. 'I consider it a kind of magnetism. It is like investigating why some materials make better magnets than others. Something about the structure of the atoms reflects the force of the magnetic field. But human beings are all made of the same atoms.'

'It could be chemical, Professor Lodge,' said Ernest eagerly. 'Different people have different chemical compositions in their brains, don't you think?'

I looked at him with renewed interest. So this was Ernest's

mentor, Sir Oliver Lodge, the professor of physics from Liverpool who studied the ether.

'Certainly,' said the Professor. 'But the transmission: how does it work? If only you could remember what it feels like, Kate. What happens in your brain before you begin speaking with the voice of another?'

'I can't remember a thing, you know that,' she replied. 'Everything I know about my own trances, other people have described to me.'

'It must be waves,' said Sir Oliver. '*Electric* waves of some kind. Because the lights came on.'

'Did they really? No, I just turned them on myself.'

'No, during your trance they flashed on and off without anyone else touching the switch. Could it have been your maid, by any chance? Is there another switch to your lights?'

I admired the purity of the Professor's mind. Did he really think that if Mrs Thorne had arranged with her maid to flash on the lights, she was about to tell him? But she merely replied,

'No, dear, the only light switch is right in here.'

'So they *are* electromagnetic waves,' he said firmly.

'I am disappointed,' murmured Ernest into my ear, as we stepped out into the darkening street a short while later, having bid our hostess goodbye exactly as though we had been invited for a perfectly ordinary tea rather than a conversation with the spirits of the dead. 'I hoped – I truly hoped that we might learn something important, something definitive.'

'The – the spirits don't seem to give a lot of factual information,' I said hesitantly.

'No,' he admitted. 'I didn't really expect Ivy to name her murderer. The spirits are far removed from our daily world of living beings. But I thought she might say something about the circumstances of her death.'

'Ernest, I will try to discover them, I promise you, even if I do have to resort to more down-to-earth methods,' I said.

'But how?' he groaned. 'I was so sure…'

'Well, I will begin as I always do, by collecting information,' I reassured him. 'Tomorrow I will visit her theatre company. There are many things I need to learn about her life. And there are many questions that I will have to ask you. For instance – do you know where Miss Elliott lived?'

'No, I don't,' he replied glumly. I glanced at him quickly. It was obvious that he had been in love to the point of sickness, yet it was not at all clear what the material circumstances of that love had been. I did not know whether the two had ever exchanged even a single word, or whether it had all been the passion of a spectator for an actress upon the stage. And it seemed extremely difficult to ask directly.

'You'll never be able to find all the people she knew,' he said. 'I mean, all the people who knew her. There are too many, they are too anonymous.'

'What do you mean?' I said, surprised and confused by this odd remark. 'Are you talking about spectators?'

'Not spectators,' he said. 'Don't you understand? She was an actress, Vanessa. An actress is – I mean – known to many people. An actress is public. Don't you understand what I'm saying?'

'But it can't be a member of the public who killed her,' I said. 'It must have been someone who knew her more closely than that.'

He turned away, sweeping his hand through the air in a gesture of despair.

'An actress is public property,' he said. 'It's a hopeless task. But after all, she was killed in Cambridge. Shouldn't you be looking for the murderer there?'

'Oh, I am going to do that,' I said quickly. 'But her murderer must have come from her own circle. I need to find out more about it. More about *her*.'

We composed our faces into cheerful politeness as we entered Ernest's flat. Kathleen was still up, waiting for her husband. She looked thin and tired.

'Did you enjoy it?' she asked me. 'Ernest always wants me to go, but I just don't believe in those things.'

'Oh – it was extremely interesting,' I said. 'I don't know yet whether I am a believer or not. I would need to see more.'

'Who was there?' she asked him.

'Professor Lodge and the other usuals, minus a few,' he said. 'We're all members of the SPR, you know,' he added, turning to me, 'the Society for Psychical Research. We are dedicated to pursuing any hint of psychic activity that we hear of. Mrs Thorne is a fairly recent discovery of ours, although she has been having trances for years. She is remarkable. So simple about it all; no pretension, no pose, no properties. No Ouija board, no tricks, no wires.'

'The lights did go on,' I remarked.

'Well yes, but that was the effect of the electromagnetic waves,' he replied. Quite exactly as though this were an established scientific fact.

It was already late, and Kathleen rose and showed me to the small spare bedroom. I settled myself in bed, looking around me a little sadly; it was obvious that the pretty Morris wallpaper, the white ceiling, the fresh curtains in front of the window protected by white-painted iron bars, had all been arranged with the intention of making the room into a nursery. But there were no children in it. I fell asleep with the image of the twins in front of my eyes, hearing the echo of their quick little feet as they went trotting across the room on some errand of fundamental importance to their infant minds.

I was awoken from deep sleep in what seemed to be the darkest part of the night, by a hand laid gently on my shoulder. I started awake, and sat up. Kathleen was kneeling by the bedside, faintly visible in the gloom in her white nightgown.

'I am sorry to wake you, Vanessa,' she whispered. 'Please forgive me. But I can't sleep, I am so worried. What happened in Cambridge, while Ernest was staying with you? Why did he return so changed? What has come over him? He has been like a sleepwalker since he came back. I am beside myself with worry. What is going on? You were there – you must know!'

I sat up straighter, and rubbed my eyes. I felt myself in a most difficult moral predicament. What was I supposed to do? Hide the truth from her, or tell it? My ability to make swift, accurate decisions was hindered by the sleep which seemed to fill all the pores of my brain, as Newton had described the ether filling the pores of all solid materials.

'I love him, Vanessa,' she urged me. 'But he won't talk to me. It's like he's gone somewhere else. I can see he's suffering, but I don't know why. I'll go mad if this goes on. I can't bear it.'

'I do know what the matter is,' I said finally. 'He has received a bad shock. A woman was found murdered in Cambridge several days ago, and I am working on the case. Ernest was present when we discovered that the identity of the dead woman was none other than an actress he greatly admired.'

'Ophelia,' she breathed, with sudden understanding. 'I know the actress you mean.'

'Yes, the actress who played Ophelia, and was to play Titania when we went to see *A Midsummer Night's Dream*. Do you remember how we discussed whether or not she was wearing a wig? Well, she was, because it wasn't the same actress. The actress Ernest knew was already dead on that day.'

'So she's dead!' she whispered, with an emotion which emerged as a strange little squeak. 'I see it all now. Vanessa, I can't thank you enough. I was desperate. I was thinking – you can't imagine what I was thinking. I thought maybe Ernest had fallen in love with *you*. He came back this morning, and could talk about nothing but you for the whole day, and how he wanted you to come to the séance in the evening. Ernest can't help talking, talking, when he is upset. Yet he doesn't say what's on his mind – he'll go all around it. Oh, I know him so well! I see now why he wanted to go there – and why he wanted you to come. *She's* dead. He must have thought that she would speak.' She stopped, thinking for a moment, and then added, 'Did she? Did she appear?'

'Yes,' I said, 'but she only said strange, incomprehensible things like "the dark box".'

'Horrible!' she said, shuddering. 'The dark box. It's nightmarish. I must go to him. Forgive me for having woken you, Vanessa. I am more grateful than you can imagine.'

She slipped away, and I lay down again, feeling that I had been as tactful as the situation permitted.

A gentle hand touched the woman's shoulder as she lay sleeping, the early light of dawn shut out from her room, but for a glimmer round the edge of the heavy dark curtains. She opened her eyes sleepily, and catching the hand of her son in hers, she looked up at his tall figure.

'Shh, Mamma, don't make a noise,' he whispered. 'Don't wake Papa. Come upstairs with me, quickly. I have to show you something wonderful. But it's a secret.'

She followed him up the stairs to the enormous, empty room under the rafters, and observed him wordlessly as he drew her to a small and curious construction of wood and metal. His eyes shining, he stretched out his finger and pressed a crude button. A little bell tinkled shrilly at the other end of the room.

It was cold in the vast, empty chamber. Mother and son held each other close for a long time before returning to their beds.

I woke early, and rose and dressed as soon as I heard movements in the adjoining bedroom. I was in a hurry to leave; I was afraid to find the domestic situation too tense for my liking, and I wished to begin my investigations at once. However, when I emerged from my room upon hearing Kathleen enter the kitchen, I found her in high spirits, humming as she made tea. She turned a radiant face to me, but said nothing. Indeed, she could hardly ask me how I had slept, or I her! I watched her for a few moments, admiring the sturdy, well-built yet very feminine body Nature had seen fit to bestow upon her, moving with vigour and purpose inside a close-fitting bodice. When Ernest entered the room, she caught his arm and drew him towards her briefly, in passing, then let it go; a mere butterfly caress. Her reconquest of her husband was clearly underway.

I waited till Kathleen had left the room to ask Ernest what I most desired to know, namely whether the Outdoor Shakespeare Company was still playing in Hampstead, or had moved to another location. He did not know, but fetched the morning paper from where it had been delivered on the doormat, and spread it out among the teacups. We bent our heads together over the announcements of theatre productions.

'Why look,' said Ernest, 'they're going to be playing in a

real theatre. The Acropolis. It's been closed for ages for renovations. I expect they got it temporarily – and inexpensively.' He spoke quite normally, but his hand trembled as he refolded the paper.

'I am going there at once,' I told him. He nodded without comment.

In spite of the improved conjugal atmosphere, I sighed with relief as I emerged into the sunny street. London! I never set foot in it without feeling a surge of excitement caused by the busy immensity of its populous thoroughfares and byways. It was a joy to me to walk and walk, even as the streets became narrower, the houses seedier, the pavements dirtier and the people more unkempt. I had located the position of this unknown theatre in the East End of London, and it took me more than an hour to reach it, but it was an hour well spent. I arrived somewhat dusty, but feeling refreshed and renewed.

It was, nevertheless, with a feeling of timidity that I hesitated in front of the door of the dilapidated building located at the address corresponding to the Acropolis theatre. There was no sign over the door to indicate the nature of the building, although traces remained of a sign that had hung there and been removed. It was pressed closely between two peeling tenements, and the large wooden door was worn, scratched and discoloured by inclement weather and total lack of care. Two broad windows, one on either side of the door, bore cracked and broken panes, some of which had been summarily patched with canvas, and sheets of yellowed newspaper covered them on the inside so that it was impossible to obtain a glimpse of the interior.

I remained in the street for a few moments, contemplating this unwelcoming door. It did not seem to be equipped with any kind of bell, but finally the staring eyes of a little group of street children impelled me to move, and I stepped forward, laid my hand upon the knob, and pushed. The door creaked and yielded; it was not locked.

I entered a foyer running the whole width of the building. It was not especially large, yet its dimensions were fair enough to give an impression of spaciousness, especially in the dimness produced by the covered windows, which caused the walls to recede into vagueness. A stone floor which could have been quite impressive if swept and polished rang under my feet. The space was entirely empty except for a counter along the length of one of the side walls. Counter and floor were strewn with old programmes, newspapers and scraps of all kinds. I thought that it might have been a decent entrance to the theatre, and could again become one with a little effort; a thorough cleaning, new glass and curtains at the large front windows, and reasonable lighting would suffice. The idea of light caused me to glance upwards, and I found myself admiring an enormous chandelier covered with cobwebs and hanging somewhat askew.

There were two doors in the far wall, a double door in the centre and a little one off to the side. I advanced slowly towards the double door and tried it very delicately. It yielded; I opened it a crack, and found myself looking straight into the theatre itself.

Curved rows of fixed, wooden folding seats faced the stage, watching, like silent spectators, the scene unfolding thereupon. These hundreds of seats were occupied by two or three people only. On the stage, an actor and an actress were reading some lines, standing with their texts in their hands. A young man, following the shouted directions of one of the seated gentlemen, drew chalk lines and circles upon the floor. The back of the stage was half-collapsed, partly open into the backstage area beyond, where several other people could be seen occupied at different tasks. At least two men stood upon ladders, one hammering away with rather gentle taps, as though he were not on familiar ground, or did not wish to disturb the actors, another tearing away strips of peeling paper from what might have been an old backdrop. A row of electric lights, several of which were not functioning, lined the edge of the stage.

The actress on the stage, a tall, well-built girl, lifted her head, and I recognised Helena from *A Midsummer Night's Dream*, although today, instead of Greek drapery, she wore only a simple walking skirt and a modest blouse waist with unfashionably small sleeve puffs no greater than my own. No doubt she, like me, belonged to a small sisterhood of those who willingly sacrifice fashionability in order to avoid wearing frighteningly gigantic leg-of-mutton sleeves which require special cloaks and refuse to pass through ordinary doors.

'Let's move to the confession scene,' said the director sitting in front of the stage, and the young woman turned her head towards the area behind the stage, and bellowed unceremoniously,

'Mrs Warren's wanted now!'

Immediately, there came a middle-aged woman dressed in a skirt fitted closely around her generous hips, and a blouse whose fantastic decorations turned her shoulders into the widest part of her body – no mean feat, considering the rest of it. I slipped into a seat at the very back of the theatre to watch the continuation of the rehearsal.

The young man left, and joined one of the workmen at the back, standing at the bottom of the ladder and reaching tools up to him. I could make them out through the partially destroyed backdrop. The two women fetched a pair of wobbly chairs and sat on them, facing each other, holding their scripts in their hands. They read from these, but lifted their faces to look at each other whenever they could, having taken in a whole line or two in a single glance.

The young woman played a character by the name of Vivie Warren, a person who appeared to consider herself vastly superior to her mother. The older woman expressed this by acting querulously hurt as she spoke her lines. Vivie began by criticising her mother and her mother's friends, but after a short time moved to what was obviously the uppermost question in her mind: the identity of her unknown father. At this point, the dialogue was interrupted and recommenced more than a dozen times, as the play's director seemed to be seeking a way in which to allow Vivie's mother to pronounce an admission so bold that I was doubtful that such a play could be performed on the London stage at all, and not only because of the scandal, but also because of the artistic effect. It seemed impossible that the entire audience should not immediately feel, as I did, that the whole play had been written uniquely with a view to pronouncing exactly these words and exposing those facts in a public place.

'Listen, you're describing your youth,' said the director to Mrs Warren. 'You need to take a kind of calm but slightly wailing tone, as though you're going through these old memories which are drab and wearisome to you, but not acutely painful any more. The important thing is to speak *without* emphasis.'

I sat back, unnoticed, and went on listening.

Mrs Warren: *The clergyman got me a situation as a scullery maid; then I was a waitress, and then I went to the bar at Waterloo station; fourteen hours a day serving drinks and washing glasses for four shillings a week and my board. Well, one cold, wretched night, when I was so tired I could hardly keep myself awake, who should come up for a half of Scotch but my sister Lizzie, in a long fur cloak, elegant and comfortable, with a lot of sovereigns in her purse. When she saw I'd grown up good-looking, she said to me across the bar, "What are you doing there, you little fool? Wearing out your health and your appearance for other people's profit!" Liz was saving money then to take a house for herself in Brussels, and she thought we two could save faster than one. So she lent me some money and gave me a start; and I saved steadily and first paid her back, and then went into business with her as a partner. Why shouldn't I have done it? The house in Brussels was real high class: a much better place for a woman to be in than the whitelead factory where girls get themselves poisoned, or the scullery, or the bar, or at home. Would you have had me stay in them and become a worn out old drudge before I was forty?*

Vivie: No; but why did you choose that business?
              Saving money and good management will
              succeed in any business.

Mrs Warren: Yes, saving money. But where can a woman get
              the money to save in any other business?
              Could you save out of four shillings a week
              and keep yourself dressed as well? Not you.
              Of course, if you're a plain woman and can't
              earn anything more; or if you have a turn for
              music, or the stage, or newspaper-writing:
              that's different. But neither Liz nor I had any
              turn for such things at all: all we had was our
              appearance and our turn for pleasing men. Do
              you think we were such fools as to let other
              people trade in our good looks by employing
              us as shopgirls, or barmaids, or waitresses,
              when we could trade in them ourselves and get
              all the profits instead of starvation wages? Not
              likely.

Vivie: You were certainly quite justified – from the
              business point of view.

Mrs Warren: Yes; or any other point of view. What is any
              respectable girl brought up to do but to catch
              some rich man's fancy and get the benefit of
              his money by marrying him? – as if a marriage
              ceremony could make any difference in the
              right or wrong of the thing! Oh, the hypocrisy
              of the world makes me sick! Liz and I had to

work and save and calculate just like other people; elseways we should be as poor as any good-for-nothing drunken waster of a woman that thinks her luck will last forever. I despise such people: they've no character; and if there's a thing I hate in a woman, it's want of character.

Vivie: *Come now, mother: frankly! Isn't it part of what you call character in a woman that she should greatly dislike such a way of making money?*

Mrs Warren: *Why, of course. Everybody dislikes having to work and make money; but they have to do it all the same. I'm sure I've often pitied a poor girl, tired out and in low spirits, having to try to please some man that she doesn't care two straws for – some half-drunken fool that thinks he's making himself agreeable when he's teasing and worrying and disgusting a woman so that hardly any money could pay her for putting up with it. But she has to bear with disagreeables and take the rough with the smooth, just like a nurse in a hospital or anyone else. It's not work that any woman would do for pleasure, goodness knows; though to hear the pious people talk you would suppose it was a bed of roses.*

'This is rubbish, Alan,' said the actress playing Vivie, jumping out of her chair and throwing her script to the floor. 'We can't play this stuff! It's all very well to say "without emphasis". But the emphasis is there, in the words. The whole thing is just wrong.'

'It can't be done without seeking effect,' agreed the older woman. Rising, she walked to the edge of the stage and squinted down at the man called Alan, whom I now knew to be the Alan Manning that Ernest had mentioned. 'It's missing the human aspect, Alan. What Shaw is doing here is trying to prove a point. I'm not saying the point he's trying to prove is wrong. But the authenticity of any dialogue is bound to be lost when you try to use it to *prove* something.'

'I do see what you're saying, of course,' said the director, standing up and stretching. He was in his shirtsleeves, having thrown his jacket over the back of his seat. 'It doesn't dig deep enough, does it? I didn't realise that when I read the script at home. It seemed to hit pretty hard. But now it's starting to sound a bit like a social tract. Still, maybe we're spoilt by Shakespeare. Don't you think we could save it?'

'It's risky,' said the older woman. 'If the play were really good, we could overcome the public anger it's bound to produce. But with a play as poor as this, it doesn't stand a chance.'

'I hate it!' cried the younger actress vehemently, joining her colleague at the edge of the stage. 'What does he think he knows? How does any man dare write about such things – as though he can possibly understand! How dare he – how dare he even pretend to imagine!' She stamped her foot, and continued furiously. 'He wrote these lines to be spoken by *actresses*. And what will the effect on the public be? It's – it's like a betrayal in the midst of our struggle. Our profession is only just beginning to be perceived as...honourable. No, that isn't even true yet. No decent girl would be allowed to go on the stage, even today. But the subject is being *raised*, at least! There are *some* playwrights who are trying to tell the public that our profession is *not* to be confused with—'

'The oldest profession in the world,' broke in Mr Manning calmly. 'All right, that's enough, I understand your point. It was just a try, remember? Let's take a break, and have a bit of a read of Act III after elevenses. If we all agree it won't work, we'll chuck it. I've got three others under consideration, remember?'

'I'll get a pot of tea,' said the older actress, putting her arm around the younger girl's shoulders. The one or two seated spectators rose, and scrambling directly up onto the stage, they crossed over to the back and disappeared. Only Mr Manning remained, shuffling together the pages of his own copy of the script, upon which he had been making notes. I went over towards him.

'Excuse me,' I said softly. He turned abruptly.

'Who are you?' he said.

'A friend of Ivy Elliott,' I said.

'A friend of Ivy's!' he exclaimed. 'But what are you doing here? Don't you know that Ivy is dead?'

'Yes, I know,' I said. 'I have simply come to talk to you about her, if you will let me. Or rather, to ask you to talk to me. I – I wanted to meet the people she worked with.'

He walked towards me and squinted directly into my eyes, unpleasantly.

'You're no friend of Ivy's,' he said. 'What could she have had to do with someone like you? What are you – a journalist prying for information? I've nothing to tell about Ivy. I spoke to the police for two hours yesterday – that's enough for me. She disappeared without warning, and we had no idea what had become of her till they came yesterday to tell us that she was dead.'

'Alan!' shouted a voice, and one of the young men who had been working in the backstage area came out onto the stage and looked down at us. 'Tea! Who's this?' he added, moving forward to peer at me over the lights.

'Some so-called friend of Ivy's,' said Mr Manning with a sneer of disbelief. The young actor jumped lithely off the stage to the floor and approached us.

'What about Ivy?' he asked quickly. 'Anything new? You can say what you like, Alan, but it's just unbearable, not knowing what happened to her. Do you know anything?' he added, turning hopefully to me.

'Not a lot, but more than you do, perhaps,' I told him, thinking that sharing some information might be a small price to pay for learning more about this strange company.

'Come along and join us for tea,' he said. Then, noticing Mr Manning's lowering brow, he added, 'Oh, were you just chasing the lady off? Sorry! But you didn't tell us a syllable about what the police said yesterday, and we're still all in the dark. All we gathered was that Ivy is dead; not the how, not the where, not the why. Come on, don't be so close.'

'That's all they told me. I didn't hide anything from you,' said Alan crossly.

'Yes, but maybe this lady knows more.'

'I do,' I said quickly. 'I come from Cambridge, and that is where she died.'

'Come on then,' he said, and I found myself awkwardly

manoeuvring my way up onto the stage and through the rent in the backdrop, to where the actors were grouped around a large table on which had been placed a steaming teapot, several chipped cups without saucers, and a plain pound cake.

'Folks, this lady has come unexpectedly to tell us something about Ivy,' said the young man. There was a collective murmur of surprise, and everyone drew closer, even Mr Manning, although he still frowned.

'I know that you are all aware that Ivy Elliott is dead,' I said respectfully.

'Well, we weren't,' said a young lady with bright eyes and dark hair, 'only since the police came yesterday.'

'That doesn't matter, Jean. The point is: how did she die? What happened?' asked a man who, now that he had descended from the ladder, I saw was extremely tall. I recognised the two of them as the actors who had played Hermia and Theseus.

'She was murdered, and her body was found in the Cam,' I said. 'The exact circumstances of her death are not clear, but the post-mortem clearly shows that she was strangled shortly after midnight on the 21st of June, and her body placed in the river some three or four hours later, where it was found in the early morning by a passer-by.'

'Oh, that's horrible, too horrible. She was strangled? Who did it? Who could have done such a dreadful thing?' cried the girl called Jean, turning pale.

'Nobody knows at this point.'

'What was Ivy doing in Cambridge?' said the elderly lady who had been playing Mrs Warren. 'Who took her there?'

'She had a friend there, who invited her from time to time,' I said. 'She had just left his home when she was killed.'

The woman sat down suddenly and placed her forehead in her hand.

'It makes me feel queer,' she said. 'Ivy, dead. I can't get used to it. I can't get it into my head.'

'We all feel that way, Paula,' said the tall man, laying his hand on her shoulder. 'It won't be the same here without her.' But she was sobbing quietly.

'To think she was killed on the twenty-first,' she said. 'Her one free day.'

'Why was she free then?' I asked.

'We alternate plays,' replied the tall actress. 'Tuesdays and Sunday evenings we play something modern. We've been doing *The Wild Duck*. Ivy wasn't in it. Oh God. We must have been playing while she was being murdered.'

'Not playing,' said the actor. 'If she was murdered after midnight, we would have been finished.'

'Finished, but not gone,' said Paula. 'We never get out of here before one o'clock on the days we change plays, with all the dismantling. We were all right here. Oh, to think that if only we'd given her the role of Hedwig like she wanted – she wouldn't have died!'

'Don't say that,' said Jean quickly. 'It makes me feel as though you all think it's my fault she was killed!'

Mr Manning turned towards the group and spoke rather sharply.

'Nonsense, Paula' he snapped. 'If somebody wanted to murder the girl, a time and a place to do it would have been found. It has nothing to do with *The Wild Duck,* nothing to do with us at all. Come,' he added, beckoning me to follow him. 'I think we had better talk in private.' He was obviously not at all pleased at the emotional storm I had caused within his well-controlled company.

I followed him over to a set of doors leading to a row of smaller rooms, no doubt actor's lodges or something of the kind. One of them had been set up as a working room for Mr Manning, with a desk, a chair and a large number of papers, plays, books and notes scattered about. He offered me the chair and sat down on the desk himself.

'Just what, exactly, did you come here for?' he said.

'I came to learn more about Ivy,' I told him. He hesitated, and I thought he was going to challenge me to tell him why, but he suddenly changed his mind. Instead he said,

'We don't know much about her. She worked here, but kept her personal life very private. What kind of thing do you want to know?'

'First of all, have you her address? Do you know where she lived?' I said. For answer, he wrote it out on a little scrap of paper and handed it to me in silence. I read it and thrust it into my dress.

'Then, I would like to ask you how long you have known her, and when and how she came to join your company,' I continued.

He cast his mind back.

'Let's see, she came in…in June? No, in May. Last May, just over a year ago. We had put in an advertisement, actually, for two young ladies and a man. There are not many of us in the company, you see. We're twenty all together; seven or eight main actors and actresses, and then a bunch of irregulars we call on occasionally to fill in the minor roles. At the time, we were just beginning. I put the Company together a few years ago with two or three of the people you have just met; they brought in a few friends. We put down what money we could, and found a sponsor. Our first plays were out in the country, and we made a success of them. As soon as we were able to hire enough extras, we started putting on Shakespeare. Our idea was that the country folks should be able to have as much Shakespeare as they need, without going to London for the purpose. After a couple of seasons we did well enough to try for the London audiences, and it worked. We did comedies first. Then we decided to try Hamlet. That was my decision. I've been waiting all my life to direct Hamlet.' By this time, Mr Manning appeared to have forgotten my original question. His eyes were shining with an intense gleam. His words came tumbling out. 'It's dangerous, Hamlet, you know. It can make you or break you. Everything has been tried; the greatest actors have played Hamlet. If you can't find something new to say, there's no point to it. I wanted two things. One was the nature aspect. I wanted to do the play outside. I knew we could accomplish things that had never been tried before, by choosing the right spot and taking advantage of its possibilities. There are scenes in Shakespeare – the rehearsal scene in *A Midsummer Night's Dream*, the forest scenes in *As You Like It* – which take place among trees. Nothing like making them take place among real trees. Then I wanted something else which has been abandoned, I find, in all recent performances. I wanted something like simplicity; something classical, which has been lost with all the experimental performances we've had lately. Have you seen Ellen Terry playing Ophelia? A madwoman – that short hair standing all on end, her eyes staring crazily. She went to a lunatic asylum, they say, to study the behaviour of the madwomen there. The public drinks it in. But that's not what

I want. Ophelia doesn't mean raving lunacy, not to me. What's left in the human being when reason goes? Something meaningful – meaningful, I'm telling you. There's a truth within us that goes far beyond reason; strip reason away and that's what you'll find. The human individual. Ellen Terry's performance hurt me. I wanted to give Ophelia her truth back; the intelligence, the feelings, the innocence and the poetry that gleam all the stronger through the ruins of reason. But we didn't have a good Ophelia. Carrie is fantastic in certain roles, although she's a little typecast, being so tall. But she wasn't what I had in mind. I put in the advertisement and got dozens of answers. Jean came then, the girl you saw in there. She wasn't Ophelia, but I hired her; I knew she'd play a hundred roles to perfection. When I saw Ivy Elliott, I felt hopeful for a moment. She had the right physical appearance. But her acting experience was limited. She'd played only a few small roles. I asked her how she got her start and she said she answered advertisements and went to auditions; she wanted to be an actress more than anything she'd ever wanted in her life. She'd had no experience at first, but they taught her and she learnt quickly. Acting is a profession, you know. You can't just stand there and spout words and gesticulate! Every tone, every gesture, every movement is meticulously planned by the director. The actor has to understand and execute. It isn't easy. But I took a chance on Ivy, because she had something captivating about her that I thought might make up for her lack of experience, and her – her manner. She had the face, the hair, the figure. And something more.' He stopped, lost in his own mental images.

'What was she like?' I asked to give him a little prod.

'She was remarkable, in her way,' he replied. 'Her manners

were common, her speech was common, her behaviour with men was worse than common; it was familiar. Yet she wasn't vulgar. By her accent, she wasn't from London originally. No Cockney there. In fact, I've no idea where she came from and what her background was, and I think I'd rather not know. What she had was what I was talking about before; she had a certain inner truth that lay deeper than all the cheap squalor life had surrounded her with, and the surprising capacity to let it come out when she acted. The Ivy we knew used to just fall away as soon as she walked onto the stage. I had to teach her a lot about *where* to walk and *why*, but not about *how*. She had a very jaunty step usually; not modest, you know. Ladies used to cringe sometimes, just brushing past her in the street. But she knew instinctively never to use it on stage. She had a grasp of complete simplicity that made her much easier to direct than some others I could name. There were a lot of roles she wouldn't have been able to play, certainly. We couldn't have found a place for her in *Mrs Warren's Profession*. The characters are too bold.'

'Is that the play you were reading just now?' I said. 'I wondered what it was.'

'Bernard Shaw,' he replied. 'You don't know it? It was published some years ago, but it hasn't been performed yet. Too shocking. The mother a brothel-keeper, the daughter a smoking Cambridge graduate working in the City. I thought we could make something exciting of it, but you probably heard what Paula said. It might not be so easy.'

'It is difficult to write and speak publicly about such things,' I murmured.

'And privately,' he added, looking at me. 'But the stage can help. That is one of its purposes. Some people think of it as being an artificial venue, a place where life is imitated. But it can be the contrary. Thanks to the screen of artificiality, truths can be said that can't be stated in intimacy. Ibsen grasped that fact, and that's what made his fame. The public is captive, silent – slam it into them while they're sitting in the dark. Let them ferment and complain afterwards.'

'But plays can fail if they offend,' I said.

'Certainly. That's why *Mrs Warren's Profession* may not be a good idea for us now. Yet it's an interesting play in its way. Say it out loud! Shakespeare's safer, of course. He said everything as well. Nothing is missing, yet nobody gets offended. And Shakespeare is full of roles for Ivy's type. I hired her as a permanent member on a hunch, and it played out well. I was pleased with her work, and the public was quite fond of her. Over and above her acting, she had an excellent memory and she was accurate and businesslike. I liked that in her. She was always on time, always knew her lines, never had moods.'

'She must have been pleased to be hired as a permanent member,' I said, 'if she were hoping only for a part in one play.'

'Oh, she was pleased as Punch,' he said. 'Jumped at it. But I had to tell her we couldn't pay her much. She was upset for just a moment, but then she accepted. And she scraped by. She supplemented it somehow or other; I don't want to know more.'

'Dare I ask how much you were able to pay her?' I said.

'Two,' he said abruptly. 'Two shillings a week during plays, three when she had a big role, one and six when she understudied, nothing when she was off. I couldn't give more. I would have if I could. We're practically running at a loss as it is,' he went on defensively. 'The trailer and tent are expensive; the travel and horses are expensive; we all need salaries. I told her she wasn't expected to buy her own costumes. We have a fairly large collection here that she was free to use. She occasionally took things home with her, but as long as she altered them to fit herself and didn't spoil them, that was all right with me.'

'Such a salary is really not enough for anyone to live on,' I said thoughtfully, without adding that salary was the wrong word – slave-wages would have been closer to the mark.

'I know that; yet she lived. I didn't ask questions. I'm too busy just trying to survive. Getting this theatre is a stroke of luck; we've been offered it free for a month if we renovate. That costs us money as well, of course, but we're doing as much as we can by ourselves. Losing Ivy is a blow, you know,' he added. 'A blow to the Company, and a personal one as well. I liked the girl. She wasn't easy to come to know. She was pleasant, yet she kept herself to herself. But she was a good hard worker. She'd have enjoyed being here now.'

He shrugged, and then rose, clearly intending to put an end to our conversation. I would have liked to speak with the others, but he guided me firmly across the stage.

'We must get back to work,' he said, as he gave me his hand to deposit me over the edge and pointed firmly towards the exit. I made my way among the seats to the aisle, crossed the foyer and stepped out into the street, closing the door behind me. I should have liked to talk to the members of the company a little more, yet I had food for thought already. And something else.

I removed the scrap of paper bearing Ivy's address from my pocket, smoothed it out and read it again, then walked until

I spotted an empty cab idling near the kerb. Entering, I gave the man the address in Bayswater and settled back in my corner to think.

The house in front of which he deposited me surprised me. I had expected something quite different, although I was not sure exactly what. I knew, of course, that Ivy did not live on the money from the theatre alone. Mr Archer, for one, had given her three pounds by his own admission, and from the description of one of the witnesses, it sounded like it might have been an even greater sum in fact. So it was not that I expected to find that she lived in a miserable hovel. But neither did I expect to find a neat stone house, converted into small flats, with clean front steps, geraniums at the windows, a well-swept area with trimly painted railings, and a highly polished brass doorknob. The house was eminently respectable, and so completely different from the image that I had evolved in my mind that I even wondered briefly if she had given a false address, or if I had come to the wrong place.

I rang, and the door was opened by a plump lady wearing a housedress and an apron. Her waist was cinched rather tightly, and below and above it her body burst out like a pillow upon which no stays could have any truly significant effect. Her white hair was piled under a cap.

'Are you looking for a room? I haven't got any empty right now,' she said, 'but I've got a beautiful one'll come free in a day or two, if you can wait.'

With a flash of intuition, I realised that she must already know that Ivy was dead – after all, the police had already been to the theatre, and they had almost certainly been here as well – and felt certain that the room to come free was Ivy's. I wondered why it was not free already, and then thought that perhaps she needed time to clear away the dead girl's things.

'I am very interested in taking a room here. May I see it at once?' I asked, seizing the opportunity.

'Well,' she said dubiously, 'it's not free yet. It's very nice,' she added, 'one of the biggest ones. Just up those stairs. It looks out over the back and has got two large windows.' She hesitated for a moment, then said, 'Well, there's no one there right now. Come with me. I'll show it to you.' Her eyes swept approvingly over my dress, my gloves, my parasol and my hat.

I followed her up the short flight of stairs, impatient, wondering. She took a key from a large ring hanging at her waist, and unlocking the door, she opened it and held it for me to enter.

The first thing I saw was that the room in front of me was shared by two occupants. A curtain of some dark stuff hung loosely from a stretched cord dividing the room in two; to each side of this curtain was placed a narrow bed of iron scrollwork painted white, a chair, a dresser with a mirror on it, and a washstand. The room was quite large enough to contain this furniture without appearing crowded. Each tenant had a trunk under the bed, as well as a number of articles of clothing arranged on shelves and in drawers, and hanging on a row of hooks on the wall. I looked carefully on both sides, and walked over to peer out of one of the windows, in order to gain a little time. The lady joined me without haste.

'The view's not so bad,' she said. 'There's plenty of light.'

The view showed nothing but the backs of the houses across the street, into whose windows one could see a little too clearly. I looked around.

'The ladies who live here are moving away?' I said, feigning polite interest.

'Ye-es,' she said with a flash of hesitation. I began to feel sure that this room was shared by Ivy Elliott with another girl, and I conceived a tremendous desire to discover her name.

'They – they'll be gone in another day or two,' she continued. 'We'll arrange the furniture for one person, of course. We can take one of the beds away. It'll be a lovely room for one, won't it?' In order to increase my perception of its spaciousness, she pulled the dividing curtain all the way to the back of the room. I had already determined, by a few small details, which side of the room must have belonged to the dead girl, for only one of the washstand bowls was wet, and there was dust on the other mirror, something no girl will allow. I fixed my attention on that side of the room, and walked through it thoughtfully.

'Yes,' I said, longing desperately to open some of the drawers, 'I should like to keep this bed. If we take away the bed and dresser from the other side, perhaps I could put in a small sofa?'

'Certainly,' she was beginning, when Providence suddenly intervened in my favour, and the doorbell downstairs rang.

'I'll be right up, ma'am,' she said, hurrying ponderously, if such a thing is possible.

My movements were quicker than light. I first handled the clothes hanging from nails, seeking anything written: letters, documents, a diary in the pockets. There was nothing, though the dresses themselves flashed sequins, rhinestones and feathers. I then slid open the drawers one at a time and ran my hands through the contents. I was looking for anything written, yet could not help noticing, in the blink of an eye, that the top drawer held chemises, petticoats, corset-covers and corsets in two heaps; white cambric and cotton to the right, flower-patterned, and lace-trimmed and black silk to the left. The right-hand items looked new, the left-hand ones well-used. I stored this information in the back of my mind for later, closed the drawer, and opened the one below. It stuck – I gave it a little jerk – and it came out in my hand, bumping onto my lap as I sat on my knees in front of the dresser. I lifted it hastily to push it back in, and that is when I felt a little rustle of paper against my dress; a bundle of letters had been hidden underneath the drawer, slipped into a crosswise band of wood. I pulled them out and thrust them into my dress, then pushed the drawer back into place just as I heard the landlady come puffing up the stairs – not before having had time to perceive, at a glance, that my hunch was correct. The letters were addressed to Ivy Elliott.

When the landlady returned, she found me sitting calmly upon the bed, observing the room from different angles.

'How long has the room been let to these young ladies?' I asked as we descended the stairs.

'They've had it for a year,' she said, frowning.

'And why are they leaving?'

Her frown deepened. 'I can't say exactly,' she said. 'They've given notice, so it will be very soon.'

'What is the rent of the room?' I finally asked. She looked me up and down, and said,

'Five shillings a week.'

It seemed expensive, but I suspected that it might suddenly have been increased for my benefit. I wanted more than ever to know the name of the young woman who was sharing Ivy's room. It seemed to me that no one, if not she, could tell me the details of Ivy's private life. But I could not think of a good way to induce this lady, whose friendliness was fast evaporating, to tell it to me. I began to wonder if I should spend the following days hovering in the vicinity in the hopes of catching the mysterious tenant as she entered or left. But the landlady, feeling, no doubt, that I had spent sufficient time in a private dwelling not yet my own, was ushering me towards the door.

'I'll take the room!' I said impulsively. 'When can I have it? Do you think tomorrow would be too early?'

She looked pleased.

'Well,' she said, 'I'll see if I can arrange it.'

'I don't want to put the ladies – what are their names? to excessive inconvenience,' I said.

'I'll speak to – them,' she replied, and I detected the microscopic hesitation before the word 'them'.

'If they have paid through to the end of the week, or have not been able to find new lodgings yet, I hope they will allow me to offer some compensation,' I said, still hoping to find some way to enter into contact with the remaining occupant of the room. 'Perhaps I can discuss it with them tomorrow?'

'I'll take care of that,' she said again, 'I'll see how I can arrange things.'

I felt that she was going to try at all costs to prevent a meeting, and I could understand why. She very likely thought that no one would want to rent the room of a dead girl, little imagining that this was my dearest wish. But I could hardly tell her so.

An idea struck me, and I quietly withdrew a banknote from my purse.

'Then let me at least leave this, as some compensation for my haste,' I said. 'I should like to put it in an envelope, and leave it for the young ladies with a note explaining the circumstances.'

She yielded, and allowed me to enter the drawing room and avail myself of paper, ink, blotter and seal. Alas, she stood over me as I wrote, although I tried to shift my shoulders in such a way that she could not see the words. This was most annoying, since I would have liked to write something of the truth, and beg the young woman to contact me at once. Thus observed, I found that I could not write exactly what I wished. So after a moment's thought, I composed the following.

'I am very sorry for any inconvenience I may be causing you by my urgent need to take over the room you are vacating as soon as possible, preferably tomorrow. Please let me know at once whether or not you agree to this plan. I may be able to be of assistance to you, in finding a new lodging, or otherwise.' I added my name and address, folded over the paper, and looked up at the landlady with as much authority as I could muster.

'What names shall I put on the front?'

She hesitated, then said, 'Address the note just to Miss Wolcombe. That will be enough.' I wrote the name, pleased to have finally extracted it and wondering if by some ruse I could manage to obtain the Christian name as well. The landlady took the note from my hand, and accompanied me to the door with a great show of friendliness masking a state of apparent nerves. Strange? perhaps not, in view of the fact that she had very probably learnt of Ivy's fate only that morning, and it must certainly have afforded her a severe shock. I was in a state of nerves myself, although I hid it, forcing myself to keep a staid pace until I had turned the nearest corner. Then I pulled Ivy's letters from my pocket and turned them over feverishly.

Alas, they were most grievously disappointing. A milliner's bill, two or three letters from a dressmaker with questions about a costume design, and several brief notes from Alan Manning containing information about rehearsal schedules comprised the whole of the little packet. And the one item that could have indicated something out of the ordinary refused to yield up its secret. An envelope postmarked Cambridge, the address inscribed in an educated hand by a pen of excellent quality, had somehow slipped inside another envelope. I pulled it out and opened it with a thump of excitement. But it was quite empty, and though I examined it hopefully from every angle, there was nothing to indicate who had addressed it.

Well, there was the handwriting. I supposed that it might be identifiable eventually. But I thought sadly that it would probably turn out to be no more than the handwriting of Mr Geoffrey Archer. And what could one conclude from that? Why, nothing at all, except that he occasionally wrote to her, as he himself had freely stated.

I wondered why there were no other envelopes or letters from him. Probably Ivy simply did not keep them. Perhaps she did not care for them, or feared the landlady's prying eyes. I put the little bundle away with a sigh and took stock of what information I had gathered so far.

The theatre people seemed to know her only somewhat distantly, or professionally. It seemed difficult to imagine a motive for the killing, although professional jealousy can always be evoked. But that would mean a woman. Obviously Jean was the closest thing that Ivy might have had to a rival, although Mr Manning seemed to consider them as very different. However, there had clearly been at least some discussion as to who was to play one of the characters in *The Wild Duck*, so a rivalry was not out of the question. On the other hand, if Jean had been playing on that very night, then she could not have been murdering Ivy in Cambridge. I remembered how the woman called Paula had claimed that the whole company remained to dismantle the stage sets. She must have meant all of those who had roles in the production. I wondered how many there were, and determined to examine the dramatis personae as soon as I could find a copy. After all, anyone who had not been cast could still remain as a suspect.

Apart from the actors and Mr Manning, I now knew of four people personally acquainted with the dead girl: Mr Archer and Miss Wolcombe, whom I had not yet met, the landlady, and Ernest. In order to obtain information from the landlady, I would have to install myself in her room and work upon her for days, but this did not seem to me to be a priority, as she probably knew very little. Much the greatest chance of learning about the private life of the dead girl lay with Miss Wolcombe, who must have been a very close friend of hers if they had decided to set up house together. I very much wondered what kind of a woman Miss Wolcombe would turn out to be. Two young women living independently in rooms indicated a working-class background, and from what I had learnt of Ivy Elliott, she could be said to be situated on the margins of decent society. Yet what did that reveal? Those margins, as every other class, contain an immense variety of human beings.

Mr Archer was an unknown quantity, and I could only continue hoping that Mrs Burke-Jones would be able to find or create an opportunity for us to meet. There remained Ernest. Ernest could hardly be the murderer, since he had charged me with the solution of the crime. Of course, the occasional murderer has been known to make such a grandiose gesture as a bluff, but such an act would make absolutely no sense in Ernest's case. He had only to keep silent about his acquaintance with the girl and it was quite unlikely that it would ever have been discovered.

Yet, after all, I reasoned, it was not entirely unimaginable. If the girl had been expecting *Ernest's* child – I shuddered at the thought – then she might have told her friends, and she may even have threatened to make a scandal. Ernest knew Cambridge well, he came quite often. And in fact, he came regularly to our house, and was familiar with the area...and with the Cam in that part of Cambridge.

But no! Ernest's behaviour made no sense, if he were the murderer. He talked of the girl constantly – surely he would have kept away from all references to the pretty actress in his conversations with us. Surely he would not have called upon my services – and as much as told me that he loved her.

Of course, people cannot always control their obsessions.

The image of Kathleen suddenly started into my mind. *She* could be said to have a motive, if anyone did. She was aware of her husband's habits in the matter of love. She was a strong, well-built woman. But on the other hand, how could she have known where Ivy Elliott would be spending her evening off? It was easy to find Ivy when she played at the theatre, but it *might* not be so simple at other times. Still, she might have followed her. All the way to Cambridge? Yet why not? What better way to deflect suspicion than killing your enemy in a faraway town?

I thought over Kathleen's behaviour. Had it been in any way incompatible with the idea of her being the murderer, as Ernest's obviously was? No, it had not. She had woken me in the night to ask about him, but that did not prove that she was unaware of the girl's death. What had she said when I told her? *Ophelia*...She had known at once to whom I was referring. A creeping horror began to overtake me at the thought that I had meant to spend a second night in her home, before returning to Ivy's house the next morning in the hopes of catching Miss Wolcombe.

I shook myself impatiently. Kathleen couldn't be the murderer – she was my friend! It was unfair to even think of her that way. It made me wonder if people would so easily assume that I could be a murderer. In fact, I soon began to ask myself the question. If I discovered that Arthur was in love with an actress, might I...? No, out of the question. I saw myself, rather, living like Mrs Burke-Jones in lonely dignity, bringing up my children, keeping a pleasant home, and holding up my head proudly day after day in front of an entire society aware of the whole sordid story. But Mrs Burke-Jones's husband had left, gone to live in France with the governess of her children. I wondered what I would do if I discovered, or realised, that Arthur was pursuing an affair while continuing to live tranquilly (or nervously) at home. I found it impossible to imagine him behaving thus. I was presented with a vivid mental image of Arthur delicately peeling away the arms of a seductive lady in a black lace corset, with painted lips, and extracting himself from them with a tinge of distaste. I burst out laughing at myself.

Kathleen was not the murderer; she was my friend. But I am a professional, and as such, there was no better way to spend the evening than with her, attempting to detect evidence of any kind. I set my feet firmly in the direction of the Dixons' flat.

I felt much cooler and more self-possessed by the time I reached the flat and rang the bell. I had entirely prepared what I meant to say to Katherine. My plans, however, were immediately foiled by the fact that it was Ernest who opened the door.

'Are you staying on?' he said, in a timbre of voice for which it was obvious that Kathleen was not at home, and that he meant to talk at once about the subject that most interested him. 'Did you have a fruitful day? Did you find out anything important?'

'A few things,' I said, 'But Ernest, I need to talk to people who *knew* Ivy Elliott. I've been to the theatre, but the problem is partly that the people there really didn't seem to know much at all about her private life. And also, on the night of the murder, they were putting on a play. Ivy didn't have a role, but everyone who did obviously has an alibi.

'Who was in it?' he asked.

'I don't know yet,' I replied.

'Well, do you know which play it was?'

'Ibsen's *Wild Duck*. Do you happen to have a copy here?'

'Of course. I've got all Ibsen; I've got complete works of all of the world's great playwrights,' he said. Going over to the bookshelf, he browsed for a moment and then pulled out a volume and opened it. We studied the list of characters together.

'The young girl, the mother, and the housekeeper,' I said,

'that accounts for the three other women in the company. They are definitely excluded. But I am afraid the same holds for the men, because there are quite a number of male characters. They must all have been cast.'

'I can find that out easily enough,' he said, throwing down the book.

'So we may assume, unless you discover something unexpected, that the members of the theatre company are not involved, as they were acting,' I said. 'Except for Mr Manning, perhaps? He does not act.'

'But he must have been there,' he said at once. 'The director is there every night, every minute of the play.'

'Well then, subject to your verification of the cast, that means that the theatre people are out of it. I will need to investigate the people she knew outside of her professional life.'

He winced at my words.

'What is the matter?' I said.

'Vanessa,' he said, planting both hands on the table and leaning on them heavily. He looked at me hard, turned his head away, and then looked back at me again, with something like aggressiveness. 'There's something I have been trying to make you understand,' he said. 'I have to tell you this, I have to spell it out, because you don't seem to understand it, and you must.' There was an uncomfortable silence.

'What?' I said stimulatingly.

'Ivy was a prostitute, for God's sake!' he cried. 'What do you think she lived on? The shillings and pence she got from that half-cocked director? Find me an actress in this country who doesn't do it, unless they have the luck to be born in an acting family. How else do you think they live? Not on their salaries, I can tell you! An unknown actress doesn't even earn as much as a – as a servant, or a barmaid. There isn't enough work in it. A barmaid who works twelve or fourteen hours a day may make four or five shillings a week and barely survive – so what do you think a girl can earn if she works only six or seven hours, and not every day, at that? And anyway – what kind of woman do you think gets up on a stage and shows herself half-naked to a hall full of people? What I keep trying to tell you is that it's no bloody *use* your saying you want to find the people who knew Ivy. She had a hundred – clients – whose names she didn't even know!'

I remained silent for several moments. Was *this*, then, the true image of the Ivy I had been imagining so differently? Certainly, I had not perceived her as an angel of virtue. Her background was vague, and Mr Manning had described her manners as somewhat immodest. It had seemed clear enough that she was Mr Archer's mistress, partly kept by him. He invited her to Cambridge, he bought her jewellery, their relations were transparent even to the shopgirl Estelle. But it was one thing to be the occasional mistress of an elderly man, and another to live as Ernest described. This was totally different, beyond my imagination. And it seemed incompatible with the little I knew of her life, her hard work as an actress, her modest, shared little room. Yet I remembered the drawer full of French corsets that no decent woman would wear...

'Are you sure?' I said timidly.

'Of course,' he snapped.

'But how – how can you know such a thing?'

'How do you think?' he challenged me.

I remained silent, rejecting and then accepting the obvious explanation.

'Now, don't start judging me,' he said, with a raucous edge to his voice that made me feel most disinclined to judge anything. 'You probably can't even imagine how it was. I saw her on stage – I admired her, yes, I admired her to obsession. I must have seen her perform fifteen, twenty times, often in the same play, again and again, before I got up the courage to go and speak to her backstage. I had a note delivered: would she meet me? I – I wasn't thinking of anything particular, you understand? I wasn't thinking at all. I just wanted to meet her, to be near her. She accepted at once. She was friendly, familiar. Too familiar, really. I wasn't at all sure whether I really liked it, at first. I thought I didn't. I thought I would have wanted something different. Yet I kept going back. Finally – I don't even remember how it happened – but we agreed to meet outside. And we did. I took her to a little restaurant...'

'And?'

'Why am I telling you this?' he said abruptly. 'I wasn't going to. I haven't told a soul, not a single, solitary soul about this.'

'You are telling me because I need your help to find her murderer,' I said quietly. 'I cannot work without knowing anything about her. I need answers to my questions.'

'I probably can't answer most of them,' he said. 'But you can try asking them. What do you need to know?'

'Facts first,' I said. 'You saw her often?'

'I – we – a number of times,' he replied hesitantly. 'But she stopped seeing me all of a sudden.'

'Really? When was that?'

'Two or three weeks ago. She suddenly asked me not to come backstage any more. I went to see her act several times, and I tried to speak to her, but she refused. Don't ask me why, because I've no idea. She wouldn't tell me.'

'Did you guess? Did you have some theory?'

'Well, it occurred to me that she had come into a source of money, somehow,' he admitted uncomfortably. 'I thought perhaps she had found a rich man to keep her, something of the kind. She did say something – something about beginning a completely new life. But she wouldn't say what she meant.'

I thought of Mr Archer, then of the pretty bedroom shared with Miss Wolcombe, and the newly purchased modest white underwear. Beginning a completely new life. I wondered why she had chosen to wear precisely those fresh, new undergarments to visit Mr Archer, rather than the flowered or black silk. I remembered my sharp suspicion, in the train, that after leaving his house, she had simply returned there. I still had to take up that matter with Inspector Doherty. Yet somehow, the petticoats seemed to speak up in denial of this idea. They told me that she had left his house for good.

Not three weeks ago, Ernest was still seeing her. And then suddenly – nothing. It was strange.

'I visited her lodgings today,' I told him. 'Did she – did she ever take you there?'

He hesitated.

'She took me to a flat,' he said. 'I think it might not have been the place where she actually lived. It was rather large and luxurious, but we never went into the drawing room or the other rooms. We – she used to – we only used to go into one room. I think it must have been the servant's bedroom. It was next to the kitchen.'

'The servant's bedroom?' I said, surprised. 'Did she work there also?'

'No, I'm sure she didn't. In fact, I don't think the flat was occupied. It was furnished, but there was never anybody there and it was never disarranged. I don't know why she had a key.'

'Where is the flat?' I asked quickly. 'We need to find out what she was doing there and to whom it belongs.'

'I don't know exactly – somewhere in Mayfair. I'm sorry. I would tell you if I could. But – it wasn't very often. It wasn't that far from Piccadilly, I think – in a block of rather modern flats. We used to go there in a hansom, just the two of us...and...well, I was paying more attention to her than to the streets. Recently, I wanted to find the flat, but I couldn't remember how to get there. I hardly even remember what the building looked like, though I suppose I would recognise the entrance hall if I could go in. The trouble is, when I went there with her, my head was spinning so I just wasn't conscious of anything around me.'

'What made you suddenly want to find it again?'

'She – she wouldn't see me any more at the theatre. I, well, I wanted to stand in front of the house, watching, to see if she was going there with – someone else. I wanted to catch her, to force her to tell me why she didn't want me any more. I thought I was going mad. The days seemed as long as weeks, months.' He stopped and closed his eyes.

'How much did she tell you about herself, about her life, her friends or family?' I asked him.

'Very little,' he said. 'She was not in the habit of talking about herself at all. I didn't know where she lived, nothing about her past. I believe she told me she had no family. I don't remember anything about friends, either, although – wait a moment. No, she did mention a friend. What did she say? It was nothing – I liked her hat, and she told me she had borrowed it from a friend. It's not much, I know, but one could build on it. Somewhere out there is a girl who knew Ivy well enough to lend her a hat. She mentioned this girl once or twice. It wasn't one of the actresses, for I knew them all. I think her name might have been Jenny. But I can't remember anything more about her.'

'But what did you talk about, all the time you were together?'

'Well – did we talk? Yes, I suppose we talked at dinner, when – well, Kathleen thought I was having dinner with my acting friends...well, I suppose I *was*. Oh, what nonsense. God, it's awful, sordid.' He passed his hand over his eyes, and continued abruptly. 'Anyway, we only ever talked about the theatre. It's my passion and it was hers. She told me how she had wanted to act ever since she was small, and I told her what I admired about her playing. We discussed interpretations of Shakespeare and other roles. She had an interesting grasp of characters. She told me that she knew immediately whether she would be able to play a role or not, and there were many that she couldn't play. She said she had something inside that told her whether she could identify and *be* the character, or not. I learnt a great deal about acting from her, even though she considered herself a mere beginner. It was all fascinating for me. But I don't see how it helps you.'

'It does and it doesn't,' I said. 'It does help give me a picture of the way she was. But I need more. More understanding, and more facts.'

'I can't think of any more facts. I'd give

my right arm to know more, to know who killed her. You know that, don't you? I've just given up my honour.'

'Not at all,' I observed crisply. 'You haven't given up your honour just by *telling* me about all this. Telling has nothing to do with it.'

'Then why does it feel exactly as though it does?' he said. 'I've felt a hundred times more ashamed telling you this than I ever felt while doing it.'

'Something is wrong there,' I remarked, 'but I have no time to figure out what it is. It's a job for someone in the church, not for me. What I want you to do is to identify the flat where you met her. You said it was near Piccadilly. Take a map and go up and down every single street on both sides until you find it. Peer inside every door. I'm going to look for "Jenny".'

Two young men emerged on the edge of the sun-drenched field which rolled away in front of the imposing stucco villa, to the cypress-covered hills in the distance. One of them thrust a tall pole decorated with a homemade white flag into his brother's hands. A servant followed them, puffing under the weight of a large apparatus.

'Run, run all the way to the other side of the field!' he cried. 'Giovanni will carry the stuff. Set it down on the other side, and as soon as you hear the signal, raise the flag, way up high so I can see it.'

Thursday, July 7th, 1898

This morning began rather dully. I ruminated over a gloomy sense of failure in the train to Cambridge, in spite of all that I had learnt. I had not been able to see Kathleen alone; she returned home quite late, and Ernest was present at breakfast. I could only stare at her, but for all that I did so, I could see nothing but a woman whose happiness and gaiety, while not intact, still held the upper hand in her temperament. Her attitude towards her erring husband was both tender and cheerful. Her kindness to myself, her friendship, the generosity with which she insisted on preparing a small lunch basket to carry on the train, all seemed to form a screen in front of my eyes behind which I was simply unable to perceive a murderess. Yet there is a motive there – and one which might be even deeper than it looks. Perhaps Ivy had written to her, demanding that she divorce her husband; perhaps Kathleen's refusal to do so was the cause of Ivy's recent coolness towards him. Maybe – although it wouldn't square very well with the significant words *beginning a completely new life.*

I tried in vain to resort to that basic element of the detective's work: establishing the alibi. I asked her about her regular theatre nights and her other social activities, but there was no getting an accurate picture of her Tuesday evenings. Tuesday was her regular bridge night, she said, but before I could sigh with relief, she added cheerfully that as often as not, she didn't go. And I felt uncomfortable asking directly about the 21st of June. I filed the bridge evening away in my mind for future reference if necessary.

Before boarding the Cambridge train this morning, I did make another attempt to establish contact with the mysterious Miss Wolcombe, whom in my mind I had already identified with the 'Jenny' referred to by Ernest. I rose extremely early and made my way quickly to the house, hoping that the young woman would not yet be abroad. But I learnt from the landlady that she had packed her things and left already, late in the night.

I found myself in a most annoying position. The landlady proudly displayed the empty, carefully swept room to my eyes; one of the beds had already been replaced by a small chintz-covered sofa.

'Miss Wolcombe came last night, and I gave her your note,' she explained. 'She got all her things together at once—' I did not say anything, but imagined clearly enough that the landlady had exerted strong and immediate pressure to obtain such a result, 'and went off somewhere in a cab. I guess she had found new lodgings already.'

'Did she not leave an address, for you to forward her post?' I said.

'No,' she replied. 'She said to keep it for her, and she would come back in a little while for it.'

'I am sorry,' I said, 'I quite wanted to make her acquaintance, because a friend of mine spoke to me recently of a young woman called Jenny Wolcombe. I thought it might be she. Is her first name Jenny?'

'Yes, it is,' she told me, a little surprised.

'She must be the same person,' I said. 'Do you know if she has a profession?'

'A profession? I don't think Miss Wolcombe has a profession. She didn't go out to work, if that's what you mean. She had rather irregular hours. She even spent a day or two away from time to time, but other times, she would spend the whole day in her room, sometimes not even getting out of bed until evening. She had very strange habits; I'm not sorry she's gone.'

'And her friend who shared the room?' I asked, following a sudden impulse. 'Was she strange as well?'

'Oh,' she said, taken aback. 'Miss Elliott was all right. She was a theatre actress. A funny profession, that, strutting about like a peacock in fancy dress. But she was a nice enough creature. At any rate, she's gone, they're both gone, now. Are you going to bring your things here today?'

'I have only this bag for today,' I told her. 'I need to bring down more things from Cambridge. Let me pay a week's rent, and I will go up to Cambridge today and return as soon as I can.' I rather reluctantly handed her five shillings, consoling myself with the notion that they should be considered as inevitable out-of-pocket expenses. And it did give me a place to stay next time I should come down to London. Ernest's flat was becoming a most embarrassing place for me to be.

I went up to the room, closed the door, and opened my small case upon the bed. Out came the combinations, the petticoat, the stays, the collar, the nightdress, the ribbons, the extra shoes in case it rained, the hairbrush and the pins. I laid them out on the bed and looked at them with the eye of a detective, interrogating them, asking them what they revealed about their owner. They looked back at me, reassuringly, neither too new nor used to excess, worthy and reliable, reasonably fashionable, yet not suggestive. I read from them an accurate picture of my own social status.

I picked them all up and arranged them carefully in the wardrobe and in the drawers of the dresser. I ran my fingers to the very back of the latter as I did so, and peered underneath them as well, hoping against hope to find some further trace of her sojourn, some abandoned scrap, but there was nothing.

Having thus taken possession of my new lodgings, I went out again, taking only Kathleen's little basket, and making my way to Liverpool St, where I caught the next train to Cambridge, with a peculiar feeling of passing from one life to another. Once settled back in a corner seat with nothing to do, my frame of mind descended progressively into gloominess. I had lost all trace of Jenny Wolcombe, unless she chose to communicate with me in writing, and I had not succeeded in meeting anyone else who could tell me the kind of thing about Ivy Elliott that I really needed to know. Ernest, while giving me a piece of information which completely changed the fundamental basis of the problem, had also proved incapable of furnishing me with the only concrete fact that, I felt, might truly lead me to the grasp of the circumstances of her daily life which alone could yield the solution of her murder: the address of the flat where she used to take him, and where it was to be assumed that she pursued that part of her professional life which was not devoted to acting.

And as for what I had learnt about her from him, it only made things more difficult. He had used the word *prostitute*, a word which conveyed no real knowledge to me, which induced nothing more than the automatic reflex reaction of a high-minded shudder accompanied by the dutiful feeling of Christian pity which society has engraved into our mentalities, obscuring all efforts at true understanding.

What do I know of the life of a prostitute, the mentality of a prostitute, the people and places frequented by a prostitute? How does one learn about such things? Had I encountered Ivy Elliott in life, would we, in reality, have exchanged even a single word? How, then, could I manage to perceive her voice and thoughts, after her death? I wanted to do so; I longed to do so. Could death, in a case such as this, remove rather than create a barrier?

I suddenly remembered the séance – the table, shuddering and tilting under my fingers, and the strange knockings, and the young, wailing voice.

'No, but that can't have been real,' I told myself firmly. 'It must have been Mrs Thorne, moving the table with her knee or some such mechanism.' Although I could not see how one could produce such movements, or such sounds, with one's knee...and surely a famous physicist like Sir Oliver Lodge, well-known for his important researches on magnetic waves, could not possibly be taken in by crude, foolish trickery! I really did not know what to think. I gave up wondering about it, and determined to ask Arthur's opinion as soon as I should arrive home.

It was a joy to find myself there finally, and I relieved my feelings by describing the séance to him in detail. I explained as frankly as I could – searching inside myself to the very best of my ability – that it seemed equally impossible to me to believe that I had witnessed a manifestation of spirits, or that the strange phenomena had been caused by some kind of complicated, unimaginable system of cheating. He laughed.

'In cases like this, one might as well simply suspend disbelief,' he said reassuringly. 'I'd be amazed if the thing yielded any useful piece of information, though. According to what I've heard, they're usually vague enough to be irritating. Still, you're not the only person puzzled by such things. No physicist can resist at least wondering how it might work. Some declare they have found explanations, and others that those explanations are insufficient. And so it goes on.'

'Who claims to have found an explanation?' I asked. 'What is it?'

'The most famous by far is Michael Faraday's,' he said. 'He was England's foremost researcher on the relation between electricity and magnetism until Maxwell. Faraday was an experimentalist, and I remember that he did some controlled experiments with table-tipping in his old age, and published some articles refuting the spiritualists claims. I really don't remember where he published them, but I can try to find out for you tomorrow if you like.'

'Oh, I would like that,' I said. 'I don't think the table-tipping is the most important aspect of this case, to be sure, and yet...I don't wish to leave any stone unturned.'

'Perhaps this is another stone, then,' he said, handing me a letter. 'It came this morning. It's addressed to Miss Duncan, here in your very own house. Isn't that strange? Who could possibly know you by your maiden name and yet know that you live in this house?'

Taking up a paper knife, I sliced open the elegant envelope. Out fell a neatly printed dinner invitation:

Mr and Mrs Geo. Darwin
have the pleasure of requesting your company for dinner
on the twelfth of July

followed by a prettily handwritten message from Mrs Darwin, professing to be delighted to meet a young friend of her dear acquaintance Mrs Burke-Jones.

I blessed Mrs Burke-Jones inwardly, and showed it triumphantly to Arthur.

'Our nearby neighbours, just up at the bridge,' I told him.

'The brood of very active children, you mean?' he asked.

'Yes, the Darwins. He is the son of Charles Darwin, I learnt recently. Oh, I do wish you could come with me, but it's really impossible this time. What a bother. I'm sure they're most interesting people. But Mrs Burke-Jones organised this for me, and I asked her to introduce me to them by my maiden name – I really *cannot* be known for who I am. It's for detecting purposes!'

'But they might recognise you,' he said. 'I mean, I know we don't know them, but I know who they are from seeing them pass in the street and it is to be supposed that the process is symmetric.'

'Oh, I don't think they know me,' I said. 'We hardly ever see the parents, and when we do, I don't think they see us. Mr Darwin is always fussing over his rugs and trying to make sure he's well-wrapped. I think he must be either ill or hypochondriac. As for Mrs Darwin, I've seen her only rarely, and she seems always in a great hurry. And even if the children do recognise my face, how should they know what my name is? I'm not worried.'

The handkerchief was adequate to signal success from the fields in front of the villa. It would not be seen if Alfonso went to the far side of the hill behind the house. For this he was armed with a hunting rifle, and he marched sturdily off, up the narrow path past the farm buildings. It was the end of September now, and the vines were heavy with purple grapes, the air golden. The walk over the rim of the hill took twenty minutes. Alfonso led, followed by the farmer Mignani and the gardener Vornelli. Finally Guglielmo, watching tensely from a window, lost sight of the small procession as it dropped over the horizon.

In the distance, a shot echoed down the valley.

Friday, July 8th, 1898

Experimental investigation of table moving, by M. *Faraday*, I read, sitting on the garden bench, perusing the yellowed copy of *The Athenaeum* which Arthur had managed to locate and borrow for me.

'He did this in 1853!' I remarked. 'And yet people still continue with spiritualism, so his reasoning doesn't seem to have convinced the public.'

'I suppose not,' smiled Arthur.

'What fun it must be to be a physicist,' I said. 'I wish I could simply tell Mrs Thorne that I should like to make some experiments to verify her statements. But I could hardly ask her that, and even if I did, I admit I can't see what experiments to make.'

'Well, there were two physicists there already, according to what you told me,' he answered. 'Perhaps they are investigating the phenomenon.'

'Ernest and Professor Lodge? They were there, certainly. But they don't seem to be investigating much. I mean, Professor Lodge certainly *thinks* he is investigating, but he believes so completely in the phenomenon of communication with the dead that it doesn't occur to him to question it. So it's not the same kind of investigation.' I turned over the page of *The Athenaeum* and began to read Mr Faraday's report.

I obtained the cooperation of participants whom I knew to be very honourable, and who were also successful table-movers. I found that the table would move in the expected direction, even when just one subject was seated at the table. I first looked into the possibility that the movements were due to known forces such as electricity or magnetism. I showed that sandpaper, millboard, glue, glass, moist clay, tinfoil, cardboard, vulcanized rubber, and wood did not interfere with the table's movements. From these initial tests, I concluded that: No form of experiment or mode of observation that I could devise gave me the slightest indication of any peculiar force. No attraction, or repulsion could be observed, nor anything which could be referred to other than mere mechanical pressure exerted inadvertently by the turner. I began to suspect that the sitters were unconsciously pushing the table in the desired direction. However, they firmly maintained that they were not the source of the table movements. Therefore, I devised an arrangement to pin down the cause of the movement. I placed four or five pieces of slippery cardboard, one on top of the other, upon the table. The sheets were attached to one another by little pellets of a soft cement. The bottommost sheet was attached to a piece of sandpaper that rested against the table top. This stack of cardboard sheets was approximately the size of the table top with the topmost layer being slightly larger than the table top. The edge of each layer in this cardboard sandwich slightly overlapped the one below. To mark their original positions, I drew a pencil line across these exposed concentric borders of the cardboard sheets, on their under surface. The stack of cardboard sheets was secured to the table top by large rubber bands which insured that when the table moved, the sheets would move with it. However, the bands allowed sufficient play to permit the individual sheets of cardboard to move somewhat independently of one another. The sitters then placed their hands upon the surface of the top cardboard layer and waited for the table to move in the direction previously agreed upon. I reasoned that if the table moved to the left, and the source of the movement was the table and not the sitter, the table would move first and drag the successive layers of cardboard along with it, sequentially, from bottom to top, but with a slight lag. If this were the case, the displaced pencil marks would reveal a staggered line sloping outwards from the left to the right. On the other hand, if the sitter was unwittingly moving the table, then his hands would push the top cardboard to the left and the remaining cardboards and the table would be dragged along successively, from top to bottom. This would result in displacement of the pencil marks in a staggered line sloping from right to left. It was then easy to see, by displacement of the parts of the line, that the hand had moved further from the table, and that the latter had lagged behind – that the hand, in fact, had pushed the upper card to the left and that the under cards and the table had followed and been dragged by it.

'That seems to be that,' I said after having read this paragraph aloud.

'He doesn't say it's fraud, you notice,' said Arthur. 'He absolutely believes in the good faith of the table-turners. They were actually all friends of his. It's just that he attributes all the strange phenomena rather to their own unconscious movements, whether psychological or muscular, than to transmission through the magnetic field.'

'Which means in particular that messages purporting to come from spirits of dead people might just as well emanate from deep within the mind of the medium,' I said. 'Yet the things that Mrs Thorne said were strange and eerie, and the voice was so far away – all the voices which spoke through her were so completely different from each other in tone and accent. I wonder if the words she said had any real significance. I don't suppose we'll ever know.'

I jumped up from my seat, pushing the papers off my lap.

'What I really need,' I said, 'is to stop thinking about this, and visit a bookshop to obtain serious information about serious matters. And I *must* see Inspector Doherty.'

I went up to the nursery and peered into the two little beds where the children were taking their afternoon nap. They were sleeping deeply, their soft, regular breathing making two little rhythms on either side of me. The room was dim, but not completely dark; the soft glow of sunshine gleamed through the drawn curtains, printed with elephants and giraffes, giving a fuzzy outline to the furniture and the toys scattered about: the wooden rocking horse, the Lilliputian table and chairs, the doll's bed with its bonneted occupant.

Cedric's long eyelashes fluttered, and he opened his large dark eyes and looked up at me.

'Are you finished sleeping?' I asked him softly. He nodded seriously.

'Do you want to come to the shop with Mamma?' I suggested. In a single movement, his compact little body was standing upright in the bed, his arms raised to be lifted. I scooped him up, removed his little nightgown and took up the sailor suit that was hanging neatly over a chair.

'Come,' I said, 'we'll get dressed in Mamma's room, and then we'll go out.'

Several boot buttons and a glass of water later, we were on our way, hand in hand down the summery street. We took an omnibus into town, a great adventure for an active little boy both fascinated by and a little frightened of horses, and alighted in the centre, where we began by looking in at the police station to ask if Inspector Doherty was in.

'He's out,' said the young man at the desk. 'He left word that he would be back in an hour, though.'

I left a note, and wended my way with Cedric to my favourite bookshop, a dusty hole containing hundreds of ancient books and magazines piled upon shelves, upon chairs, and upon each other, kept by Mr Whitstone, an equally ancient person with a wrinkled face, sparse white hair and twinkling eyes which appear to know everything. Mr Whitstone has been of invaluable help to me for at least ten years, since I first began teaching in Cambridge.

I found him alone, sitting on a stool behind his grubby, much-marked wooden counter, and reading. He looked up as I came in, carrying Cedric in my arms in order to preclude his causing any untoward accidents with the rather precarious piles of books which left little room to navigate.

'Ah, Mrs Weatherburn,' he said, nodding. 'A pleasure. What can I do for you today?'

I hemmed and hawed for a moment. But Mr Whitstone is a man of experience, and there was no use in beating about the bush.

'I need to learn about prostitution,' I said, more firmly than necessary in order to compensate for my extreme embarrassment, not at the thing itself, but simply at the speaking of it aloud. Our culture acts more strongly upon us than we could wish, at times. And interestingly, my own predicament reminded me of Ernest's words, when he had said that the speaking of his acts aloud had brought home to him a feeling of loss of honour more strongly than the acts themselves. I seemed to recall that I had been rather sententious with him.

'You want novels? Or serious works?' asked Mr Whitstone, not batting an eyelash at my request.

'Serious works, if such things exist,' I replied at once.

'You want to understand the sociology of the phenomenon?'

'Yes – I think so,' I said.

'Parent-Duchâtelet's study of prostitution in Paris is the definitive scholarly work on the subject,' he informed me. 'If that is the kind of thing you want. Statistical information, you know, about the social origins of the women and so on. I don't have it – you would need to order it from a French bookshop. Let me see now, I seem to remember...why, yes, I might have something else useful for you, however.'

He puttered about in a corner. I peered over his shoulder.

'What about that?' I said, pointing to a book interestingly entitled *Fanny Hill, Memoirs of a Woman of Pleasure*.

'No, no, no,' he said, hastily taking that book and pushing it behind a pile of others. 'That is not what you think. It is not memoirs. It is a novel from the last century. Not right for you at all. No, no, no.'

He inserted his body between me and the titles he was examining, and appeared to become somewhat anxious, so I stepped back and let him finger over his books by himself. After a moment he turned back to me, holding a pile of sensible tomes called *A Social History of Women in Rural*

England, The Woman Question, a Collection of Pamphlets Advocating Suffrage, and *Fabian Essays.*

'You do read French?' he asked, holding out a book by Alexandre Dumas.

'Yes, reasonably well,' I replied, surprised. Surely if an English novel was deemed unfit for my eyes, a French novel could hardly be better!

'You know Dumas, of course,' he said.

'Oh, yes.'

'But you very probably do not know of this book,' and he took out and handed to me a leather-bound little volume with its binding partially falling away.

'*Filles, Lorettes et Courtisanes,*' I read.

'It is a brief and somewhat more literary summary of Parent-Duchâtelet's work,' he said. 'Dumas was not only a very prolific writer, but he wrote about much more varied subjects than most people realise. The French littérateurs are more fascinated by the subject than our English writers,' he added. 'You might – ah, you might want to look into Balzac. And for what has been written by our British authors...' He ceased speaking momentarily and glanced suspiciously around the perfectly empty shop, then continued in a hushed voice. 'You may remember the Stead affair of 1885?'

Although I was seventeen years old and no longer a child in 1885, I knew nothing of the affair he referred to, having lived a sheltered life. I raised my eyebrows questioningly and allowed him to continue without interruption.

'No greater indictment of the evils of British...ah, prostitution, has ever been written,' he told me. 'Stead discovered, Stead published, Stead offended and was punished for making known what was not meant to be known. I cannot tell you more. You would have to manage to locate an old copy of the Pall Mall Gazette.'

'I will search for one,' I said. 'In the meantime, I will take the Dumas.'

I purchased it and carried it out of the shop, leading Cedric by the hand.

The sun was bright after the dark interior of the shop. I found myself walking towards Petty Cury. I wanted to go to Heffers, partly to examine their English translations of Balzac, and partly just to see the younger Mr Archer. Not that merely seeing him could provide me with any information of any kind, but I felt that as he had very probably been acquainted with Ivy Elliott, any contact with him might bring me, however infinitesimally, closer to her, and thus to the truth. I entered the shop and looked for him, but he was not to be seen either at the counter or in the little glass-windowed office behind it. I led Cedric among the many shelves, reading over their labels until I located the French literature. I stopped, and Cedric immediately sat down on the floor and pulled three books out of the lowest shelf.

'No, no,' I whispered quickly, trying to remove his little fingers and replace the books without becoming too noticeable or obnoxious to the many customers frequenting the large, quiet shop. He let out a kind of screech and prepared to follow it up with several more. Hastily, I scooped him up and plumped him into a large, well-used leather armchair placed among the shelves for the convenience of the browsers.

'Stay here and watch Mamma,' I told him firmly. 'If you're very good, we'll go and have a bun after the shop. All right?'

Always willing to eat, he assented and sat down. Less than

ten seconds later, however, he was standing on the seat and performing gymnastics over the back of the armchair. It stood solidly and showed no sign of tilting and spilling him to the ground, so I allowed myself to look away for a moment and read over the titles of Balzac's novels. Having discovered and taken up *Splendours and Miseries of Courtesans*, I glanced back at Cedric, who was now sitting on the seat, engaged in thrusting his hands deep into all the cracks between the seat cushions and the arms and back.

'Look, Mamma,' he said proudly. I hurried over, and removed a small, dusty but originally green sweet from his fingers. He looked about to rebel, but contented himself with fingering the rest of his treasure trove: three dustballs, a key, a crumpled ball of paper, a not-very clean handkerchief, a cheap tie-pin and the disgusting remains of another sweet. He sat contentedly, his legs straight out in front of him, his boots only just at the edge of the seat, this collection of delights spread out upon his lap. I swept up the little pile and glanced around, but there was nowhere to deposit it, and it didn't feel right to push it all back into the chair, so I gave up and to his great satisfaction, tucked everything back into his chubby hands.

'These things are dirty,' I told him. 'When Mamma is finished here, we'll go outside and throw them away.'

But when the moment came to separate him from them, he proved stubborn.

'Me keep this,' he said, clutching the half-sucked sweet which filth had fortunately rendered no longer sticky.

'No, Cedric,' I said firmly.

'Well, me keep this,' he said, attaching himself to the crumple of paper.

'All right, you keep that,' I said with relief, brushing everything else into the gutter.

'It's got witing on it,' he told me, showing it to me.

The merest glance, and my heart gave a jolt of surprise. A crumple of scribbled paper lost in a bookshop armchair – if I had thought at all, I would have expected a reference or a list of titles, brought in for some useful purpose and discarded. Instead, what Cedric displayed to my astonished eyes was a letter – and, looking more closely, a love letter.

My darling, I read,

You don't even know how near I am to you, but I will see you in a moment! Oh, even if the words I long to say to you directly cannot be spoken aloud yet, I cannot resist writing them down for you, here and now, black on white. I will slip them into your hand when nobody is watching and my heart will know you have heard them.

I love you.

I love you.

I love you.

I never thought I would find love like this, in this way. But now I have found it, I know it is love, because I think about you all the time. Other people have found so many wonderful words for this, words that I have spoken aloud a thousand times. But even if my own words are poor in comparison, I know you understand them as they are meant, not as they sound. Tomorrow we will stand up and say the truth to the whole world! And tomorrow is already today.

Your own Ivy

Ivy?? Ivy? Ivy! Was it possible?

Ivy is a fairly common name.

And yet, there was a connection between Ivy Elliott and Heffers bookshop. Mr Archer himself constituted a connection. Mr Archer's *son* constituted a connection. Was I mistaken, or did he not live just upstairs, over the shop? *I will see you in a moment...*

Of course, the letter might not have been written in Heffers – might not have been written moments before her death at the hands of her murderer. Yet as I stared down at the simple words, I felt that it must have been. For clearly, *tomorrow* and its truth had never come. And whatever that truth might have been, was it not also the cause and reason of her murder? Could Julian Archer have promised to marry her, and have murdered her instead?

I felt an anxious tugging at my skirt, and looked down. Cedric was waiting for the return of his treasure, his eyes anxious, his hand outstretched.

'Mamma needs to keep this,' I told him, bending down to speak to him face to face. 'You're a good boy to have found this wonderful thing. Will you give it to Mamma as a present?'

He looked up at me, his generous little heart already willing, though still slightly suspicious.

'Can I still have a bun?' he asked timidly but hopefully. 'With raisins in it?'

'Raisins in it, and sugar on top!' I promised, tucking the letter away. 'Let's go and get it this very minute.'

A three-and-a-half-year-old man is still a man, and we have all been told a thousand times that the way to a man's heart is through his stomach.

'Inspector Doherty,' I said, seated across from him half an hour later, holding a somewhat grubby and rather tired small boy on my lap. 'I hope you don't object to my coming to see you about the Ivy Elliott case. There are a few things that I feel I simply must ask you about.'

'Well, Mrs Weatherburn,' replied the inspector, 'I'm ready to hear whatever you have to say.'

'First of all, I want to ask you – this has been troubling me for some time now – if it is not possible that Ivy Elliott never really left Chippendale House after all. I mean, she was seen to go walking down the path, but could she not have simply returned to the house a few minutes later on, and waited for Mr Archer somewhere within?'

He smiled.

'Not bad,' he said. 'But Mr Archer has an alibi.'

'He was at the party in his own house,' I argued. 'He could easily have left it to go upstairs for just a few minutes – that's all it would have taken him.'

'But he didn't leave. Didn't you read what the witnesses stated?' he reminded me.

'I did read over them quickly,' I said, 'I know they said he remained at the party, but...'

Taking out the same folder of statements that he had already shown me, he extracted one and put it in front of my eyes. I read it; the words seemed familiar.

The party took place in Mr Archer's drawing room, which has large windows giving over the front garden. Miss Elliott was in the drawing room for most of the evening. She did not exactly act as hostess, but took care of the material aspects of the service, telling the servants when to bring liqueurs and biscuits, which curtains to draw and which to leave, when to light the outdoor lanterns and so on. She left quite late. I did not look at the time, but it must have been near midnight. She seemed tired, and going up to Geoffrey, she told him that she thought she would be on her way. She said she was going to a friend. He asked her if she was sure she wanted to leave, and pressed her to stay a little while longer. She did so, but after a few minutes she said that she was very tired, and would leave. He went out into the hall with her to bid her goodbye. He cannot have been out of the room for more than five minutes. She left, and Mr Archer returned and remained with us for the duration of the party, which continued until past 2 o'clock. He did not leave the room again. I am certain of it, as I was sitting on the sofa next to him for the entire time. He simply rose to his feet once or twice to say a few words to the butler.

'And you believe this absolutely?' I insisted.

'Several others say the same,' he replied. 'Yes, we believe it. Apart from his alibi, he doesn't appear to have any motive. Of course we considered him as a major possibility from the start. We thought the girl might have been threatening to make some kind of a scandal about the child she was expecting. But we soon learnt that there was and could be no possible proof that Mr Archer was the child's father. Given what we discovered about Miss Elliott's life, she could not have made any statement on the subject that would have carried the slightest weight. Mr Archer had neither opportunity nor motive.'

'Perhaps he hated prostitutes, like Jack the Ripper,' I suggested meekly.

He looked at me sharply. He had almost certainly thought me unaware of the details of Ivy's life. However, he shrugged, and answered,

'By all accounts, far from hating them, he liked them very much. Very frankly, Mrs Weatherburn, you're barking up the wrong tree here. I suggest you leave Mr Archer aside as a suspect. Have you no other ideas?'

The image of Kathleen flashed in front of my mind, but I put it aside resolutely.

'Even if Mr Archer has an alibi,' I persisted stubbornly, 'could he not have hired a killer to wait outside the house for Ivy to leave?'

'Too dangerous, because of the risk of blackmail, for what seems a weak motive. And extremely expensive as well,' he replied.

'How expensive?' I asked, wondering at the insanity of such a question, and passing my hand half-consciously over little Cedric's ears, although he could certainly not understand what was meant by the term 'hired killer'.

'A small fortune,' he replied. 'It's not enough to purchase the act itself. One must purchase the silence of the murderer. And that silence is never really certain. But in any case, we know that the girl did not return to the manor, nor was she murdered directly on leaving it. We did a large-scale search for anyone who was in the streets between midnight and two o'clock on the night of her death. There are not many people out and about at that time of night, but we did find a few. And we have two statements describing a woman we think must have been Ivy Elliott. Listen to this.'

He shuffled them out of his desk drawer and read them to me aloud.

We were on our way home down Newnham Street. I can't say the exact time but it was certainly between twelve and twelve-thirty. I came home at twelve-forty-five, so I guess it could have been close to twelve-fifteen when I saw the woman. She was walking along the street, and I remember feeling surprised to see a woman alone and on foot at that hour. I hesitated about offering her a place in my carriage, and told the driver to slow down. But then when I saw her more clearly, I thought that she might be a kind of woman I should not want to know. It wasn't that she was painted or flagrantly dressed. She was wearing a peculiar gown, loose and flowing. But she looked up at me so boldly as the carriage passed her that I changed my mind and told the driver to go on.

'That's the first one,' said the inspector. 'The other is even clearer.'

I was out walking because I couldn't get to sleep. I thought I would just take a turn outside. I live on Market Street. I went down the street to the end and turned left along King's Parade. There was almost no one about. That's why the figure of the woman in white struck me. She was coming up King's Parade towards me. She passed me right about in front of the Senate house, and turned left onto St Mary's behind me. I was struck by her attitude; her hands were clasped together, she seemed excited. I turned and followed her for a moment. I walked back up to St Mary's and looked around the corner, just in time to see her going around the front of the church. I didn't approach her, as I thought she might take fright, and that it would be a cruel thing to do, to appear to be following a lady around in the dark of the night. So I just glanced around to the front of the church. The woman was kneeling in front of the church, praying. She remained there for several moments, and then she jumped up and scurried off very quickly around the Market Square. I let her alone and resumed my walk. I did not see her again.

'Market Square,' I said thoughtfully. 'Where could she have been going?'

'That is exactly what we would like to know.'

There was a short silence, then I asked,

'Have you any other suspects?'

'Other than Mr Archer, you mean? My dear Mrs Weatherburn, I really think you are going to have to relinquish that idea once and for all. At this time, we are giving particular consideration to the angle of Miss Elliott's friends, and in particular, the "friend" she mentioned at the party as being the one she was staying with. Surely she was on her way to this friend when she crossed the Market Square. We have advertised for the friend, but as yet nothing has been forthcoming, and that is suspicious in itself. In the meantime, the police in London are investigating her life there. How about you?'

'Well,' I said, a little reluctantly, but struck by a sense of duty, 'I have an idea about the "friend" that Ivy was going to see. I think she might have been referring to Mr Archer's son, Mr Julian Archer. He lives in Petty Cury, over Heffers bookshop – Ivy could very well have been going there, couldn't she?'

'Petty Cury? Yes, from what the witness describes, of course she could have. But that is not a sufficient reason to suppose that Mr Julian Archer had anything to do with her murder. Decidedly, Mrs Weatherburn...' I quickly interrupted what resembled the beginnings of a lecture, and taking out the letter, I handed it to him directly.

'I found this stuffed down in the armchair at Heffers,' I told him.

'I found it, Mamma!' Cedric corrected me loudly. The inspector cast him a glance which quelled him instantly, then read the letter quickly through.

'Now this is interesting,' he said, 'and also, perhaps, important. You really found it in the bookshop? When did this happen?'

'Not an hour ago,' I told him. 'I was looking for a book, and Cedric was playing in the armchair. Of course, we don't know that it is the same Ivy. I don't have any examples of her handwriting. But I feel that it must be.'

'I'll be able to have that verified soon enough,' he replied. 'My London colleagues must have access to some handwriting samples of hers. Now, just proceeding for a moment on the assumption that the letter really was written by Miss Elliott, what does it mean? Who was it written to, and when?'

'It isn't easy to guess,' I said. 'But the letter must have been written after midnight, given that she says "tomorrow is already today". And since she clearly refers to something very important happening "tomorrow", and this thing, whatever it was – it sounds like a public declaration of betrothal, or something of the kind – does not seem to have happened, I infer that it was written on the very night that she died.'

'Hardly,' he objected. 'The thing, whatever it was, could have been meant to happen weeks or months ago, and may not have come off for any number of possible reasons.'

'Indeed. But if so, one can imagine that the letter was sent and received, in which case I can't imagine how it could possibly have ended up in the armchair.'

'I am wondering how it came there in any case.'

'Ah,' I said. 'Well, now that I have learnt from you, or rather, from your witnesses, that she was seen in the vicinity of the bookshop after leaving Mr Archer's house, it is not difficult to imagine an explanation.'

'Such as?' he said.

'Well, for example, let us imagine that Ivy Elliott and Mr Julian Archer were in love, and that he had given her a key to the bookshop, perhaps even some time ago, to facilitate their meetings. Suppose, though, that she insisted on marrying him, and that he had let himself be trapped into a promise he had no desire to keep. He may have told her to come to the bookshop after the party at his father's house and wait for him there, then come down and killed her.'

'It doesn't hold water,' he said.

'Why not?' I asked indignantly.

'Well,' he said, 'first of all, you say he told her to come to the bookshop, and she says in the letter that he doesn't know she's there.'

'True,' I said. 'All right, she came without telling him, as a surprise. Or else, he told her to come, but imagined that she would arrive much later, towards two o'clock, so he could have no idea that she was already there when she wrote those words.'

'And you think she wrote this letter while waiting to see him?'

'It could be.'

'Doesn't that seem odd to you?' he continued. 'Why write to him at all, if she was about to see him? And how could she be sure of seeing him in a moment, if he was expecting her an hour or two later?'

'I don't know,' I said slowly, 'but she does clearly say that she is writing to him although she will see him in a moment. People in love do odd things. I know – perhaps what she meant to do was to write the letter, then carry it upstairs to his rooms! That would explain it. Although I admit that I can't quite see why she should not speak the words rather than writing them – and why she should secretly slip the letter into his hand. Perhaps he was not alone, and she knew it?'

'Well, that makes sense,' he admitted. 'Mr Archer doesn't live alone up there.'

'Well, then!' I exclaimed triumphantly.

'Well what?' he challenged. 'How do you see what followed? If she did go up, then what did she do with the letter?'

I reflected for a moment. 'She can't have gone up,' I said, 'otherwise she would have given it to him. Maybe she went up and he was not in...but no, even then she would have kept or destroyed the letter, or left it for him. She can't have gone up. Mr Archer must have come down and killed her.'

'That's all very well,' he said, 'but we just agreed that he didn't know she was there.'

'Oh,' I said. 'Well...maybe he was looking out of the window, and happened to see her coming down the street?'

'So he hopped down and killed her? Just like that? On an impulse?'

I cast about desperately.

'Well, maybe he had premeditated that she would come at

two o'clock and he would kill her then,' I said, 'and when he spotted her earlier, he just did what he had planned to do anyway.'

'But if he had planned to meet her at two o'clock,' he argued, 'why would it have been in the bookshop at all? Why, if there was any plan to meet, couldn't she simply come upstairs directly? Don't tell me that he didn't want to see her in his rooms, or that she wasn't supposed to come there. Because if that were true, she wouldn't have meant to go upstairs after writing her letter.'

'Er,' I said.

'And for that matter,' he went on inexorably, 'if he did come down and surprise her, how did the letter end up in the armchair?'

'Maybe,' I scrabbled, 'maybe before she could give it to him, he told her that he didn't want to marry her after all. Then, if she had been sitting in the armchair, reading it over, say, she might have crumpled up the letter in a fury and thrust it away.'

'She'd have been more likely to tear it up and throw the pieces in his face, don't you think?' he said.

I did think so.

'And in any case,' he continued firmly, 'I still don't see any real motive.'

'Well,' I mumbled timidly, 'because maybe he had promised to marry her and no longer wanted to...'

'My dear Mrs Weatherburn, do you see any reason why he should not simply have told her that he had changed his mind?'

'Breach of promise...?'

'Mr Archer's word against a woman like hers, in a court of law?' he said, and laughed outright.

'Maybe she was blackmailing him,' I ventured, in a last, desperate attempt.

'What for? Julian Archer doesn't possess the kind of social status for which an affair with a prostitute can destroy him. And for that matter, blackmail hardly seems compatible with such a letter.'

It was hopeless. My idea made no sense, no sense at all. And yet – she *must* have been in the bookshop – she *must* have written the letter there – and given the time of her death, she may well have been killed there...

I looked at the inspector. He was staring thoughtfully at me.

'Nevertheless,' he said, 'I will question Mr Julian Archer. We might as well see what he has in the way of an alibi.'

A boy and his mother – a break with the past.

Left behind: father, brother, old family servants. A white Tuscan villa, green slopes covered with cypresses, a sky always bright with Italian sunshine. A life of joyful security in familiar surroundings. But also, the paternal authority, the frustration, the rejection, the lack of interest, the incomprehension, the disapproval. Finished, all of that.

In the future: uncertainty, doubt and anxiety. Endless fog and rain and storms, heavy grey stone buildings, iron railings around the areas. Chill winters and hard work. But also, support, admiration and appreciation, and practical, material assistance. At least, so Guglielmo had been promised.

He shook the dust of Italy from his shoes, and stepped aboard the train.

I sat at the beautifully decorated table, laden with porcelain, silver, crystal and flowers, playing my role to the hilt.

My wedding ring had been left at home, my stays tightened a full inch more than usual, and a certain strand of hair left to curl along the side of my face instead of being treated as no more than a bother and pinned away as usual. My dress, also, had been selected with the greatest care. I wished to choose one which was both youthful and fashionable, but unfortunately today's fashion seemed to make these two qualities become contradictory, the large sleeves and intricate decorations lending an air of poise and maturity to the female figure which was exactly what I desired to avoid. I hesitated between distinguished silk and innocent muslin, between roomy, gathered skirt and gored, shaped skirt, between waist-emphasising sash and close-fitting buttoned bodice, and it was only after several sessions of secretly reading Dumas that I realised that neither the elegant ladylike appearance nor the modest, girlish look were correct for the situation. Finally, I settled for adding a double garland of small silk rosebuds in green leaves to the front of my plain pink silk skirt, and chose a petticoat with a ten-inch lace border to go underneath it. I attached a similar garland to a wide-brimmed straw hat after having removed the feathers that had been sewn onto the band, and wore white boots at the risk of soiling them on muddy footpaths. My most unusual jewellery – the large pieces that I actually never wear – completed the ensemble, and I left the house feeling positively daring.

The early evening was balmy, and I arrived to find the party gathered in the garden, the table having been set out-of-doors. The house was placed so near the river as to leave only a kind of swath, or band of garden between them, but a wooden bridge had been constructed leading to the odd little island that crowds into the narrow river just below the Silver Street bridge. Upon this island, a couple of youngsters could be perceived running about and hiding between the trees, calling to others whose heads hung dangerously out of the windows of a kind of large grange which stood along the road next to the house. This grange, which could easily have been turned into a residence nearly as large as the house itself, seemed to serve essentially as a playground. As I entered the main gate to the drive, a tall wooden structure which completely hid the goings-on within, I noticed a bicycle leaning against the half-open door of the grange, and a pile of balls, bats, kites, rafts, oars and other equipment for outdoor enjoyment just within. I looked around for Mrs Burke-Jones and found that she was already there, which was fortunate as I was counting on her to introduce me to the host and hostess. They were standing together near the table, nodding their heads, shaking hands, and addressing a few polite words to each guest.

Mr Darwin looked at me penetratingly as he greeted me, and I supposed that in spite of my optimism, he must surely find my face familiar. However, he seemed uncertain how to place me, which suited my purpose well enough. I supposed there was a risk that he would realise who I was the very next time he saw me out walking with Arthur and the twins. But I put this thought away and contented myself with smilingly answering his quiet,

'Delighted to make your acquaintance, Miss Duncan.'

'I'm so pleased you could come. We've heard so much about you,' cried his wife, an energetic and very beautiful lady whose speech betrayed her American origins, although their echo was somewhat dimmed by years, if not decades of living on this side of the Atlantic. 'I know you used to be a teacher. Such fascinating work, and so important to influence and educate the new generation. What made you stop?'

I bit my tongue to remind myself that the word 'marriage' was forbidden, and murmured something anodyne about preferring privacy and wishing to work at home. However, she pressed me further, no doubt out of genuine interest, so that in the end I had to invent – with a hesitation due to the unpleasantness of lying but which she took for modesty – that I was an aspiring writer. Given that I was almost certain to meet the Darwins again in the future, I felt that I was running myself into difficulties. But there seemed nothing to do about it.

I knew Mr Archer the moment he entered the gate. A tall figure followed him, and turned to close and latch the gate behind him; I recognised his son, the younger Mr Archer from Heffers. Seeing the two of them together, I noticed a similarity which had not struck me when I had briefly glimpsed the father in the half-darkness, standing on the garden steps of his house. Of an equal height, both men were well-built, with handsome, rather angular faces. The younger one, however, had an easy, pleasant manner which in his father seemed to take a sharper, more purposeful form; his smile was slightly toothy and carnivorous. I felt I did not like him very much.

He has an alibi, I recalled to myself firmly. *You are here to*

meet him and eventually learn more about Ivy. Not to prove
that he is a murderer.

Either because Mrs Burke-Jones had interceded, or purely
by chance, I found myself seated at table upon the elder Mr
Archer's left. On my other side was a girl of fifteen looking
sulky and uncomfortable in an obviously new dress,
somewhat tight under the arms, and Julian Archer sat across
from me, with Mrs Burke-Jones on one side and an unfamiliar
middle-aged lady on the other. This lady had briefly been
introduced to me as Mrs Darwin, not my hostess but another
Mrs Darwin; it seemed that there were a number of Darwin
sons, all married. There were five or six young people around
the table; Darwins, it seemed, were also prolific reproducers,
as, indeed, it seemed somehow natural that they should be.
Mr Darwin sat at the head of the table, and his pretty wife at
the foot.

The conversation began by turning on the subject of sports,
health, hygiene, exercise and costume. The members of the
Darwin family were great exponents of the advantages of
bicycle-riding, and the women of the family were experts on
the new style of 'bicycle-clothing'.

'It's all much more sensible than this stuff,' said Gwen, the
girl on my left, plucking disagreeably at her dinner gown,
which was really a very beautiful and well-made dress,
although it seemed to cause her acute annoyance.

'Everyone, but everyone knows about the benefits of
exercise,' said Mrs Darwin. 'There isn't a soul in the world
who doesn't feel the better for a spin on a bicycle, or just a
long walk.'

'Except for me,' said her husband. 'I come home feeling like
death and have to lie down for an hour with a cold compress.'

She merely laughed.

'The only annoying thing is that there are not more sports open to women,' she continued. 'We can paddle at the beach, and go on walking holidays and bicycle rides, and play tennis in a mild way. And I don't say that this is not a marvellous improvement over the constricted lives our poor mothers and grandmothers were obliged to lead. But just think of all that men are able to do! Running races, weight-lifting, swimming, gymnastics – all those sports that we heard so much about two years ago, when they revived the Olympic games!'

'Lifting weights does surprising things to the muscles,' observed the other Mrs Darwin with a slight frown. 'They get all hard. We wouldn't want that happening to our daughters, now, would we? It's hard enough to make them keep their hats on when they play tennis or run about on the beach!'

'And there is a question of dignity,' said Mr Darwin. 'We don't want to see women out of breath and excessively warm with messy hair and red faces.'

'Who doesn't want to? I do,' murmured Gwen in an audible undertone. I felt a certain sympathy for her point of view, and recalled my own happy childhood in the country, of which many hours were spent gambolling freely with my sister in the sunny meadows, unobserved and uncommented. It seemed to me that faces reddened with effort, tangled, windblown hair and for that matter also bare feet and loud shrieks – in other words, the complete absence of attention paid to decorum – had been an essential ingredient of the sense of boundless freedom and joy connected with our escapades. But before I could open my mouth to express even a very subdued version of this feeling, I realised that the older Mr Archer, the object of my interest, was speaking.

'As far as I am concerned,' he was saying, 'the noblest and most magnificent sport in the world is boating. And women may participate in it with no loss of the lovely beauty we all delight in.'

'Boating can't be much of a sport, then, if girls can do it,' observed one of the Darwin boys.

The modern headmistress in Mrs Burke-Jones could not resist such an opening.

'My dear child,' she said, 'the natural superiority of men over women is a deep question; the reasons for which the whole of society appears to unanimously perceive this superiority are complex and interesting, and they are to be taken seriously. Surely no true man wishes to preserve a semblance of superiority simply by *forbidding* women to do what otherwise they would be fully capable of doing, in order to *pretend* to himself that he alone is capable – yet in a large measure that is exactly what society does, collectively speaking.' And as the child looked confused by this somewhat theoretical discourse, she clarified her meaning by adding, 'Before you reject any sport that girls are capable of doing in favour of one which you suppose they are *not* capable of, ask yourself honestly if they are truly incapable, or merely forbidden?'

He stared at her silently, and Mr Archer intervened smoothly.

'I assure you that boating is an extraordinary sport, with room for every kind of effort and every kind of ability.' Warming to his theme, he continued, 'A real sportsman will need every ounce of his athletic ability to master a light sailing-boat in rough weather, whereas in yachting, passengers may perform no other office than that of feeling the rush of the tangy sea air and admiring the splendour of the silver waves.'

'That sounds beautiful,' I said, gazing at him as he spoke. He turned to me, and smiled.

'Have you never been on a yacht?' he asked me eagerly.

'No, never. The only boats I have ever been on are the ferries that cross the Channel going to France.'

'An interesting ride, with many a pleasure waiting on the other side,' he replied kindly. 'But the sensation is utterly incomparable. You know nothing about yachting?'

'I wish I did,' I said, seizing eagerly upon this topic which appeared to be a kind of opening through which I might eventually reach the man himself.

'There are splendid opportunities for an observer to become acquainted with the sport,' he said. 'Why, the two best regattas of the year are just coming up. You know which ones I mean?'

'The Cowes Regatta!' shouted several voices.

'I have heard that spoken of,' I said meekly.

'Yes, the Cowes Regatta is in early August. And before that, the Kingstown Regatta, in Ireland. Why, that's on the 20th of July, just a week from now! The best yachts in the world come to race there, and each year reveals astounding new tactics and new technology. It seems as though the progress will never end.'

'Do you own a yacht? Are you a racer?' asked one of the boys.

'I own a yacht on which I spend many a delightful weekend,' he replied, 'but I do not race with it. I haven't got the technique of these champions who spend much of the year in training.'

'Training,' said Mr Darwin, 'pah. Training is the ruin of the true meaning of sport and sportsmanship. Winning in sports should be a brilliant combination of luck and talent – a gift from the gods. Not a matter of plodding strain to gain a tiny fraction of a second's advantage each day.'

'Yet nothing is more inspiring than that effort for advancement, for improvement, each tiny drop of which leads the entire world towards progress!' exclaimed the elderly gentleman with emotion. 'I admire the concept of sportsmanship you describe, but I do not think the search for new technology goes against it. The miracle of machinery is the key to progress.'

'You're talking about improving the boats, I take it,' said Mr Darwin. 'I suppose that's necessary enough. I was talking about training the body; about these people who run every day, and hop and jump for hours to get their muscles to learn to run or swim faster than Nature intended them to.'

'And yet it's the training, and the work and the effort that go into any sport, whether technological or physical, that yield the astonishing results we see year by year,' disagreed Mr Archer.

'It's Father's favourite topic,' said his son, exactly as Mr Darwin's son said,

'It's Father's pet grieve.'

There was a general laugh, and Mr Darwin made a face in his beard.

'Then why do you not engage in technology yourself?' said Mrs Darwin politely. 'Surely you could put together a team to improve your boat enough to race it?'

'Oh,' said Mr Julian Archer, 'the answer to that is the story of the Archer family fortune. It puts us all in a very peculiar situation; I don't believe there is another family in England like ours.'

'Do tell it,' said Gwen, perking up and looking up at the laughing gentleman opposite with the first sign of interest she had shown that evening.

'Well, the story begins in the seventeenth century. We Archers are an old family; our genealogical tree goes back, with precision, a great deal farther than you might think; quite to the Middle Ages. The family was an important one, and a fabulously wealthy one, until the appearance of a certain James Oliver Archer in the year 1663. This young man, the eldest son of his father, grew up horrendously dissolute and "shewed Signs of destroying the Prosperity of the Archers and their Future with it", as is written in his father's diary, which still remains in our family's possession. James's father believed that the boy was evil because his mother was evil. She wasn't English; he had married a Spanish woman with splendid black hair and a temper, and he lived to regret it. She ended up in an asylum, quite mad – one can almost sympathise, what with the combination of English weather and an English husband. At any rate, the father was convinced that James was growing up with bad blood, and that he would transmit that blood to all future Archers. And he determined to rescue the family fortune once and for all from such a risk. So he made a most remarkable will. The entire fortune was to be left to the eldest son in each generation, or failing sons, the eldest daughter and then her eldest son. But the Archer enjoying the inheritance should never, as long as the Archer family existed, be allowed to manage it himself. It would invariably lie in the hands of trustees, who themselves would name successive generations of new trustees, "always to be chosen Instructed and Worthy Men known for their Honesty and Temperance in all Things". The Archers successively inherit the house, and various other properties that previous Archers managed to persuade their trustees to add to the estate; the farm, the yacht, the London flat. The costs of the upkeep of the estate, the servants, the labourers and so on, are entirely paid by the trustees. In fact, every single thing the Archer heir spends must be paid for by the trustees, on presentation of full accounts. Archers never have money in their pockets; no more than a couple of hundred a year as pocket money. Any more significant expense must be agreed with beforehand by the trustees. And if they overspend without warning, they're liable to find themselves doing a stint in debtor's prison. It's happened – my great-grandfather spent a few months there, though both Grandfather and Father appear to have toed the line.' He smiled at his father.

'Yes, my Grandfather showed a bit of a streak of that evil Spanish blood,' said the elder man. 'He'd had to wait for the inheritance; his father died at ninety, and he himself was already well over sixty at the time. That didn't make the trustees any more lenient with him! They knew he was an old rake and they meant to rein him in. They were all over eighty themselves.'

'What had he been doing up until he inherited the money?' asked Gwen.

'Working for his living,' replied Mr Archer. 'The will provides for the education of all the Archer sons, but then they are supposed to find "an honest man's Profession until such Time as their Father is deceased".'

'Did you have a profession?'

'Certainly. I was trained as an engineer. I could have put together a team to turn my yacht into a racing yacht; I did, in fact, make the request. But the present trustees decreed that that was not a fit use of the family fortune.'

'Oh, too bad,' cried Gwen. 'What do they think is a fit use?'

'Increasing the fortune itself, of course!' intervened the younger man with a laugh. 'The fortune must continue to make a fortune. They invest it.'

'As it happens, I have a good head for that type of thing as well,' said his father. 'I've had some successes in that line, and they take my advice now. It's good to feel some control.'

'Yes, Father's made some interesting discoveries,' added his son.

'And what about you, then?' asked Gwen. 'You must have a profession too, don't you?'

'Yes, indeed I do. A very bookish one, I fear,' he told her. 'Nothing to do with boats, technology or investments in the City.'

'Go on then – what is it?' she insisted, tantalised.

'I manage Heffers bookshop. You probably go there from time to time, don't you? I quite enjoy it, as a matter of fact. Books are much more in my line than machines, I'll admit. And it does give me my independence, after all. I live in the rooms over the shop – no one knows about my comings and goings!' He smiled at his father indulgently.

'Rooms over a shop?' cried Gwen, shocked. 'But – but – you'll give all that up, won't you, when you become the Archer heir? You're like a sort of gentleman Cinderella.'

'You're stupid, Gwen,' shouted the smallest of the boys rudely. 'Cinderella Minderella!'

'Oh, be quiet,' she answered back with no less rudeness. 'Brothers!' she added with a flash of contempt, then turned back to Mr Archer for sympathy. 'Do you have any?' she asked him.

'Ah, yes,' he replied, with what seemed to me to be a slight shade of reluctance. 'I do have a brother.'

'Is he as awful as mine?' she said. 'Must he work for his living also? What does he do?'

'He isn't at all awful,' said Julian. 'He's an invalid and a scholar. He stays at home and writes books, very long ones, each of which takes a huge number of years.'

'Oh – that's too easy,' she said with some disappointment. 'I thought you Archers were all obliged to have real working lives. If he's a scholar, then why can't you all be scholars?' She glanced over at her father with the air of someone who knows all about scholars and is not excited by them.

'My brother is an exception,' explained the young man. 'He cannot get around without his invalid chair; he hardly goes out. So the trustees made an exception for him. He has an allowance.'

'Oh,' she said. 'I'm sorry. Why is he an invalid? What happened to him?'

'We don't really know,' he said. 'Either it's because he fell down the stairs when he was a baby, or because of an illness he had when he was one. But he grew that way; he's always been like that. Off I had to go to school, while he stayed home being pampered by Mother!' He smiled.

'Lucky you – I'd love to go off to school!' exclaimed Gwen. 'With me it's the opposite. The boys get to go, and I have to stay home and have a governess. And she teaches me to *sew*,' she added in a tone of disgust.

'Too bad,' he said sympathetically, while her mother frowned and tried to make signs for her to stop at once, which young Gwen superbly ignored. 'You sound like a young lady prepared to attack one of the Professions yourself. Which is it to be?'

'I mean to be an artist,' she said firmly. 'I like to draw.'

Between boating and family history, my relations with the two Mr Archers were, by the end of the meal, of the most cordial; in fact, on the part of the elder Mr Archer, they may well have been somewhat more than cordial. It was what I had wished for and tried to obtain, yet it made me uncomfortable. Throughout the evening, I had displayed a keen interest in everything he had to say on every subject. I had admired his multiple experiences as a man of the world. I had showered the sunniest smiles upon him, and fed his ego to the best of my ability. But as I did so, my dislike of the man continually grew; he reminded me of a predator seeking for tender flesh. I hid this feeling, happily accepted an invitation to tea, and threw myself eagerly into plans to join a group of his friends to travel over to Ireland to attend the Kingstown Regatta on the 20th. He seemed devoured by the need for attention, and I believed I need only manage to be alone with him to persuade him to talk about Ivy. And, determining to accomplish this at the first opportunity, I arranged to visit him 'for a look at the famous Chippendale gardens' no later than tomorrow.

I looked at Mr Archer, observing how his eyebrows met over his beaky nose, and the odd, carnivorous-looking teeth. Inspector Doherty had been formal, yet how could I not wonder? Was Ivy Elliott in love with Julian Archer? Was the father, whose mistress she was, aware of the fact?

Would that be a motive for murder?

But, I reminded myself with annoyance, motive or not, Mr Archer's alibi is unshakeable. He did not murder her.

Yet I really cannot, *cannot* bring myself to like him.

A mother and her son, alone in London. No husband in sight, no family in the city, and suitcases that, if one were to examine their contents closely, contained plenty to excite surprise and suspicion. Respectability was the first priority, and for this very reason, Bayswater became their first home. Rooms to let in Bayswater were searched for and found, and found in the Talbot Road; very bourgeois rooms in a very bourgeois house, rooms filled with china dogs and shepherdesses, with Chinese fans decorated with tiny coloured ostrich feathers, with glass-beaded chandeliers, and at all the windows and over the doors, thick heavy velvet curtains. Those curtains were their shelter and their protection. They drew them closed, shutting out the damp grey London weather, and set to work. Guglielmo unpacked his suitcase, the one with the apparatus, and began setting pieces on the shiny dining table. His mother took paper and pen, and began writing the letters that would introduce her son into the wider world.

Wednesday, July 13th, 1898

Tea with Mr Geoffrey Archer of Chippendale House, Cherry Hinton, was one of the most unpleasant experiences of my entire life.

It all began decently enough. A trim little maid brought in a carefully prepared, well-laden tea-tray, and Mr Archer told her to go, and to make sure that no one entered the drawing room on any pretext unless explicitly called for. He then invited me to pour, and asked for four sugars. This was exactly what I had been hoping for and counting on, for to tell the complete truth, fearing that the situation might get out of hand, I had taken the precaution of bringing a small dose of laudanum with me from home; Arthur takes some now and again when his mathematical ponderings keep him awake. This I managed to slip quietly into his cup, after which I stirred it carefully and handed it to him with an engaging smile.

There were small iced cakes and biscuits, and the teacups were of egg-shell thin porcelain, white with a fine gold border. I admired how the light glowed through them, and Mr Archer told me that they had been in the family for four generations and virtually none of the pieces had ever been broken. I led the talk to his family, and displayed the greatest interest in the mad Spaniardess and her son. It was easy to see that Mr Archer took pride in his ancestry. This was understandable, for the story was quite fascinating, and the quantity of old diaries and papers preserved through the generations quite unusual.

'Day by day for twenty years, the old gentleman wrote down his son's misdeeds,' he told me. 'I should like to show you the book, but the trustees insist upon its being kept in the bank, of all places, together with a number of other family heirlooms. My wife was allowed to keep her jewellery in the house when she was alive, but she passed away many years ago, and the trustees took back the entire collection and put it in the bank vault as well. Do you realise that the entire house is inventoried regularly?'

'Goodness,' I said sympathetically, 'you can't call your soul your own.'

'No,' he agreed. 'It's the price we Archers pay for having a colourful ancestor behind us. If I wish to make any significant purchase, I must submit it to their approval. They are not unreasonable, of course. I was allowed to offer some most beautiful gifts to my wife. However, they were all then inscribed in the estate book and I am no longer allowed to sell or dispose of them freely.'

'James Oliver must have been a dreadful spendthrift,' I said.

'Oh, he was a spendthrift and worse. It's hard to imagine a misdemeanour, or even a crime that he didn't at least participate in.'

'Not any crime?' I said, opening my eyes very wide. 'Surely he was not – a murderer!'

'Not openly, otherwise his life would have terminated at the end of a rope, rather than in his bed, as it did – a nasty old man, I've no doubt, with a miserable wife and a large number of legitimate and illegitimate children. But it wouldn't surprise me if he were the one responsible for a certain number of rather peculiar deaths that his father noted down in the diary. You see, his father kept him on such a tight rein financially that in order to satisfy his depraved tastes, he simply had to get money elsewhere.'

'How did he do it?' I asked, hoping to lead him on. For apart from its historical interest, I felt that Mr Archer took an intense though secret delight in identifying himself with his amoral forebear, and I felt I was coming closer to his real nature.

'Women were his weakness,' he told me, his wolfish smile appearing. 'He couldn't seem to see a girl or woman who didn't stimulate some ancient reflex of possession within him. Yet he was no Apollo, unfortunately. Women were repelled by him, and that led him into an infinity of trouble.'

'How do you know what he looked like?' I asked, surprised.

'Why, there's a portrait of him in the study. Every Archer heir is painted. Come, I'll show it to you.'

He took my arm, and I allowed him to do so, although his touch displeased me strongly, and the pressure of his fingers through my sleeve struck me as being firmer than absolutely necessary. We crossed the room, went through a plush-covered door, and found ourselves in the study, a large room equipped with a burnished oak desk covered with glass, upon which were a lamp, an inkstand and other articles for office-work. The panelled walls were divided by oaken mouldings into sections, and in each section hung a portrait.

'That's James' father,' he said, and I found myself staring into the eyes of a bust portrait, darkened with age, of a gentleman with an enormous quantity of facial hair and the kind of look of fanatical intensity that I have always imagined on the faces of Protestant preachers such as John Knox, inflamed with exacerbated morality.

'And there's James,' went on Mr Archer, now pointing to a full-length portrait. I stared at it; it showed little or no resemblance to the present Mr Archer, but much inheritance from the Spanish mother. Black hair and sharply marked black eyebrows in the shape of an inverted V; black eyes with an intense gaze, as though to a specific point or goal, and thin lips pressed together, surmounted by a moustache not very different in shape and style from the eyebrows. While not positively ugly, the face was rendered disagreeable by an insufficiently pronounced chin. Such chins are usually associated with weakness of character, but in this case the weakness appeared to have taken the form of an incapacity to resist yielding to lust or whim rather than a problem of indecisiveness. In his hand he held a whip, the cord dangling negligently from the handle, and at his hip was a short dagger.

'Yes, women were his downfall,' Mr Archer mused, gazing upon his ancestor. 'He couldn't see one but he had to have her. He was the terror of the countryside. A dozen times or more, his father found himself confronted with peasant families of the neighbourhood whose daughter's life and future had been destroyed by his son. He remarks once, bitterly enough, that he was turning into a matchmaker among the farming families of the area, for once James had finished with them, the girls were only fit for marrying old widowers or invalids, and even that was possible only thanks to the dowry the old man provided out of a feeling of moral rectitude. The entire area around here lived in terror of James;

if he found out that a young man was courting the girl he had his eyes on at the moment, he'd go out and flog him within an inch of his life. Every month a scandal broke out during the time he was growing up. Yes, he had a streak of evil in him, all right.'

These words were pronounced in a tone of such intense satisfaction that I glanced up at him; the egotistic smile on his lips revealed his thoughts as though his head were made of glass. This was all to the good, I supposed, in view of the fact that my purpose here was to make him talk about Ivy.

'Where is *your* portrait?' I asked flatteringly. He was pleased at the question, and led me to a vividly coloured painting in which he, as quite a young man, posed in hunting costume with one foot on a stool, a hound at his feet and – a whip in his hand.

'Is the whip a family heirloom as well?' I asked, pointing to it.

'No,' he laughed. 'Not an heirloom, but a family symbol. Archer men like to dominate.'

My dislike of the man was intensifying by the minute, but for some inexplicable psychological reason, this feeling gave me the strength to play my role all the better. I fluttered my eyelids to signify admiration of masculine domination. I have always possessed a certain talent for acting, but it is something I feel to be a bit shameful and unworthy, like a talent for lying. Not good…but occasionally extremely useful.

'I recognise that one,' I said, noticing the portrait hanging next to Mr Archer's. It was a painting of Julian Archer, also a full-length portrait, in an interesting pose. The subject was standing with his two hands on a table, leaning a little forward, and looking straight into the viewer's eyes with a twinkle of amusement. It was an excellent painting. I was making some comment to the sitter's father about the likeness between them, when my eyes were momentarily arrested by another bust portrait hanging nearby, showing a pale, rather long face, markedly different in aspect and expression from all the surrounding portraits, sorrowful, melancholy, burdened, perhaps, with the weight of the Archer evil. I was about to ask who he was, when Mr Archer yawned prodigiously, covering his mouth politely with his hand and turning away from me, and I perceived that the draught was beginning to take effect, and began to feel in a hurry to lead the conversation to the point where I wanted it.

'I have a nice little flat in London, where I go whenever I need a little change of air,' he remarked, moving back in the direction of the sitting room and glancing at me significantly. 'I travel to the Continent quite regularly as well.'

'Oh, how *exciting*!' I said. 'Do you go to Paris and Rome? The women must be so beautiful there.'

He smiled vainly. 'Women are beautiful everywhere,' he said, 'but different everywhere. Every flavour is worth trying. The fresh, home-grown product is just as delicious as the hothouse import.'

The already plain meaning of this sentence became much plainer as he placed his hands on my shoulders and bent his face down to mine with an intention that was perfectly clear. Thoughts rushed through my mind. He repelled me. I did not want his touch. But if I played my game carefully enough, I should tempt him sufficiently to keep him talking, and defend myself enough to keep out of danger. I knew that my whole strategy with this man was a risky one – how long could it be before he discovered that I was a married woman with children, living in a cottage not so very far from his own manor? If I wanted to find out anything from him, it would have to be in a very short time.

His lips were already on mine. I repressed a shudder, and allowed him a judiciously calculated moment before twisting away with a purposely artificial look of shock.

'Oh, Mr Archer,' I gasped, 'how can you?' I sent him a look which meant, as clearly as I could make it, that he might obtain what he desired from me, but that he should have to fight for it. That self-satisfied little smile played over his lips again. He relished the combat.

'Why, you can't do that, Mr Archer!' I cried. 'You mustn't!'

'And why not?'

'Because you don't *love* me – do you?'

'I do,' he replied, entering into the game at once. 'I'm in love with you, upon my word, Miss Duncan. It's struck me all of a heap.'

'I don't believe it,' I pouted, stepping back from him, and moving through the door into the sitting room, I scooped up my fan which I had left on the sofa, and fluttered it. 'It's too quick.'

'Love at first sight is the Archer way,' he purred.

'Then you must be in love once a week,' I said.

'Well,' he said, 'we Archers have susceptible hearts. You heard what I told you about James.'

'Goodness, I hope you're not *too* much like him!' I cried.

'Oh, no. I've inherited that fiery streak, but I respect women,' he said. 'I'm dearly fond of the creatures, and would never mistreat them.' He sat down on the sofa next to me, and put his hand on my knee. I took it off.

'You must tell me about everyone you've been in love with before me,' I said.

He burst out laughing.

'No, I can't do that! There are far too many!' he said.

'Oh, you wicked man,' I flirted, feeling thoroughly ashamed of myself, and behaving all the more brazenly in compensation. 'Tell me about the last girl you loved before me, then.'

'You don't want to know about other girls,' he coaxed, leaning into me.

'No, I do, I do. Where is she now? Why aren't you in love with her any more? I shall be fearfully jealous if you don't tell me it's all over with her,' I said with mock severity, 'and if you don't explain to me exactly why you don't love her any more, I'll be frightened that you'll treat me the same way.'

'Oh, you silly creature,' he said. 'There *was* a very lovely young girl, but...she is dead.' And for a moment he looked extremely sorry.

'Dead!' I leapt away from him, feigning a great fear. 'Why – that's just like your ancestor James! Why did she die? How did she die? Of love?'

He rubbed his eyes and stifled a yawn. The laudanum was definitely having its effect.

'No,' he said. 'I don't know exactly. She was here for a party, and she said goodbye and left, and later I heard that she was dead. I really know nothing about it. But I do miss her. She was a good girl, and very pretty, though not in the same way as you are. But then – no two women are alike,' and he once again proceeded to resemble a wolf.

I nestled up to him with the outer shell of my body, while the inner portions shrank away in disgust. A tense, awkward giggle escaped me as I imagined myself observed at the present moment, and suddenly remembered some pages from

Dumas' little book which had caused me to laugh uncontrollably by asserting that the lovers of the loose women known as *lorettes* are all uniformly known as 'les Arthurs'. I am not a *lorette* – in spite of my behaviour with Mr Archer I am most definitely *not* a *lorette* – but my beloved is certainly an Arthur. And Ivy? Ivy was a lorette...a flower with as many lovers as petals.

'Who was she?' I asked him suddenly.

'Oh, she was just a little actress,' he replied with a shrug. 'A sweet, good girl, but not important. I was very fond of her, but I don't pretend for a second that she was fond of me, or rather, that she was fond of me only. A girl like that has to earn her living as she can. Not like you. You're a good girl, anyone can tell that.' He settled closer to me and laid his head on my shoulder. 'Goodness, how tired I am,' he remarked, closing his eyes.

'Oh,' I said kindly, 'do take a little rest.' And I petted his white hair, willing him to sleep. It was not long before he sank into a deep, drug-induced slumber. I disengaged myself, deposited the old gentleman on the sofa, and stood up. I had a little time to explore freely, for the maid had been told not to enter. The sleeping draught was by no means a strong one, and Mr Archer might be awakened by any loud noise, so I slipped out of the room silently and closed the plush-covered door to the study behind me.

This was the room that interested me. Here, I might find examples of handwriting – Mr Archer's own handwriting, to identify the empty envelope I had found in her room, or Mr Julian Archer's writing, or perhaps even Ivy Elliott's own writing, to identify her letter. And here, I might also find financial information sufficient to prove to me, as Mr Julian had asserted, that Mr Archer was not able to spend his money freely, could not access any significant sum without its being known...could not, under any circumstances, allow himself to pay a hired murderer, let alone put himself at the risk of blackmail.

I pulled open a drawer of the desk, and then another and another, glancing at the papers they held, riffling through them quickly. I saw nothing unusual and nothing private. Everything seemed to treat of financial affairs of one type or another. Which suited me well enough.

I rapidly went through one after another of the well-organised, neatly docketed folders arranged in the drawers. I examined and turned over every single paper. Long experience has made me able to read and understand such papers quickly and accurately. After twenty minutes of searching, I had found nothing to contradict Julian Archer's description, and everything to confirm it.

Letters from the trustees approving or rejecting various payments, statements of bank accounts, copies of Mr Archer's own correspondence, everything was there, and everything was in perfect order. As well it should be, since he was periodically obliged to go through it all in detail with the trustees.

I looked with especial interest through a folder labelled *Investments*. Apart from statements of earnings, it contained an exchange of letters between Mr Archer and the trustees going back over some thirty years. It emerged clearly from these documents that Mr Archer had been allowed, many years ago, with trepidation and disapproval, but upon his own insistence, to invest a modest sum of money in a firm whose enterprise he greatly admired. This investment had turned out extremely profitable, and over the following years, I saw that Mr Archer's expertise and intuition in the matter of investment had convinced the trustees to place larger and larger sums in the companies that he recommended. It was, however, equally clear that no money connected with these investments was ever transferred to Mr Archer directly, neither the sums invested nor those earned. All passed through the trustees, all went directly to swell the Archer fortune, which by now controlled many thousands of pounds invested in a dozen companies, most of which appeared to be inventors of technological products which had obtained Mr Archer's approval. I scanned the list briefly.

Wagner Typewriter Co.
Herreshof Yacht Manufacturing Company
Friese-Green London Ltd.
London Telegraph Company
Dickson Kinetograph, Baltimore
Emile Berliner Gramophone Company
Raff and Gammon Co.
Thomas J. Lipton, Tea Planter
The Marconi Company
Lanston Monotype Printing
Gaumont Cinéma, Paris
General Electric Company, Schenectady, New York

I could not help but admire Mr Archer's knowledge of technology and his flair. It did seem rather unfair that he should not freely profit from a single penny that was made through his own efforts. He himself protested the situation in a number of letters. However, the trustees invariably responded that such were the terms of the ancient will, that increasing the Archer fortune was a worthy goal in itself, and that of course all money he requested for any reasonable activity should be forthcoming with their approval immediately. And they did accede to a number of requests, for voyages, sojourns in hotels in various cities of the Continent, dinners hosted in elegant London restaurants. It seemed that it was not money which was lacking in his life, nor even the freedom to spend it; it was privacy. Yet that very lack was exactly what condemned my idea of a hired killer to hopeless impossibility. And to make matters worse, the numerous examples of his handwriting I examined intently did not correspond – not in a single, solitary, detail – to the writing on the envelope I had found addressed to Ivy Elliott. Nor was there even a scrap of correspondence concerning her to be found in the desk.

I closed the last drawer, disappointed, and slipped quietly out of the french window, down a few steps and onto the lawn. I was about to walk around the house and down the path to the gate, when suddenly and unexpectedly, I perceived a gardener coming towards me, pushing a wheelbarrow.

Afraid that he would stop me, and feeling strongly that I really had no business to be where I was, I pulled back hastily and scampered around the same tree behind which I had been hiding with Estelle the first time I laid eyes upon Mr Archer. But the gardener came around the house, stopped, and began clearing a space to put in some flowers, not two yards from where I stood. I waited on tenterhooks for a moment – he stood up again and went off to fetch something. I took two steps in the direction of flight – he was already coming back! I glanced up into the tree; it stood very close to the house, but on the other hand it was leafy enough to provide a reasonable hiding place. In no time I was silently perched amongst its lower branches.

I was compelled to remain there for nearly an hour as the gardener worked below me. By peering through the leaves, I found that I could obtain a reasonable view into Mr Archer's sitting room. I fell to wondering what he would do if he woke up and discovered my departure. My curiosity was eventually satisfied.

I saw him sit up, rubbing his forehead and looking confused. He stretched, and looked all about him. I could not hear him at all, but I believe he called out something, quite probably my name. Then he arose and began to look for me. I shrank back into the branches.

He crossed into the study and looked there, then opened the french window and peered out onto the lawn. I held my breath, expecting him to ask the gardener if he had seen me. But he said nothing; presumably he did not care to advertise his amorous adventures to the servants. Finally, he returned indoors and departed towards the interior of the house. I waited another quarter of an hour, watching the progress of the gardener's planting with interest; he had set in nearly all the plants, only two were left, only one, none were left, he was finished. He fetched water and watered them copiously, then swept up the scattered leaves and put them in the wheelbarrow. He stopped for a while, taking the sun and fanning himself with his hat while I waited impatiently, then finally moved away, wheeling his now empty barrow.

I shifted on my branch and began climbing down the tree as silently as possible. 'Ouch!' I exclaimed under my breath, pulling my arm away sharply as my sleeve became caught on a twig. I expected it to snap, but it didn't, so I reached up with my fingers to disengage it. To my surprise, it was not a twig, but a wire which was caught in my sleeve buttons. My fingers unwound it and followed it; almost invisible, it continued upward towards the top of the tree and downwards along the trunk. I took care not to trip over it as I reached the ground. I wondered vaguely if it was a trap of some kind. Magpies, I know, are very annoying when they come to attack the nests of other birds.

Looking about me to make sure there was not a soul in sight, I sped onto the path and away. I hurried all the way home, and as soon as I arrived, I flung myself into a chair and penned a note to Mr Archer so that he should not take my disappearance amiss. In spite of my complete failure to have discovered the slightest incriminating factor, I did not want my acquaintance with him to come to an abrupt end.

Dear Mr Archer,
  You seemed very tired, so I slipped away quietly. I hope you forgive me. I spent a perfectly lovely afternoon.
Yours truly,
  Vanessa Duncan

I sealed this, went out to post it, and returned home to find Arthur waiting for me. He seemed delighted to see me, came towards me warmly, and put his hand on my arm. I felt horrendously guilty, remembering myself with Mr Archer's repulsive lips pressed upon mine, suddenly seeing the scene as though through Arthur's eyes. I blushed to the roots of my hair. He looked at me, a little surprised, then suddenly took my hands in his.

'You're very beautiful today,' he said unexpectedly. I looked at him, and suddenly, as he saw me with different eyes, I saw him with different eyes. I mentally compared him with Mr Archer, and Mr Julian Archer, and was happy. I am really very lucky in my husband.

'Oh, Arthur, come – let's go out for a ramble, just the two of us,' I said. And we left the house behind and walked into the countryside, down lanes and through fields, along streams and under trees. He filled my arms with wild flowers and I filled his hair with kisses. But it was a long time before I felt really able to look him straight in the eyes. When I did, what I found there caused my guilt to be submerged by a rush of other feelings.

1897

'It's all very well,' snorted Lord Kelvin, *'but I'd rather send a message by a boy on a pony.*

The message from Ernest was brief: a telegram containing nothing but the words *I found the flat*. Not even a signature. But of course, I didn't need one.

'I'm going back to London for a couple of days,' I told Arthur.

'Staying with Ernest and Kathleen?' he asked.

'Not exactly,' I admitted. 'I've taken a room.'

'A room?' he asked, surprised. 'How did you come to take a room when there are both friends and hotels?'

'It was Ivy Elliott's room', I admitted. 'I thought it might help me discover something, to stay where she lived, and meet people who knew her.'

'Oh,' he said. 'And has it?'

'Not much yet. I've met the landlady, but she hasn't been very helpful. Still, I did find out that Ivy shared the room with another girl, only she's gone. I'm going there now to follow up a different clue.' *I mean to find out how a flat near Piccadilly came to serve as a meeting-place for prostitutes and their clients*, were the words I did not add aloud.

I gathered some clothing into a case, more to furnish my new room convincingly than because I actually needed it. Then I kissed the twins goodbye – they considered me with large, tear-filled eyes but allowed themselves to be consoled by Papa's complete and undivided attention – and took the omnibus to town, where I telegraphed to Ernest to meet me at four o'clock on the steps of the Royal Academy.

As soon as I arrived in London, I made my way to my new home. The landlady seemed pleased to see me. I arranged my things, and descended to have a little chat with her before venturing forth on my errand. I wanted to ask her about Miss Jenny Wolcombe.

'Oh, I'm well rid of her,' she said, her features suddenly clouded by a look of huffiness and resentment. 'She came back here just a day or two after you took the room and made a terrible scene. Right here in the house – and people listening!'

Clearly her fury at the unpleasantness she had been put through, and her sense of grievance, far outweighed any discretion on the subject of the previous occupants she might have felt. I put on my very best listening expression.

'A scene? How dreadful!' I said commiseratingly. 'What about?'

'Accusing me – me! of stealing some letters. As though I ever stole even a farthing from a single one of my lodgers. Why, I treat them like my own children. All that I did for that Miss Jenny, and her to come and accuse me of stealing letters! I told her it must have been the po—'

She broke off suddenly. But whether or not she wanted to mention them, I knew well enough that the letters had not been taken by the police.

'It certainly isn't *my* fault, at any rate,' she went on quickly. 'How dare she accuse me?'

'Oh, she has made a silly mistake!' I cried, struck by a sudden idea. 'The letters she was looking for stayed in the room; I believe I have just found them, as I was putting my clothes away!' And I took the little bundle from my reticule where I kept it.

'You, miss?' she said, amazed. 'You found them? But where were they? I cleaned that room out for you myself.'

'They were underneath one of the drawers,' I said, pleased to be truthful for once. 'I pulled one out completely by mistake, and these fell into my lap. But they are addressed to Miss Elliott, not to Miss Wolcombe. Shouldn't they be given back to Miss Elliott directly?'

This was a stab in the dark; I wondered what she would say. But she shrugged, and merely contented herself with replying,

'Miss Wolcombe said to give them back to her.'

'How can we? Do you know where she is living now?' I said, trying yet again to pin down that elusive person!

'I made her tell me,' said the landlady, still indignant. 'She didn't want to. She wants nothing to do with the po – I'm sure she wouldn't want me to tell anyone.'

She stopped abruptly again, but not before I had quite understood. Naturally, a young woman of Jenny Wolcombe's type would want nothing to do with the police, and just as naturally, the police would want to find her in order to question her about her friend's death. I extracted a note from my handbag, which changed hands.

'She said 14 Shepherd's Mews,' she murmured, mumbling a little as though that might make her betrayal less complete. 'I've no idea where that might be,' she added hastily, as though that, also, could make a difference.

'I will find the place and leave the letters there for her,' I said placidly. 'And I do hope she will offer you an apology. Accusing you of stealing – why, it's unheard of!'

My radiant good humour (due to having managed to obtain this morsel of information) soon got the better of her indignation, and I left, looking at the clock to see if I had time to locate and visit Shepherd's Mews before meeting Ernest. It was, however, later than I thought, and I had to to hurry to find a cab and be driven to the Royal Academy, arriving a few minutes after the hour. Ernest was already waiting there, holding his hat on in the gusts of hot, dusty wind which lifted the women's skirts and shawls and sent papers flying over the pavement.

'The flat's not far from here,' he said after greeting me. 'Shall we go? It's not that hard to find it from here, yet I assure you it took me hours of searching. The most confusing thing was that after I'd spent so much time looking around on every single street in the area, they all began to look familiar. I got so mixed up I was about to give up. And that's just when I found it, of course.'

'Yesterday?' I asked.

'Yes, yesterday. I telegraphed you right away. I'd been going down every street methodically, peering into windows and things. I've been scolded plenty of times! I was lucky; I was just standing in front of it, wondering if it could be the one, when a fellow came out. So I just pushed past him into the hall. And then I was certain right away.'

We went down Piccadilly, turned right on Bolton Street and left onto Curzon Street, along which we walked for some little distance.

'This is where it's complicated,' he said finally, looking around and turning left into a little tangle of conflicting lanes. 'It's right here somewhere – what's this? Pitt's Head Mews? Yes, it's along here a little, then left again...ah, here we are!'

He stopped, and pointed at a wedge of street containing just a few tall, rather elegant brick buildings, and with no name indicated at all. I peered about me.

'I asked what the street's called,' he told me; 'they call it Shepherd's Mews.'

'Shepherd's Mews!' I cried, staring at him. 'Shepherd's Mews – really? Why then – why then, it must be at number 14!'

Now it was his turn to stare.

'You must be a magician,' he said. 'How could you possibly have known that? How? How?'

'It's simple,' I said, resisting the temptation to imitate Mr Holmes's famous technique of not revealing his methods, the better to impress. 'Ivy Elliott's landlady knew where Ivy's friend Jenny Wolcombe went to live after giving up the room they shared. Jenny gave her the address when she went to move out their things.'

'And she came here?' he said, gaping.

'Well, yes,' I said. 'I suppose it isn't very surprising, is it? Miss Elliott had a key, and Miss Wolcombe may have taken it, or possessed her own.'

'But it wasn't their flat,' he said. 'That was obvious; they were just using it.'

'Well, if Miss Wolcombe had to move out of her room in a hurry,' I said, 'and if she knew this flat to be unoccupied, she might well take refuge there temporarily while looking for something else.'

'You must be right,' he replied. 'Let's go and see.'

Number 14 was handsome, with a well-polished front door equipped with an imposing brass handle. It was quite large, opening out into two wings on either side of the main hall, with each side divided into several flats.

'The flat that Ivy used was on the left side here, up the stairs, looking out at the back,' Ernest told me.

'If only we could get in,' I remarked.

'Let's wait. Someone will surely come out by and by.'

We waited patiently for half an hour. Ernest tried to extract information from me about the progress of my investigation, and I tried to find out more from him about Ivy. But like a man, he was incapable of giving me a real picture of the girl. He had created a romantic image which he served up to me upon a garlanded platter.

We both jumped as the door swung open and a lady emerged; a lady of a certain age, her hair dressed fashionably though severely. As one, Ernest and I pretended to be just arriving, and made to enter the building through the door she had held open just long enough to pass through.

But to our surprise, the lady wedged her generous frame in the doorway to block our entrance.

'Oh, no, you don't,' she said angrily. 'We have enough of you people here. This is a decent house.'

'I – we are only coming to visit someone we know, who lives here,' I stammered.

'Don't lie to me, young lady,' she said. 'You think I don't know what you're going to do up there in 4B? You think I haven't seen this gentleman here before, with that other baggage, the blonde? You should be ashamed of yourself!' she added, shaking her beaded handbag at Ernest. 'It's a scandal, and it's perfectly disgusting! Why, I've written a dozen letters – I've only just put one in the box, but what's the use? I've never had the shadow of an answer. I suspect you bad girls of simply stealing them! We've all had enough; I mean to see the end of this! It must stop at once or I will call the police!

Heaven knows I don't want the police here, but the situation is getting worse by the day – why, you, sir, are the fourth gentleman I've seen going up to 4B since last night! You'd better be on your way at once, this minute, for you're not getting in here today, to pursue your shameful activities. You be gone, or I'll call the police this instant!'

She pulled the door closed behind her with a bang, and stalked off past us down the path without so much as a further glance. I looked at Ernest. He was beet red with shame and consternation.

'I am really sorry,' he managed to enunciate between closed teeth.

'Well,' I said drily, 'it is all part of my job. Please do not worry about my feelings. I assure you much more unpleasant things have happened to me than being accused of being a woman of easy virtue.' I thought of Mr Archer's repulsive kiss and repressed a shudder.

'What shall we do?' he asked, as we continued to stand on the front path.

'We are going to wait until someone else comes out,' I said. 'Or no, perhaps I had better wait alone, since you seem to be known here already. I think you should go, Ernest. I will manage it better by myself.'

'But what will you do?' he asked.

'I don't know,' I said. 'Something or other. Just go, and let me see what I can discover.'

'All right, I'll go,' he said, 'but – please do come to our place for supper. Perhaps you can slip me a word about what you find out.'

He left, still red, and I remained calmly waiting on the path until the door opened again. This time a young man came out. He breathed heavily as though he had been running, and his hat and tie were askew. He held the door for me as I entered, without even looking at me. In fact, he turned his face away. I, on the contrary, followed him with my eyes until he turned into the street and disappeared. Flat 4B?

I entered the hall and hesitated, noticing the residents possessed individual letterboxes, arranged in neat rows along the walls. Each letterbox was marked with a name and a flat number. Immediately, I looked for the name attached to 4B – and this is what I saw!

Mr G Archer, 4B

Mr Archer's flat! It was in *Mr Archer's London flat* that Ivy and Jenny met their clients! Could the old gentleman have been aware of this use of his flat? It seemed scandalous, unthinkable – to be sure, Mr Archer had hinted at using his own flat for some unavowable purposes, but surely that was not at all the same thing as allowing it to be used as a…a…

Through the narrow slot where letters were inserted into the box, I perceived a gleam of white. The letter of the irate neighbour, no doubt. Having only just been called a bad girl who stole letters, I felt an irresistible desire to oblige.

I looked around carefully; the hall was empty. Taking off my gloves, I tried to slip my fingers through the slot, but it was too narrow for them them to enter. I could actually touch the letter, but it was impossible to seize hold of it, although I tried for some little time.

Suddenly I thought of a pair of small pincers I always kept in my reticule. They had served more than once on similar occasions. I took them out, and manoeuvered the tips into the slot, grasped the letter and levered it carefully out. I hesitated for a moment – should I steam it open discreetly and put it back tomorrow? But no. It was too important (or I was too impatient). I tore it open unceremoniously.

Mr Archer,

I feel compelled to address myself to you yet again on the subject of the ill-frequentation of your flat number 4B.

I have attempted to inform you many times, without ever receiving an answer, that this is a decent house and such goings-on cannot be tolerated. It is unacceptable for me to be unable to emerge from my own flat and cross the hall without encountering a flaunting female shamelessly accompanied by yet another of her men friends, entering your flat.

I have told you many times that this use of your flat must cease at once. However, lately it has actually become worse. Whereas it was previously clear that the flat was not used at night-time, it now seems that permanent quarters have been established there. As my flat adjoins yours, I am able, and indeed, obliged, to overhear sounds from your flat both day and night, and I assure you that it is quite intolerable. I demand that you react instantly to the situation, or I will have the occupant bodily thrown out by the police within the week.

Sincerely,

Ada Furze (Mrs)

Flat Number 4A

I put this letter into my reticule and took my way up the left-hand flight of stairs till I reached the landing upon which gave both flats 4A and 4B. I stopped in front of the door and knocked on it strongly and abruptly, then listened carefully. I thought I heard the sound of a door opening within, and a rustle. I knocked again, and waited, thinking of the panting young man I had seen rushing hastily away, his face averted.

I waited, knocked again, and waited some more. No one opened the door. After a while, I called out gently.

'Miss Wolcombe? Are you home? I need to talk to you about Ivy. Please open the door.'

But nothing happened. Further knocking and waiting produced not the slightest effect. It was only after half an hour of gentle knocking and coaxing that I gave up and left, walking down the stairs slowly, still vaguely hoping. Nothing happened, however, and I made my way to Ernest's flat feeling both frustrated and disappointed.

He looked at me quickly as he opened the door, then glanced behind him and sketched a finger in front of his lips. I heard voices emanating cheerfully from the dining room.

'We have a guest,' Ernest whispered. 'Tell me quickly – anything?'

'No,' I said, 'I believe she was there, in fact I believe she is living there, and I'm quite sure I heard someone inside. But she wouldn't open the door even though I knocked...and talked.'

'I should have stayed,' he said. 'I could have persuaded her, I'm sure I could. Listen, I'll – I'll go there and try my luck tomorrow. If she's there, I'll find her, and I'll talk to her. I'll make her see that she *must* help you.'

'Give her these,' I said, and handed him the little bundle of bills and letters addressed to Ivy. He looked at them hungrily, but then thrust them quickly into a pocket as a voice spoke in the hall behind him.

'Is that Vanessa?' said Kathleen, coming up to us and reaching for my shawl. 'Do come in – what are you doing here, standing out on the mat? Professor Lodge is here, do come and be introduced.'

I recognised the Professor at once, of course. Bearded and jolly, he radiated an atmosphere of conviviality throughout the room much in contrast with the tension I often felt at their home. The table was already laid; Ernest ushered me to a chair at once, and Kathleen kissed me warmly, disappeared into the kitchen, and returned carrying a large tureen. The Professor looked up sharply as I sat down across from him.

'Ah,' he said, before Ernest had a chance to make introductions, 'why, we've already met, haven't we? I recognise this lady – she's the Doubting One!'

'Me?' I said, surprised.

'Yes, you,' he thundered heartily. 'I saw you the other night at Mrs Thorne's – watching, analysing, reasoning – it was all there in your eyes! Why do you think you didn't receive any messages? The spirits can tell, you know. They won't address any but receptive hearers.'

'Oh,' I said, 'but I *was* receptive.'

'You may have *thought* you were,' he smiled, digging vigorously with a spoon into the large dish of stew that Kathleen had placed in front of him. 'Consciously, I mean. But unconsciously, I can assure you that you were not.'

'Oh,' I said, reflecting that what he said was very probably true. 'Do you think it's possible to change one's unconscious attitude?' I added meekly.

He looked up at me thoughtfully.

'An interesting question,' he said, 'not often asked. It is possible, yes, indeed it is. But it takes work and effort. It's not enough to simply decide or desire it; such feelings affect nothing but the conscious state. The subject needs to uncover the causes for the unconscious doubt and remove them progressively.'

'Actually,' said Ernest, 'I've seen more than one doubter become completely convinced by a single astounding manifestation.'

'Oh yes,' agreed the Professor, 'but those are not the same type of doubter as this lady. Those are the people whose doubt proceeds from the conscious, whereas unconsciously they desire nothing better than to believe. Therefore, in spite of appearances to the contrary, such people are receptive. It is much easier to overcome conscious than unconscious doubt.'

'But I think I would be convinced,' I argued, 'if I were to perceive an astounding manifestation.'

'I think not,' he said.

'Why not?' I insisted.

'Because, dear lady, you did perceive an astounding manifestation the other evening!' he responded.

'Oh, well,' I said. "But that – it was a little vague – I thought—'

'You thought of something which would be more convincing to a mentality such as yours,' he completed my sentence. 'Accurate factual analysis of the past, for instance, or an incontrovertible instance of thought transference, or what is sometimes known as "telepathy", is that it?'

'Yes,' I nodded, not adding my secret further caveat of the manifestation in question involving only people that I absolutely trusted, like Professor Faraday with his friends.

'I would love to witness something of the kind myself,' said Kathleen. 'I would like to believe, yet I can't seem to. I can't help believing that human beings are made to keep their thoughts private.'

'As indeed they are, in general' replied the Professor, happily accepting a second helping of stew. 'Yet there are extraordinary exceptions. Have you never had any experience of thought transference?'

'Not that I can remember,' she replied. 'Of course, there are some funny things...but one always just puts them down to coincidence, doesn't one? Or else, to the fact that one knows the other person extremely well, so that one's guesses about their thoughts or actions can be very accurate.'

'When exactly does an accurate guess qualify as thought transference?' I wondered aloud.

'The typical question of a Doubter,' he replied, twinkling in my direction. 'I take such an attitude as a challenge.'

'Please do!' I encouraged him.

'Anyone can be a medium, you know,' he explained, 'even a Doubter. Amazingly, they can be just as good mediums as anyone; I've seen it happen often. The quality of being a medium is, I believe, entirely independent of the subject's conscious or unconscious attitudes and beliefs. It is a different capacity altogether. Some people are just naturally gifted with it.' He sighed, and went on, 'Some of the best telepathic mediums I have ever met are identical twins. Too bad we don't have one here tonight.'

'We do,' I told him, smiling. 'I am an identical twin.'

'Really!' he exclaimed, almost jumping out of his seat. 'But this is ideal! You have a sister? Where is she?'

'She lives in Kent,' I said, 'where I grew up. It is quite far away. Does that have anything to do with the thought transference?'

'Not necessarily,' he replied. 'Telepathy can occur with anyone, not just between twins. However, it seems to occur particularly often between twins, which is probably why twins make better mediums in general. Tell me, have you never had any telepathic experiences with your sister?'

I paused for a moment, pondering.

'You have, but you never recognised them as such,' he prompted me. 'You think, like Mrs Dixon, that they were nothing but coincidences.'

'No-o,' I said. 'There have been such flashes of understanding between us that no coincidence could explain it. But then, we are so alike on the outside, that it is understandable that sometimes we also think alike.'

'Is it really?' he said. 'You look alike, but are your personalities alike?'

'Not really,' I told him, 'I have always been the more adventurous of the two of us, Dora the more poised. But we understand each other perfectly.'

'And there have been moments when you felt something about her, although she was far away?'

'Well, yes,' I admitted, 'and things that we did for the first time on the same day – and letters we wrote to each other at the same time, about the same thing, that crossed.'

'Ah,' he said, 'and yet you don't believe in telepathy?'

I hesitated, and he pounced.

'Let us give it a chance,' he suggested, his eyes shining with eagerness. 'I too rarely have an opportunity to work with a twin as medium. If you are willing, let us try some experiments after dinner.'

Thus I found myself seated, one hour later, in a comfortable armchair, facing Kathleen similarly installed, and observed with fanatical intensity by Professor Lodge and Ernest.

'Now, concentrate hard on a single idea,' the Professor instructed Kathleen. 'Mrs Weatherburn, you must empty your mind of your own thoughts entirely, and make yourself receptive. Fixing your eyes on Mrs Dixon will help you to concentrate and keep distracting sights out of your vision.'

I sat obediently, staring at Kathleen and trying to empty my mind. This proved oddly impossible; I succeeded in stopping the train of conscious, directed thought, but the result was that I felt myself more aware than usual of the little voice that ran through my head permanently, producing a continuous stream of observations.

Don't think how silly all this is, and how self-conscious you feel, I instructed myself silently. *Don't think anything. Watch Kathleen.*

I stilled myself and watched her, and immediately became aware of how much one can perceive if one truly concentrates on careful observation. Kathleen was still settling into her seat; I saw her eyes flicker around the room, and as clearly as if I were thinking it myself (as indeed I would have been if I had been sitting in her place), I saw her wonder what item to think about and concentrate on. She glanced at her husband, her expression changed slightly, and all of a sudden a peculiar look crept into her eyes. It took me a moment to identify it; then she turned her gaze straight on me, and I clearly read defiance.

She's going to test me, I thought, *she's going to test the whole notion.* How? By doing exactly what I might well have done myself: by courageously, brazenly, defiantly thinking the most forbidden thought of all, in full view of the telepathic observers. She was throwing down a gauntlet in defense of the privacy of thought. Our eyes met. A moment of indefinable length passed.

Suddenly my mind was filled with a storm of images so powerful that the room faded away completely behind their sudden reality. I saw the blonde actress, Kathleen's face twisted with hate, an impression of hostility and terrible violence, an arm raised to strike – all rushing confused through my brain as though glimpsed through a wild tempest of wind and snow. Starting out of my chair with the shock, I stumbled towards Kathleen, my hands out to stop her...

'Ophelia!' I heard myself gasp.

She stared up at me, startled, and I became aware that she had never moved from her chair, that I must have looked as though I were about to attack her. I withdrew hastily, feeling slightly stunned.

'What did you see?' Sir Oliver demanded eagerly. 'Ophelia? Is she right, Mrs Dixon? Is that what you were thinking about?'

'I – I—' she began. 'Ophelia? No – I wasn't thinking about Ophelia.' She looked at me edgily, warily. What was I to think? Had I just experienced thought transference, or had it all been nothing but a startling visual representation of my own repressed fears and suspicions?

The Professor's face fell.

'What were you concentrating on?' he asked her. There was an instant's fluttering, or else I imagined it, and Kathleen said,

'On my husband.'

'Well,' said the Professor, 'let us not be discouraged. Mrs Weatherburn received an astonishingly strong impression, did she not? It may have come from someone else, from someone nearby – why, perhaps it came from your sister!' he added, turning to me with renewed excitement. 'Why, that must be it! You are more in tune to her thoughts, even when she is far away, than to the people about you, are you not?'

'I don't know,' I said reluctantly. 'I know Dora well enough to guess her thoughts effortlessly sometimes, and in certain ways we are similar enough to think similar things at the same time. I have always supposed that to explain the various coincidental experiences we have had. But this is certainly something different. How could a thought travel hundreds of miles instantaneously? And how could it be perceived?'

'How can light travel hundreds, thousands, millions of miles? And how is it perceived?' he responded instantly. 'The answer is the same, it must be. You need to understand that light is but a form of electromagnetic waves; it is *visible*, that is, perceived by the eye, simply because our eye is a machine able to perceive certain wavelengths and not others. The wavelength of the visible electromagnetic waves is extremely tiny; a few millionths of an inch, no more. Such waves exist of every wavelength, no doubt – all that is missing is our ability to detect them with suitable apparatus that nature has not provided to our living bodies. Still, machines can be created to detect them. I have done a great deal of research on this subject; I was the first to show that electrical impulses could be transmitted along wires, but I was not satisfied with my work, for I wish to study waves transmitted through the ether. The discovery which changed my whole life was made by Heinrich Hertz; he succeeded in building the first apparatus to detect the emission of enormously long waves – wavelengths as great as four inches – in his laboratory. He accomplished this astonishing feat ten years ago and I have worked on it ever since; I have improved his *machine* greatly;

not so much the emitter of the waves, which works simply by an electrical discharge from a Leyden jar, but in the truly delicate and subtle part of the thing: the wave detector. I have a machine now which detects and reacts instantly and powerfully to any Hertzian wave. Unfortunately, the waves die out as they go away; my machine is unable to detect them from more than a few yards away, whereas light comes to us all the way from distant stars. I cannot seem to detect the long waves from any serious distance away. This is why I am fascinated by telepathic phenomena. I am convinced that we are perceiving nothing more than an extraordinary natural apparatus, granted to but a few, to perceive waves transmitted, I dare hope, by every human being, alive or dead. Telepathic experiments seem to work better at close quarters, leading me to the impression that the telepathic waves have extremely long wavelengths and die out even sooner than the Hertzian waves I have worked on. But incidences of distant telepathy, such as what you have perhaps just experienced, indicate that a different physical reality may be at play: the waves are transmitted over great distances, and my apparatus is simply not good enough. No one in the world has been able to detect the Hertzian waves at a greater distance than I have, although some of the world's greatest scientific minds have attempted it: Hertz himself, Branly in France, Popov in Russia. Many people believe the waves simply die out too soon to be detectable at any distance. Yet my intuition contradicts this; I cannot help but feel that the world is only waiting for a new kind of scientific genius to emerge and invent the apparatus to detect them.'

'No one can do it if you can't, Sir Oliver,' said Ernest with enthusiastic devotion. Kathleen, instead, responded to the

Professor's speech by playing a little ostentatiously with her beads and repressing a yawn. I remembered that she disliked scientific conversations, and hastened to relieve her by rising to leave. Sir Oliver bid me goodbye with great eagerness, vehemently expressing the hope of seeing me participate ever more actively in the sessions of the Society for Psychical Research of which he was a key member, and of which I had attended one of the sessions, without knowing it, at the home of Mrs Thorne. He pressed a pamphlet into my hand, which I perused upon my road home.

Society for Psychical Research

The original Sidgwick Group, founded in 1874, consisting of Henry Sidgwick, Frederic W H Myers, Edmund Gurney, Walter Leaf, Lord Raleigh, Arthur Balfour, Eleanor Balfour Sidgwick and Lady Raleigh, created the Society for Psychical Research for the purpose of investigating mediums and Spiritualistic séances with total objectivity, whether exposing frauds or discovering new truths. Since the founding, numerous new members have joined the society, including a number of esteemed public figures: Sir Oliver Lodge, physicist, William Crookes, chemist, Arthur C Doyle, physician and author.

The SPR contains six distinct research committees, each devoted to the study of a particular aspect of Spiritualistic and psychical phenomena:

1) Thought transference, or 'telepathy'.

2) Mesmerism, hypnotism, clairvoyance, and related phenomena.

3) 'Sensitives' and 'mediums', being people with the ability to communicate with the dead.

4) Apparitions of all types.

5) Levitations, materialisations, and other physical phenomena associated with séances.

6) The collection and collation of data on the history of the above subjects.

I hesitated for a long time before consigning the pamphlet to the wastebin.

Experiments of the last summer have made perfectly certain the possibility of using captive balloons on the high sea. In place of balloons, without doubt one might use the modern kites, brought to such a pitch of perfection in America. I owe it to the kindness of an acquaintance in New York that I know something of these excellent kites. Altogether, we are face to face with very peculiar phenomena. Nature has opened a new door for us. It is the mission of science at present to bring light into the opened room.

Monday, July 18th, 1898

I hardly dared believe that Ernest would succeed where I had failed, and was thus surprised and amazed to receive not one but two letters today, as though in answer to my prayers. I opened Ernest's first. It was short and to the point.

Dear Vanessa,

As promised, I confronted the dragon's lair and laid siege to Miss Wolcombe's door until she let me in. You were right; she is no other than Ivy's friend Jenny, who shared lodgings with her until last week. Vanessa, should you have further contacts with Miss Wolcombe, as knowing you I am sure you will, I want to warn you: she is a good creature, she is, indeed, but her life and her circumstances have been so vastly different from yours, and indeed, from my own, as to make her thought processes appear totally foreign to us. Her instantaneous reaction upon learning from her landlady (who learnt it from the police) of Ivy's death, was to raid her friend's boxes and drawers in order to remove anything personal from prying eyes, and to then proceed to remove herself bodily from the path of the police. I expressed amazement at her reluctance to aid them in their legitimate enquiry into Ivy's death, but she simply stared at me as though I were suggesting she aid wolves in their legitimate quest to devour her. Women such as Miss Wolcombe keep as far as possible from the police at all times, and it is a kind of fundamental rule of existence for them, from which no deviation is conceivable.

When I explained that no one was involved in the present investigation other than you and myself, and pressed her to help us, she still hesitated, but yielded when I painted a grim picture of Ivy's murderer still wandering the streets. Still, I got no more from her than a promise to write to you directly; she told me nothing, in spite of all my coaxing and entreaties. Being aware that she knows more about Ivy's life than anyone else, and that she now holds any private letters Ivy may have received before her death, made it torture for me to accept her refusal with equanimity, but I forced myself to do so, for men, in the eyes of women such as she, are natural enemies and sources of harm, to be mistrusted, hated, vanquished, and at the very best, used. I put my trust in you, therefore, to tell me what there is to be known.

With my very sincerest regards and prayers for your success,

Your devoted servant,

Ernest Dixon

I put down this missive, seized the second letter, which was actually a rather heavy envelope obviously containing several documents, and tore it open at once. Out came a letter from Miss Wolcombe, as well as other older, somewhat crumpled and folded letters – letters to Ivy!

Dear Mrs Wetherburn,

I am writing to you because Mr Dixon said you are trying in good faith to find out who killed Ivy Elliott who was my best friend and the best friend anyone could ever have. I dont want to be mixed up in anything. But Ivy was strangled and drowned Mr Dixon told me and I am ready to kill the person who did it with my own hands. I was never going to tell anybody about this but I will tell you in case you can find out who it is, because Mr Dixon says you can find out anything and you wont tell anyone. Just before she died Ivy was engaged to be married and she was the happiest girl in the world and her whole life was going to change. She was in love and he was in love with her. I know this because she told me, and they were going to be married very very soon. I dont know if this has anything to do with her dying. Maybe it does and maybe it doesnt. Maybe I have another idea about this. Im not sure but I am trying to find out. I hate to think he killed her or she died because of him, because she loved him and was so happy in those last two weeks you cant imagine, like I never saw her, but the trouble is that from his letters I found in her droors he lives in Cambridge and that is where she was killed Mr Dixon says. But I know she went to Cambridge to see another old man as well, him that wrote one of the letters. If you could find out who the man was, the one she was going to marry, maybe that would help you do what you are trying to do. I dont know who he was. Ivy beleeved he loved her and he did give her real happiness before she died, but if he killed her Ill kill him. I am sending you his letters which I took.

Yours from Jenny Wolcombe, Ivy's friend

The spelling, the uneducated handwriting and the passionate attachment to her friend which glowed from between the lines combined to make this missive strangely moving. I picked up one of the enclosed envelopes and took out not one but two folded letters, whose thin, onion-skin pages I smoothed out with a feeling of triumph. The handwriting corresponded exactly to that of the empty envelope that had somehow been left behind amongst the bills. Refined and expensive paper; elegant handwriting, filled with character; a good-quality quill.

My love, my beloved, my heart,

Three days before I can see you, three days of burning impatience, three days of waiting, every minute wasted in which I cannot tell you, by look and word and gesture, what you are to me, what you are: you, radiant with the glow of youth and loveliness, scarred with suffering, fragmented but not destroyed, come into my life like light into the eyes of a blind man. This is what I want to say to you: come to my arms with all the baggage of your life, all that which renders human a being as beautiful as an angel; all those things which are unspeakable and about which I make no myth, believe me: your past, with all its acts, its experiences, its memories, and above all, above all, my beloved, the child within you; come to me with everything, I want all of it, such as it is; there is nothing else in this world that I desire. If you can possibly consider it, if you can turn your forget-me-not eyes in my direction, say one word, just one single word, and I will marry you as soon as the law allows – I believe it takes no more than a few days – and under any conditions you want, anything at all that you request, require, demand or need; I want nothing but to keep you safe from harm.

And at the bottom – a scribbled, totally illegible signature! I flung the paper onto the table in fury after scrutinising it in vain, then snatched it up again, guilty for my momentary anger, then put it down and quickly unfolded the second letter.

My beloved,

It is done, it is settled, it is fixed for the twenty-second; one life until that day, another one, thereafter. Your hand in mine, my darling, your heart near mine, your child mine also – ours, to raise together in love and tenderness, in front of the whole world: I, a husband, a father! You, the bringer of this miracle! This banal, common condition that is yet a miracle each and every time an individual man attains it.

I have wondered and questioned to exhaustion whether I can bring you happiness. You could offer me no greater gift than the words you sent me, which restored my joy, my peace, my very life, stained and burnt by the acid of doubt. All is well, all is ready; come to me on the twenty-first, and do not breathe a single word to anyone.

I stood stunned, holding these two letters in my hand, and absorbing, with a shock, the idea that somewhere in Cambridge beat a heart shattered, in total silence, by Ivy's death. I had wondered if her own innocent words of love were not addressed to a perfidious Julian Archer, but I found that hard to believe now. Could he be the author of these desperately sincere words? Was he as passionately in love with Ivy as these letters indicated? Was he planning to wed her secretly, no doubt in order to avoid the angry and, I suppose, partially justified interference of his father? He did not appear to be a man shattered by the death of his beloved, but that meant little; we British are past masters at hiding our feelings, and have made it into a source of pride to boot.

I sat down, trying to restore order to my thoughts, but could get no farther than the urgent need to determine whether or not he was the author. It would be easy enough to do, surely, on the basis of the handwriting. I put the letters into my bag and issued forth without further delay, not pausing until I stood in front of Heffers bookshop. I pushed the door and went in, ready with my ruse; I meant to ask Mr Archer for detailed information on some book or other, and get him to write it down for me. The bell tinkled and a clerk emerged from the office; Julian Archer, however, was nowhere to be seen.

'Is Mr Archer in?' I asked the young man, a vacillating and uncertain personage of an obviously inferior position.

'No, ma'am,' he replied, 'he's in London today, taking care of purchasing. He's due back later this afternoon. Can I help you in any way?'

'No, thank you,' I said, repressing my frustration at not obtaining an immediate answer to my question. Various plans for seeing some sample of his handwriting from the back office flashed through my mind, but all of them were too complicated and could not fail to arouse suspicion. No, there was no help for it but patience. I went back out into Petty Cury – and found myself standing at the door leading to the upper floor. Mr Archer's rooms over the shop! Without conscious thought, my finger flew to the bell and pressed it firmly. I then stood awaiting the consequences of my actions, wondering what to expect.

After only a few moments, a manservant opened the door and gazed upon me enquiringly. Improvising rapidly, I asked him if Mr Archer was in, even though I knew full well that he was in London. This made my surprise all the greater when he responded with a nod and invited me into the narrow entrance hall, which contained nothing but a small table set against the wall, and a staircase leading to the upper regions.

'Yes, he is in. Your name, please? Will you wait here? I will go and enquire whether he can receive you.'

'Miss Duncan,' I said meekly, wondering how on earth to justify this sudden and impossible visit, and I almost considered dashing out into the street and away, except that I had already given my name. I fluttered, dismayed – and then something suddenly caught my eye! On the table just at my hand, in a salver, lay two letters, addressed and ready to be carried to the post. I moved them gently with my finger, staring hungrily at the written addresses. Yes, it was – yes, they were – surely! Surely? I opened my bag, extracted the envelopes from inside it, compared – yes – yes, the same! I was in luck, one of the letters was addressed to a Professor Iverson at Emmanuel College. That capital I – yes, this was the same handwriting. Julian Archer was the author of the letters hidden in my bag – he must be!

But what could it all mean?

The manservant's hurrying feet were heard on the stairs, and he stood at the bottom, beckoning me upwards. Even though my task was now accomplished, there was nothing for it but to go.

I followed the manservant up not one but two flights of stairs, to the top of the house, where he opened a door and ushered me into an agreeable, sunny and pleasantly furnished sitting room. Plump armchairs stood about the fireplace, a grand piano stood at the far end from the street, and near the windows was a large desk, at which was seated a curious figure. The pale sunshine glanced over a hunchback as round as a stone; from between two narrow, jutting shoulders, a head seemed to grow forwards rather than upwards. This head turned as I entered, heralded by the manservant's stolid enunciation of my name, and revealed an interesting, not unattractive face.

'Oh,' I said in confusion, 'I expected to see Mr Archer.'

'I am Mr Archer,' he replied with a slight smile. 'But I suppose you wanted to see my brother Julian.' As he spoke, he pushed himself away from the desk with his hand, and I saw that he was seated in an invalid's chair with wheels. This he swivelled to face me.

'Please sit down,' he said kindly. 'I rarely receive the pleasure of a visit; perhaps I can be of some help to you instead of my brother.'

I sat down upon the sofa; I felt slightly shy, and also foolish to have completely forgotten about the existence of Julian Archer's invalid brother. I looked at him now, resisting the natural impulse to avert my eyes from his grotesquely deformed body. His shrivelled legs, encased in well-tailored trousers, seemed almost useless; his arms were strangely long, with sensitive and elegant hands. I noticed a smudge of ink on the inside of the middle finger, and glanced over at the desk where he had been working. It was piled high with tomes and papers; I tried to make out the title of the one nearest me, but it was in Greek. Mr Archer used his arms to propel his chair towards me until he was facing me at a reasonable distance.

'May I offer you some tea?' he asked.

I stammered a refusal, not at all sure that I was going to stay long enough to partake of a cup. I was intrigued by his face, which, while bearing not the slightest resemblance to his father and brother, seemed somehow slightly familiar to me. It was not displeasing, yet there was something strange about it; it was a face that was extremely hard to read, a veiled face. Why did I feel as though I recognised it?

'I wonder if we have ever met before?' I mused, almost absently.

'Undoubtedly not. I am afraid that I rarely set foot out of doors,' he replied. 'And if I had already encountered you, I should not be likely to have forgotten it.' He smiled rather sadly, then went on, 'Do tell me in what my brother could have been of help to you? If you need some advice or information about a book, I might be able to replace him.'

I stifled a nervous giggle which rose to my throat at the idea of telling him the truth, seized eagerly upon the fiction of a book, and suddenly, moved by an urge to probe without revealing myself, I said, 'Yes, that is what it was. I am looking for a book by someone called Alexandre Parent-Duchâtelet, a book in French – that is, I wanted to know if this book has been translated into English. I haven't been able to find it anywhere.'

I cringed inwardly as I realised that if he knew the book, my question would be most embarrassing. I regretted my impulse and tried to console myself by hoping that he couldn't possibly have heard of it. Surely, surely not. How many invalid scholars read books entitled *De la prostitution dans la ville de Paris?*

His reply showed that apparently, some do. However, he preserved a quietly professional attitude which revealed nothing at all.

'Parent-Duchâtelet?' he said. 'You won't find his research at Heffers. It hasn't been translated into English at all. England has its own social researchers. You've read William Acton? I suggest you do – although, of course, being English, he is a moral crusader as Parent-Duchâtelet is not. Acton wants to cure the social phenomenon, Parent-Duchâtelet to understand it. I agree that the French attitude is often preferable. However, you will have difficulty finding a copy of the book here. You would need to go over to the Continent.'

He blushed unexpectedly as he said these last words, turned his head slightly and uncontrollably as people do when they are specifically *not* supposed to look in a certain direction, then fixed his eyes firmly upon the region of my knees. My eyes followed his naturally, his expression and movement having led me to an unerring conviction that a copy could be found no farther than the room we were in, or at most, the room beyond. I was distracted, however, by the sight of something completely different: a pair of crutches, propped in a corner of the room near the desk. I stared at them, then looked back at him, down at his legs, which were so thin that the trousers appeared nearly empty. Could he stand, then, and even walk? My eyes guessed his height; standing, I thought, he would barely reach my forehead. Yet he was not helpless; those long arms were used to handling all the normal actions of his life...

He knew all about books, he could replace his brother with advice and counsel; surely he often went downstairs to the bookshop.

Had *he,* then, been the one to discover the secret of his brother's love and imminent marriage? And determined to put a stop to it?

Ivy, in the bookshop, sitting in the armchair, writing a few words of passion before hurrying upstairs to press them secretly into her lover's hand – the sharp tinkle of the opening door – the startled girl thrusting her letter down the side of the seat – the tap of crutches...the deformed figure entering, mad with jealousy, in love with her, perhaps, himself, twisted with the repressed resentment of years, determined to annihilate his brother's happiness...

I looked at the man sitting in front of me, and my eyes fell on the long fingers resting on his knees. The fingers of a strangler?

'Thank you for your help,' I gasped confusedly, rising from my chair. 'I must go – I must go.'

'Let me ring,' he said courteously, rolling his chair over to the bell-pull.

'Please don't bother – I can let myself out,' I cried, opening the door myself in my haste and fleeing down the stairs to the street with a feeling of desperate escape from an accursed presence. And I made my way, almost running, to the police station, and asked for Inspector Doherty, terrified of hearing that he was not available.

But he was in his office, and received me benignly.

'Inspector,' I said, 'I know who killed Ivy Elliott now – it wasn't old Mr Archer or his son Julian – it's the other son, Philip! I'm sure of it!'

There was a long silence, during which I thought he was absorbing this piece of information with amazement, until I became aware that he was slowly shaking his head.

'I'm sorry, Mrs Weatherburn,' he said. 'But we have already investigated both Julian and Philip Archer. You remember our previous discussion, in the course of which you advanced what I considered a rather unbalanced theory about the guilt of Julian Archer. You made some legitimate points, however, and we questioned both him and his brother about their alibis. They were together on the night of the murder. They are both well and truly out of it.'

I sat down in the hard wooden chair across from him, and slumped my elbows on the desk.

'I don't believe it,' I said. 'They are shielding each other.'

'Mrs Weatherburn,' he said patiently, 'how many times do I have to tell you that these difficult cases are not for amateurs? The two Archer brothers were together for the entire evening and part of the night of the girl's death, together with a friend and their manservant Simpson. Here, let me show you their statements directly; it will be simpler.'

He took out the usual folder, the sight of which by now recalled what appeared to be a series of dreary failures, and opening it to the end, extracted the latest documents.

'Perhaps you should come and see me more often,' he admonished me, 'although, as you well know, I think you would do best to leave the case to me altogether. However, don't think I'm forgetting the service you rendered me with the girl's identification, not to speak of the interesting letter you found. I'm grateful for that, which is why I'm still sharing my information with you. Here you go: the sworn statements of the four witnesses.'

Mr Julian Archer: I did not feel like attending my father's party, although he had kindly invited me to do so. Most of the people there were not really in my circle of friends. I preferred to stay home, and proposed to spend the evening with my brother and a friend or two. We dined at eight, and Mr Trevelyan came to join us after the meal. We spent the evening talking and playing music; both my brother and I play the piano, Philip much better than I, of course, and Trevelyan pipes on the flute. We also played several rather amusing parlour games, charades and so forth. We spent the entire time upstairs in my brother's rooms on the upper floor. My own rooms are on the lower floor, just over the shop. The flat is reserved for the manager of Heffers, but I am perfectly happy to share it with my brother. My brother walks with great difficulty, so that it is much more convenient for him to live in town. Simpson remained with us until a little before one o'clock in the morning, when we sent him to bed. Trevelyan left at about two. It was late, but we were having a most enjoyable time. Did we leave the sitting room at all? Well, naturally, over the course of several hours, we all must have left the room more than once, but not for more than a couple of minutes. I myself stepped down to my own rooms once or twice to fetch items for the charades or look up a word in the Philological Society dictionary; Philip only uses Richardson's, whereas I find that the Philological is often more up-to-date. As far as I remember, neither Trevelyan nor my brother actually went downstairs, nor do I think Simpson needed to at any point. Beyond my brother's sitting room is his bedroom, then Simpson's bedroom, and the kitchen and bath; when Simpson was not in the room with us, he was over there. After Trevelyan left, I spent the rest of the night in my brother's bedroom. I do that on occasion, because he sleeps very badly and sometimes needs help at night. Usually Simpson is within call, but we'd sent him to bed so late I thought it would be better not to disturb him. I myself need very little sleep. It doesn't bother me at all to spend the night on the camp bed.

Mr Samuel Trevelyan: I spent the evening of the 21st of June at the flat of my friends Philip and Julian Archer, whom I have known since we were boys. Both Julian and I have become quite busy lately with work, so that we don't see each other as often as we used to. I was delighted at his suggestion that we spend an evening all three of us together. For obvious reasons, that could only be at Philip Archer's rooms. We enjoyed ourselves a great deal; both brothers were in an excellent mood. I don't remember anyone leaving the room for any significant amount of time. Well, Julian popped down to his room for charade things once or twice, but he was certainly never absent for more than five minutes. And Simpson was in and out all the time, with drinks and cigars and things, but I think he kept going through to the kitchen; I don't remember him actually going downstairs for anything. As for Philip, I'm sure he didn't go downstairs at all; it's difficult for him, so I'd have noticed if he had.

Mr Philip Archer: I spent the entire evening in my rooms with my brother and a very good friend of ours, Sam Trevelyan. He did not leave until well after one o'clock. I did not look at the time, but it must have been closer to two, because we sent Simpson off to bed at about ten minutes before one, and Trevelyan stayed a good while after that. My brother had been sitting at the piano playing comic songs, but he stopped singing when Simpson went to bed, and then we played charades and word games. About going downstairs? Well, Simpson was in and out all the time, but as far as I remember he didn't actually go downstairs for anything. Julian didn't leave either; he just went to his room for a couple of minutes now and then to look up words, and to get things for our charades. We were all together for the entire evening. After Trevelyan left, my brother and I went on talking for a while, as I felt incapable of sleeping. I suffer very seriously from insomnia, because of my enforced lack of activity, and painful backaches which prevent me from sleeping for many hours in the night, although I resist the use of laudanum, fearing to become weakened and dependent. Julian ended up spending the night in my room, as he does on occasion. I didn't sleep until the sky became quite light, though Julian did.

Michael Simpson, manservant: All three gentlemen stayed upstairs from nine o'clock through until I went to bed a little before one. The whole time I was in and out of the sitting room, to the kitchen, to the dining room. As for the gentleman, Mr Julian Archer went in and out a few times; he also went downstairs. Mr Philip did not go downstairs; he generally needs assistance to use the stairs. When I wasn't needed I sat in my own room till I was rung for. It's the room adjoining Mr Philip Archer's bedroom, looking out at the back. That way I can easily hear if Mr Philip needs me. As I said, I went to bed at about one o'clock, but I left my door ajar. I sleep lightly and am used to being called at night for Mr Philip's needs; he doesn't always call, but sometimes he needs his medicine. I vaguely heard the gentlemen going to bed about an hour after I did. Mr Julian stayed to sleep in the upstairs bedroom on his camp bed, but I left my door ajar as usual just in case. I believe I would have heard if anyone had risen and gone downstairs during the night. I am sure that nobody did so.

I perused these four statements carefully, then turned to the inspector.

'Thank you for showing me these,' I said. 'I have something to show you, as well. Let us see what we can make of our combined information.' And I took the two letters out of my reticule and handed them to him.

'These were written to Ivy Elliott and found by a friend of hers amongst her effects after her death,' I told him. 'I received them from her only today. It seems certain that the letter she wrote, that I found in Heffers, was addressed to the person who wrote these.'

'I had that checked, by the way,' he told me, 'and you were right. The letter was undoubtedly written by Ivy Elliott.'

Taking up the letters, he turned them over and read them with the same attention I had devoted to his testimonies.

'Who wrote these?' he asked finally, after staring at the signature. 'Do you know?'

'I believe it was Julian Archer,' I told him. 'I've seen his writing and it is the same.'

He stared at me.

'So what you are saying is that these letters tell us that Julian Archer was in love with his father's mistress, and planning to marry her secretly on the very day after the murder. Well, Mrs Weatherburn, that sounds very like the theory you expounded last time you were here.'

'Yes,' I said, 'but then I suspected him of being entrapped into an undesirable marriage and wanting to get out of it. These letters make me feel differently. They are compellingly sincere; he needn't have written them so, he *wouldn't* – I think he *couldn't* have written them so, if he didn't really desire to marry her, even less if he were secretly planning to kill her.'

'Perhaps,' he mused, toying with the letters. 'So how do you see things now?'

'I think that Mr Philip Archer discovered his brother's love affair somehow, perhaps by reading his correspondence. He probably found out about the planned wedding.'

'And so?'

'Well,' I went on thoughtfully, 'suppose that Philip Archer is wildly jealous of his brother. Would it not be understandable, given his condition? Now, he rarely goes out, and probably has almost no contact with young women; imagine that he became acquainted with his father's mistress and conceived a strong attraction for her. There is a book – well, anyway. What I mean is that in a man compelled to physical inactivity and used to repressing all overt signs of both physical and mental pain, jealousy on such a score could spill over into insanity. I've been asking myself why Julian and Ivy felt they had to keep their marriage entirely secret until it was a fait accompli. I understand that Julian felt his father might be angry, given that Ivy was his father's mistress, after all, but my impression is that Mr Archer is very fond of Julian, and was not passionately in love with Ivy himself. Of course, he might have been very angry that his son should make such an incorrect marriage at all, but he has no power to disinherit him, and he could be just as angry after the marriage as before. But if Julian feared that his brother's maniacal jealousy might destroy the wedding ceremony itself, I can understand his desire for secrecy better.'

'Fine,' he said, 'jealousy may be a weak and entirely hypothetical motive, but it is admissible. Still, though, how do you think Philip Archer actually murdered the girl? Given that the statements say he never went downstairs, added to the problem we discussed in detail last time: how could he possibly have known that the girl was there?'

'According to the witnesses,' I said, 'she must have arrived in Petty Cury at about one o'clock. Now, up until almost that moment, Julian Archer was sitting at the piano playing comic songs. I've been in their sitting room; the grand piano is at the far end of the room from the window, so that precludes Julian Archer standing staring into the street watching for her to arrive, as I conjectured last time we talked. But it doesn't preclude Philip's having seen her through the window, either because he knew she was coming, or simply by coincidence. Mr Trevelyan noticed that both brothers were in a very good mood. For Julian, it would be understandable, given that he was going to be married to his beloved the very next day, but for Philip, such a mood might better express a state of manic overexcitement.'

'So you think he saw the girl, slipped down and murdered her, came back and went on as though nothing were amiss?'

'Yes,' I assented.

'Well, but Mrs Weatherburn – *what happened to the body?*'

'Julian went out in the middle of the night and put it in the river,' I replied. 'He must have realised what had happened, or Philip told him. However horrible the deed, I believe that Julian would protect his brother, has always protected him, has looked after him all their lives; in spite of the horror of the act, he cannot bring himself to betray him now.'

'And Michael Simpson's evidence that no one went out at night?'

A crack appeared in my carefully constructed edifice, but I resisted.

'He must have been sleeping, no matter what he says,' I asserted firmly.

'But all the witnesses agree that Philip Archer never went downstairs,' he objected. 'And that he could hardly manage it without assistance. Even if he could, surely it would take him some little time, and it could hardly fail to be noticed by his brother, his friend or the manservant.'

Another little crack appeared.

'Mr Trevelyan doesn't know the house well, and he was drinking liquor and enjoying himself; perhaps he didn't notice that Philip slipped discreetly out of one door rather than another,' I said hopefully.

'Mr Trevelyan knows the flat perfectly well,' he argued, 'and anyway, I assure you that Philip Archer cannot "slip" anywhere discreetly. Don't you know how he walks? He has to collect his crutches first, and then each step is an effort. Believe me, it cannot pass unnoticed. When he moves from room to room in his own flat, he uses his chair.'

My edifice began to crumble.

'He may have been pretending to be more helpless than he really is...' I said.

'For years? In preparation for this murder?'

'Oh, I don't know. I don't know. I must think!' I cried. My mind was in a turmoil. Somewhere, somewhere in this tangled mess the truth *must* lie.

Silence, for the first day.

Silence, for the second day.

Minute after minute, hour after hour, nothing to be heard but the crashing of the waves on the beach below, and the cries of the gulls flying over the cliffs.

Silence, for the third day. And on the fourth day – the unmistakable, tiny signal.

I left the inspector, wondering if his objections and his discretion would prevent him from acting, or if he would do something – anything – even without telling me. I walked blindly, thinking – yes, surely it would be strange for Philip Archer to behave more helpless than he really was – yet nobody had said that he *could* not negotiate the stairs alone, only that he generally requested assistance...

But it was not merely a question of stairs. Stairs to the street, entering the bookshop...murder...and then mounting the stairs back to the room, all in a time so short as to make his absence go unnoticed?

Well, Simpson may well have been away in his own bedroom or in the kitchen, and as for Julian, if he noticed, Philip may have said he would explain later – and have done it. Only Mr Trevelyan must be supposed to have noticed nothing...it was odd, but couldn't it be?

My feet stopped automatically, and I realised with startled amazement that they had carried me back to Petty Cury. I stood facing the bookshop, not knowing why I was there. The door to the upper rooms was in front of me, hermetically closed. And behind it sat a murderer, like a hunchbacked, long-armed spider in the centre of his web. I could not tear myself away, nor ring the bell. I stood there for many minutes, confused, reluctant to leave, incapable of acting.

People walked past me along the street, and some glanced at me. I searched around for some place to be less conspicuous, and noticed that the two buildings just across from Heffers were separated by a tiny, narrow alley; an odd thing, since all the other buildings on that side of Petty Cury are joined as one. But it suited my purposes, and I withdrew into it and stood watching the door, not knowing exactly what I was doing it for, wondering, hoping, for some reason, that Philip Archer would emerge.

Instead, someone entered.

With a quick, sharp step, a woman walked up to the door, stopped in front of it, and rang the bell with a violent gesture.

She was tall and black-haired, her lips were pressed together, and she held a crumpled paper in a gloved hand which shook with tension. The other hand was hidden under her cloak. Her mass of hair was disarrayed underneath a hat set askew, whether by art or by haste I could not tell. Her forehead was burning, her cheeks flushed. Simpson opened the door, and she pushed past him into the hall; I glimpsed her storming upstairs.

I did not hesitate now, but crossed the street and rang again. Apparently unruffled by the unexpected sequence of female visitors, Simpson admitted me and preceded me up the stairs, informing me courteously of the presence of another visitor. The woman had been there for less than a minute. He opened the sitting room door, smoothly announced my return and left, closing it behind me. Philip Archer was sitting in his chair, at his desk, exactly as he had been when I first saw him. The woman was staring at him with a mixture of amazement and contempt; she barely vouchsafed me a glance.

'Why, you mangy dwarf,' she said to him, her voice low

and vicious. 'So *you're* the "young" Mr Archer? Now I understand everything. Now I understand why you never showed yourself, you sick, deformed little monster.'

He stared at her for a moment without replying; a shadow passed over his face, nothing more. Then he reached for his crutches, which leant against the wall in the corner behind him, and, awkwardly struggling to his feet, he approached her. Because of the withered legs and hunched back, he was significantly smaller than she; yet he looked up at her with a certain authority.

'May I ask who you are,' he said quietly, 'and what you want from me?'

'I've come here to kill you,' she said, and suddenly her hand came out of the cloak, and it was grasping a large kitchen knife. 'I'll do it – I don't care if they hang me!'

Mr Archer's eyes fixed on the knife, and an expression of utter bewilderment painted itself on his features. He looked as though he had not the faintest glimmerings of an idea why this dark-haired Valkyrie wished to do away with him.

The sight of the blade pinched me with a cold fear. She looked like a madwoman. I kept my eyes fixed on her, ready to pounce if she pounced.

'But why?' said Mr Archer after a moment.

She took a step towards him, and I tensed. But her next words were startlingly unexpected.

'Because you're a filthy pimp,' she said between clenched teeth. 'Why, you evil scum – a pimp and a sick little hunchback murderer, disguised as a Cambridge gentleman. I know your secrets! Just look at you – an angel face on a devil's body – pretending you don't even know what I'm talking about.'

'But I don't,' he protested, still seemingly unable to muster anything more urgent than a tone of courteous though disbelieving politeness. His body, however, began to shake violently on the shrivelled legs which refused their support, and, yielding to necessity, he collapsed onto the sofa and stared up at the woman who towered over him.

'Well then,' she said, doing something in her rage which might almost be described as gnashing her teeth, and taking yet another step towards him, 'I'll tell you. And I'll tell *her*,' she added, gesturing towards me with her chin, 'though I don't know who she is. Because I'll be happy to have a witness. I *want* a witness. I want the whole world to know that a dirty little rat from Cambridge who couldn't ever have had a woman no matter how much he might have wanted one, enjoyed himself working women to the bone, forcing them to sell themselves on the street to pay him. Oh, you're no ordinary pimp – *you* wouldn't know how to strike a girl or force her to satisfy your depraved imaginings – when she's already exhausted from night after night of work, if you can call it work, and sick of the very sight of a man. You never showed your face and I've often wondered why. But now I know. Who could set eyes on *you* without laughing themselves sick, you deformed little midget? What girl would work for you if she once set eyes on you? If a man's going to live on a girl's work, crush her, take everything from her, wring her dry, then he'd better not be a contemptible laughing-stock in her eyes. Who could feel fear – who could feel anything but loathing for a *thing* like you, that can't even be called a man?' Her eyes narrowed, and her look of manic hatred increased as she stood nearly on top of him, fingering her knife. But it was obvious that she still had a great deal to say.

'Oh, you must have felt wonderful, squeezing us dry, taking everything we had, while you sat here in your nice chair, in your pretty rooms. It must be all so easy, when you don't see anything of the filth and hardship, mustn't it? You're a new kind of pimp, aren't you? A dirty little rat like you – *you* taking money from us for sleeping with other men! It doesn't bear thinking about!'

And she let out a horrible, hysterical peal of deranged laughter.

'No, no – this is all an awful mistake,' stammered Mr Archer, glancing at me awkwardly. But she didn't even listen to him. The flood of words continued to pour forth.

'We were getting out of it, that's what we were doing,' she said. 'We were getting out of it – you knew you couldn't hold us any longer. You knew it, you knew it, you knew she was going to be free from you, and you were afraid she would reveal everything! That's why you killed her, isn't it? Don't think I don't know – I know it now! I have the proof!' And she agitated the crumpled paper she held in her left hand. '*That's* why Ivy had to die, isn't it?' she said again in a kind of raucous whisper, leaning towards him, brandishing both the paper and the knife in his face.

'Why Ivy had to die?' This time Mr Archer reacted; the words emerged like a raucous croak, and he half struggled out of his seat again. 'What are you talking about? What does all this mean? What do you know about Ivy's death?'

For the first time, a shade of doubt crossed the woman's face, and she withdrew a step.

'*You* killed her,' she said, but her voice wavered a little.

'Mr Archer,' I said, stepping forward and speaking firmly

and gently, 'please allow me to intervene. I am a detective, and I am investigating Miss Elliott's murder.'

'Oh,' said the woman, paying attention to me for the first time, and understanding swept over her features. 'Are you – are you Mrs Weatherburn?'

'Yes,' I said, 'and you must be Jenny Wolcombe.'

'Yes, I'm Jenny Wolcombe, who's lost the one thing that made her life bearable. Jenny, who's lost her best friend, her only friend. And you're *here* – so you've understood as I have, then?' Unconsciously, she lowered the knife which she had been brandishing crazily.

'Ivy was your best friend,' I said, gently trying to draw her attention, to distract her from Mr Archer, whose chest was no more than a few inches from the blade, which she still gripped firmly, although no longer pointing it at him. 'Tell me about her, tell me everything you know about what happened. I need to know – I need to know about Ivy, how you came to know her, what your lives were like.' I moved closer to her, holding her eyes with mine, concentrating, soliciting her attention. She reacted slowly, turning towards me, and her words came in a rush. Her hand raised the knife again, as though to convince herself that she would not lose her advantage, but her attention was diverted to me, and she began to speak in a rush. It was, perhaps, the only tribute her dead friend would ever receive, and the only chance she would ever have to speak about her.

'Ivy and I worked together for years,' she began. 'We made friends back when she first started. I helped her then. She came up from the country, and I saw her just wandering the streets – wandering the streets. I saw tears on her face, she was just lost, didn't know where to go, what to do. She saw me watching her, and begged me for help. She was only fifteen, I was already eighteen, I'd been on the street for years, there was nothing about it I didn't know. She'd been in trouble out where she came from. Got a little too fond of some slick gentleman or other and her family threw her out, wouldn't have anything more to do with her. And neither would he, of course. What could she do? She came up to London and just wandered all over town crying until she talked to me.

'I took her home, I taught her everything. We worked in a lodging house then, and paid the landlady practically everything we earned; the rest had to go on clothes and food. Ivy used to keep telling me we had to get out of it. "I want a future," she used to say. "I'll get us out of this, I swear it." She wanted to become an actress. She took to going out and trying for all the parts advertised in the papers; she went to all the theatres in London asking for parts. She was so pretty, and there was something about her. She could act. Don't ask me how; I couldn't do it if my life depended on it. But she had something in there that came out when she stepped onto the stage. Like another person inside her; maybe the person she was before she met the slick one. She got a few little parts, and then, a year ago she was hired by a real company.

'Oh, she was excited. They didn't pay her much; a girl couldn't live on it, let alone two. But she told me it was the beginning. "We're going to get out of here now, Jenny," she told me. "We're going to become decent girls." "*You* are," I said to her. "You're the actress. What can I do? Kill myself in a factory for fifteen hours a day and fall deathly ill for my pains?" "No," she said. "We'll do it little by little. Let's move out of this place first. We'll get a room in a real lodging house, a decent one. We'll get a nice room, Jenny, and no one will know about us. That will be the beginning." "You're crazy," I said to her. "What are we going to live on? Your two shillings a week?" "No," she said, "we'll have to go on working. But not in our room! I know a gentleman that has a flat in London he almost never uses. I think I could get him to lend me a key, and we could go there for work. We'll just pay ordinary rent, Jenny, we won't have to pay the extra – we won't have to work as much. We'll be free agents. And we'll get better from there, you'll see. I'll become a star. And you'll go to the Working Women's College and get an education." That's what she used to say.' She turned back to Mr Archer, and her lip curled. 'Girls like us can dream, too, can't we? And it could have been as she said, except for you.'

'No,' he said, sketching an indefinite gesture with his hand.

'Oh, yes,' she said. 'Because Ivy's old Mr Archer didn't want to give her the key to his London flat, did he, even though she used all of her sweet wiles on him. She was going to give up and look for something else, until his son, that she called *young* Mr Archer, learnt of the story. "Oh, you want the key," said *young* Mr Archer, "well, I'll give it to you on some conditions, and here they are: you never go into any room except the servant's quarters next to the kitchen; you never say a word to Father about this; I'll wire you whenever Father's coming to London, and you clear out of the place at once till he's gone; and you pay me rent." What kind of money do you think we could make that way? Well, I'll tell you. Nothing, or next to it. *Young* Mr Archer needed our money. And young Mr Archer's rent was more than what we made. People like you don't even think we girls are human beings, do you? You look at us, but you don't see us. You see flesh, naked flesh to lust after and to spit on. We don't even have souls to people like you. We're invisible; *our* profession is a screen that hides us. A person can't look at us and see what we are – nothing, ever, except what we *do*. How could you ever know what that feels like?'

'How could I know?' he interrupted, with a sudden flash. 'Do you really think people ever look at *me* and see anything of the man that I am? Don't you see that if anyone in this world can understand what you mean, I am that person?'

She hesitated, struck by his words, but they seemed only to inflame her more.

'So that's why!' she cried. 'It's always a comfort to find worse than yourself, isn't it? Oh, I begged Ivy to get out of it all. I told her it was even worse than the old lodging house. The days when old Mr Archer came to London, sometimes he asked Ivy to stay with him and gave her a few shillings. He was all right, that old man; I met him, he liked Ivy well enough. Thank God he did, because we couldn't work on those days. Sometimes he didn't need Ivy because he had guests or went out. Then we starved. I had to work more than I ever had. Ivy's earnings with the theatre were less than what she could have made by working, and her rehearsals took up hours of the day. I was struggling to pay the two rents by myself. I couldn't take it any more! I begged Ivy to give it up. But she swore that she'd find a solution, that she'd earn more money in the theatre, that we'd find a way. She didn't want to go back to the old house, where the clients came up to our rooms. She wanted to separate her life in two, cut the bad side off from the good side, and make it smaller and smaller until it was gone. And you know, I kept on with it, even though it was harder than it ever had been. I kept on with it because I loved Ivy, and I loved our secret life, that pretty room we shared, with all those nice, ordinary people who had no idea about anything, and the time we spent there, brushing each other's hair, just like two nice girls. And Ivy kept promising me it would get better. She'd make Mr Archer see reason. She'd ask him to lower the rent. She did ask, and you know what he said?' Her demented voice imitated a kind of mincing cruelty as she quoted, '"Oh no, I'm sorry. I can't make it any less. In fact, you haven't been too punctual lately. I might just have to take that key back from you if this goes on."'

'And then Ivy got pregnant,' she went on, without the slightest pretence of obscuring this brutal fact under the euphemisms that we habitually use for it. 'We thought everything was up with us. A few more months and she'd lose both her jobs, plus the baby to keep. She was sick about it. We spent the whole night crying in each other's arms. It was the loss of everything we had gained; back to the mud for me, even worse for her, the loss of her work as an actress. I never saw her so desperate. She went up to Cambridge to see the old gentleman, with some idea of telling him what was happening and begging him for help. He was never a very generous old fellow; he never gave her more than a few shillings, but he was fond of her, and very rich. It seemed like her last chance.

'She stayed away three days and came back radiant. She threw herself in my arms and told me everything was going to be all right. It was better than she could have dreamt of. The old gentleman had given her nothing but a pat on the back and a few coins – but something much, much better had happened. In those three days, Ivy had fallen in love, and someone had fallen in love with her. She'd left desperate, she came back wildly happy. "I love him, Jenny," she told me. "I can't believe it. You wouldn't believe it. Maybe even you wouldn't understand." "Of course I would," I told her. "Except it sounds too good to be true." "It's true," she promised me. "Only we can't tell anyone. It has to be a secret till we're actually married. He's getting a licence – we can marry in a week or two, and then everything will be all right. It will be all right, Jenny! He has some money – not too much, but it'll do. We'll leave all this right behind us and move away." She wouldn't tell me anything more; wouldn't tell me his name, anything about him. But it was like she was walking on air. He wrote to her twice in the next week, telling her the marriage was fixed. I started to believe in this unbelievable piece of luck. Ivy was so beautiful, anything was possible. She'd even told him about the baby. He wanted to adopt it, bring it up as his own. He must have been wild about her. A week later, the old gentleman asked her to come up to Cambridge to host some party of his. "I'll go," she told me, "it's for the day before my wedding, Jenny! It'll be like a goodbye to him. He's been good to me." She never came back. She didn't write or wire. I didn't know anything; I just thought she'd got married, and perhaps the new husband had whisked her off on a honeymoon somewhere. Only I couldn't believe she didn't write to me. I wanted to find her so much that I looked through her letters and read the ones he'd sent her, trying to figure out who he was. But I couldn't tell, I couldn't make out his name and there wasn't an address.

'Then the police came to see me and told me Ivy had been murdered in Cambridge, the very night she went up there. She'd been dead for days and I hadn't known it! Oh, I was sick, there aren't any words for what you feel when you find out that your best, your only friend is dead, and you had no idea. She was on the threshold of her life and she was killed. I tried to think who could have killed her, and why. Then I knew that it must have been the young Mr Archer – him, there, that I had never seen, that I didn't know where he lived. Who else could it have been? Once she didn't need him and his bloody key any more, she could have told everyone about what he'd been doing. She could have told his father, and got him cut off without a shilling. I made sure he'd done it; I swore I would kill him myself. I saved up every penny to buy myself a train ticket; I vowed I'd find out where he lived and kill him with my own hands. It was easy to find out where he lived. I looked in a Directory.'

As though the fact that her story had suddenly reached the present moment, she seemed to remember that she was in Philip Archer's presence. She turned back to him suddenly and stiffened, and raised the knife again. 'I never expected to see a helpless rat like you,' she said. 'But who cares? I'll kill you anyway.'

'You don't understand,' said Philip Archer suddenly. 'You've got it all wrong. I was her fiancé. I was going to marry her.'

His words fell into a stunned silence, that lasted. We both stared at him.

Was it possible?

'You're a liar,' said Jenny Wolcombe. 'Even after Ivy was engaged, she went on hating young Mr Archer. We talked about him – she said she'd *never* speak to him again. I told her we could get revenge, but she said she was too happy now, it would be enough to forget he had ever existed.'

I saw Philip open his mouth and close it again. *Julian*. His own brother.

'I loved her,' he said. 'She was going to marry me. I wrote the letters you found.'

I stepped forward quickly, removing the two letters from my bag, and held them out to him.

'Here they are,' I said. 'You say you wrote these? Can you prove it?'

His forehead flushed as he saw them; he took them from me with a look of unspeakable pain.

'The handwriting?' I said gently. With a gesture of his head, he indicated the writing-table, covered with his manuscripts. Jenny took the letters and moved over to it. I followed her.

The handwriting was Philip's – it was absolutely identical! I had assumed the letters I saw on the hall table were Julian's, when in fact they were Philip's. I had made a horrific mistake, and I reproached myself bitterly, because it had never occurred to me...not for one second, that the ardent lover who wrote passionately to the beautiful girl might have been one and the same as the man who now sat on the sofa in front of me, automatically excluded from my mental image of what a lover should be. I felt ashamed.

'Look at these,' said Philip, reaching into the pocket of his jacket and removing a wallet, from which he extracted three or four small, ill-written notes. Jenny snatched them from him, trembling. All were identical in handwriting to the crumpled letter that little Cedric had found in the armchair in Heffers. All were modest little missives bearing the same essential content – *I can't believe I have found love...I would never have thought it...I thought I had seen too much of men to ever love...this is happening because you are different from all the others...in just a few days I can tell the world that I love you...it happened so quickly that I still can't believe*

*it...yet I believe you...perhaps one has to suffer as you have
to be what you are...your Ivy, your loving Ivy, your Ivy
forever...*

The knife fell to the ground with a clang. No one picked it
up. Jenny let her arms fall to her side.

'It was you?' she said softly. 'You?' She looked down at
him, at his ravaged face. 'But then, I don't understand. Who
killed her? Why did she have to die?'

'Jenny,' I said, 'listen to me. I won't let her killer go free. I'll
find him. I swear it.' *How could the murderer be anyone but
Julian Archer*, I thought, *alibi or no alibi*? But I was afraid to
mention his name. Clearly it had not yet occurred to Miss
Wolcombe that Philip Archer might have a brother, but it
could not be long before she learnt it or thought of it by
herself. I was anxious to avoid this. Such a man should
undergo the full rigour of the law, not swift death by the
violent blade of an angry girl ready to yield her own life in the
taking of his.

'Listen to me,' I said again, with all the calm I could muster.
'I need your help. You have helped me a great deal already by
everything you have told us here. I need to ask you more
questions. I want you to go straight to my house and remain
there. Look; here is the address, and here is some money to
take a cab. Go there and tell my husband or my housekeeper
that I have told you to wait for me. I will come as soon as I
can. You will help me, and we will find the murderer
together.'

I handed her a card, and she took it docilely. Her passion
was entirely spent and she seemed exhausted. Glancing at the
address, she nodded wearily, moved toward the door, passed
through it and reached back to close it behind her. Then she

paused in the doorway and stared back at Philip for a long moment.

'I was wrong,' she said very softly. 'You're the only one who brought her any happiness. Forgive me my words.'

'There is nothing I wouldn't forgive Ivy's friend,' he said. She turned to go, and he buried his face in his hands. It is rare, but there are times when men weep.

1897

As an observer remembered it:

Cowering together against the wind, anxiously attentive, we waited. And suddenly, after the raising of the flag, we perceived the first tickings! Silently and invisibly, the message had been borne across the space from the rocky coast, ferried across by that mysterious medium, the ether

I stood near him, feeling absolutely helpless. What can one say or do in the face of such distress? I stretched out my hand to lay it on his shoulder, then took back the pathetically insignificant gesture. I wanted to talk about Julian, but dared not speak his name.

I remained hesitating for no more than a minute before my thoughts were distracted sharply by the sounds of shouting and turmoil in the street below. I started up at once. I had sent Jenny away, because it seemed urgent to me that she leave before the thought that Philip Archer must have a brother became concrete in her mind, with the possibility of instant verification to hand.

'Get away, get away!' I heard the shouted words outside, 'or we'll call the police! Creatures like you are not wanted here!'

I bounded down the stairs and ran into the street, in time to make out Jenny, running at full tilt and already at the far end of Petty Cury, disappearing around the corner, and a flushed, angry group of customers clustered at the door of Heffers.

'What happened?' I asked.

'A crazy woman came in here and threatened the manager,' was the reply.

'I saw her first,' said a lady. 'She came out of that door right there and stared into the shop window, then she strode in, and went up to him and asked him his name. When he answered, she flung herself at his throat like a wildcat, screaming and scratching!'

'It was all we could do to push her outside,' added another gentleman, pulling down his cuffs and smoothing his hair.

'Like a jilted lover,' said the lady. 'She must be quite mad.'

'Didn't you come out of the same door just now?' someone else suddenly asked. 'Do you know who that woman is?'

'Ah, n-no,' I stammered, deeply dismayed by this turn of events. My confusion and horror was increased by the sight of Julian Archer himself stepping into the doorway of the shop, clearly back from his expedition. His face bore a long, scarlet scratch, but he seemed calm. I stared at him with fascination. I had found this man charming and pleasant; I had not noticed in him the traces of cruelty so perceptible in his father. And they were still as invisible as they had been. His face lit up with a warm smile upon seeing me. I bit my tongue and forced myself to stretch my lips in return; then with a little nod, I turned on my heel and hurried off after Jenny as fast as was seemly and before any awkward questions could be asked.

I made my way home, talking to myself to calm my anxiety. I didn't know if Jenny would have gone to my house or not, but I was afraid of the girl; I thought her mental state dangerous, and feared what she might do both in my house and out of it. I was more certain than ever that Julian Archer must be the murderer, yet still unable to put together a convincing version of the chain of events. At every point in my story there was some little, niggling contradiction necessitating an unrealistic explanation. *How could he have known Ivy was in the bookshop?* He could not have seen her arriving, and from what Jenny had told us, it did not seem possible that she would have exchanged even a word with Julian Archer, let alone arranged a secret meeting. And even if she had accepted such a meeting for some reason (some kind of blackmail?), surely she would not have sat down comfortably to pen a letter to Philip at the very moment she was expecting his brother to enter the shop? What was she doing in the shop at all? Writing a letter and preparing herself to go upstairs and – as was now clear – slip it into the hand of her beloved behind his brother's back, in order to afford him a moment of joy before the morrow.

Reaching home, I hastened inside and found Arthur on the sofa reading the newspaper, no sign of a distraught woman to be seen. Quickly I sat next to him, removed the paper from his hands, set it aside to gain his full attention, and told him the gist of everything that had occurred.

'Arthur, I didn't know what to do with her! I'm afraid she'll do someone a mischief, or get herself hurt,' I said.

'What are *we* to do with her?' he replied with understandable dismay.

'Please watch over her for a day or two, if she comes here,' I said. 'Do not let her wander away by herself. She has realised who Julian Archer is; I believe she realised on her way downstairs that Philip Archer must have a brother – I expected her to see it even sooner. Then she must have spotted him through the shop window and recognised him by his physical similarity to his father, whom she met in London. If she did not thrust her knife into his breast to the hilt then and there, it is only because she had left it upstairs. I am afraid she is stalking him even now. I wish I knew where she was.'

'Is he the girl's murderer?' he asked me.

'Oh, Arthur, I think he must be, but he has a perfect alibi. I don't know what to do! But even if I can prove that he is, she mustn't be allowed to attack him. Keep her from harming him and herself, Arthur. If only she would come here.'

We sat down to dine together; Arthur was exactly as always, but I was unpleasantly tense with waiting. And finally, she came. The knock snapped sharply on the door, I flung it open, and she dropped almost into my arms, dishevelled, exhausted and in a state of mental disturbance bordering on despair.

'You didn't tell me he had a brother,' she said immediately.

'It is not for you to act!' I said severely, preparing a drink for her to which I added a dose of laudanum.

'I waited all this time for him to come out, the rat, but he never did,' she said, trembling. 'It got dark, so I came here. But he won't escape me.'

'You did right to come,' I said gently but firmly, handing her the drink and ringing to ask Mrs Widge to provide her with dinner on a tray, and Sarah to prepare the spare bedroom for her.

Sarah and I got her to bed soon after, and I did not waste much time in following, taking the precaution of leaving the bedroom door open, however, in case she might think of sneaking away during the night. I slept badly, my confused dreams circling obsessively around Julian's alibi, his alibi, his alibi. The alibi came entirely from his brother – well, his brother and the guest – but how tightly did it really hold? Philip had spoken to the police with no inkling of his brother's guilt. Would he now realise that he must think over the evening again? I resolved to visit him again as soon as the morning was reasonably advanced.

I rose early, shaking the night's cobwebs from my brain, and took my early morning tea out into the garden to think. Arthur and Jenny were both still asleep; I could hear Sarah moving about in the nursery. I wanted to wait a little longer before going to see Philip, at least until Arthur should be up and alert to watch over Jenny.

'Miss Duncan!' I started as I heard the bright, eager whisper from some distance away, in the street. If the voice had said 'Vanessa', I might almost have taken it to be Pat in its muffled enthusiasm. I jumped up and approached the garden gate.

'Mr Archer!' I gasped. The old gentleman was standing there, leaning on the gate, peering in.

'So this is where you live?' he said, flashing his toothy leer in my direction. 'I got your address from the Darwins.'

I nodded quickly, awkwardly. It could only be a matter of time before my different identities amongst the members of this circle came to a clash. A matter of time which might easily be reduced to no more than a few seconds, should Sarah happen to emerge into the garden with the twins now, and should they, as they undoubtedly would, run to me calling out 'Mamma!'

'Listen,' he said, 'I came to see if you still meant to come to the Kingstown Regatta with me. It's tomorrow, you remember? I'm taking the train up today. I couldn't get away earlier, but I'll join with a couple of friends there who sailed up in my yacht. It's a wonderful event; you'd enjoy it enormously, you know. You promised you'd manage to get away from here for the day. Do you think you can?'

'Oh,' I said, recalling suddenly that I had indeed made such a promise, at a time when it seemed expedient, and wondering what I ought to do. I looked at Mr Archer, thinking rapidly: Ivy had come straight from *his* house to Heffers – carrying *his* money. So much money – why so much? He had spoken of three pounds, one of the witnesses had said a roll of bank notes; yet Jenny had said he never gave her more than a few shillings. She had gone to the bookshop carrying all that money. Why? Why?

Could the elderly gentleman in front of me have played some part in her death, in some way that I could not yet completely comprehend?

It was not certain, but it was possible; it would have been enough for him to wait for her perfectly natural, voluntary departure from his party, at the hour of her own choice, witnessed by any number of his guests, and then as she left, to communicate the exact time to his son. He would know just how long it would take for her to walk the distance, something very close to half an hour; they must have done it together any number of times. Certainly I knew almost to the minute how long it took me to walk to town from my own house, ten minutes or so nearer than his.

And if he received such a message, Julian would have no need to look out of the window or feel anxious about her arrival; he would know to within a minute or two when she was likely to arrive, he could content himself with slipping downstairs at the right time and either finding her there or waiting for her.

Yet what kind of a message could the father have sent to the son, across a town, instantaneously?

Telepathy?

'Yes, I'll come,' I said abruptly. 'I'm free tomorrow, but I can't get away today. Can I get up there by a night train?'

'Of course,' he said. 'Night express to Liverpool, and early morning ferry over to Dublin. Then there's a short train to Kingstown. Look about for me, my girl; you'll find me easily enough, I think, and if you don't, meet me at the Anchor Hotel at midday.'

'I'll be there!' I promised. 'But oh, please go away now. I'll be in trouble if anybody sees you.' And I cast an anxious glance over my shoulder at the house, which was still silent.

He winked at me and left, to my great relief, and I went inside and found Arthur seated at the dining room table, enjoying coffee, toast and sausages. I extracted his promise to look after Jenny for the next two days. He did not look enthusiastic, but I sketched the situation clearly enough to make him understand that it was no joke, that it might indeed be a matter of extreme danger, and in spite of his obvious doubts, he squeezed my hand and promised not to let her out of his sight. And I scrambled into my boots and snapped off a button with the button-hook, in my haste to return to Petty Cury.

I arrived in front of the flat trembling with haste and anxiety. A glance told me that Julian Archer was already working in the bookshop, and I rang at the door of the flat, pressing myself against the wall in case he should look out. Simpson opened it, and I rushed into the hall and told him that I must speak to Mr Archer at once. He went up, and I followed on his very heels.

Philip was standing at the head of the stairs when I reached the second floor, supported on his crutches. He held out his hand to me, and gripped mine with a grasp full of nervous, bony strength.

'I hoped you would come back,' he said. 'I still don't understand – I need to understand.'

I entered the sitting room, and he struggled after me and sat down in his wheeled chair. I sat on the sofa, and leant towards him. An electric current flowed between us, much stronger than the feeling Sir Oliver had managed to induce in me with all his experiments.

'Mr Archer,' I said, grasping the nettle, 'who murdered Ivy Elliott?'

'Don't you think I've asked myself that question?' he said, his mouth twisted. 'If I could tell you, I would.'

'But you can, can't you?' I said. 'The police say that you gave him a complete alibi.'

'You're talking about *Julian*?' he said, looking up sharply. 'My brother did not kill her – it's impossible! Even if he did do the dreadful, horrible things that Miss Wolcombe told us yesterday, making them work in my father's flat, forcing them to pay him, that doesn't make him a murderer, for God's sake! Not my own brother! Anyway, I *know* he did no such thing. The police told me that she was killed between midnight and one o'clock in the morning of the twenty-second, and he was here with me for that whole evening, and the whole night. He can't have killed her, no!' He stopped for a moment, heaving, looking not unlike a man who has just run a long distance. Suddenly his lips parted and he murmured almost inaudibly, 'And yet...'

'And yet?'

'There is something,' he said. 'I believe now – I am sure – that he had found out about the marriage. Once I found Ivy's letters to me disarranged on my desk, and wondered about him. But I didn't ask, and he never said a word. Still, the more I think about it, the more I am certain that he did know. I know him so well!'

'And you think that would constitute a motive?' I asked gently. 'I mean, a stronger motive than what Miss Wolcombe surmised, that Ivy might tell others about his – his, ah, activities?'

'That wouldn't be a motive at all,' he replied. 'Ivy would never have spoken of all that again once she had got right away from it. She was not vindictive.'

'You may be right,' I said. 'But why would your brother kill her rather than let her marry you?'

'Rather than let *me* marry *her*,' he said bitterly. 'Don't you see? Ivy was expecting a child, who would have become *my* child. A son, perhaps. She was sure it was a little boy.'

'A son?' I repeated slowly, wonderingly. 'A son? To inherit? Do you mean that *your* son would inherit the Archer fortune if Julian did not have a son?'

'No,' he said. 'My son would inherit the Archer fortune in any case. I am the older brother, not Julian.'

I was stunned. Why had I never even thought of this?

'You?' I said. 'But – but Julian talked about the fortune at table...I understood that he was the heir...and I saw his portrait in your father's study at Chippendale House! I thought that only the Archer heirs were painted there.'

'My portrait is there as well,' he replied. 'My father had us both sit for the American, Sargent. He had Julian painted because the doctors told him I might die at any age; according to some, I was not likely to live past the age of twenty-five.'

'Of course!' The portrait I had noticed in Mr Archer's study leapt suddenly out of my memory, as clearly as if it stood again in front of my very eyes. Now I knew why Philip had seemed familiar to me when I first saw him, although so different from his father and brother. I remembered what I had thought of his portrait when I first noticed it. I had thought it the face of a burdened man – burdened by the Archer evil...

'She was desperate when she found out about the child,' he said suddenly. 'She told my father, she told Julian, she begged them for help. She didn't know what to do; she had no money, no one who could help her; she was going to lose the work as an actress that she cherished. She came here to the flat to see Julian – to beg him yet again! I knew her already, of course; I'd seen her often with my father. She was so beautiful...But we had never really spoken together. She had such eyes...She came to see Julian, and he wasn't here, and she talked to me instead; she talked to me for hours; she laid her head on my knees and cried; she told me everything about herself, and I think...I think I told her everything also, about myself...words that I had never before spoken aloud. And I asked her to marry me then, at the end of that afternoon. When I think it was barely more than a month ago. It seems forever.'

He stopped, drew a deep breath and continued.

'We were to be married the very day she died; did you know that? It was all planned. She was to come upstairs in the night, after leaving my father's party. She didn't have any things with her, she didn't want anyone to suspect what she meant to do. She had chosen her Ophelia costume from the theatre for a wedding dress; she didn't possess anything else remotely suitable, and she wouldn't hear of my offering her anything before the wedding – I had enough ado persuading her to accept just a little, simple pearl engagement ring. I would have kept her here for the rest of the night, and first thing in the morning after Julian went down to work, I would have sent Simpson out for something, and she would have helped me get to the church. But she never came. She was killed on her way here, and I only found out about it weeks later, when the police came to tell me. For all that time, I knew nothing of what had become of her; nothing, not one word. I thought that she had just changed her mind, and couldn't bear to tell me. God knows I wasn't even surprised. I thought that she couldn't go through with it – that she couldn't face marrying a – a *thing* like me. After all…no woman could.'

'You are wrong,' I said. 'She could have, and she would have. She loved you. Didn't you hear what Jenny said? Haven't you read her letters? She was going to marry you, and she was killed for it.'

'I loved her,' he said, 'loved her and was in love with her. Strange, isn't it? That can happen even to a man like me. The body is ill, but the heart is just like anyone's heart. After those hours we spent together, I was like a madman. I told her so; she stared at me; I'll never forget her look full of amazement and tears. I didn't want to force her or blackmail her into marrying me out of despair, if she didn't want to of her own free will. I told her I would give her money; I have an allowance of my own, I could have kept her decently. I would have had her child brought up at my expense and never asked anything of her. But I took her hand in mine and told her that if she could accept it, I would marry her. I would adopt her child and make it legitimate. I knew what she felt about men and the love of men, the physical, bodily love; I knew she felt nothing but revulsion. I swore to her that our marriage would be exactly as she wanted; nothing, or everything – or anything. And she told me I was the first man in the whole of her life who had spoken such words to her. I remember what she said – many of those she had taken home with her for money had spoken of love, but not one had ever spoken to her with generosity. I'll treasure every one of her words until I die. I had so few of them! I wanted her – I wanted her child. Can you understand that? I wanted her child, to hold and cherish; I, who will never have a child of my own. That's why we chose not to tell Julian until the thing was done. He's always known that I cannot live long; he had but to wait, and the family fortune would be his. He's known that all his life; he wouldn't have accepted this.'

Julian – his name, inevitably, had reappeared.

'Did the police tell you where she was killed, and what we believe she was doing when she was killed?' I asked him suddenly.

'No,' he said, glancing up at me, surprised. 'I know she was found in the Cam, in the Lammas Land. I didn't know they knew anything about what she was doing when she died.'

'You should know,' I said. 'It concerns you closely. It seems virtually certain now that she was killed in the bookshop just downstairs. I don't know why she went in there or how she had a key, but I believe that she was there, writing a letter to you, which she meant to slip into your hand as she came upstairs a few minutes later, so as not to let your brother hear any special words pass between you. I found her letter to you; she thrust it down into the armchair. I gave it to the police, so I don't have it here, but I can tell you what it said.' And as closely as I could remember, I quoted the words of Ivy's last little note. He bent forwards to catch my words.

'Can I have the letter back?' he asked softly.

'I will get it for you,' I promised him. 'But – now we *must* talk about your brother – I have to ask you the most difficult question of all. Given that Ivy was in the bookshop, do you not think that your brother could have slipped down and killed her there during one of the times that he briefly left the room?'

There was an awful silence. When he spoke, his voice was no more than a low croak.

'It is horrible to say…Julian – my brother! Is it possible? No – it's too horrible.'

It was not enough. I waited, but as he did not speak again, I urged him gently.

'No one knows Julian like you do,' I said. 'No one but you can answer this question: *would he have been capable of it?*'

'I thought he would go to any lengths to prevent my marrying Ivy. I thought it, and feared it, and did everything to hide it,' he admitted. 'He *could* have done it, perhaps – yet no! I told you, he spent the whole evening with me.'

'Except for a few minutes now and then,' I reminded him. 'And she was just downstairs. It would have taken no more.'

'But he couldn't have known she was there!' he said, as though with a last surge of energy in the defence of his brother. 'Even I had no idea she meant to stop down there before coming up here.'

'Couldn't they have planned it between them?' I persisted gently. 'Could he not have asked her to meet him for some reason?'

'Impossible,' he replied. 'Ivy would never have agreed to meet him anywhere, day or night. She hated him; her one desire was never to see him again. I didn't know why, I thought she had some inkling of the difficulties he might put in the way of our marriage; she never told me about my brother's role in her life; I believe she kept silent about it to protect my feelings. But she told me she hated seeing him. And besides, if she had meant to meet him down there secretly, she wouldn't have written to me while waiting for him.'

'I know, I've thought of that,' I admitted. 'Listen, perhaps he did not find out that she was going to the bookshop from Ivy herself. Might it not have been your father who sent her there, and told Julian?'

'My father?' He stopped, stunned, and stared at me. 'Why would my father do that?'

'Why would he send her to Heffers? I don't know, but he could easily have found a pretext. He gave her quite a lot of money before she left his house, a whole roll of bank notes, according to a lady who saw him do it. He admits it, and says it was a gift, but it seems like too much money...'

'She wouldn't have accepted a gift from him, not on that day,' he said. 'She no longer needed it! When she begged him for help the week before, he gave her just ten shillings – and she was in desperate need!' He covered his eyes with his hand.

'Well,' I said, pursuing an idea that had been vaguely in my mind, 'do you think it is possible that he asked her, as a favour, to bring that money to Heffers? Could he have borrowed it and meant to return it, or told her some such story, and lent her the key to get in and put the money there?'

'My father doesn't have the key to the bookshop,' he said weakly.

'Julian could have given it to him,' I said.

'But *why*?'

'To save his son from losing the family fortune to a bastard child...' I said wearily. I hated saying the words, but he *must* know. He stared at me.

'Are you saying that my father would have sent Ivy there on purpose to be killed?'

'I don't know,' I said, unable to speak my honest thought: *yes*!

'It can't be,' he said, echoing the logical objections that hovered in my mind, contradicting my own intuitive conviction. 'Even if Julian gave him the key and knew he meant to send her there during the night, how could he have known exactly when she would be there? He didn't spend his time listening or looking out for her, I swear it. He sat at the piano and played waltzes and...comic songs...' His voice trailed away, trying to reconcile the memory of that cheerful moment with the murder.

I was struck by a sudden revelation. 'The *telephone!*' I shouted suddenly, springing to my feet! 'I've been wondering how your father could have let Julian know exactly when Ivy left his house – just that one detail would make it easy for him to predict her arrival at the bookshop and slip down within a few minutes of the right time! I've been so stupid, thinking about telepathy. Mr Archer – do you have the telephone installed?'

He looked at me blankly, and shook his head.

'No,' he said. 'The shop downstairs has one, but we don't, up here.'

My face fell utterly. 'Is there *any* other way your father could have communicated with your brother on that evening, without leaving his house, without your knowing anything about it?' I said.

He did not answer. He looked utterly wretched.

1898

'They've offered us to cover the Kingstown Regatta in a boat,' he said, showing the letter to Kemp, his eyes dancing. 'Let's do it. It will be the best publicity we've ever had, by far!

Wednesday, July 20th, 1898

The darkness was agitated around me, its peace shattered by the incessant rumble and chug of the train, the rolling movement imparted to the whole of the sleeping car, the sensation of proximity of a world of living humanity enclosed together in a series of wagons, all engaged in the communal business of trying to get some rest, not many, probably, succeeding. The train was the Irish Mail to Holyhead, which after stopping innumerable times to pick up the mail bags suspended for collection alongside the track, disgorged a group of dishevelled and exhausted passengers at the landing stage at the unholy hour of two-thirty in the morning.

I was on my way to the Kingstown Regatta. Mr Archer, who meant to return home in his own yacht, sailed by his friends, had naturally invited me to join him for the trip, but I had pleaded the necessities of my daily life and refused. Spending a festive day in town together was one thing; spending a night enclosed on a boat with no possibility of escape an entirely different one.

The decision to make the trip at all had not been taken lightly. I had thought long and hard, and I continued to do so, interrogating myself pitilessly as I lay, eyes open against the darkness, broken by flashes of light, bumps and shouts, as the train stopped at Harrow, at Hempstead, Bletchley, Nuneaton, Tamworth, Stafford, Rhyl, Bangor.

Logic, reason and Inspector Doherty told me that my entire investigation of the Archers must be a mistake; the alibis were too solid, the instantaneous message that would have solved the mystery remained inconceivable, Sir Oliver's experiments in telepathy had done no more than convince me that the thing was impossible – and the Archers did not possess the telephone. Yet at the very moment when I was wavering, almost convinced by all these objections, Philip had revealed to me an overwhelmingly strong motive for the murder, of which I had suspected nothing. And Ivy had been killed in Heffers, or at least I was convinced that it was so. Then how could the Archers be unconnected with her killing?

I promised myself that this trip to Dublin represented my very last, final attempt at finding out the truth. If the Archers were guilty, I must discover it *now*, and if I failed, I must accept their innocence and either search for the murderer elsewhere against all my intuition, or give up the search altogether. Coming here at all seemed tremendously dangerous. If Mr Archer were guilty, then by questioning him too closely, I risked making myself suspicious to him. If he were innocent, then it was a frightening risk to go away leaving Jenny behind; Jenny, in the same town as Julian Archer, aware now of his role in her past life, filled with hatred and violent fury. Whatever I undertook seemed fraught with danger.

The sky was dark and cloudy when the train pulled into Holyhead. My eyes, which had firmly refused to shut for the entire duration of the journey, now protested vigorously at the necessity of remaining open. The other passengers and I trudged across the landing stage that floated along the banks of the Irish Sea and embarked on the Royal Mail Steamer. For several hours, I lay in a berth in the ladies' cabin, snatches of dreams mingling in my mind with moments of waking during which I perceived the slowly lightening sky through the porthole. Towards seven o'clock I gave up all pretence of sleeping and went above onto the deck.

The sight of the sea, infinite and twinkling, reflecting even the meagrest morsels of sunlight accorded to its purling surface, moved and awakened me to the sense of the largeness of the world. My own task gained in sharpness and perspective. I suddenly realised that outside the necessary contact with Mr Archer, the regatta might turn out to be one of the unforgettable travelling experiences of my life. I know nothing about boating, but who cannot be struck with admiration at the sight of a splendid yacht, manned by expert sailors exhibiting the kind of rapid, precise motion that one usually expects from horses or acrobats? I found myself looking forward with eager purpose to the coming day, and my sense of purpose began to share space in my breast with a sense of impending beauty and excitement.

The little train from Dublin to Kingstown, the first railway constructed on Irish soil, revealed to me a landscape whose dominant colour was a vivid green, produced, I thought sadly, by an enormous quantity of rainfall, which we were not absolutely certain to avoid that very day, since the sky overhead was becoming increasingly grey as the train progressed through the countryside. The ride was short; no more than six or seven miles later all passengers were invited to alight, and I found myself in Kingstown.

It was unmistakably a festival day, reminiscent of Ascot. The crowd that milled in the streets surrounding the port were dressed in clothes so elegant and fashionable that my own carefully chosen muslin gown and bonnet appeared countrified and even, in spite of my best efforts, slightly wrinkled. I smoothed out my skirts as well as I could, adjusted my shawl and proceeded to the Anchor Hotel.

It took some courage before I could persuade myself to enter, but when I did, I saw that the dark, quiet interior contained almost no clients, and my awkward shyness diminished. Mr Archer was nowhere to be seen, as it was still long before midday, but a kind gentleman pointed the way to the port, and told me that everyone had already gone there, as the race was about to begin.

The scene on the docks was impressive. A throng of passionate spectators crowded together so solidly that the sea was invisible behind them; their hats and umbrellas formed a screen impenetrable even to the tallest viewer. The jostling was indescribable, and only the masts of the boats could be perceived. The tall lamp posts surrounding the area in front of the dock were all covered with clinging and climbing boys, and these served as the only useful source of information about what was happening on the water.

'They're off for the Queen's Cup!' a voice cried; a general shout went up, and the boats sailed away – but only, as I soon understood, to take up their starting positions for the first race. This placing in position took up what seemed an immense amount of time, which was relieved by the boys on the lamp posts shouting out descriptions of the boats as they manoeuvred. Finally, when I had tired of moving around the edge of the crowd, waiting and trying unsuccessfully to find a loophole through which I could perceive the water, I heard the report of a gun, and knew the race had begun. I gave up on the waterfront altogether and moved to the outskirts of the crowd, hoping to hear something interesting, at least. But no.

'There's too much fog,' shouted the boys to the people massed below. 'We can't see a thing – they're already out of sight! If there's as much fog out to sea, they'll have to cancel the whole race!'

A collective groan went up from the rearguard formed by those, like myself, unable to push to the front of the crowd. But our disappointment was certainly less than that felt by the people who had struggled to obtain the best viewing places for the start of the race, some of them by arriving, with campstools, in the dark that precedes the dawn. Murmurs of discontent were heard from all sides, and there were some movements of departure.

Half an hour later, the crowd had thinned considerably, as people went off to console themselves with promenades or drinks, in the hopes that the mist would soon lift and that some distant trace of the boats could be made out with telescopes, or at least their return perceived. It was then that I spotted Mr Archer, standing amongst his friends, one of the last of the faithful, still eagerly peering out to sea. And as the crowd dissolved, I saw that the fog rendered it impossible to see the departing boats, even though they were probably still not out of sight of the starting point.

'Goodness, what fog,' I exclaimed, as I joined him. 'I wonder how the sailors can see to sail!'

'Miss Duncan!' he exclaimed, greeting me with more warmth than I might have wished. 'So you have managed to join us! This is delightful! I hardly dared hope!'

I applied a look of enthusiasm to my face.

'I wouldn't have missed this for worlds!' I assured him. Then, glancing out over the sea, I modified, 'At least, I didn't expect it would be like this.'

'The weather is rather unfortunate,' he agreed. 'And if the sailors cannot see to sail, they will have to put it off until tomorrow. But we may hope that there is little or no fog twenty miles out. It is difficult to know what is happening – quite a mystery! Well, let us make the best of it, now that you are here. Munroe, let me introduce you to my charming friend Miss Duncan. Miss Duncan, Mr Munroe, and Miss Eaglehurst.

Miss Eaglehurst was a young woman who corresponded physically much better to the type I was pretending to be than I did myself. Young and pretty, but tainted by a brash and forward manner, she shook my hand boldly. Apparently this young woman was beyond the need for a chaperone, unless, indeed, we could be considered to be chaperoning each other. But perhaps the mores and customs of the yachting world are different from those of the towns and villages, and chaperones are not considered necessary. As incorrect as I was well aware my own situation to be, Miss Eaglehurst's was certainly much worse, since she had obviously come there together with Mr Munroe on the yacht. I hoped that Mr Archer was not going to renew his suggestion that I join him on it for the trip home, fingered my return ticket within my glove, and set myself to be as charming as he had announced me to be.

'Do let's take a turn; there's nothing to see here,' said Miss Eaglehurst in a rather petulant voice.

'My dear girl, the fog may lift at any moment,' replied Mr Archer optimistically. But his companion was less confident.

'Oh, let's go,' he said, drawing the woman away on his arm. 'We can come back soon enough, but in any case there's nothing to see when the boats are distant. At any rate, we'll all meet for luncheon at one, shall we?' And they moved away, leaving me uncomfortably alone.

'Well, well,' said Mr Archer, instantly taking advantage of their departure to lay his hand undesirably upon my shoulder. 'So here we are, are we?'

'Oh, yes,' I said, adopting a hypocritical look once and for all and willing myself not to depart from it even for a second. 'How lucky you are, to come to such interesting events every year, and several times a year.'

'Today is not the best example,' he said, 'although it might improve. Last year was much more splendid, with coloured flags waving from all the masts.'

'Oh—' I said, 'but last year, you weren't here with me. Still, I'll wager you weren't alone. Don't lie now; I know you are very naughty, aren't you? You must have been here with some other lady!'

'I was,' he said, pretending not to like having to admit it, but showing his pleased vanity clearly enough.

'Was it the actress you told me about?' I said, pouting jealously, and hoping I was not proceeding too quickly, too obviously.

'Yes it was, as a matter of fact,' he answered briefly, and a shadow crossed his face. He did not much want to talk about her, that was clear. My task was not going to be especially easy. Now that I had broached the subject, I thought that I had better forge ahead with it, for coming back to it later on might seem even more annoying and suspicious.

'Oh dear,' I said, 'I feel bad at taking the place which

legitimately belongs to someone who died.'

'It's not your fault,' he replied shortly.

'Of *course* not,' I assented, fluttering my eyelashes. 'It's just sad. It isn't my fault or *your* fault, either, that she died.'

I scrutinised him intently from under the brim of my hat as I pronounced these daring words, wondering if the slightest sign of awareness or knowledge might not flash however briefly across his face. I did not expect him to turn towards me, suddenly black with fury, and shout,

'Shut up, you imbecile!'

'Oh,' I said, stepping backwards and covering my mouth with my hands. There was a time when I had clearly suspected *him* of being the murderer. The idea came back to me sharply now. A frightening look shone from his eyes.

'I am so sorry,' I said quickly, soothingly. 'Here I am, causing you pain by reminding you of it, when I should be helping to offer you a lovely, pleasant day. Please forgive me. Let us talk of other things.' And I went so far, in my fear, as to lay my hand upon his arm.

'Yes,' he agreed, recovering his calm and squeezing my gloved fingers. 'You're upsetting me, harping on about that.' He paused, then forced a smile, in an attempt to erase the negative impression his violence had left upon me. Then he leant towards me, and the smile converted itself into his usual strange leer, which always made me feel just a little bit like a piece of red meat.

I stared at him, fascinated as though by a serpent, and suffered him to provide me with an unwelcome caress, only pushing him away after a moment to remark feebly that 'people will see us'. He appeared aware that although but few people were left on the docks, they were not of the sort that one might freely offend. We were surrounded by proper ladies, families with children in stiff frocks, monocled aristocrats and elegant dandies. The number of little boys in sailor suits was quite a bit larger even than the number one usually sees about the streets, and several little girls were wearing sailor-type collars over the shoulders of their navy-and-white dresses. Their image imprinted itself on my retina as though I were watching them through a glass. On the far side of the glass, the gay throng pressed in the streets to participate in the festivities. On my side, the inner side, a different scene proceeded: Mr Archer, asking Ivy to get him out of a scrape, by putting some money back into the till at Heffers before its loss was noticed. Ivy assenting willingly, used to rendering service, pleased to make a last gesture for the man who had at least treated her with kindness. And then, Mr Archer waiting calmly until she expressed the desire to leave – no hurry, no pressure – handing her a roll of bank notes, closing the door behind her, glancing at his watch, and then – then *what*?

Philip had claimed there was no telephone in the flat. But he had said there was one in the shop below. Could a wire not be brought upstairs? If the elderly gentleman had one in the manor, then might one not believe that it had somehow been done so?

'Mr Archer,' I said suddenly, 'I know you're very interested in machines. I wanted to ask you – do you have the telephone at home?'

'No, I haven't had one installed,' he said, surprised at my odd question. 'The Darwins have, though; they were one of the very first families in Cambridge to get it. Number 10, I believe they are, and they highly recommend it.'

'Do they? And what do *you* think?' I improvised quickly. 'I wanted to ask your advice, because my parents were wondering if it would be a useful thing to have, and not too difficult or peculiar to use.'

'Well,' he replied, 'it certainly isn't difficult. And it's absolutely fascinating, technologically speaking. But as to usefulness, it has its disadvantages, I find. As far as calling the tradespeople is concerned, they come to the house for their orders and deliveries, and for anything particular, I have servants who can just as well go and call upon them. And for any private communication, I prefer the post. There's no privacy over the telephone, you know. The girl at the Exchange hears everything, to say nothing of other families, if you have a party line. It doesn't tempt me.'

'I wonder what it is really like to live with the thing,' I said. 'It is strange to think that a girl one doesn't even know can listen to everything one is saying. Do you mean that a telephone call can never be secret in any way?'

'Not even the fact that you made one,' he answered, with a smile that struck me as smug.

The flame of hope that had suddenly awoken in me died down. Not only was every telephone in Cambridge apparently registered by number, so that it would be impossible to hide the fact of owning one, but the girl at the Exchange would know about and quite possibly remember precisely any call that had been made. One could not be sure that she would remember, of course, but the risk was far too great for him to have even considered using such a method.

Then *what*? What had he done?

'Let's do like Munroe,' said Mr Archer, becoming impatient with my thoughtful silence and pulling me by the arm. 'We'll take a turn and see what's happening in the streets.'

It was after a long time of strolling about the streets and lanes, punctuated by a pleasant cup of tea, that we began to notice that a large portion of the crowd that had previously been at the water's edge was now headed inland, seemingly all in the same direction. A little automatically, we took to following them.

The moving stream thickened as we advanced, and there was a sense of expectation. The few people we crossed who were coming the other way were in animated conversation.

'It's some kind of hoax,' said a man who passed us, speaking loudly, 'to keep people from becoming bored with the whole race because they can't see it.'

'I wonder what's happening?' I said. 'Shall we follow all these people and find out what the hoax might be?'

Mr Archer merely smiled enigmatically.

After just a few moments, we discovered the place where the stream of people had converged into an excited, milling pool. They all stood in front of a long, low, cream-coloured building, elegantly built in the style of a Palladian villa, its two Ionic porticoes linked by a colonnade, which ran down a great length of the street. People were pressing and crowding under the porticoes, in front of the enormous windows giving out on them. The words

Royal St George Yacht Club
Founded 1838

were emblazoned over the main entrance, which was further decorated with a triangular flag, red with a white cross in the centre of which was a crown.

Starting on the fringe, we worked our way forwards as people looked and departed, until we finally reached the window which was the main feature of attraction. As it came into my field of vision, I saw a young man adding, from the inside, a piece of paper to a long column of papers already gummed to the pane. The top paper read

Queen's Cup Reporting
By The Irish Daily Express

Underneath was a list of handwritten messages describing the progress of the yachts in the race. Mr Archer began to read them eagerly.

10:55 The RAINBOW having crossed the line before the gun was fired was recalled thereby losing 3 1/4 minutes,

stated the first one. All were brief, technically worded descriptions of the movements of the various boats.

11:00 Time round Rosberg buoy: AILSA 10:54, BONA 10:54:33, ISOLDE 10:58, RAINBOW 10:59:10, ASTRILD 10:59:42

11:15 The AILSA stayed, and went away on the port tack, as did also the ASTRILD. After going a short distance the BONA also stayed, following the example of the other two.

11:36 The RAINBOW and the ISOLDE standing in under Howth.

11:55 Yachts heading for Kish BONA leading by five minutes, AILSA second, RAINBOW 3rd, ISOLDE 4th and ASTRILD last. Breeze freshening

12:5   BONA had to go about unable to fetch ship but still leading. ASTRILD ahead of ISOLDE.

12:13 BONA rounded Kish

12:17:29 AILSA rounded

12: 24:29 RAINBOW turned the lightship

12:36:41 ISOLDE rounded

12:45:42 ASTRILD following

'And it's nearly one o'clock now,' said Mr Archer, taking out his watch and glancing at it. 'They'll be more than an hour finishing the loop and starting the second round. Let's go get something to eat, shall we? We're to meet the others at a very nice little place – you'll like it.'

'I should love to,' I said. 'But do tell me how the Yacht Club can know all this, when nobody can see anything?'

'They've got a boat out there watching,' he said shortly.

'But...' I stopped, staring at him, my heart pumping suddenly. 'But...but how can the boat out there tell the people here what is going on?'

He hesitated, but before he could say anything, a lady standing near me, wearing a very large hat decorated with ostrich feathers, intervened excitedly. 'Don't you know?' she asked. 'Why, this is the work of the Italian boy genius Marconi. Don't say you haven't heard about his astounding discovery? It's been in all the papers!'

I felt Mr Archer pulling on my arm, and a tiny alarm seemed to go off inside me. I wanted to know about Marconi – the name, already, reminded me of something – and I felt that Mr Archer did not want me to know. I resisted his pressure, and opened my mouth to put some questions to my informative neighbour, but I was forestalled by a gentleman standing close by.

'Nonsense,' he said. 'It's all nothing but a great trick to keep us busy till the boats come in! Messages transmitted from the water twenty miles away! What will they expect us to believe next?'

'I read that they are transmitted by waves travelling through the ether,' cried the lady.

I felt a great shock of disappointment. The ether – why, Arthur had told me that modern physicists no longer believed that it even existed! This was no better than Sir Oliver. I shrugged gloomily, and followed Mr Archer.

'Then it really is some great hoax?' I said to him as we emerged into the street, in which the mist was lifting slowly, allowing glimmers of pale sunshine to seep through.

'Oh, I don't know,' he said brusquely. 'We'll see what is going on later on. It's sure to be better by two or three. The Queen's Cup will not be over until after four o'clock, so we'll have plenty of time to go back down to the waterfront to watch the end. Do you like oysters?'

I admitted to a fondness for oysters, and allowed myself to be taken to a open-air restaurant looking directly out over the water. Mr Munroe and his lady friend were standing in front of it already, waiting for us. We were seated together at a table for four, and oysters duly arrived, followed by cod, Atlantic salmon and halibut. Mr Archer order conger eel.

'We've been on a ramble,' said Mr Munroe. 'Can't see a thing. Dead boring.'

I wanted to ask him if he had seen the messages at the Yacht Club, but I felt that the subject annoyed Mr Archer, perhaps because of the foolishness or pretence surrounding an activity to which he clearly attributed the highest importance. However, I soon became aware that two gentlemen at the table next to ours were discussing nothing other than that precise topic. Showing nothing, keeping up a light flow of conversation, I lent an ear to their words over the clink and scrape of glasses and forks.

'The Flying Huntress is a good little tug,' remarked the elder of the two, who was elegantly dressed in summer flannels and wore a close-cut beard. 'Marconi did well to choose her. He's a good sailor; he and his assistant will be able to follow the manoeuvres as accurately as it's possible to think of doing.'

'Yes, we're in luck,' replied the other. 'Marconi knows as much about yachting as any good amateur; he and his assistant can handle the sailing, the messages and the transmission all by themselves.'

'And know what to write,' said the first. 'Not that he couldn't have taken an expert on board if he'd needed to. But he's a loner, that fellow. Have you ever met him?'

'No, have you?'

'Once, at Cowes. The fellow's a regular yachting maniac. He'll change the future of yacht races with this system of his. It was a splendid idea of the paper's, hiring him to report on the race. And they've got even more than they bargained for. They couldn't possibly have guessed how foggy it would be.'

'They say it's all for the best,' said the bearded gentleman. 'His system works better in fog and stormy weather, so I've heard. Something to do with conductivity. I wonder what's happening now? Just look at the time – they'll be well into the Sovereign's, and the Queen's will be starting the second round. Let's go and get some news.'

They paid, rose and left, leaving me filled with an odd confusion, increased by the impossibility of thinking clearly and calmly while sitting at a white-clothed table, covered with dishes containing the bony remains of aquatic creatures, together with a man who might or might not be the father of a murderer, a lady who had very clearly applied rouge to her cheeks and redness to her lips, and her swain who clapped his hand too familiarly upon her arm and drank at least four glasses of wine during the meal. The gentlemen at the neighbouring table took the messages *seriously* – and they continually mentioned *Marconi*. And the name appeared familiar to me. But where had I seen or heard it before?

A creamy syllabub concluded the meal. Mr Archer summoned the waiter with a lordly gesture and paid the bill, while I tried to pretend that this was perfectly normal and not a shameful and inadmissible proceeding which I would never dare to admit to any human soul. I felt more uncomfortable than I ever had, for money spent in one's favour creates a debt towards the spender which is more dreadfully difficult to erase or forget than that created by words, smiles or even (Heaven forbid!) kisses. It was a relief when we arose and made our way back to the dock, but a disappointment to find that although the fog had turned to no more than a light mist inland, the worst of it appeared to have drifted out to sea, so that the horizon was still as invisible as before.

'What shall we do?' complained Mr Munroe, 'We're not going to stay here, are we? Why, we might as well be lying in bed!'

'Let's go back to the Yacht Club and look at the messages,' I suggested quickly. 'If you want to know how the race is going, you can find it out from there.'

He did not know about them. 'What are you talking about?' he asked me, surprised.

'They have information on the course of the race, that they are putting up on the front window for all to see,' I said. 'We were there just before lunch.'

'What is this cock-and-bull story?' asked Mr Munroe, turning towards Mr Archer.

'I don't know the details,' he replied. 'She's correct that there are messages proclaiming the progress of the race, though I don't know how accurate they can be.'

'Well, let's go and see!' exclaimed Mr Munroe. 'It's almost three o'clock; the race is practically over anyway.' He turned on his heel, and off we went, the four of us, back in the direction of the Yacht Club.

The list of messages on the door had become considerably longer, and another list had been started next to it, this one giving the progress of the Sovereign's Cup race, which had started some two hours later than the Queen's.

2:13:13   BONA rounded Rosberg, standing on

2:20:22   AILSA

2:28:50	RAINBOW gone about starboard tack
2:44:30	ISOLDE rounded. The vessels are very much scattered. BONA alone about on the port tack with a very long lead.

'What do you make of all this?' exclaimed Mr Munroe, with real amazement, when we had worked our way to the window and read over everything from the beginning.

I was beginning to answer him by some reference to the scientific impossibility of such a thing, but he had quite other ideas in his mind. Turning towards Mr Archer and gesticulating with annoyance, he cried,

'Why, it says here that Bona's ahead by seven minutes or more! I was certain Astrild couldn't fail this year – she's been so completely overhauled I thought she was primed to win!'

'Astrild looks to be last,' laughed Mr Archer. 'Better luck next time, old fellow.'

The young employee of the Yacht Club, wearing his smart cap and buttons, appeared behind the window holding a rather large sheet and placed it carefully below the preceding one.

3:16 BONA keeps spinning out her lead turning to windward in the smooth water and barring flukes she may fairly calculate on winning the Queen's Cup. Coming up to the Kish on the second round although there was more wind the sea was lighter and more suitable therefore for the smaller boats. BONA has rounded Kish, holding a 20-minute lead.

'Twenty minutes! It's all over,' said Mr Munroe.

'Let's go back and see if we can see the boats coming around for the finish,' said Miss Eaglehurst. 'I'm sure the fog is gone by now, aren't you?'

A great many other people had the same idea. Parasols went up in the street as a more and more shafts of sunlight pierced through the mass of grey clouds.

'If they only rounded Kish ten minutes ago, they won't be coming in for another half an hour,' said Mr Munroe.

'No, but if the fog keeps thinning we'll be able to see them when they're still quite far out. In fact, I wonder if we can't make them out already,' replied Mr Archer, as we came in sight of the sea. 'Look, Munroe. Can't you see those moving shadows way over there?'

'Yes, by Heaven, I think you're right!' he exclaimed, and the cry was taken up by a hundred voices and as many pointing fingers. Ten minutes later the first of the returning boats was clearly visible. Comments burst forth all around me.

'It's the Bona,' said someone. 'But which is the second boat? I don't recognise it.'

'It isn't a yacht,' someone else answered. 'Look, you can see it now. It's just a tug.'

'Oh, that must be the Flying Huntress, following the race! Yes, there it comes. Just look at the mast!'

'Seventy-five feet it must be. That's where the wires are. It has to be so high, they say, to transmit over ten or twenty miles. For a mile or two you don't need nearly so much.'

'Wires? Does he use wires? But they call it *wireless transmission*, don't they?' exclaimed another voice.

'Do you mean to say it's true?' said a lady who stood so

near me that the fragrance of the fresh violets she wore in her corsage wafted across my face, mixed with the strong, salty, fishy odour of the sea water and all the other nameless odours of the throng. 'Do you mean to say it wasn't all a big joke, those messages on the Yacht Club window?'

'Of course not,' replied a man near her. 'It's perfectly real! The messages are sent in Morse code, by electrical impulses which go up the wire there and out into the air, where they are captured by another wire set up in a tree next to the Yacht Club. The wire is connected to a Morse printer that reads the electrical impulses that come down it, and the messages are then copied out in longhand and handed to the Yacht Club and to the *Irish Daily Express*. The newspaper ordered up the whole operation. Oh, Marconi's fame is going to multiply by a hundred after this publicity!'

All grew dark before my eyes. The sensation of loss of consciousness, of fainting, was so powerful that I believed I *had* fainted, and was almost surprised when my vision returned, no more at first than a little hole in the centre of which the Flying Huntress rose and fell on the waves. Two young men were now discernible on the boat; one was working at a machine set up on a table, and the other peered at the Bona, and then at the boats which were following behind, and made notes. A great cry went up from the crowd as the boat passed the finish. But it was not the Bona which was being thus acclaimed.

'MARCONI! We want MARCONI!' went up from every throat, and the applause swelled into a great thunder as the tugboat approached the dock and the smaller of the two young men stood on deck, waving at the people. A gaggle of journalists wriggled their way to the forefront of the crowd and began shouting questions at him before he was within earshot.

And in my mind, everything suddenly came together in a dreadful picture, terrifying in its simple completeness.

The wire in the tree!

A wireless transmitter: whatever that was, it was the machine which stood on the table on the deck of the boat now floating before me. And Mr Archer had one of them in his house. Of this I was now as certain as if I had seen it at work.

The *Marconi Company*; I remembered now that I had seen that name on the list of the companies in which he invested! Mr Archer, fascinated by all new technological inventions, had invested in the Marconi Company before the general public had even heard about it, and learnt all the details of the existence of this strange, incredible, unheard-of machine. Mr Archer was supposed to possess an immense talent for choosing intelligent investments. In this one, he had apparently surpassed himself.

The crowd pressed thickly forward, hats were thrown in the air, parasols were waved, and the man called Marconi was hailed as a triumphant victor and welcomed to land on the shoulders of a crowd so excited by his prowess that the skipper of the Bona stepped off his ship onto the dock practically unnoticed. With great aplomb, however, he shouldered his way to where Marconi was being celebrated and interviewed, moved up to him, and shook his hand, offering a great smile to the photographers as he did so.

I stared transfixed at the man who had succeeded in realising what Sir Oliver had made sound nothing more than a myth on the level of fairies and spiritualism séances. He had sent messages over the sea, through the air, from one wire to another; messages which had been encoded and decrypted, and then read and understood by hundreds or thousands of people. He had accomplished something which seemed but a dream. And there he stood, astonishingly young, barely more than twenty, his fair hair slicked back, his fine-featured face serious one moment, laughing boyishly the next.

There was no doubt about it: Marconi's invention was more important than the boat race, more mysterious than telepathy, more powerful than the telephone, more astonishing even than electricity. For telephones and electricity run along wires, and our human brain is capable of comprehending transmission along a concrete object linking us to our destination. But wireless transmission – waves travelling, whether it be through the ether, through the air, or through absolute nothingness – *this* was something which, it seemed to me, would change the future of the world more than any of those.

The magnitude of the discovery thus revealed to me was so exhilarating, that it took many long minutes before I came to the realisation that I was finally in possession of the undoubted truth about Ivy's death. I stared at Mr Archer as he gazed out over the sea, watching the slower boats arriving. He had pretended all day that he knew nothing about the wireless transmission. He had lied – but it would be easy to get proof!

Without attracting his attention, I slipped off through the close-packed crowd and made my way along the streets to Kingstown's little station, where I boarded the first train to Dublin. I had only one idea in my mind: I must return to Cambridge instantly, at once, now. There was no time to be lost.

July 1898

Telegram for Guglielmo Marconi:
 Urgent Her Majesty Queen Victoria having been informed of recent success of wireless transmission requests immediate wireless service communication between Osborne House and royal yacht where HRH the Prince of Wales is recuperating after knee surgery.

MARCONI TRIUMPHS:
TRANSMITS MESSAGE OVER TWENTY-FIVE MILES

Telegram for Guglielmo Marconi:
 Have heard of astonishing accomplishment re reporting Kingstown Regatta New York Herald would like to request similar reporting service for upcoming America's Cup next autumn

Telegram for G. Marconi, President, Marconi Company:
 Construction of receiving station for cross-channel communication proceeding as planned in Wimereux near Boulogne stop first experiments in cross-channel transmission should be possible within six months

SHIP TO SHORE COMMUNICATION MADE
POSSIBLE BY INCREDIBLE MARCONI
WIRELESS APPARATUS

US Navy commander considering installing Marconi apparatus on all ships if cost can be kept reasonable
MARCONI'S FANTASTIC DISCOVERY
ENDS THE ISOLATION OF THE SEA!

Stumbling in my haste and silently upbraiding my carpet-bag, which had struck me as eminently light and manageable upon the outward journey, but had now turned into a heavy and cumbersome burden. The short trip to Dublin passed quickly, but I missed the connection to Dun Loaghaire, and thereby the last steamer of the evening. The employees behind their counters looked upon me with sympathy as I tried to explain that I must return to England instantly. There was a steamer at seven in the morning, they told me. That was sufficiently early, was it not? I fretted and fumed, but there was nothing for it, so I took the last train for Dun Loaghaire, and dined late in a small hotel near the dock, where the lady was kind enough to give me a room for the night and promise to send a maid to call me at six. Of course I woke up one thousand times during the night to look at my watch, but was sleeping soundly when the rap came on the door at first light. I had to hurry madly to call for hot water, prepare myself and purchase my ticket, and finally flung myself onto the gangplank at the last possible moment; it was removed for departure almost from under my very feet as I rushed up it. I dropped exhausted onto the deck and wondered why time seemed to alternate continually between rushing headlong and stopping altogether. The morning rose bright and beautiful as we moved out over the water. It seemed forever until we reached Holyhead, and I hastened to the ticket window, then stood in a long queue, and finally asked the man the quickest way for me to get back to Cambridge. He took out a book of timetables and made some calculations.

'You wouldn't necessarily think it, ma'am,' he said finally, 'but you'd do best to take the Day Mail to London and go from there. It leaves at twelve-thirty, and will get you into Euston Station before six o'clock. You'll have to take the Circle Line to Liverpool Street – you won't find a cab available at that hour – and catch the train up to Cambridge.'

I couldn't possibly arrive before the evening! I grimaced with annoyance, then smoothed out my face and purchased my ticket with as pleasant a face as I could muster. It was the knowledge I now held which gave me such distress, such tension and such a need for hurry: the knowledge, and my enforced silence. Even though I knew that a few hours of delay could make but little difference, I felt that I could not bear the knowledge all by myself; I was driven by the need to share it without delay, in order to remove some of the dreadful burden from my shoulders.

Just thinking about Julian Archer caused me to burn inside. He had been disporting himself cheerfully for weeks since the murder, smiling and gay, apparently, even on the very *night* of the murder, and every further minute that he spent in liberty now struck me as a debt he owed to Death itself.

A debt which could no longer be left unpaid.

I believe I have never felt a horror or enmity for any human being as powerful as that which I felt for Julian Archer, while I sat motionless, my teeth clenched, hour after hour on the rhythmically shaking train. Every smile, every laugh, every dashing gesture or pleasant word I had seen or heard from him became tainted, in hindsight, with the horror of cold-blooded murder. I hated him and I was angry with myself for having thought him quite likeable. I remembered the first time I had seen him, when I stepped into Heffers full of my question about the old gentleman with the silver-topped cane. I remembered noticing his kindness and courtesy as he helped the customers, and thought that Ivy was already dead, and his heart already full of the secret horror. For the first time in my life, I desired to see a man arrested, tried, and condemned.

Not one man, but two. A father and son as diabolical as the mind can contemplate.

My mind turned over and over these thoughts with the persistence of a nightmare, till I ended by dozing off. I was awakened by the sound of bustle and argument about me. The passengers in my compartment were in the process of being told by a conductor with a most deprecating expression on his face that no specific duration could be given to the delay, which was due to a technological problem.

'We'll be going when they've mended it,' he was saying for the fourth time as I came fully to myself. 'No, ma'am, I cannot tell you when that will be.'

A glance out of the window told me that we had stopped at Rugby. So near Cambridge – a mere sixty or seventy miles, I thought – and yet so far! Oh, why was there no direct train from Rugby to Cambridge?

Like the other passengers, I descended onto the platform and took to walking up and down, trying to get some idea of the progress of the work that a group of men were engaged in about the locomotive. Nearly an hour passed as I fumed and fretted, and then something happened. The stationmaster was hastening along the platform, holding something out – to me? No, to a woman standing near me, in the grip of an impatience as frenetic as my own.

'An answer to my telegram?' she said, snatching it from his hand and reading quickly over the contents. 'Oh, thank God!' And she hastened towards the barrier, while I followed her, curious to see what she had arranged.

She waited for some moments at the barrier, and then a couple arrived, and came towards her, nearly running.

'Oh, I think the train has stopped forever!' she moaned.

'It's all right,' said the man, 'everything is arranged. We've got as good a pair as you could wish for to start off with, and my man is arranging the relays as we talk. We'll have you there sooner than you could have arrived by train to Cambridge and then the carriage afterwards.'

She flung her arms around his neck with a sob. 'Oh, thank you,' she said, 'I am so frightened, so frightened of arriving too late! Oh, you are so good to me. How can I thank you enough? But it's such a long way to go there and come back. How will you do it?'

'We'll leave you in Huntingdon and spend the night in Cambridge, with friends,' said this blessed gentleman, as she gave up her ticket and passed through the barrier to join his wife and him. 'It's nothing, my dear. Don't put yourself out. Richard is ill, and of course we'll do anything we can to get you to him quickly! Come along outside now. We ought to leave this very minute.'

'Wait!' I cried in a panic, giving up my ticket and swinging past the barrier to run up behind them as they moved quickly away. 'Wait, please! Are you really going to Cambridge? Can you take me with you, please? I'm in the same situation as you are – I *must* get there tonight!'

Their natural reluctance to suddenly adopt a total stranger for a journey of several hours in necessarily rather intimate conditions was, I believe, shunted aside by their own preoccupation and haste. It would have taken them longer to explain politely to me why this was not possible than it did to simply accede to my request. In less than two minutes, therefore, I found myself seated in a handsome brougham, assenting with almost excessive eagerness to the gentleman's explanation that he must leave his sister at the house where her husband lay grievously ill, and that our arrival in Cambridge would necessarily be somewhat delayed. After some discussion of our relative destinations, they agreed to drop me at my home, and I settled into my corner and remained more or less silent for the remainder of the journey, while the sister, sister-in-law and brother analysed and prognosticated over the symptoms of the sick man. At any other time, such a conversation would have held much to interest me, as do all human affairs. But under the present conditions, Richard's inflammations were as foreign to me as if he were suffering from them in far-away China. I was walled up within myself, and had to force myself to make what friendly conversation I could, as we stopped various times to change the horses, and once, rather late in the evening, when our host insisted absolutely on his wife and his sister taking some dinner at the inn. At any other time, such a pleasant and unusual adventure would have been most delightful to me, and the succulent dishes which were laid before us a welcome variation to our usual fare. But images of the dead girl filled my mind, and I saw the hours pass, and evening blend into night, with increasing dismay. I had thought we might arrive in Cambridge in some six or seven hours, but I had counted without the lengthy halts for the relays and the dinner, the detour to Huntingdon and the time spent there in farewells and taking news of the sick man. Long before our journey's end, I was annoyed with myself for not having waited for the mail train to be repaired. But I knew that in the absence of any certainty as to when that might be, I should probably always act the same again.

It was the darkest part of the night when we finally reached Cambridge, and I was deposited in front of my house with the kind wishes of my benefactor. The night was black as pitch: black, and utterly still. There was not a soul to be seen, not even an animal; the only sounds were those of the breeze sighing through the leaves, and the occasional gentle whush of what might have been a small animal. I thought of Ivy, who had walked this very street, that other night, filled with joy and thankful anticipation, unaware of her mortal danger. I wondered painfully if she had realised what was about to happen to her when she saw Julian entering the bookshop, and how many of the last minutes of her life were spent in fear and anguish.

When I entered the house, I found it as silent as though it were utterly uninhabited. Unlocking the door with a feeling of relief, I tiptoed inside, removed my boots and hat, and hurried upstairs into the bedroom to reach the safety of Arthur's arms. Quickly, I removed my jewellery and the pins from my hair and dropped them on the dressing table, then turned towards the bed, visible as no more than the darkest patch in the darkness. It was only then that I became aware of the complete silence in the room. There was no sound of breathing; no sound of anything at all.

I moved to where Arthur should have been lying asleep, and felt with my hand. The bed was empty. Startled, I felt for the matches, lit the bedside candle and looked around me. The bed was not unmade, but not perfectly smooth. It looked as though he had lain down on it without undressing. He must have been taking his surveillance of Jenny seriously enough to be too worried to go peacefully to bed.

I hurried out into the hall: the two doors on the opposite side leading into the twins' room and the nursery, and the door next to ours leading to the spare bedroom were all closed. Jenny should have been in the guest room, but all of my instincts told me that she was not. I hesitated a moment, then opened the twins' door and let a little glow from the candle shine in. They lay in their cots, their cheeks flushed with sleep. The door communicating directly with the nursery was open, and Sarah was sleeping there near the door. I could not see her, but I heard her stir and quickly closed the door. Then, in a quick gesture, I opened Jenny's door.

Nothing. She had gone, of course. There was no other possible explanation for Arthur's absence.

If events of such importance had occurred earlier in the day that the two of them had not come home at all, then his bed would not have been disarranged. Yet I could not believe that he had allowed her to go out at such an hour, or accompanied her purposely. I could only conclude that she had pretended to go to bed and then slipped out, and that Arthur, lying prepared for such a possibility, had heard and gone after her.

Where would she have gone? To find Julian Archer, of

course. She wanted revenge; she meant to kill him. She was quite mad.

In my haste, I ran straight out of the house in my stockinged feet, my hair falling down, then dashed back and tugged on my boots, ignoring the buttons. On an impulse, I snatched up a box of matches and thrust it into my dress, then hastened straight down the path to the gate.

It was while I was feeling in the blackness for the latch that I thought of the Darwins' bicycle. I had found it difficult to take the quaint-looking toy seriously enough to want to purchase one for myself, and could not really imagine myself riding it around in public. But the thing had become all the rage amongst young people recently; both men and ladies had taken it up as a sport. Our neighbours, always on the crest of the wave of fashion, had enthusiastically made the purchase for their large family of youngsters, and I had frequently seen them wobbling up and down Silver Street upon it, practising riotously. I was tempted.

I had noticed the bicycle in their garden when I was at their house; they kept it leaning against the old granary, just within the street gate. To run there was a matter of a few short minutes; to hurry on foot all the way to the centre of town would be much longer. I hesitated no longer, but hastened down my lane and up the Newnham Road in the darkness until I reached Silver Street, my eyes growing progressively used to the dimness around me. I soon made out the large square of the gate set in the dark mass of the high garden wall, unlatched it, and felt around tentatively within – there was the bicycle! I dragged it out carefully and closed the gate, hoping that I would be able to put it back without mishap before the night was over. But if I could not, the explanation for my act would be, I believed, sufficient to justify it.

By the time these thoughts had gone through my head, and I had emitted a nervous gurgle of laughter at the mental picture of myself trying to explain why I was doing what I was doing, I had balanced myself upon the machine, hair wild, skirts hitched into a bundle to free my ankles, and was pedalling unsteadily over the bridge and on up Silver Street, then left on King's Parade. It was fortunate that I was the only vehicle on the road, and even more fortunate that I did not happen to encounter any rock or obstacle over which I should certainly have taken a spill. But the road was smooth and silent, and glided away beneath my wheels, which turned faster and faster as I grew used to the rhythm of the movement. I was driven by fear; I do not believe I could have learnt nearly so quickly or so well if I had been doing it for pleasure.

Not five minutes later, the dark shadows of the Cambridge buildings loomed against the slightly paler sky sprinkled with tiny stars.

Once I perceived something like a delivery cart moving along ahead of me, and once I heard something coming up the road behind me. I dismounted in a tumble, and stood waiting silently and tensely at the side of the road until the vehicle had passed far enough ahead to pose no further risk of collision. Then I sprang back onto the machine and pedalled swiftly onwards.

I stopped the bicycle just before turning into Petty Cury, half-fell off it, leant it silently against a wall, and stood still, listening and peering down the street as best I could. I perceived neither sound nor movement at first, and began to wonder if I had made a mistake by coming here. Then I became aware of muffled noises. Quickly and silently, I crept towards them.

As I approached Heffers, I realised that the sounds were actually proceeding from across the street, in the narrow alley separating two neighbouring buildings where I had waited and watched secretly just yesterday. Confused grunts were interrupted by a whispered imprecation, and diverse sounds of a struggle could be heard, as well as heavy breathing. I hastened to the opening, pulled out my box of matches and struck one.

In its momentary flash and glare, I made out three human figures cramped in the tiny space. Two were stretched full length upon the ground. The flame illuminated Jenny's body as she lay unconscious, a dark mark across her throat, while a figure whom I identified as none other than my very own husband was kneeling on the back of a man lying on his stomach, his body half over hers. Arthur had planted his knee in the small of the man's back and was pressing him down by the shoulders, while the man was struggling violently. At the flash of light from my match, Arthur looked around, and Julian Archer took advantage of his second of inattention to writhe violently foward, throwing Arthur off balance.

'Be careful!' I cried, stepping forward.

The match burnt my fingers and I dropped it and reached for another, which I lit in time to see Julian struggling away from Arthur's grasp, reaching out his arm, stretching it out to its full length, away from me, towards Jenny's head which lay beyond him – no, not towards her head, but next to her head. I held the match out over him and perceived a metallic gleam.

'The knife!' I screamed. Arthur lunged, and grasped Julian's arm, pulling it back. They struggled for a few long seconds, Julian gaining inches towards the knife, which I had suddenly and incongruously recognised as one of our very own best kitchen knives, much approved of by Mrs Widge. It lay well out of Arthur's reach, but only just beyond Julian's fingers. If he once grasped it, death lay in his hands.

I dropped the match, hurled myself over the two of them, a tangle of bodies and arms and legs, landing in a completely disorganised heap on the other side. Julian Archer swore as my skirts covered his head, Jenny's body and the knife. But I disentangled my arm and and felt for the blade in the darkness, where I thought I had seen it. His fingers reached it just as mine did, and I snatched it out of his reach and scrambled back. Then I lit another match.

He looked up at me, recognised me and unexpectedly burst into a short, barking laugh.

'Why, Miss Duncan,' he said, 'you here, joining this little party? At such an original hour, too. What might you be doing here, I wonder? Joining in the attack, perhaps? This lady here rang at the bell, woke up my servant and had me called out of the house, then pulled me in here and tried to stab me! Just as I was fending her off, this other ruffian came and jumped on me from behind. I thought it was some kind of robbery. Can you be connected with it all? What on earth is going on here?'

'He was strangling her,' said Arthur quickly.

'Nonsense, man – she was trying to stab me, the vixen! I was just holding her off!'

'We need the police,' I said.

'No, no,' said Julian Archer quickly, and I heard his smile preserved in his voice as the match once again flickered out, leaving us in darkness. 'There's no need for the police now. This woman has not been badly hurt, I hardly touched her. If this person could just get off my back, we can have a look at her and set her back on her feet, and then perhaps we can all be on our way without any further disturbance.'

I struck another match. Arthur looked at me questioningly. I looked back at him, willing him to remain where he was.

'No,' I said. 'We must summon the police at once.'

'Well,' said Mr Archer with a show of annoyance, 'I must say that I don't see how you're going to manage to get them here. I intend to shake off this fellow and get up; I've had quite enough of the dust, thank you very much.'

'Don't get up,' I said, and grasped the knife threateningly.

'My dear girl, that knife in your dainty little hand doesn't frighten me in the least! A little bluff, a little feminine drama; it makes me laugh! Go on then, get the police, if you can manage it without going anywhere!' And he attempted to roll over, but Arthur made himself heavy, and because of the extreme narrowness of the alley, he could not escape to one side or another.

I well knew that I would be utterly incapable of stabbing him, yet his words provoked me to an indiscretion.

'Oh,' I said coldly, 'I can get the police here very quickly without going anywhere. I could do it quietly, if I had a nice little *wireless machine*. But as I don't, I'm afraid I'll have to be a bit noisy about it.'

His eyes swung to my face, his jaw dropped. I believe I truly understood only at that moment what was at stake. It might have been safer to keep him in ignorance – but his reaction nailed the lid to my certainty. Fixing my eyes on his

face, I inhaled deeply and forced myself to produce an
extremely long, loud scream.

It was not an easy thing to do, in that dark city street, at
that dark hour. If one has never tried it, one cannot know that
it is necessary to overcome an immense, almost overwhelming
inhibition. In fact, in order to do it at all, one must
gigantically overdo it. My scream turned into a wild,
primeval, unstoppable ululation.

'Poliiiiiiiiiiiiiiice! Heeelp!!!!! Poliiiiiiiiice!!! Murder!!!!!!!' I
shouted and screeched into the darkness.

Lights flickered on in windows up and down the street.
Some of the windows opened, and heads peered out.

'Help! Call the police! Murder!' I shouted again and again.

A man wearing a nightcap on his head emerged from one
of the nearest houses, carrying a candlestick in one hand and
a weapon of some kind in the other. I saw him start towards
the sound of my voice; then he was overtaken by a horse and
cart which came clopping up the street and pulled to a stop
just in front of Heffers. Totally ignoring the man with the
candlestick, the lights and heads at the windows, and my
continuing cries, an elderly man climbed down from the cart,
slowly extracted a key from his pocket, and proceeded to fit
it into the door of the bookshop.

Startled, my attention was momentarily distracted by this
man, and I missed Julian Archer's swift movement. With one
violent lunge, he freed his arm from Arthur's grasp and
snatched the knife out of mine. Then he was on his feet facing
Arthur.

'Get out into the street,' he snapped. Arthur moved back
three or four steps, and Julian followed him, threateningly. By
now two or three people had congregated at the entrance to

the little alley; we heard them gasp as they saw him emerge, the knife in his hand.

I stood up to follow, then stooped down and quickly laid my hand on Jenny's breast. She was breathing; her eyes fluttered as I touched her. I left her there and followed Julian onto the street.

'It's all right,' Mr Archer was saying tranquilly to the shocked, startled neighbours. 'I was attacked by the crazy woman in there, but I managed to seize her weapon and all is well.'

'Are you sure you're all right, Mr Archer, sir?' asked the man with the candlestick, and I realised that obviously all these people were his neighbours; they were well acquainted with him and would certainly take his part rather than ours.

'Quite all right,' replied Mr Archer calmly. 'I'm not sure why this gentleman attacked me; I thought he was together with the woman, but I suppose he just saw me defending myself and leapt on me, believing I was harming her. Quite understandable, I'm sure, and I'm very sorry we conflicted,' he added, lowering the knife and stretching out his hand to shake Arthur's.

'No!' I cried, hurrying forwards. Arthur's steady gaze met mine, then Mr Archer's, and he did not lift his hand. Mr Archer drew his own back, and turned to stare at me inimically.

'What's the matter with you?' he snarled in a low voice.

Ignoring him, I crossed the road and addressed myself directly to the delivery man, who was now engaged in stolidly removing labelled and addressed crates of books from the interior of the shop and loading them onto his cart.

'Do you come here every morning at this time?' I asked him.

'No miss,' he replied, attending calmly to his work as though it was perfectly normal to be surrounded by people wearing caps and nightgowns at four o'clock in the morning. 'Only Mondays and Thursdays or when I'm asked for special.'

Ivy's corpse – *the dark box*. It was all so devastatingly plain; Ivy's strangled corpse had been placed into a crate, casually prepared beforehand by the manager in the interior of the shop and placed amongst a number of other crates ready for delivery, surprising no one...and all picked up and taken away by a man with a cart, early, early on the Wednesday morning, when the usual delivery man would not be there. This one would be a different man; no other than Mr Archer senior, I could no longer doubt it; Mr Archer senior dressed in a working man's overalls and cap after bidding goodbye to his elegant guests...driving slowly into the centre of town with his gardener's cart and pony, lifting and packing the crates, taking away the corpse in full view of any chance nocturnal passers-by without arousing the slightest suspicion, while his son rested peacefully in his camp bed upstairs, enjoying his perfectly organised alibi. Delivering the boxes, and above all, the last one – delivering it first, when no one would be walking through the Lammas Land for pleasure; driving straight there and emptying the contents of the box into the river, then clopping calmly away to the next place. Completing the other deliveries, if there were any, then returning home and burning the unwanted crate on the refuse heap at leisure. Just an old crate of books from the shop.

The dark box! The bride, the bride will never see the church!

Had it been Ivy's voice, then, that I had heard? Can such things ever have any rational explanation?

I turned and looked at Julian Archer. He was staring at me, shaken by my question to the driver, following my mention of the wireless. His mouth was twisted strangely and his lips were dry. He moved towards me and I felt danger approach as thick as electricity in the air of a storm. Yet surely he would not stab me in front of all these people – would he? How strange to stand watching, wondering, as though someone else's life was at stake. He was approaching me, his face was leaning into mine.

'Just who are you and what do you want?' he whispered.

Arthur came up beside me and took my hand in his.

'This is my wife,' he replied, addressing Julian, but speaking clearly enough to be heard perfectly by the assembled group of neighbours. 'And I believe that she is preparing to level a grave accusation against you. You would do well to listen.'

Julian's glance shifted rapidly to Arthur and then back to me. As he realised that the situation was more complex than it had seemed, his sense of his own danger increased, and from being defensive he became aggressive.

'You poor sod,' he said, 'if you knew what your wife does when you're not there to see.'

'I do know,' replied Arthur coldly. 'She makes a practice of detecting criminal activities.'

His words confirmed what the murderer had already begun to understand. A hunted look flashed across his face; for a moment I feared he might run away, and wondered if the neighbours would give chase if he did. I wanted to keep him there, just a few minutes, just a minute longer.

'My husband is quite right,' I said steadily, capturing his eyes with mine to hold him.

'You just be careful what you say,' he said, his lips curling back. 'People like you are easy victims. Easy. You know that, don't you?'

The threat was spoken low, but it was overhead – by Jenny, who had come to her senses and now flung herself suddenly out into the street. Her dark hair seemed lit around the edges by the flicker of the candles held by the people standing behind her. Ignoring them, she approached him and pointed a finger directly at his chest.

'You rotten criminal,' she said, causing him to jump and turn around suddenly, 'you pimp, you murderer, I'll get you yet!'

The gathered neighbours drew in their breath in a collective gasp of shock.

'This woman is a slut; she's raving,' cried Julian Archer.

'Yes, I'm a slut,' she shouted. 'I'm a slut, and who made me one? Who makes sluts of girls like me? Men like you, who take our money and keep us down in the filth while they get rich! Yes, that's what he does,' she went on, her voice rising, and she turned towards the onlookers and advanced towards them, thrusting out her chest so as to provide them with the full benefit of her shocking manners and appearance. And indeed, her height, her pose, her loud voice and her dark, tangled hair, her wild face, her torn clothing and the bruise on her throat caused the white-clad group to shrink back from her with hushed horror.

'Go away,' said a bearded man harshly. 'We don't want women like you here, with your shrieks and your hysteria and your lies and your immoral habits. We don't know what you're doing here and we don't want to. Go back to wherever you came from!' He gave her a sharp push. She shrieked.

At that moment came a sound I had been hoping and waiting for, a sound which was music to my ears.

'Now, now, what's all this?' said a strong, authoritative voice, and a police officer came loping up the street. 'I heard screaming down this way just a couple of minutes ago. Was that from here? Who screamed? Just what is going on here?'

I was about to answer, when Julian stepped in front of me, took the candlestick from his neighbour, and faced the constable openly and directly. By the light reflected on his face, I perceived with astonishment that he had erased all traces of disturbance from his features. Truly, this man possessed aplomb beyond measure. Putting on an air of dignity which has been offended by the sight of vulgarity, but which remains above the fray, he spoke.

'I have been attacked, Officer,' he said. 'These two women have insulted me publicly, and one of them tried to stab me with a knife, causing me to have to defend myself and take it from her. Here it is, Officer. I am of course extremely sorry to have had to lay hands upon a female, but I trust I did her little harm. These women should not be here, disturbing our quiet streets.'

'Arrest them, Officer!' said the angry bearded man, playing nicely into Mr Archer's hands.

'Is this true, ladies?' said the policeman, glaring at us severely.

'Yes,' cried Jenny, her eyes flashing. 'He's a murderer and a filthy pimp, and I pulled the knife on him and I'll do it again! It's him you should be arresting!'

'Now, now,' said the constable, 'I think you're going to

have to come along with me, miss, and stop bothering this gentleman. And you gentlemen and ladies should all get back to your beds. There's nothing to see here,' he added with a nod towards the assembled group of onlookers and a complete and obvious disregard for the truth. 'Come on, then,' he went on, addressing both Jenny and myself. 'You ladies should not be here. Leave this gentleman alone and come along to the Station where we will try to untangle whether you have been guilty of nocturnal breach of the peace or more serious illegality.'

I saw, or thought I saw, a tiny little look of triumph flash through Julian's eyes. If we went with the officer now, he would be out of the country in a matter of hours.

'No!' I cried.

'What do you mean, no? You can't talk to me like that,' said the policeman. 'Otherwise it'll be the handcuffs on you. Now you be careful how you behave.'

'I'll just be going back home, now, Officer,' said Julian with a courteous nod. 'I live right here. I will be available in the morning, of course, should you need me for anything.'

'Don't let him go!' I said, grasping the officer by the arm. 'He's a murderer!'

'Ah,' said Julian, in a tone of weary, half-intolerant impatience, 'there they go again.'

'Now, miss,' the officer scolded me, 'be careful what you say. You can't go throwing around accusations like that.'

'I am not throwing around accusations,' I replied, and taking a leaf out of Mr Archer's book, I drew myself up to my full height, pushed back the worst of the catastrophically half-unpinned hair which was falling into my face, and assumed my most distinguished accent.

'I accuse him formally of murder,' I pronounced firmly. 'Inspector Doherty is in charge of the case and fully cognisant of all details. He should be called as soon as possible. This man strangled Ivy Elliott, the young woman whose body was found in the Cam on the morning of the 22nd of June. Don't allow him to return inside his house – he will destroy important evidence!'

The police officer's face changed; he stared at me. 'Who are you?' he asked.

'Let me answer that,' replied Arthur, whose quiet distinction covered me like a protective blanket. 'My name is Weatherburn, I am a don of the University, and this is my wife, Mrs Weatherburn. She is a private detective who has been investigating the murder of the girl named Ivy Elliott. Inspector Doherty is fully aware of her activities in the matter. Please allow me to repeat her suggestion that he be summoned at once.'

Calm masculine tones succeeded where feminine efforts failed. The constable turned to the delivery man, who had finished his work of loading crates and was standing motionless, watching the scene. 'Go straight to the police station on St. Andrew's Street, my man, and tell them to fetch Inspector Doherty here as fast as possible,' he snapped sharply. 'Now, and don't lose any time about it! Do you hear?'

'Yes sir,' said the delivery man, climbing into his cart and clopping off with no sign of emotion.

During the time it took us to convince the officer, Julian had once again slipped towards his own door; as the cart rolled down the street, I saw that he was about to enter, and feared that he would lock it behind him and make his escape while we waited for Inspector Doherty. I saw with dismay that the house door already stood open, and I jumped forward, determined to try to prevent him from closing it behind him. But he did not enter; indeed, it was not he who had opened the door, but Philip; Philip, who stood motionless, framed in the darkened doorway, listening. How long had he been there? After a moment's hesitation, Julian made as if to push past him.

'Wait,' said Philip, barring his way. 'I heard everything she said.'

'It's rubbish, Phil,' said Julian quickly, warmly. 'That woman's mad. You know as well as I do that I was with you the entire evening that Ivy was killed.' He tried again to squeeze past, but Philip dropped his crutches and opened his arms to grasp the doorframe with both hands.

'I know that you were,' replied Philip, but his look was as cold as stone. 'That is exactly why she should be allowed to speak. Stand aside.'

Standing on the doorstep raised above the level of the street, he was as tall as his brother; their eyes were at a level, and locked into each other in what seemed a duel of silent wills. His crooked, deformed body obviously had difficulty remaining upright without the crutches, yet so steady was his look and so strong was the impression of power that emanated from his stance and his gesture; so strong, perhaps, also, the ingrained habit of respect – and perhaps even pity – for his handicap, that Julian did not dare to use violence to pass him. And I, watching, was awestruck by Philip's act, for he knew exactly what he was doing. If Julian could once enter the house, his destruction of the evidence, and even his escape out of some back window, were practically certain. There was nothing passive in Philip's unmoving stance. Without words, it said clearly that if his brother had murdered his beloved, he would deliver him up to justice with his own hand. It wrenched me that he should be forced to do this, *this*, to the brother with whom he had grown up. Yet it could not be avoided; it was the only way. I began to worry that as the seconds passed he would begin to doubt, and yield. I turned to him and spoke.

'He strangled her here, in the bookshop,' I said. 'He placed the body into a crate of books, and your – er – his father came dressed as a delivery man in the early morning and carried the body away. It took him no more than a few minutes to hurry down to the bookshop to kill her, since he already knew exactly when she would be there – because your father sent her from Chippendale House directly to Heffers with some story or other about putting money back into the cash register there, and sent a message to Julian by *wireless transmitter*, informing him of the exact time at which she had left the house. So he didn't need to watch for her coming. He *knew* to within a couple of minutes when she was going to arrive.' I felt a peculiar sensation as I spoke these words; it was strange to be so completely sure of myself, while having no real notion of what a wireless transmitter might actually be! Neither, apparently, did anyone around me.

'What did you say? What is that?' asked Philip.

'It – it is a machine with a wire,' I said. 'I don't know exactly how it works, but I know that it can send messages silently, directly and instantaneously through the air from one house to another over quite a long distance. It is a recent invention, but your father knows all about it. He invests in the company which created it. I have not been into Mr Archer's rooms here, but I will guarantee that there is a machine there, with a wire running upwards, probably out of the window. I have already noted the existence of such a wire in a tree in the garden of Chippendale House.'

'Is it true?' Philip asked Julian. 'Do you have such a machine upstairs?'

'I have a machine with a wire,' he said, 'but this young lady doesn't understand what it is used for.'

'Show it to me,' said Philip.

By this time, the police officer had advanced towards the brothers; he was now standing directly behind Julian. And the other spectators had followed him, so that we were all grouped around the doorway where Philip still stood. As though in a strange procession, we entered and mounted the stairs, preceded by Philip, who climbed with excruciating slowness, one painful step at a time, then Julian, then by the police officer (who was now holding the knife he had removed opportunely from Julian's hand), myself, Arthur, Jenny, and the other neighbours. We stopped after the first flight, and entered into a room which was obviously Julian Archer's sitting room. It contained nothing out of the ordinary. We crossed it and entered his bedroom, which looked out over a miserable little lane to the back. There, on a large table in front of the window, sat two peculiar machines, one at each end of the table, separated from each other by nearly two yards. They were quite large, and one of them was equipped with two white buttons, connected by wires to a kind of jar. The machine was completed by a large brass rod bent nearly into a circle, at the ends of which were fixed two brass balls facing each other, separated by no more than a tiny space. The other machine was fitted with a glass tube containing what seemed to be a little pile of metal filings. Something looking like a small spoon lay over this tube, and a wire went up from this machine, through the crack at the bottom of the window, and outside. This machine was also connected by one short wire to an ordinary electric battery, and by another to a tiny printing machine with an inker and a long, thin roll of paper. The glass tube formed a kind of hole in the electrical connection between the battery and the printer.

'This is it,' I asserted.

'What does this apparatus do?' asked the policeman, addressing Julian.

'It's scientific,' he replied coldly. 'It's difficult to explain to a layman.'

On an impulse, I reached out and pressed one of the round white buttons with my forefinger.

There was a crack of electricity, and a spark jumped between the two brass balls. Instantaneously, the metal filings in the glass tube on the other machine seemed to come alive, leap up from the bottom of the tube and cohere into a single mass, exactly as though they had been suddenly attracted by a magnet. This newly formed metallic link completed the path of the electric current, connecting the battery to the tiny printer, which immediately purred into action and inked a small dot on the roll of paper, which then advanced by a quarter of an inch. The spoon then suddenly leapt up and lightly tapped the glass tube. The metal filings fell away into a little pile of powder again; the current was broken, and the printer fell silent.

'What is the meaning of this?' said the police officer.

'It's for Morse code,' I cried, remembering what I had heard in Kingstown. And reaching out again, I pressed down the other button. The spark flew as before, the metal filings cohered, the printer printed, the tapper tapped, the connection was again broken. But this time the printer had printed not a dot, but a short segment.

'You see?' I said. 'These two machines are separated by the whole length of the table. No wire connects them to each other, yet by pressing a button on one of them, I can transmit a message which is printed in Morse code on the other.'

'And you claim that this machine can send a message to another one situated a mile away?' asked the police officer doubtfully.

'Over ten or twenty miles. I have seen it with my own eyes,' I replied.

'This is a miracle,' said the police officer.

'No,' I said. 'It is a stroke of genius.'

'He's a devil!' shrieked Jenny suddenly. 'I'll kill him with my own hands! Let me! I want to kill him! I want to kill him!'

She tried to throw herself on Julian, but many pairs of hands held her back. The attitude of the people, however, had changed completely. She was held away protectively, while Julian now stood abandoned in the centre of the room like a loathsome serpent.

'I think you had better come along with me, sir,' said the policeman to Julian, taking out his pair of handcuffs.

I saw his eyes dart – backwards, forwards, to the sides. There was no chance of flight, no chance of escape. Already people were stepping forward to come to the assistance of the officer in his duty.

'You'll pay for this,' he snarled suddenly, turning to me.

'No. *You* will pay,' said Philip to him, and his low voice contained a vibration of bitterness beyond description. 'You and father. You will pay between you for a life destroyed.'

'You fool,' said his brother, 'this is all your fault. If you hadn't taken the grotesque idea into your head of forcing a beautiful girl to marry a snivelling runt like you just because she was in trouble, none of this would have happened.'

'That's a lie,' cried Jenny suddenly, 'he didn't force her – *you* did! You forced her beyond bearing, and then you killed her, not even for money, just for nothing – nothing at all! What did you care? She wasn't even a person to you. She wasn't a person to anyone, I think. Men thought she was too beautiful – she was Ophelia – she was a whore – she was an idol – she was less than dirt, and all the time she was just a girl, an ordinary girl, who had the right to life like everybody else – and you took that from her. And now you're on your way to Hell where you belong. Go burn in Hell! Burn! Burn! Burn in Hell!'

'Hell?' said a voice on the stairs, and Inspector Doherty arrived, looking just as disorderly and half-dressed as the rest of us, clearly fresh from his bed. 'What's going on here? Do I understand that some new evidence has appeared in the case?'

'It's incredible,' said the police officer to Inspector Doherty. 'This young woman has shown us how that machine over there can send an instant message through the air without a wire.' He hesitated a moment, then reached out and pressed one of the buttons himself. The printer immediately obliged. Both policemen stared. Inspector Doherty ran his fingers over and under the tables, searching for a wire.

'It's Morse code,' breathed the constable admiringly. 'This machine sends and that one receives. And she says it'll work even if they're miles apart.'

Inspector Doherty was not slow to understand. The officer's description too clearly corresponded to the missing link in the case against Julian Archer that we had discussed at such length. He glanced at me, raising his eyebrows. I gave a quick nod towards Julian. His eyes followed my look.

'The body?' he asked.

'The father,' I answered at once. He hesitated no longer, but turned to Julian Archer, taking the handcuffs from the constable as he did so.

'You are under arrest for the murder of Ivy Elliott,' he said. 'You will accompany me to the police station at once.' And the two policemen hustled Julian out of the door. 'I'll thank you to join us there as soon as you can, Mrs Weatherburn,' the inspector threw back at me over his shoulder as he disappeared. 'We will need your statement.'

The street door banged below, and an odd silence established itself in the dim bedroom. Then the neighbours began leaving, gathering together and disappearing little by little down the narrow stair with the fluidity of a stream. Arthur and I remained together in the darkness. I looked around for Philip, but he was gone; I heard his steps going up the stairs to his own rooms, creakingly, wearily. Thump, drag, pause. Thump, drag, pause. Thump, drag, pause. There was a little swish, and a quick step suddenly followed his. Perhaps Jenny could find some peace in those rooms upstairs, darkened by the mourning that she shared.

I let my head sink onto Arthur's shoulder. He made a gentle attempt to restore some symmetry to my hair.

'I don't want to go,' I said.

'You must finish what you began,' he replied. 'They need to

know what you know, Vanessa. What about the other man, the father? Where is he?'

'He's on a yacht,' I said. 'I don't know how you arrest a person on a yacht.'

'They watch all the ports,' he said.

'It's strange, isn't it,' I said, 'that until today one might have thought that it was absolutely impossible to communicate with someone on a boat. This machine will change all that – it will change the world around us more than we can imagine. It is the most modern thing I have ever seen.'

I reached out and pressed the little round button one last time. Together we watched the flash of the spark, and the reaction of the other machine as the invisible wave crossed the air. The metal dust flew together, and the little printer stolidly grunted out its single dot. The spoon tapped, the dust fell, and all became quiet.

'This truly marks the end of an era,' I said.

'Come along,' said Arthur, touching my elbow. 'We must go.'

'You're coming with me, aren't you?' I said.

'Of course,' he answered, linking his arm through mine.

The passages in italics contained between each day's diary entry, describing the childhood and youth of the Italian-Irish inventor Guglielmo Marconi, leading up to the day of his extraodinary triumph at the Kingstown Regatta on July 20th, 1898, are all entirely historical and were researched from various biographies and articles on Marconi.

Marconi's career as an inventor and businessman continued brilliantly, Cross-channel transmission was achieved in 1899; an article from *McClure's Magazine*, authored by one Cleveland Moffatt and dated June 1899 is blazingly entitled: 'Messages sent at will through space – telegraphing without wires across the English channel'. The article begins: 'Mr Marconi began his endeavors at telegraphing without wires in 1895, when in the fields of his father's estate at Bologna, Italy, he set up tin boxes, called "capacities," on poles of varying heights, and connected them by insulated wires with the instruments he had then devised – a crude transmitter and receiver. Here was a young man of twenty hot on the track of a great discovery, for presently he is writing to Mr W. H. Preece, chief electrician of the British postal system, telling him about these tin boxes and how he has found out that "when these were placed on top of a pole two metres high, signals could be obtained at thirty metres from the transmitter"; and that "with the same boxes on poles four metres high signals were obtained at 100 metres and with the same boxes at a height of eight metres, other conditions being equal, nearly up to a mile and a half. Morse signals were easily obtained at 400 metres." And so on, the gist of it being (and this is the chief point in Marconi's present system) that the higher the pole (connected by wire with the transmitter), the greater was found to be the distance of transmission.' In fact, as was later discovered, the height of the pole is not directly correlated to the distance of the transmission; rather, this distance increases because of the stronger currents and longer wavelengths resulting from a larger antenna's greater electrical capacity. In December 1901, he received the first trans-Atlantic radio transmission, from Poldhu, Cornwall to Newfoundland, Canada, using a 400-foot kite-supported antenna. Over the coming years, Marconi was responsible for the equipping of all ships with radios, although unfortunately the ships' radio operators went off duty at night; however, one chance operator still at work caught the last messages from the sinking Titanic in 1912 and his ship was able to rescue those survivors who had managed to get into lifeboats.

Before Marconi's work, several other brilliant physicists and inventors had managed to detect waves at distances of a few yards, such as Edouard Branly, Heinrich Hertz, Alexander Popov and of course, Sir Oliver Lodge. The latter was, as described, a passionate believer in telepathy and communication with the dead, a member and sometime president of the British Society for Psychical Research; much later, after the sad death of his son Raymond in World War I, Lodge wrote *Raymond, or Life and Death,* a book which begins with an account of Raymond's youth, continues with a description of the family's successful attempts to contact him after his death through mediums, and ends with a discourse on Lodge's philosophy about the Afterlife. The concerns of the British Psychical Society and the scientific study and analysis of séances in the Victorian era are faithfully represented; the brochure and Faraday's article explaining table-turning as a result of unconscious movements on the part of the participants are true documents.

The Darwin family – and their house, and their granary, and their bicycle, and their telephone – are real people who resided in the house which now forms Darwin College; all these things are described in the delightful autobiography of Gwen Raverat née Darwin, *Period Piece: A Cambridge Childhood*. Finally, many thanks are due to Mr Peter Kenyon, whose critical advice was useful in innumerable places, above all in ensuring that all travel described in the book, whether by carriage, train or steamer, could have occurred at the tail end of the nineteenth century exactly as described.